THE LAST
Confession
OF
THOMAS
HAWKINS

THE LAST

Confession

OF
THOMAS
HAWKINS

ANTONIA HODGSON

H

**HODDER &
STOUGHTON**

First published in Great Britain in 2015 by Hodder & Stoughton
An Hachette UK company

1

A CIP catalogue record for this title is available from the British Library.

Hardback ISBN 978 1 444 77545 7
Trade Paperback ISBN 978 1 444 77546 4

Typeset in Adobe Caslon by Hewer Text UK Ltd, Edinburgh
Printed and bound by Clays Ltd, St Ives plc

Hodder & Stoughton policy is to use papers that are natural, renewable
and recyclable products and made from wood grown in sustainable forests.
The logging and manufacturing processes are expected to conform to
the environmental regulations of the country of origin.

Hodder & Stoughton Ltd
338 Euston Road
London NW1 3BH

www.hodder.co.uk

For David and Chris,
even though they prefer the twentieth century

'All you that in the condemned hold do lie
Prepare you, for tomorrow you shall die'

*Words called beneath Newgate Prison
on the eve of a hanging*

PROLOGUE

No one thought Tom Hawkins would hang. Not until the last moment.

Gentlemen don't hang; not even ones found guilty of murder. Hawkins wasn't much of a gentleman, that was true, but he came from a good family. A good family with good connections. The pardon would come. Sometimes the Marshal kept it hidden deep in his pocket, only to pull it out with a flourish when the procession reached the gallows. A bit of drama for the mob. A lesson, too: an act of mercy is always a lesson.

This is what Hawkins tells himself as his cart rolls slowly out of Newgate Prison. *The pardon will come. I've kept my side of the bargain. I've held my tongue.* But Hawkins has a gambler's instinct, and he can feel the odds rising with each turn of the wheel.

He should have been freed hours ago. If he could only catch someone's eye . . . but the Marshal is riding up at the head of the procession, followed by a band of constables armed with staves. Their boots pound hard against the cobbles as they march up Snow Hill. He can't see them. He is a condemned man, and condemned men must ride backwards to their hanging, on carts swagged in black crêpe. He sits with his back to the carthorse, chained in iron, long legs stretched out in front of him. He sees only what he has already passed: the muddy road beneath him, the houses, the crowds of people.

The great bell of St Sepulchre tolls low and heavy as the devil's heartbeat, summoning the town out on to the streets. *Hanging day.* He has heard the bell toll many times before. He has followed the carts to the gallows. He has watched men die slowly, blind beneath a white hood, their legs kicking the air. Now it is his turn to dance upon the rope, while the world cheers him to his death.

No. He must stay calm. The journey to Tyburn will take two hours through all these crowds. There is still time. He has done everything that was asked of him. Surely his loyalty, his silence, will save him now? A thin, snake's voice whispers in his head. *There's nothing more silent than a corpse.*

He pushes the thought away, concentrates on his breathing. This, at least, is still his to control. There is a smudge of dirt on the ankle of his left stocking. His eyes fix upon it as the cart arrives at the steps of St Sepulchre.

The horse gives a sudden lurch and he is flung forward, then back. He winces in pain as his shoulders slice against the sharp edge of his coffin. They have tied it behind him for the journey. *Breathe.*

Four prisoners will hang today. Higgs and Oakley are footpads, betrayed by a fellow gang member. Mary Green was caught lifting a few yards of mantua silk from a shop in Spitalfields. Cherry red, the newspapers said, as if such a thing mattered. Hawkins is the only one convicted of murder. He is the one the crowds have come to see. Even with his head down, he can feel them staring. They hang out of every window; line the narrow streets five or six deep, on the brink of riot. They curse his name, tell him he will hang like a dog. The two guards flanking his cart grip their javelins hard, watching for trouble.

Sometimes the town shows pity, but not today. Not for a man who won't confess his crime. Violence smoulders in the air, ready to catch flame. It would be safer to keep the carts moving, but there are traditions that must be observed on the road to Tyburn and this is one of them. *Perhaps they will push the cart over.* His arms are pinioned, but he could still run. He lifts his eyes to the crowds; sees only hatred, fear and fury. Aye, he could run – straight into the arms of the mob. They would tear him to pieces.

The church bellman appears on the steps. He is a narrow-boned, fretful man, and the hand bell is too big for him. He rings it twelve times, holding onto the handle with both hands. It is a struggle and he looks relieved when it's over. The crowd, delighted, applauds him as if he were a comic turn at Sadler's Wells. He frowns at them. This is meant to be a solemn moment and they are ruining it. 'Pray heartily unto God for these poor sinners,' he pipes, fighting to be heard over the din, 'who are now going to their death.'

'My thanks for that reminder,' Hawkins mutters. The guard at his left bites back a smile.

The bellman calls upon the condemned to repent. The other three prisoners have admitted their guilt – they have an air of calm acceptance that draws approval from the crowds. Young girls throw sprigs of white flowers on to their carts. White for forgiveness. White for rebirth. Oakley is so convinced God will grant him mercy that he is going to his death dressed in his shroud; the long white smock and ruffled cap a sign to all that he is eager to leave this wicked world and ascend to heaven.

Hawkins is wearing a sky-blue velvet coat and breeches, and a white silk waistcoat trimmed with gold thread.

A plump, pretty girl trembles her way towards him as if he were a caged tiger and pushes her last sprig of flowers through the wooden rails of the cart. As he takes them from her their fingers touch. She gives a start, half-thrilled, half-terrified, and hurries back to the safety of the church steps. He sighs under his breath. Perhaps later she will tell her friends how she met the notorious Thomas Hawkins on the road to Tyburn. Will she say that the devil shone out of his bright-blue eyes? That his touch burned her skin? Will she pay a shilling for an inch of the rope that hangs him, and keep it for luck?

I will not hang, he reminds himself. *The pardon will come.* But he is no longer sure.

PART ONE

Chapter One

It began with a scream in the dark.

It was early January and I was limping my way home through Covent Garden. No longer the dead of night, not yet morning, but the secret hours before dawn, when rakes tiptoe from tight-shuttered bedrooms, and thieves slink back to the slums of St Giles. A time when good, respectable men are fast asleep, their houses barred and locked.

Long, uncounted hours earlier I had slipped out for a bowl of punch and a game of cards. I won three guineas. Such things must be celebrated. I bought a late supper for a ragged band of new friends, and a good deal more punch. The night continued. I spent the three guineas. Then I spent some more. At some point, I lost a shoe.

The first of the market traders were dragging their carts into the piazza, hunched double against the cold. They swung their lanterns into the shadows, searching for their allotted place. I saluted one or two as I passed, but didn't linger. The weather was dismal yet again, the air damp enough to leave its trace upon my skin. Still – at least it wasn't raining.

In fact, given that I had lost my shoe and my winnings, I was in a remarkably cheerful mood. I pulled out my silver watch and held it up to the moonlight. Almost five o'clock. Kitty would be at least half-awake by now; she preferred to rise early. We enjoyed such different hours it was a wonder we had ever met. I imagined her now, taming her wild copper curls with pins. Perhaps I would untame them again, pull out the pins and let her hair spill down over her shoulders. Or perhaps she would shout at me for staying out all night again. Yes, now I thought of it, that was more likely. Kitty had a fearsome temper. When the meek inherit the earth, she will be left quite out of pocket.

We had met the previous autumn, when I was thrown in the Marshalsea for debt. For the past three months we had been living beneath the same roof. Some of our neighbours thought it a scandal. The rest did not think of it at all, not in this disreputable part of town. I had spent the first few weeks recovering from a sickness of body and spirit that had left me weary and out of sorts. I had been tortured, beaten and betrayed in prison, witnessed murder and almost met my own death. It was the betrayal that lingered in me, an infection that would not heal. I kept old friends and acquaintances at a wary distance, wondering, wondering ... Kitty was not without her faults, but I knew this much – I could trust her with my life.

Slowly, I recovered my strength. I read and worked quietly at my desk, strolled about the town in the daytime, and spent my nights with Kitty. I was content – for a while. Yes, yes, damn me for a fool, but a man of my temperament may grow tired of anything. Put me in heaven, and after a short, blissful period I would be knocking at the gates of hell, asking if anyone cared for a game of cards. Lessons that had felt so sharp and certain on my release from prison began to fade. What harm could it do, one trip to the coffeehouse? One short visit to the gaming tables? And perhaps another? I was not so bad – not quite so bad as I had been. Surely that was enough? I was not a monk, damn it.

Kitty did not mind this so very much – better to let me ramble about the town than have me sit scowling into the fire. What troubled her was that I had begun to slip out alone, without her.

'It isn't *fair* Tom,' she had said, the last time she caught me sneaking from the house. 'I am not some timid song bird for you to keep locked in its cage.'

'That is true,' I agreed. I had heard her singing. 'But tell me what I must do, sweetheart? The world is how it is.'

'Well you might look a little less pleased with it,' she muttered.

I'd sighed and lifted my hands. A weak apology, but it was not my fault the town was made for bachelors. The women who frequented the coffeehouses and gaming tables and taverns could not be called *respectable*. Kitty didn't care, but it troubled me that I couldn't protect her in such wild places. Nor did I like the hungry looks of the men, slavering like dogs around her. I knew what they saw when she arrived upon my arm – a rich, unmarried wench sharing her bed with a penniless rogue. A whore, in other words. And men do not treat whores well, in the main.

'Perhaps if we were married . . .' I'd added, slyly.

I turned down Russell Street, leaving the piazza and the market behind me. I had asked Kitty to marry me a hundred times, and she had refused me a hundred times in return – with good reason. A few months ago she had inherited a fortune from her guardian, Samuel Fleet, including the house and print shop where we now lived together. If she married me, the business and all her fortune would fall under my control. How could she trust me not to gamble away her inheritance? She had never admitted her concerns to me, but I could see the doubt in those sharp green eyes of hers, whenever I asked for her hand. Given the choice between being rich or respectable she had chosen to keep her money and let her reputation fend for itself. I couldn't blame her for it. I'm sure I wouldn't marry me either.

A blurred shape leaped down from a wall into my path, startling me from my thoughts. A cat, out hunting. It pounced hard into a pile of stinking rubbish a few feet ahead. There was a scuffle, and then a long, vicious squeal. A moment later the cat trotted past, triumphant, a huge rat dangling in its mouth. I skirted the rubbish heap with an anxious eye. I had almost walked straight through it.

Russell Street is like a young country girl, fresh arrived on the London coach. It begins with good intentions – smart coffee-houses, handsome private homes. Then after a short distance it takes on a pragmatic but profitable air – an apothecary's, a grocer's store. After that comes a fast, sordid descent – a grimy gin shop, a gaming house, a brothel with broken windows and a rotting roof. And opposite the brothel, a bookseller's and print shop, selling filth and sedition under the counter. A sign hangs above the door – a pistol tilted at a lewd angle. And underneath the pistol: *Proprietor, S. Fleet*. No longer. *S. Fleet* was dead – burning in hell or causing havoc in heaven, who could guess? This was Kitty Sparks' place now.

The Cocked Pistol is set back from the street, as if ready to slink away at the first glimpse of trouble. It is also narrower than the houses upon either side, which gives it the appearance of being squeezed slowly to death by its neighbours. I paused at the dark-green door, preparing myself for Kitty's wrath. It could be a fearsome thing to behold, and rather thrilling for us both. Her face would flush and she would bunch her fists tight into her gown, her chest heaving. She would call me a selfish dog, a scoundrel, an inconstant son of a whore. At some point the questions and accusations would falter and she would grab me or I would grab her and we would fling ourselves up the stairs. She had the most bewitching way of slipping her fingers beneath the band of my breeches and pulling me into bed, while staring deep into my eyes. A simple thing, but my God it was worth all the shouting.

'*Thief!*'

A muffled scream, close by. I gave a start, and peered up and down the dark street. There was no one there; not that I could see. The street fell silent, as if holding its breath. I felt the hair prickle along my neck. Was someone hiding in the shadows? I reached for my sword, drawing it smoothly from my side.

Someone shouted again, a sharp cry of fear. '*Help! Help! Oh, Lord, spare us!*'

A young woman's voice – a maidservant, I thought. She was calling from the house I'd just passed – Joseph Burden's home. The very last place I would expect a commotion. There were churches that were less quiet and respectable. I ran back to the door and thumped my fist against it.

'Holla! Mr Burden! Is all well?'

No one replied. I could hear shouts and screams within, and footsteps on the stairs. Burden bellowing angrily for more light. The girl was still weeping. '*I saw him! I swear I saw him!*'

A housebreaker, it must be. January was their favourite month – long, dark nights and no one out on the frozen streets to see them. Except men like me. I pounded harder on the door. 'Mr Burden!'

The bolts slammed free. Burden's apprentice, Ned Weaver, stood in the doorway, clutching a hammer in his fist. His broad shoulders blocked the view into the hallway. He ducked his head to save it from catching upon the frame.

'Thief?' I whispered.

'Aye.' He gestured with his hammer, back over his shoulder. *Still inside.*

'Is someone hurt? I heard screams . . .'

He shook his head. 'It's just Alice. Gave her a fright.' An odd, rather sour look crossed his face. 'He woke her up. The thief. He was standing over the bed.'

I took a step towards the piazza to fetch help.

'Wait!' Ned seized my arm and pulled me back to the front step, almost lifting me from my feet. It felt as if I were held in the jaws of some great hound. Burden was a master carpenter and worked his apprentice hard. 'We have him trapped. Stay here on guard, sir, I beg you. Don't let the devil pass.'

He thundered back up the stairs. *Trouble*, I thought, rubbing my arm. Well – I had a talent for it. I squared my shoulders and gripped my blade a little tighter, wishing I had not drunk quite so much punch. Or indeed been left with just the one shoe. I could still hear sobbing in an upper room, and boots thumping back and forth as the men searched the house – but nobody came back to the door. The more I waited, alone in the dark, the more puzzled I became. Why had the thief picked Joseph Burden's home, of all the houses in London? There were finer places to rob even on this street, and Burden always kept his windows and doors firmly locked and bolted at night. He was known and mocked in the neighbourhood for securing his house as early as six o'clock in winter.

The door to the Cocked Pistol swung open, candlelight spilling softly on to the street.

'Tom!' Kitty leaned out, bare feet on tiptoe. She was half-dressed in a silk wrapping gown and a white quilted cap, a few loose curls spilling across her forehead. 'There you are, you dog. What are you about? If you're pissing against the shop again . . .'

My angel. 'Housebreaker. I'm guarding the door.'

Her eyes caught light. She disappeared inside for a moment, then emerged in a pair of my boots, twirling a large frying pan in her hands. As she clopped towards me I considered ordering her back to the shop for safety. Imagined how that suggestion would be greeted. Remained silent.

'How many?' she asked from the corner of her mouth.

'Just one. I hope.'

Kitty hurried back to the shop and called up the stairs. 'Sam! *Sam!* Fetch my pistol.' She picked up her gown and ran back to me, peering eagerly over my shoulder into the narrow hallway beyond. The house was still in uproar, panicked voices tumbling through the air in a confusion of shouts and commands.

'Trapped like a rat in a barrel,' Kitty murmured. 'What will they do to him, Tom?'

I thought of Joseph Burden – devout, severe, unyielding. 'Lecture him to death, probably.'

Kitty snorted.

'They'll hang him.' A low voice behind us.

'*Sam,*' Kitty scolded, smacking the boy lightly on the arm. 'Must you creep about like that?'

Sam Fleet – fourteen years old, named for his late Uncle Samuel, my old cell mate. Looked like the old devil, too – the same short, lean build, the same black-eyed stare. A darker complexion, like a Spaniard. Thick black curls tied with a black ribbon. He was holding a pistol.

I tucked it beneath my coat. Sam had already slipped past me, poking his head through the door into the gloomy interior. Burden's house was a mystery to the neighbourhood; he did not encourage visitors. I tapped Sam's shoulder. 'Go back inside.'

A flicker of irritation crossed his face, but he did as he was told, sauntering away as if it were his own decision. I smiled after him, recognising the small act of defiance from my own youthful rebellions.

The house had fallen silent. I took a step into the hallway and shouted up the stairs.

'Mr Burden? Ned? Is all safe? Do you have him?'

'Mr Hawkins?' a soft voice replied, from the landing above. A figure descended slowly – dainty bare feet, the hem of a dress brushing the stairs, a slim hand holding a candelabrum. She did not seem quite real at first, moving with a slow, dreamy grace. Judith – Joseph Burden's daughter. She must be Kitty's age, but she rarely left the house save for church, and I had never spoken with her before.

'For heaven's sake,' Kitty muttered. 'I walk faster in my damned sleep.'

When she was halfway down the stairs Judith paused, her free hand gripping the rail tight. There was a fresh cut on her lip. She stared at us both, grey eyes lost and distant in a pale face. 'Why are you here?' Her voice was slow and dazed, as if she were emerging from a dream.

'Miss Burden – you're hurt. Did you see the thief? Did he strike you?'

'Thief? I ... no.' She put a hand to her swollen lip. 'I saw nothing.' She gave a hollow laugh. 'Nothing at all.' She sank to the stair, resting her forehead against the banisters as if they were the bars of a prison. The candelabrum slid to the floor.

Kitty leaped forward and settled it on the ground before it set the place alight. I knelt down beside Judith. She was trembling violently, her breath coming in short gasps. Whatever she had seen had shocked her out of all sense. Fearing she might faint or fall into a fit, I took her hand in mine and squeezed it gently. It was small and very smooth, the hand of a girl who spent her days embroidering cushions and pouring tea. 'Don't be afraid, Miss Burden. You are quite safe now.'

'We have a pistol,' Kitty said, arching an eyebrow at my hand linked with Judith's.

'And a frying pan,' I added, smiling.

Judith offered a ghost of a smile in return. 'You are kind, sir,' she murmured, but her hand lay like a dead thing in mine.

'Is Alice safe?' Kitty asked. Alice Dunn was Burden's housekeeper. She and Kitty would sometimes talk over the yard wall.

'Alice?' Judith withdrew her hand and curled up on the stairs, her head buried in her gown. 'Why should I care if *Alice Dunn* is safe? She is only a *maid*.'

'*Judith*.'

Joseph Burden stood at the top of the stairs, looming above us like a bear about to attack. An old fighting bear, long past its prime, but still dangerous. He was a giant of a man, with thick, strong arms from years of hard labour. His belly was vast, straining against his nightgown. He thumped down the steps and pulled his daughter to her feet with a savage wrench. Judith gave a cry of pain, stifled at once. Her father seized her by the back of the neck and with one great shove pushed her up the stairs. She slipped and scrabbled away, without a word.

Kitty clenched her jaw.

Burden heaved himself down the rest of the stairs and pushed his face into mine. '*You*. How *dare* you enter my home?'

I leaned back on my heels, avoiding his stale, hot breath. 'Your apprentice begged me to stand guard. Did you find the thief?'

His face reddened. 'There was no thief. Alice was mistaken. Foolish slut doesn't know when she's awake or dreaming.'

That made little sense to me. I'd heard the screams well

enough – Alice had sounded perfectly awake and quite terrified.

'Mr Burden. Did you strike your daughter?' Kitty asked. Her voice was steady, but she was holding the pan in such a fierce grip that her knuckles had turned white.

Burden curled his lip. 'Hawkins, tell your whore to mind her tongue or I'll rip it from her throat.'

'Coward,' Kitty hissed.

Burden spun around, aiming his fist at her. She swung the pan like a racquet, and Burden's knuckles cracked against the solid iron with a loud clang. He yelped in pain, cradling his hand. Kitty raised the pan above her head, preparing for another blow. I snatched her by the waist and led her out on to the street before she broke his skull.

'Arsehole!' she yelled, as he slammed the door on us. 'Come out here and threaten me again – just you try it! I'll kick your fucking teeth out.'

A cheer rose up from the brothel across the road. Joseph Burden was not a popular man down this end of Russell Street. Kitty glanced up at the whores leaning out of their windows, and bobbed a curtsey to them. Her temper was as fast and hot as lightning and died just as quick – thank God, or there would be no living with her.

She grinned at me and pulled me close, tugging on my coat with both hands until our bodies twined together. 'Where have you been tonight, Tom Hawkins?'

I kissed her, running my hands down her gown, finding the soft curves beneath.

'You stink of smoke,' she sighed. 'And liquor.' She slid her cheek against mine, her skin smooth against my stubble. Brought her lips to my ear. 'Kiss me again.'

I did as I was asked. The world melted away, as it always did.

And I forgot all about Joseph Burden, and his daughter's strange behaviour, and the thief who was never there.

That was my first mistake.

Chapter Two

I woke at the respectable hour of one o'clock. Kitty was long up, but her scent lingered on the sheets. I traced my hand down the mattress where she'd lain, smiling at the memory of last night's tumble. She was still a maid – well, clinging on with her fingernails. Kitty said she had spent far too much time tending squalling babies and did not want me planting one in her belly – at least for a year or so. I suspected there were other, secret reasons. I thought she might be afraid I would abandon her.

Whatever the truth might be, I had vowed to myself she would remain a maid until we were wed. I had a foolish notion of our wedding night – clean sheets, a fire roaring in the grate, good wine – every comfort attended to. It surprised me, the strength of this honourable little dream. Terrified me too, to tell the truth. A man starts dreaming of such pretty things, and what's next? An honest occupation. A home in a respectable part of town. A quiet, sober life. I might as well go home to Suffolk and turn into my father.

I did not confess any of this to Kitty for fear she would mock me, or – worse – find it charming. And so I continued to ask for her hand and she continued to refuse me, lightly, as if it were all a great joke. I could never quite find the way to say *halt this now,*

Kitty: I am quite serious. Better to be rejected in jest than in earnest.

Well, there were other pleasures to be explored for now – and I had introduced her to most of them. There was something tantalising about her strange blend of knowledge and innocence. I suspect she knew that too, and guessed at its power: to leave me wanting more at the end of each night. My own Scheherazade. But we had shared a bed now for more than three months, and I feared that there would come a night when her resolve and my restraint would buckle at the same time and all would be over. Last night, as she lay naked beneath me, I had almost surrendered to it. My God, how had I stopped myself? I stared at my reflection in the mirror, at the tiny bruises running down my arms where she had clutched me tight. My control had been nothing short of miraculous. Saint Thomas the Perpetually Frustrated.

I yawned and stretched, rubbing my hands across my scalp. My head ached from the night's debauch – too much punch and not enough supper. They will chisel that upon my gravestone, no doubt. I called down to Jenny, our maid, to fetch a pot of coffee and a bowl of hot water. Once I had washed and put on a fresh shirt and cravat, I was ready to face the day – or what was left of it. I drew back the shutters. Iron skies, the threat of rain, damp air that sank into the bones. It had been a cold, wretched winter and I was damned sick of it. My fingers hovered over an old, drab waistcoat. No, no, it would not do. I pulled out my new silver-buttoned waistcoat that Kitty had ordered for me as a gift. Much better. A gentleman must have standards, even on a grey, empty day in January.

I poured the last of the coffee and stood by the window, cupping the bowl for warmth as I watched the street below. The brothel was quiet, but there was a steady stream of folk passing by. Day folk. Ned Weaver plodded down the road, returning from a job with his bag of tools slung across one shoulder. He stared at the cobbles, his thoughts far away. Mrs Jenkins, the baker's wife, called out to him from her doorway. She was a determined gossip and could knead and pummel a secret out of a man through sheer persistence. Ned was an amiable fellow with a handsome face and a slow, bashful smile. What better way to spend the morning? She called again, but Ned pretended not to hear her, thumping hard on Burden's door. Mrs Jenkins stepped out from the cosy warmth of the bakery, pulling her shawl around her chest and hobbling across the street. By the time she reached Burden's door it was closed and Ned was safely inside. She blew out her cheeks, offended.

I rubbed my lips. Curious. Ned was a good-natured soul. It was unlike him to ignore a neighbour in such a blunt, unfriendly fashion. Strange too that Burden's door had been locked – that seemed an odd precaution for an *imagined* thief. I drew back from the window before Mrs Jenkins spied me.

Kitty and I lived in two connecting rooms on the floor directly above the shop. When we weren't abed we would leave the doors between these rooms open, forming one large space, with a sitting room and hearth at the front and the smaller bedroom at the back. I could hear her chattering to a customer downstairs in the shop, voice bright and friendly. She loved to keep herself busy and had a gift for turning a profit. And I suppose I had a gift for spending it.

I frowned at the small desk beneath the window. For the last three months I had spent much of my time translating obscene literature to sell in the shop. I'm not sure this was quite what my father had in mind when he bundled me off to school. Not sure it's what *I* had in mind either – sitting hunched over a desk for days on end. All those hours spent writing about stiff cocks, and all I gained in return was a stiff back.

I riffled back over my latest masterpiece – an intimate conversation between an experienced abbess and a naive but eager young novice, translated from the French. I'd called it *Instruction in the Cloister*. Now it was complete I must take it to a Grub Street printer to set and bind the pages. Then we would sell it, along with all the other secret books and pamphlets, the bawdy poems, the intimate drawings, the scandalised yet curiously *detailed* discussions of sodomitical practices. This was how Fleet had run the Cocked Pistol without being slung in gaol. Unlike Edmund Curll, his closest rival, he had never taken out advertisements or engaged in public spats with writers to gain notoriety. He had been discreet – and where discretion was not enough, he'd bribed and intimidated his way out of trouble.

When Kitty inherited the shop, she'd cleaned the place and brought order to the jumbled shelves. Aside from that, the business had not changed. Wary customers soon realised they could still purchase the same scurrilous material, and be served by a deuced pretty girl, too. They could even buy more respectable works if they were so inclined – political pamphlets, treatises on diverse matters of natural philosophy, poetry. Books of recipes and the lives of criminals sold particularly well. If we could find a murderous cook we'd make a fortune.

A commotion outside drew me back to the window. Half a dozen constables were marching up the street, clubs resting on their shoulders. Ahead of them strode a purposeful figure in a brown coat with old-fashioned cuffs, sharp chin thrust forward, cane striking hard against the cobbles.

Bugger the world. Twice.

I grabbed my wig and thundered downstairs into the shop. 'Gonson!'

The elderly gentleman at the counter gave a yelp of alarm and tottered out on fat legs, thrusting his parcel of books in my chest as he passed. I slung them through a hatch into the cellar below while Kitty flew about the shop gathering up anything incriminating. She pulled a hidden lever on a back shelf and dropped everything into the secret cupboard behind, slamming it shut again as the door to the shop burst open.

John Gonson, city magistrate, paused in the doorway. Towering behind him stood Joseph Burden in his leather work apron, fists bunched at his side. The guards remained on the street, poking the dirt with their clubs and chatting idly. Not a raid after all, it seemed. Kitty and I exchanged relieved glances.

'Mr Gonson.' I gave the shortest bow I could make without causing offence.

Gonson stepped over the threshold, dropping his head to pass through the door. He was a trim, energetic man with a narrow face and a clear complexion that made him appear younger than his thirty-odd years. Here was a man who slept well and drank in moderation, who never placed a bet or took a bribe. Incorruptible and resolute.

His gaze flickered across the shelves, thin lips preparing to curl in disapproval at the first sight of something immoral. Gonson was not only the magistrate for Westminster – he was also a dedicated member of the Society for the Reformation of Manners. The Society had been founded many years past to rid the city of whores, thieves, and sodomites. One might as well aim to rid the sky of stars, but Gonson was patient and determined. He had brought a new vigour and order to the Society. His spies had infiltrated brothels and molly houses, and, while most of their stories were dismissed, some had reached the courts. Two poor wretches had been hanged for sodomy on evidence from one of Gonson's informers, and he'd sent scores of women to Bridewell.

Gonson was – in other words – that very dangerous and

compelling animal: a man of vision. And the Cocked Pistol was obscuring his view. Indeed, its mere existence was offensive – and in the last few months he had considered it his holy duty to tear it down. Many of our customers were men of influence, which afforded us some protection. But Gonson made sure to visit at least once a week to disrupt business.

Having found nothing disreputable on the shelves he moved his disapproval on to me. 'I must speak with your boy.'

'The *thief*,' Burden snarled, prowling about the shop. Gonson was tall, but Burden's head almost scraped the ceiling. We were all three of us large men, crowding the shop. Kitty had retreated behind the counter, feigning boredom. Let the stags rut for a time.

'Call him at once,' Burden shouted.

Ah, now I understood. Burden was looking for a scapegoat – and for revenge. He too was a member of Gonson's reforming society, and a zealous one at that. He loathed the shop, loathed its very existence so close to his own home.

He'd also loathed Samuel Fleet, its previous owner. Sam was Fleet's nephew. He'd been living with us for a month now at its request of his father, James – Samuel Fleet's half-brother. I had been instructed to turn Sam into a gentleman, but frankly I'd have more luck shaving a wolf and wrestling it into a waistcoat. Where was he? A good question. Hiding in a cupboard? Climbing up the chimney? The boy was so quiet and nimble he could be tucked beneath my coat and I wouldn't know it.

'He's running an errand,' Kitty said.

Gonson ignored her. 'Mr Burden has asked me to write a warrant for his arrest. But I must interrogate the boy first.' Burden began to protest, but Gonson hushed him. 'I follow the law, sir.'

'For the scum of St Giles?' Burden sneered.

'For all men.' Gonson puffed out his chest, staggered by his own magnanimous spirit.

'Mr Gonson, with great respect, sir – this is a nonsense. I stood guard at Mr Burden's door last night. No one entered the house and no one left it—'

'—you let him sneak past, damn you!' Burden interrupted.

'You told me your housekeeper had been dreaming. That she was mistaken.'

Burden coloured. 'My boy Stephen swears he saw the brat. Let me fetch him, sir.' He hurried next door, calling loudly for his son.

Gonson frowned and took out his watch.

'Mr Gonson,' Kitty called to him. 'I can vouch for Sam. He was here last night.'

He looked at her for the first time, his gaze steady beneath hooded eyes. 'And what use is the word of a whore to me?' he drawled.

I took half a step forward. Kitty slipped from behind the counter and grabbed my hand, squeezed my palm in warning. I hesitated, then exhaled slowly. What was the punishment for striking a city magistrate? A whipping? A few hours in the pillory? Gonson watched me, straight black brows raised high. My temple began to throb, slowly.

Burden returned, pushing his son Stephen ahead of him into the room. I had never met the boy before – he had just returned from school. At fifteen he had the thin, tangled limbs of a young calf, and his cheeks were chafed red from shaving more often than needed. But he had the same storm-grey eyes as his father, the same strong, square face. He would be handsome enough in a year or two. I smiled to myself. Here was trouble brewing. His clothes were drab and old-fashioned – on his father's orders, no doubt – but he was without question a

24

young rake in the making. One can tell a lot about a boy from the way he ties his cravat.

His gaze darted about the shop, as if there just might be a nude portrait hanging on the wall or a couple of whores groping each other in a corner. Ah ... the disappointments of youth. I caught his eye and winked.

'Tell Mr Gonson what you saw,' his father commanded, oblivious.

Stephen hesitated, then lifted his chin. 'I'm not sure what I saw, sir. It was very dark.'

Burden glared at him, open-mouthed. Was this the first time his son had defied him? And in such a public fashion, too. He drew back his arm and gave the boy a vicious blow across the back of his head. 'Impudent puppy! *Tell them!*'

I winced, but the blow only made Stephen more defiant. 'There was no thief,' he declared. He gave his father a sly, side-long glance. 'Are you sure I should tell them what I saw, Father? What I *truly* saw last night?'

I was sure Burden would beat Stephen again for his insolence, but he seemed frozen, of a sudden.

'Mr Burden,' Gonson prompted, 'have you wasted my time, sir?'

Burden found his voice at last. 'I ... Forgive me, sir. A misunderstanding.'

'Well,' I said cheerfully. 'Thank you, gentlemen, for your visit. If you wish to purchase a book, I could recommend—'

'Damn you!' Burden snarled. 'Damn your foul books.' He reached for the nearest shelf and dashed the contents to the floor, tearing the pages from one and crumpling them with his fist.

Gonson grabbed his arm and muttered in his ear. Burden's shoulders slumped. He threw the pages to the ground and stormed out, dragging his son with him.

Kitty dropped to the floor, gathering books and ripped pages into her apron.

Gonson picked up his cane. 'You're amused by this, sir?'

'No, indeed.'

'It is a game to you – to set a son against his father. To provoke a decent citizen to violence. A neighbour.' He prodded at a book, broken-spined on the floor. 'I'm told you are an educated man, sir. A student of Divinity. Peddling filth. Corrupting the ignorant. Do you have no sense of shame? No sense of Christian duty? Those disgusting books and pamphlets you sell – fie, fie, sir – do not deny it! The men who pass through my court – the men I send to the gallows – these are your customers, Hawkins. You help set them upon that path. Can you not see the harm and suffering you cause? Do you not want your city to be free from crime? To end the *squalor* and the *misery*?'

He halted, the zealous fire dying in his eyes. He could see I was unmoved. I was a parson's son – the first skill I'd learned was how to ignore sermons. I was unsermonisable. He scowled, black brows knotted tight. 'Perhaps you are worse than I dared imagine,' he mused. 'Perhaps it is not this shop that pollutes the neighbourhood. Perhaps it is *you*, Mr Hawkins. Perhaps you lie at the heart of all this corruption and vice. A black spider in a filthy web.'

I laughed, incredulous. Was I to be blamed for all the vice in London? I was almost flattered – until I caught the quiet fury in his expression. 'Mr Gonson . . .'

'I've heard dark stories about you, sir. Dark and terrible. I've heard rumours that you killed a man, down in the Borough.'

Behind him, Kitty faltered for a moment, reaching for a book.

'I paid them no heed,' Gonson continued softly, almost to himself. 'I fear I was wrong. I shall look into the matter.' He fixed his hat and left.

Kitty sank to the nearest chair and lifted her eyes to mine. She looked terrified. We both knew the rumours were false. But if Gonson investigated the events of last autumn . . . If he talked to the wrong people down in the Marshalsea gaol . . . He just might discover the truth. 'Oh, Tom . . .' she breathed, and began to shake.

'He has no proof, Kitty. No witnesses.'

'No. But he will dig and dig until he finds *something*.' She set her shoulders, resolute. 'I won't let him take you from me, Tom. I'd rather die.'

Chapter Three

Sam was not on an errand. Kitty had lied to spare him Gonson's interrogation. But where was the boy? He was not in his room at the top of the house, nor in the narrow storeroom where he sometimes lurked, tucking himself into impossibly cramped spaces to read uninterrupted. I wouldn't mind, but the books weren't even contraband. There was something disturbing about a boy his age choosing Newton's *Principia* over *Venus in a Smock*.

I propped myself in the doorway to his room, gaze travelling across the charcoal portraits he'd sketched. There must have been twenty or more pinned to the wall, curling at the edges from damp. Pictures of his family, of neighbours and street traders. I recognised his father James – straight-backed as a soldier, with a piercing look in his eye. A handsome woman drawn in profile with a sweep of black hair about her face: Sam's mother, I guessed. A baby sister, merry-eyed and chewing a tiny fist. I searched for affection in the drawings, but there was more precision than love in Sam's pencil. A mirror that did not always catch the best angle. He had drawn me sitting at my desk, my hand resting on a book. I looked bored. Petulant.

'Mr Hawkins?' Jenny, our maidservant, emerged from her garret room across the landing. She'd learned to hide herself when Gonson appeared. She attended the same church and did not want him to discover where she worked. 'Is it true? Will they arrest Sam?'

I smiled at her. 'Heavens, no. There was no thief. Alice had a bad dream, no more.' I thought she would be reassured by this, but if anything she grew more agitated, shifting her weight from foot to foot.

'Your pardon, sir. Alice ain't a foolish girl. She knows when she's dreaming.'

I studied her for a moment, wondering how Sam might sketch her with that unflinching eye of his. She did not seem well – her complexion was almost grey, her eyes red-rimmed and sore. 'What troubles you, Jenny?'

'It's Sam, sir, he's the thief,' she said in a rush. 'He's been . . . creeping about the house.'

'Well – that is the way of him, Jenny. I am not sure he means anything by it.'

'*In the dark*, sir. When we're asleep. I woke the other night and he was stood over my bed.'

I flinched. It was not like Jenny to tell tales. Not like her to offer an opinion on the weather, she was so timid. 'I didn't hear—'

'I made to scream but he clamped a hand over my mouth. And his eyes – I thought he meant to kill me! But then he was gone so fast and it was so dark I thought I'd dreamed it. But now Alice says she saw something . . .' She tailed away, looking up at me with a hopeful, expectant expression, as if I might snap my fingers and make all well with the world.

'This is strange indeed,' I said, baffled. 'I will speak with Sam—'

'No, oh please, sir, no! *Please* don't say nothing. I'm so afraid of him. The way he stares . . . He'll murder me in my bed, I'm sure of it!' She broke down, wiping away the tears with the back of her hand.

'Jenny, come now. There is no need for this. Sam was here in the house all night. I saw him myself. He can't be in two places at once.'

She sniffed, and shot me a frightened look. 'The devil finds a way, sir.'

I promised Jenny that I would think further on the matter. I also promised to fix a bolt on her door. I was unsettled by her story, but what more could I do without confronting Sam, which she had begged me not to do? There was a chance she had indeed dreamed it all. I had my own reasons not to trust the boy, but I had seen him with my own eyes last night, while the thief was supposedly scurrying about next door. Shadows in the dark, that was all.

I headed downstairs, stomach rumbling. Dinner – that would help banish the gloom. I poked my head into the shop but Kitty had vanished, replaced by ... 'Ah, damn you. There you are.'

Sam was reading a book of anatomy, black curls falling across his face. His gaze slid briefly to mine, then dropped back down to an illustration of the heart, labelled in close detail.

I tapped the page. 'So. You're learning the mysteries of the human heart.'

'Ventricles.'

A month ago I would have been perplexed by this response. But I had learned to form sentences around the odd word he deigned to expel into the air. In this case: *'No, sir. I am not study-ing the mysteries of the human heart, but its mechanics. Including, for example,* ventricles, *a word I will now say out loud for my own unfathomable amusement.'*

His lips curved into a faint smile.

'Where's Mistress Sparks?'

Nothing.

'The magistrate paid us a visit. Mr Burden accused you of breaking into his house. He claimed Stephen saw you – though Stephen denied it. What do you say to that?'

Nothing.

'I defended you. Miss Sparks lied for you. *Sam,*' I prompted, exasperated. 'When a gentleman defends you against an accusation of theft, it's customary to express gratitude. *Much obliged to you, sir,* for example. *Thank you, Mr Hawkins, for defending my character. I am in your debt.*'

Sam closed his book. 'Bliged.'

Just one vowel short of a word. A triumph. When Sam first arrived at the Cocked Pistol I'd thought he was shy with strangers, or missing his home and family. As the days had passed, I'd come to realise that this was his natural temperament. He was a strange boy, no doubt – but I had not considered him a danger to the house. Had I been too trusting of him?

I was about to venture out in search of a decent meal when a young lad entered the shop. His clothes were badly patched but clean, and he was well fed. One of James Fleet's boys. I glanced at Sam and caught the slightest flicker of fear in his eyes. Afraid of his father? Well – he was not alone in that.

The boy handed me a slip of paper.

Hawkins. I have something for you. Come at once. Bring Sam.

I paid the boy and sent him on his way. I could feel Sam's gaze upon the note from across the room.

'Your father wishes to see you.'

His brows twitched. Ach, I knew that anxiety well enough. Tell a boy his father has summoned him and nine times out of ten it's trouble. I'd spent half my childhood in my father's study, staring at the floor while he expounded upon my failings. Weak. Obstinate. Wilful.

'I'll change,' Sam said.

I blinked, confused – as if he had somehow read my mind. By the time I understood him he had slipped around the counter and was climbing the stairs to his garret room.

'You are dressed well enough,' I called up to him.

'Too well.'

A good point. I returned to my own room and threw on my drabbest waistcoat and breeches, and a fraying, mouse-coloured greatcoat. No silver buttons, no embroidery. Not for a trip to St Giles.

St Giles is barely a ten-minute stride from Covent Garden but it might as well be another country. The Garden is not without its perils – especially at night – but the stews of St Giles contain some of the deadliest streets in the city. The last time I'd ventured in I had crawled out again upon my hands and knees, battered and bloody, lucky to be alive. I had been led there by a linkboy I'd paid to light my way home. Instead he had tricked me, leading me through the twisting maze of verminous streets into an ambush, where I had been robbed and beaten.

The same boy was at my side today.

Sam's father, James Fleet, was captain of the most powerful gang of thieves in St Giles. I would call them infamous, but their success hinged upon the quiet, secret way they went about their business. Fleet was careful not to make a name for himself, except where it mattered: whispered in the shadows. While other gangs swaggered about the town boasting of their deeds, Fleet's men were stealthy, silent and – if caught – never peached another gang member. For ten years James Fleet had ruled St Giles – and barely a soul knew it.

As we left Drury Lane and crossed St Giles's road I put a hand on Sam's shoulder. It was a little over three months since he had led me into the stews. I was *tolerably* certain I'd forgiven him. We had been strangers at the time, after all – and indeed his father had made amends, later. But I still remembered the look of pride and curiosity on Sam's face as I was beaten to the ground. The satisfaction of having pleased his pa. 'Do you remember the last time you brought me here?'

He tilted his face and looked up at me, black eyes cool and unwavering. 'Yes.'

'You've never apologised for it.'

He thought about this for a moment. 'No.'

I gave up.

The city streets are never fragrant, but St Giles wins the honour of being the foulest-smelling borough in London. It is impossible to walk a straight line – one must gavotte around the piles of shit, the clotting pools of blood, men lying drunk or dying in the filth. Sam weaved through it all with an easy tread, while I caught my heel in something so rancid I almost added my own vomit to the street. I reached for my pocket handkerchief, then thought better of it. There would be narrow eyes watching us from every alleyway, every rooftop. I did not want to enter St Giles waving my hankie to my nose like some ridiculous fop.

When Sam had first come to stay with us there had been a trace of the St Giles perfume trapped in his clothes, his hair, his skin. We had given him fresh clothes, clean linen, and several trips to a nearby *bagnio* where his skin was scrubbed and scraped and rubbed in sweet-smelling oil. I'd suggested that he might wish to shave off his curls as well, to discourage lice and other pests. Disdainful silence. Now he was back in his favourite 'old duds' – a battered hat tipped low over his face, a torn and shabby coat, thin breeches. His father could have paid the best tailor in town to stitch a new set of clothes for his only boy, but that would have drawn unwanted attention. *Where did he get the chink for such rum togs, eh?* No one in James Fleet's gang wore fine clothes. Clean and modest – that was the order. That's how I'd known the boy with the note was one of his.

Hawkins. I have something for you. Come at once. My stomach tightened.

A few nights before I had made a grave, foolish mistake. By chance I had met with Sam's father near St James's Park. It was not his usual haunt and he had looked somehow diminished, wandering through such a respectable part of town. Indeed he had seemed so lost that on a whim I had invited him to join me at the gaming tables near Charing Cross.

I did not think to wonder what he was doing in St James's. A man such as Fleet is not stumbled upon *by chance*. I am sure now that he had been waiting for me, but I did not even consider the idea at the time.

He had caught me at a ripe moment and he knew it, the cunning bastard. The Marshalsea had cast a long shadow on my soul. I had almost died, and it had changed me – I could see it when I studied myself in the mirror. I did not trust any more to: 'and all will be well'. I was no longer the careless boy I had once been. But what was I then, in truth? Not a clergyman, despite my father's wishes. So then ... what? What was my purpose? I couldn't say. And a man without a purpose is easy to trap.

I took James Fleet to the gaming house as if I were leading a pet lion upon a leash. Look! See what I have brought with me! I gambled away all the money in my purse and I drank until the floor pitched like a boat beneath my feet. All the vows I had made when I left prison fled before that cheap, seductive thought: *damn it all to hell – life must be lived!* I had won my freedom from gaol. I had won Kitty's heart. I had won my safety. The game was over. So what now?

Another roll of the dice, of course. Because the game must never end.

I sat with James Fleet in a tavern – so drunk I cannot even remember the name of it. And I confessed to him what I had barely admitted even to myself. That I was suffocating. That I had begun to suspect that a life without risk for a man of my nature was in fact a kind of slow death. Fleet had leaned forward, interested. 'I could use a man with your talents, Hawkins.' The next morning I'd woken with a pounding headache and the uneasy feeling that I had accidentally made a pact with the devil.

And now he had *something* for me.

Sam turned on to Phoenix Street, a long road that runs straight through the heart of St Giles like an arrow. Most of the houses were ruins, rotting roofs patched with tarred cloth, as if the risk of fire weren't grave enough amidst all the timber frames and gin stills. One building had collapsed into the street over-night – a couple of thin, ragged street boys were loading the wood into wheelbarrows to sell. They saluted Sam, who gave them a tight nod as we hurried on.

There were eyes upon us in every window here. Men lurking in every shadow. I could feel the stares burning the back of my neck as we passed. I stole a glance up at the rooftops, scouting the wooden planks and ropes that laced the houses together in one long, tangled forest of outlaws. The rookery, they called it – a town for thieves hidden in the skies. A man could clamber right through it without once touching the ground. We passed a gin shop, then another. And then another. At the fourth, a tattered scrap of a boy was puking his guts into the street, blind drunk. A group of older lads jeered at him and kicked him on his way. There were no old men here.

James Fleet did not live on Phoenix Street. His house was hidden, tucked away like a coin buried deep in a miser's pocket.

This was my first visit to his den, and Sam had led me on a strange, intentionally confusing route. But I had learned my lesson the last time he had brought me into St Giles, and I paid close attention to every twist and turn and double back.

Suddenly, without warning, he shoved open a door near the end of the street. It was stiff, and he had to throw all his weight behind it. Somehow he managed this without making a sound. It struck me that Sam used silence the way other boys worked with knives or their fists. I thought again of Jenny's whispered confession and felt a flicker of unease deep in my chest.

We climbed up through a tall, narrow house, its rooms partitioned with sheets and blankets to cram in as many bodies as possible. No need to guess what happened behind those temporary walls. The air stank of sex and bad liquor. Above the low sobs, the groans of pleasure and pain, I could hear a little girl crying out again and again for her mother. No one answered her. I stopped on the staircase, overwhelmed. Sam glanced back, and I could tell from his impatient expression that these sounds meant nothing to him. They were, after all, the sounds of his neighbourhood, of his childhood. He heard them the way I might hear the cry of gulls and the rush of the sea against the shore. We moved on.

At the top of the house we pulled ourselves through a trapdoor onto the roof, wind gusting fresh air on our faces. From up here we could see the city stretching into the distance, the dome of St Paul's far away to the east. Even Sam couldn't resist. He paused to look out over his father's estate, balancing lightly on a damp board that ran between two of the houses. A look settled upon his face that I recognised well – the joy and anxiety of coming home.

'Your father will be pleased to see you,' I called out.

He spun nimbly on the beam. 'Stephen. He denied seeing the thief?'

Good God, it was bad enough that he barely spoke. Even

worse when he hodge-podged conversations in such an eccentric fashion. 'He said it was too dark to be sure.'

Sam smiled. Then he padded over the beam onto the next roof.

The gambler in me found all of this exhilarating – slipping across rooftops through the deadliest part of the city. Was this not life? Was this not something to make the heart beat faster? A quieter voice counselled that such risks may be exhilarating, but were not conducive to a long life. *Oh, and for God's sake – don't look down.*

Sam was a few paces ahead of me, perched at the edge of the roof, staring down at a courtyard below. The houses huddled together to create a tiny, secret square in the middle. Sam rolled his shoulders. Stepped on to the ledge. And jumped.

I gave a shout of alarm and scrambled to the edge. Beneath me, about ten feet down, Sam had landed neatly on the balcony of a modest wooden house built in the heart of the square. Being two stories shorter than the houses surrounding it, there was no way of seeing it until you leaned right over the roof.

'What am I to do?' I called down.

Sam tipped back his hat. Crooked his finger.

'Don't jump for fuck's sake,' a voice growled through a window. A moment later, Sam's father swung out onto the balcony. A short, strong man, he was dressed in a plain shirt and waistcoat, sleeves rolled. His head was bare, scalp dark with bristle. 'You'll break your neck. Or tear a hole in my roof. Then *I'll* break your neck.' He grinned and pushed a ladder out until it lodged firmly against the roof where I stood.

I tested it anxiously with my foot. 'Will it take my weight?'

'Takes mine.'

I considered the iron muscles of his arms and chest. He was a head shorter than me, but still at least a stone heavier. I took a deep breath and climbed down slowly, conscious that I was crossing the threshold arse first. Now there's a way to make a man feel vulnerable. Intentional, no doubt.

Fleet's den was the most curious place I had ever visited – so unlike a normal home that at first I could make no sense of it. The rooms at the top of the house had been knocked into one – or had been built that way. This one large, square room stretched right up to the pitched roof, with beams left open to crack your head upon. The balcony wrapped all the way around this top floor. From here one could throw a ladder onto any roof in the square or clamber down to the street by rope. It was a building designed for escape.

I presumed that this room served as a well-guarded meeting place for Fleet's gang, but there were also hammocks slung from the beams and a grate in one corner with a leg of mutton roasting on a spit. My mouth watered at the smell of it.

Sam dropped his hat on a hammock and pushed a hand through his curls, watching his father from the corner of his eyes. Something unspoken hung in the air between them – a question or a threat. But then Fleet chuckled, and pulled Sam into a brief hug. He kissed the top of his son's head, then shoved him away.

'*Gah*! You smell like a whore. What do they wash you with, fucking rose water?'

'Lavender,' Sam replied, glaring at me as if I had spent the last month flogging him with razors.

I turned up my palms. 'You wish your son to pass for a gentleman. That includes smelling like one.'

'True enough,' Fleet conceded. He gave Sam a friendly shove. 'Run and see your mother.'

Sam hesitated. 'Pa—' He caught his father's sharp look and left at once, scrambling out onto the balcony and climbing down a rope to the next floor rather than use the stairs.

Fleet waved me over to a seat by the fire. The smell of roast meat was almost too good to bear, but I knew better than to ask for a slice. It was not wise to be indebted to James Fleet – not even for a bite of mutton. I lit a pipe to stave off the hunger while he poured us both a mug of beer and settled down in the chair opposite. He was a handsome bull of a man, with a wide forehead and a sharp jaw line. He had the same striking black eyes as his son, but Sam's features were almost delicate, set in a lean face with high cheekbones. There was nothing delicate about James Fleet. His face and hands were traced with scars – a map of old battles fought and won.

'How's Kitty?' he asked, taking a swig of beer.

'She's well.' My voice sounded thin.

He chuckled over his beer. 'Don't look so worried, Hawkins. I'm not going to eat her.'

I forced a smile. 'You have a proposal for me?'

He wasn't ready to discuss business. This conversation would play at his pace, not mine. 'So. What progress with my boy?'

'Good. Save for the incessant chatter.'

He snorted back a laugh. 'How long will it take?'

'To turn him into a gentleman?' I shrugged. A thousand years?

'No, no, no. To *pass* as one. You turn my son into a *real* gent and I'll wring your fucking neck.'

'Ah, well. That's the secret. There's no such thing as a *real* gent.' I was not speaking entirely in jest. If a man wore the right clothes and spoke in an easy, confident manner, there was a good chance he would be allowed into the court. The nobility was such a strange collection of eccentrics, fools, and fops that even the most unlikely fellow could pass.

Fleet waved his hand, dismissing the notion. This sort of subtle distinction bored him. 'There are places I can't go.

Opportunities I can't seize. Sam knows this world – *my* world. I need him to understand yours too.'

I thought of Sam, sullen and silent behind the shop counter. 'I will do my best.'

Fleet held my gaze, just long enough for me to understand what would happen if my best did not meet his expectations. 'Well then,' he said, as the sweat trickled down my back, 'can't ask fairer than that.'

I took a sip of beer. 'We had a visit from Mr Gonson today.'

'Hah. Society of Fucking Manners.'

'Our neighbour accused Sam of breaking into his house.' I paused. 'Is that possible?'

'Anything stolen?'

'No.'

'Anyone murdered?'

'Good God – no!'

Fleet settled back, satisfied. 'Shall we discuss business?'

I had already decided as I climbed over the rooftops of St Giles that whatever James Fleet wanted of me, I must find a way to refuse. 'Mr Fleet,' I assembled my most regretful expression, 'I fear I may not be able to help on this occasion—'

He stopped me with his hand. 'For pity's sake, Hawkins – stop clenching your petticoat. A proposition, nothing more. Chance to make some money.' He fixed me with a look. 'Your *own* money.'

Oh, that stung, I admit. It was true I had been living off Kitty's fortune these past few months. A fortune she had inherited from Fleet's half-brother.

'I've had word from an *acquaintance* at court. A gentlewoman has asked for my help. Needs to be done secret. Quiet. I want you to meet her tonight. Find out what she wants.'

I narrowed my eyes, suspicious. That was all – truly? Nothing more? Perhaps I could, just this once . . . Best not to refuse Fleet over such a trifling request. And would it not be encouraging, to earn a little spare coin of my own? 'How much?'

Fleet shrugged. 'If I can help her I'll pay you a tenth of the fee.'

'Half.'

A hacking laugh. 'One meeting with a fucking courtier? Let me consider.' He scratched his jaw. '*One-tenth.*'

I took a slow pull on my pipe. This was Fleet's world – he could slit my throat in here and never swing for it. But if I did not bargain with him now I would appear weak. 'If it's so easy, why not send one of your men? Why not go yourself?'

Fleet gritted his teeth, and said nothing.

I smiled at him through the smoke. 'Because you need a *real gent*. Someone who can *pass*. Someone who won't frighten the poor lady half to death.' A thought struck me. 'Your brother used to do this for you, didn't he? Play the gentleman.' A vision of my old cell mate, grizzle-cheeked and dressed in his shabby old nightgown, crossed my mind. *Forgive me, Samuel, for calling you a gentleman. I meant no offence.* 'You must have been forced to turn down quite a few opportunities these past months. Perhaps your friend at court will lose patience? Try someone new?'

Fleet scowled. 'Careful, Hawkins.'

'Half.'

'A quarter.'

'*Half.*'

A long, long pause. The blood was pounding in my ears. What was I doing, bargaining with a man who could break my jaw with one swipe of his fist? But I couldn't resist it; I was almost feverish with excitement. My God – I hadn't felt this alive in months.

Fleet leaned forward until our knees were almost touching. He stared deep into my eyes. 'Now here's a man I can work with,' he murmured. 'A third.'

I held out my hand. By some miracle, it wasn't shaking. 'Agreed.'

Chapter Four

Kitty was closing the shop by the time Sam and I returned from St Giles and a hurried chophouse dinner. She hummed to herself as she tidied books back on to the shelves, tucked a sheaf of nude line drawings into a leather wallet. I loved her more than anything in these moments. They reminded me of the first time I'd seen her in the Marshalsea, making a pot of coffee, the simple grace as she moved back and forth, the quick and capable way she worked.

She saw me and her face lit up – the warm gleam of pleasure that I was home. A blink and it had vanished. Kitty would walk about our bedchamber without a stitch of clothing and not give a damn how hard I looked at her. But she kept her deepest feelings hidden from me as much as she could, as if they were a poor hand of cards I might play against her one day.

'And are you staring at my arse now, Tom Hawkins?'

'Always.'

She grinned and wrapped her arms about my neck. 'Where have you been?'

'St Giles. Fleet wanted to see his boy.'

Kitty stiffened and glanced at Sam, who was pouring himself a mug of small beer. Sam's uncle, Samuel Fleet, had been her guardian and she had loved him fiercely, for all his faults. This was the only reason she allowed Sam to live under her roof. She did not trust or like James, his father. 'Dangerous place to be strolling about,' she said, running her fingers down my waistcoat. 'I hope you took care of him.'

'It was perfectly safe, we—'

'I was talking to Sam,' she laughed, letting me go.

Sam's cheeks flushed pink. It was hard to read his thoughts in the main, but where Kitty was concerned he might as well have shouted them from the rooftops. She was a lively, pretty young woman. He was a fourteen-year-old boy. Not everything in life is a mystery.

'You are in a merry mood,' I said, smiling down at her. I was pleased she had recovered from Gonson's visit.

'I have a gift for you.' She kissed me upon the lips, stopping the question. 'Tonight.'

A gift. My mind wandered over the delicious possibilities. Was it too much to hope she'd found a willing friend and asked her to join us . . .?

Yes, most likely it was.

She removed the apron she'd tied about her waist and shook out the dust. 'You must change before we leave, Tom. I can smell the stews on your clothes.'

I frowned, sniffing my shirt cuff. 'Leave? Where?'

Her lips pinched into a hard line. She folded the apron hard. *Snap. Snap.*

Oh, Lord. 'Supper . . .?' I guessed.

'Supper. Theatre. The Eliots.'

Damn it. I had clean forgot. John Eliot was Kitty's lawyer, and an old, trusted acquaintance of her father. He and his wife Dorothy were fond of Kitty and saw a good deal of her – at the risk of their own reputation. An unmarried woman, sharing my bed and running a notorious print shop? As far as *good* society was concerned, Gonson spoke the truth – Kitty was nothing more than a whore. 'Better a whore than a slave,' she would say with a curl of her lip. But her defiance starved her of companions. She was not a whore, nor a servant, nor a lady. She did not fit. The Eliots, thus, were precious friends. Dorothy – who was much younger than her husband – was expecting her first child in the spring. Kitty had taken to visiting her several times a week, basket brimming with fresh fruit and home-made tinctures.

The Eliots were pleasant enough company and I loved a night at the theatre, for the audience as much as the play. There was always some great spectacle or scandal, and it was amusing to watch the nobs rub shoulders with the rest of us. But I had made a deal with James Fleet and I could not free myself of it now. 'Kitty . . .'

Her eyes widened. *'Don't you dare.'*

Quietly, stealthily, Sam drifted upstairs to hide.

I reached out to touch Kitty's shoulder.

She pulled away. 'You *promised*. You don't even remember, do you?'

'Of course I remember,' I lied. 'It's just that I have an appointment tonight. I'm sorry, sweetheart, but it's important.'

'More important than me?'

Well there was a question not to be answered.

Kitty turned away so that I couldn't see the disappointment in her eyes. She began to shuffle the books upon the shelf. 'Who is it you're meeting?'

I searched for an answer that wouldn't create more trouble, but what could I say? *I was drunk and bored, so I told the most dangerous villain in London I might work for him.* 'I'll take you another night. I promise—'

'I don't give a damn about the theatre!' she cried, gripping my shirt so hard I thought she'd tear it. 'What's the matter, Tom?

Why are you acting in such a strange, sneaking fashion? Tell me! Where are you *going*?'

'For pity's sake!' I snapped back. 'Would you stop all this *nagging*. You're not my wife, damn it.'

She flinched and drew back, as if I'd slapped her.

I hadn't meant to hurt her – only to stop her questions. The words had flown from my lips without thought. But they were mean, and the message behind them was cruel. That we were not bound together after all. That I might abandon her whenever I chose – broken-hearted and ruined. 'Oh, Kitty,' I groaned, reaching out for her.

She hugged her arms across her chest, stepped beyond my grasp. 'No. It's true,' she said, cool and remote. 'I'm not your wife. And you are free to do you as please.'

With that she stalked silently from the room.

Kitty left for the theatre an hour later, too angry even to call a goodbye. She took Sam with her in my place.

I sighed and trudged slowly up the stairs to change. I knew nothing about the woman I was to meet tonight, except that she was a courtier, afraid and desperate enough to seek James Fleet's help. I selected a black silk coat and breeches, and a red waistcoat. Sober, dependable, with a military dash. That would do well enough. I tied my cravat with a flourish, gathered my hat and cane from the hallway, and stepped out into the night.

A couple of young rakes and their companions were sauntering down Russell Street, away from the Garden. I recognised one of the girls. She winked at me as they passed. That young fool with his arm about her waist would most likely find his purse missing in the morning. But for now they were a merry bunch. I stood in the middle of the street, tempted to slip into their wake. That way lay Lincoln's Inn Fields, the theatre, Kitty and the Eliots. I could still go to them – forget all about my secret assignation. James Fleet could always find another gent – *real* or otherwise – to complete his business. There was no need for me to risk my easy, contented life for a stranger. Head east. Head east and chase after Kitty.

But then I would never know who was waiting for me in St James's Park, would never learn the secret they wished to spill. A mystery left unsolved for ever. Damn Fleet, the cunning bastard. How could I resist the intrigue? It was like putting a bowl of punch in front of a drunk.

One meeting, that was all. A brief conversation with a noble-woman, no doubt about some trifling matter. A stolen bauble, a petty piece of blackmail. I would pass her troubles on to Fleet and he would resolve the rest. One meeting. And never again, of course.

West, then, to St James's Park. I did not stop to consider the Burdens' house as I passed, never thought to look up at the windows or wonder about the previous night's drama. Too much had happened since then for me to think of it. It was eight o'clock and already dark – most likely Joseph Burden had already locked and bolted the house for the night. I didn't even notice.

I hurried through the Garden with my head down against the wind, the chill air digging its fingers through my clothes like a thief searching for coins. I pulled my coat tighter, striding past Tom King's coffeehouse, ignoring the raucous shouts and cheers of its customers. I'd wasted a hundred nights in there with King's clever, dangerous wife Moll. Not tonight. She would only winkle the truth from me and use it in some poisonous way, then dismiss her betrayal with a laugh. Best to keep yourself locked and bolted against that one. She was fine company, but she'd pinch the soul from your body and flog it to the highest bidder given the chance.

Walking along the windswept Strand I prayed for a hackney cab to escape the cold, but they were all busy, horses clattering by with steaming breath, drivers swaddled in thick blankets, holding their whips in numb fingers. So I continued on, shoulders hunched, jumping over puddles of rainwater and filth.

As I reached Charing Cross I heard a gruff shout of '*By Your Leave, sir!*' and footsteps pounding hard behind me. I jumped aside, narrowly avoiding collision with a sedan chair jolting fast along the pavement, the man inside gripping the window edges hard to stop himself being flung about. The second chairman tipped his chin in thanks as he passed, but his passenger leaned out and glared back at me in outrage. He was an older man in his fifties with a red, sweating face. 'Damn fool!' he cried, spittle spraying from his lips.

I halted in surprise at his rudeness, searching for a suitable reply. A waterman turning for home watched the chair bobbing its way down the Mall. 'Twat,' he observed, cheerfully.

That would do. I touched my hat in appreciation and pressed on.

On Pall Mall, the blazing lights of St James's Palace cast a bright glow upon the pavement. Somewhere deep inside those rambling old buildings the king and his family would be playing cards or backgammon, watched by bored, obsequious courtiers. If I were king I would insist upon something fresh and new every night – a ball, a masque, a play. Or dismiss the entire court and wander naked through the palace, frightening the servants – why not? What use was being king if you could not do as you pleased? But by all accounts King George liked nothing better than routine – the same wearying pomp and ceremony day in and day out. It was said he visited his mistress at the same hour every day, pacing about outside her rooms if he were a few minutes early, squinting at his watch. I had distant cousins on my father's side of the family who spent their lives at court fighting for power and position amidst all that drudgery. My God – they were welcome to it.

I reached the end of the Mall and slipped into the park beyond, a hand resting on the hilt of my sword. St James's Park was a good deal safer than the stews of St Giles, but courtiers drove their carriages along Kensington Way late into the night. And where courtiers drove their carriages, foot pads and high-waymen were never far away – lean Highland wolves prowling amidst a flock of plump, dozy sheep.

I headed deeper into the park where the grass was higher, cursing silently as the wet mud splashed my stockings and pulled at my shoes. The lanterns along the King's Coach Way shone like jewels on a necklace. I crossed back into darkness, low and swift. I must not be seen here – not by a soul. A courtier meeting a young man alone at night in the park – reputations had been ruined by less.

Deep in the shadows of Buckingham House I took out my watch, holding the face up to the moonlight. Half past eight. Fleet's mysterious client should arrive at any moment. As a courtier, doubtless she would ride through the park from the palace itself. And as a woman, surely she would come by chair or carriage, with servants to protect her. I tucked away my watch and waited, stamping my feet to keep warm.

A few minutes later I caught the whisk of wheels along the King's Way. Out of the darkness a handsome black and gold carriage glided smoothly across the grass towards me, the driver urging on the horses with a light tap of his whip. Liveried footmen stood on either side of the carriage, guarding the doors, and a third stood on the back. The red velvet curtains at the win-dows were drawn tight. My heart began to pound, blood singing through my veins. Ahh ... this was why I had come, in truth. This brief feeling of mystery and excitement. No doubt in a few seconds the door would swing open and some trembling old dowager would tell me that her pug had run off, and might I find it for her.

I was about to step forward when someone gave a shout close by. '*Halt! Halt you dogs!*'

A shot rang out, exploding in the night air with a bright flash. I spun around in time to see a figure surge through the gun smoke. In my shock it took me a moment to realise this was the same man who had cursed me from his sedan chair near the Mall. Now he was sprinting towards the carriage, his face wild with rage.

'Run, damn you!' he snarled at the driver, who was trying to calm the terrified horses. 'Run – or by God I'll shoot you dead!'

The driver almost fell from his perch in terror, sliding to the ground and racing off into the darkness. Two of the footmen ran too, without a backward glance. Only the guard closest to the assailant stood firm – an older man, with a scarred face.

'For *shame*,' he called down. He gestured into the carriage. 'Would you attack an innocent woman?'

'Innocent?' The man with the pistol laughed nastily. 'She's a whore. The whole world knows it. Stand aside.'

With a great cry the guard leaped down from the carriage, landing heavily upon the other man. He shoved him to the ground and punched him hard in the stomach.

I sprang forward. By the time I had passed around the horses, the two men were rolling in the mud, punching and tearing at each other in a violent struggle. The horses had begun to rear up in fright, hooves thumping into the ground, knocking the carriage from side to side until the door slammed open. I caught a glimpse of a woman trapped inside, wrapped in a black velvet cloak, her face frozen in terror. As her clear blue eyes met mine, I realised with a jolt that I knew her.

Henrietta Howard. The king's mistress.

The guard was losing ground. I hesitated, not sure who to help first, then jumped onto the carriage step and held out my hand. Mrs Howard looked at me in a daze.

'Hurry,' I said. The horses were whinnying with fear, ready to bolt at any moment. I leaned into the carriage. 'Madam – please. Your hand!'

She started, as if waking from a nightmare, and slid towards me. As the carriage jolted forward she fell into my arms and I pulled her by the waist to the ground. A second later the horses took off, dragging the carriage behind them at a deadly pace.

I had saved Mrs Howard at the expense of her guard, who was bleeding from the nose and mouth, and swaying on his feet. He lifted his fists, but there was no strength in him. His attacker struck out with one last, fearsome punch and the guard thudded to the earth. He didn't move again.

Mrs Howard put her hands to her mouth. 'No,' she said, softly.

The man heard her and grinned, full red lips gaping wide. He looked half-mad, eyes gleaming with excitement. In the confusion of the attack, I had thought he must be a highwayman, but now I was not so sure. Highwaymen did not travel by sedan chair. From his clothes I thought he must be a nobleman, but he had an old rake's face, blotchy and ruined by years of debauchery. There was blood pouring from his temple down his cheek, but he didn't seem to notice it. Too drunk, no doubt – but my God he was fierce with it. He gave the guard a vicious kick to the ribs then staggered back, panting hard.

A cloud drifted apart and the moon shone bright, flooding us in silver light. Something gleamed bright by the man's boot, a glint of metal. The breath caught in my throat. The pistol. I drew my sword and prayed to God he didn't look down.

'Who the devil are you?' he slurred.

'Nobody. I heard shouts.'

'Well, Sir *Nobody*. That whimpering bitch belongs to me.' Mrs Howard gave a low sob and he leered at her. 'What – did you think you were free of me, slut? Did you think you were *safe?*' He laughed. I could smell the liquor on his breath from ten paces.

Mrs Howard gripped my arm. She was shaking with fear. 'Please, sir, I beg you. Don't let him take me.'

I pushed her behind me.

In a flash he was on me, knocking me down and dashing the blade from my hand. He was fearsome strong, despite his age and the drink – and he knew how to fight. I kicked out in panic, but he swung his fist hard, catching my jaw. My head smacked against the ground and my vision blurred. I slumped back, stunned, as the world spun about me.

In an instant he had pounced on me, fingers tearing at my throat. I grabbed his wrists and tried to struggle free, but he was too strong. I thought of the guard lying a few feet away, knocked senseless but alive. I might not be so lucky.

The man let go of my throat, raising his fist for another blow. This was my chance. I pushed up with all my strength, twisting and kicking at him in a fury. There was no grace or strategy to my blows, but I was bigger than him, half his age, and sober. As we rolled in the mud, my hand hit something hard. *The pistol.* I snatched it and aimed the muzzle at his head, pinning him to the ground with my free arm.

He fell still, staring at the barrel pointed an inch above his face. Then smiled. 'There's no powder.'

He was right – there'd been no time to reload it. I turned it around in my palm, felt the heft of it. Then I raised it high and slammed it against his temple. He gave a grunt of pain, and lay still.

I staggered to my feet, reeling. My jaw throbbed and I could feel blood seeping from my throat where his nails had torn into my skin. 'Mrs Howard,' I called out into the night. 'My lady?'

But she'd vanished.

Chapter Five

The house was dark and empty when I returned home. I heated a pan of mulled wine over the fire in my chamber, breathing in the warm, soothing scent of cloves and nutmeg.

I had been in a shocked stupor on my walk home, lurching through the streets in a daze. Now, as I collapsed into a chair by the fire, I realised how close I'd come to losing my life. I pulled off my wig and loosened my cravat. My left cheek was badly swollen and my jaw was throbbing so hard that I could only take tiny sips of wine. It did not seem broken, but I could tell it would take days to heal. So much for the thrill of adventure, Hawkins – you damned fool.

What the devil had happened? The ferocity and speed of the attack had left me reeling. I had seen men strip to the waist in the street to fight over some imagined slight. I'd been beaten and chained to a wall in gaol. I'd survived a riot, for heaven's sake. But I had never seen a man rage so far out of control and so fast. He was like a fighting dog, driven into a frenzy by a lust for blood. Could Mrs Howard have inspired such madness? Or was he cursed with an endless fury, always ready to leap into battle? Considering the way he'd spat and sworn at me from his sedan I guessed it was the latter. Either way, I prayed to God I never encountered the brute again.

As for Mrs Howard, who would blame her for running back to the safety of the palace? Whatever her present troubles, her lover could protect her far better than I. He was the *king*, damn it! I was glad to have saved her tonight, but I wanted no more part in such a dark intrigue. Court politics, James Fleet, and a raving mad man with a pistol? No, thank you, indeed.

I closed my eyes, exhausted now the danger had passed and my blood had cooled. I drifted into a fitful sleep, still sitting in the chair ... and woke in darkness. The fire had burned out. Voices drifted from the shop downstairs, snatches of laughter. I pulled myself slowly to my feet. Kitty was singing a ballad – loudly and somewhat off-key. A man begged her to spare his ears, and then they both laughed.

A shard of jealousy pierced my heart. It was John Eliot; I recognised his voice at once. Old, blissfully married, and round as a football. But still, he was alone with Kitty. I stole down the stairs, listening to their conversation. It was nothing – idle talk about the play and the devilish annoying people in the seats around them. I stood by the door and tortured myself for a few moments, even so. How could she sound so cheerful, when we had argued so badly just hours before? Did she not know that I had almost *died* tonight? That she could have come home to discover she had lost me for ever? *Well, no. She did not know that, Tom. In fact you refused to tell her where you were going, if you recall.*

Feeling somewhat foolish, I nudged open the door and bade them both a good evening.

'Ah! Hawkins!' Eliot exclaimed, rising to his feet and smiling warmly. They were seated at the table with a bottle of wine between them, lit only by a solitary candle.

'So,' Kitty said in a flat voice without turning around. 'You are home.' As if she did not care tuppence.

I took Eliot's outstretched hand.

'Brought her back for you, Hawkins,' he said cheerfully, then lowered his voice. 'She was in half a mind to stay with us tonight ... *Good God!*' He squinted at me. 'What's wrong with your face, man?'

'What's this?' Kitty scraped back her chair, then gasped in shock. 'Tom!' she cried, pushing Eliot aside and dragging me towards the candlelight. 'Is that *blood*?' She touched my cravat, saw the deep gouges beneath. 'Oh ... You're *hurt* ...'

'I'm fine,' I sighed, secretly delighted.

'Sam!' she called and a dark figure released itself from the shadows. I had not even seen him hiding there. 'Run across to Mrs Jenkins and fetch some ice. She took a load this morning.' She pushed him from the room and ran half up the stairs. 'Jenny!' she yelled, in a voice that must have woken every Jenny in a five-mile radius. 'Wake up! Mr Hawkins is hurt!'

A few minutes later I was settled on a low couch while Kitty washed the wounds at my throat with a scalding mix of brandy and hot water. I winced and gestured to the bowl. 'Could I not drink that instead? It looks ... medicinal.'

'You're filthy,' she said, dabbing hard at one of the deeper cuts. 'Have you been rolling around in the mud?'

'Yes, as a matter of fact. I was attacked in St James's Park.'

Kitty's brows rose sharply. 'A highwayman?'

'I'm not sure *what* he was. A mad man, perhaps.'

She nodded and continued tending my wounds. After a little while, she said, 'I am a good, patient soul, am I not, Mr Eliot?'

Eliot had returned to the table, a glass of claret balanced on his fat belly. 'A saint,' he agreed.

'Because I do know how you hate to be *nagged*, Tom. And of course I am not your wife, so it is not my place to ask, "and what took you to the park so late?" or "who did you expect to meet there?" It would be *most indelicate* of me to suggest that perhaps you should have taken me to the damned play this evening instead, as you bloody well promised. Gah!' She scrubbed at a spot on my jaw. 'Damn it. This dirt won't come off.'

'I think it's a bruise,' I said, weakly.

'Oh. So it is.' She stopped scrubbing. Touched her lips to it.

'Kitty . . .'

'This was James Fleet's work, wasn't it?'

I gave a small, grunt, admitting nothing.

'It's no great puzzle,' Eliot called from the table. 'Kitty mentioned your visit this afternoon . . .'

' . . . and then – all of a sudden – you had a secret, unexpected meeting,' Kitty finished. She cupped a hand to my swollen jaw and held it there lightly. 'Tom. Tell me this. Is it finished with?'

'Yes,' I said, without hesitation.

'And you promise you won't work for that bastard again?'

'*Never.*'

She reached over and hugged me close, hiding her tenderness in a grip that half-crushed my ribs. 'Well then,' she said, when she was done injuring me. 'You are forgiven. Are you not the luckiest dog alive?'

Sam materialised, and dropped a packet of ice in my lap. I shrieked an oath.

'Mrs Jenkins wants sixpence.'

'Cow,' Kitty muttered.

'Did you enjoy the play, Sam?' I asked, once I'd recovered.

Sam shook his head, curls flying.

'Oh!' Eliot and Kitty protested together.

'It was made up,' Sam shrugged. 'Don't see the point of it.'

'What was the play?'

'*The Beggar's Opera,*' Kitty answered for him, when it became clear that Sam did not know and did not care. 'We've been talking about it for *weeks*, Tom.'

'Oh . . .!' I said, crestfallen. 'I was longing to see that.'

Kitty muttered something under her breath.

Eliot slapped his hands upon the table and pushed himself up from his chair. 'I'm sure it will run for weeks. Anything that rude about parliament is sure to be a success.'

'Was it not about a gang of thieves . . .? *Ah.*'

Eliot squeezed himself into his coat, flexing his arms with a look of surprise, as if it had shrunk since he took it off. 'I doubt Mr Gay will be welcome in court from now on. But I suppose that was the point. The play is his revenge upon them all.'

'Indeed?' Eliot made it his business to read every newspaper and broadsheet he could lay his hands upon, and always knew the gossip around the court. 'How so?'

He plucked his hat from its hook on the wall. 'Gay is a great friend of Henrietta Howard. He was sure she'd secure a nice plump position for him at court one day – planned his future on it. Then old frog eyes was crowned king and it transpired that Mrs Howard had no influence over him whatsoever. It's the *queen* he listens to and no one else. Who would have guessed it? A man taking advice from his *wife.*' He winked at Kitty. 'Most unnatural.'

I smiled but stayed quiet, thinking of the terrified woman I had met so briefly tonight. I was not surprised she'd failed to help John Gay: she couldn't even save herself. Had she promised something similar to the man who had attacked her tonight? Some preferment that had failed to appear? Ach, and what did it matter? I would never see her again.

'Mackheath should have hanged,' Sam said.

'Hanged?' Eliot was outraged. 'He's the hero!'

'He's a highwayman,' Kitty corrected him, plucking his hat from his head and setting it upon hers at a jaunty angle.

'You can't kill the hero, not in a comedy,' Eliot persisted, reaching for his hat. Kitty swirled away from him, laughing. 'The audience would riot.'

Sam disagreed. 'Seen fifty or more Mackheaths turned off at Tyburn. The audience cheers.'

Later, Kitty and I lay in bed, drowsing under thick blankets as the fire dwindled to ash. I rested my head against her heart, listening to its soft beat as she ran her hand over my scalp, bristles rasping beneath her fingers.

'I must visit the barber,' I said.

She traced a finger down my bruised jaw. 'Leave it to grow a little. I like it when it turns soft. It feels like moleskin.'

I chuckled and reached for her hand.

'Tom,' she said, after a while. 'Could I have lost you tonight?'

I thought of the man's fingers tearing at my throat. The heavy thud of horses' hooves. The desperation and terror in Henrietta's eyes. 'Of course not.'

'I couldn't live without you,' she said, very quiet.

I laughed. 'You could live *very* well without me. Think of the money you'd save.'

She sighed and said nothing. The room was dark, and silent, but I could feel her disappointment in the air all around me, settling upon me like a dank mist.

There was a loud thud against the wall behind us. We both started in alarm.

Thud. Again, louder this time, something slamming hard on the other side of the wall.

'What *is* that?' Kitty whispered, crawling closer to the wall to listen.

I fumbled for my tinderbox, sparked a light. As I lit the candle, a woman cried out.

'Ahh! Ahh, God. Yes!'

Kitty clapped a hand to her mouth. Started to giggle.

The bed thumped again, and the woman yelped.

I stared at the wall in astonishment. Next door was Joseph Burden's house. People didn't fuck one another in Joseph Burden's house. We exchanged excited looks. 'Who is it, do you suppose?'

Kitty put an ear to the wall. 'Alice? Alice and Ned?'

'No. Their rooms will be up in the attic.'

She listened closer, frowning in concentration. 'It can't be Judith. I suppose it *must* be Alice.'

'With Stephen?'

There was a long, shuddering moan, then silence. Kitty pulled a face. 'Ugh. That wasn't *Burden*, was it?'

We threw up our hands in horror at the idea – then sniggered like children. Joseph Burden, proud member of the Society for the Reformation of Manners, was fucking his housekeeper. Well, well.

'Oh! Your gift!' Kitty said, then reached under the bed and lifted out a handsome wooden box. She slid it towards me, a little nervous.

I put the box on my lap and rested the lid on its hinge. Inside lay a dozen packages, narrow and flat. I took one out and opened it up, conscious of Kitty watching for my reaction. Nestling in the envelope was a long, translucent sheath folded in two and tied loosely with a thin piece of ribbon. A condom.

'I ordered them from France, for the shop. They're made from sheep's intestines.'

How arousing. 'Yes. I've er . . . I've used them before.'

She slipped her hand in mine. 'So . . . we don't have to wait, any more.'

Her face gleamed in the candlelight. So young, so pretty. This was her gift to me, then. The last of her innocence. I brushed her hair from her face. She smiled, nervous, and looked deep in my eyes.

Tell her. Tell her why you've waited this long. Tell her that you want to marry her first and take care of her. That you want it to be different from all the other times. Tell her that you're afraid if you don't wait, she will never have cause to marry you.

Tell her that you love her, damn it.

I opened my mouth ... and the words died in my throat. 'I'm ... I'm rather tired tonight, Kitty. After all that's happened ...' And it was true, save for my lie of omission.

Her eyes softened with concern. 'Oh. Of course,' she agreed, embarrassed, shutting up the box at once and slipping it beneath the bed. She touched her lips to my cheek. 'Of course.'

I blew out the candle and we lay in silence in the dark.

PART TWO

On now – the procession carries them to the narrow stone bridge and the Fleet ditch. He smells it long before he sees it: a stinking slurry of shit and offal. Not so much a river as a running sore, oozing its way down to the Thames. Thank God it is a cold, sharp day in March, not the dense heat of summer. The wind whisks the stench away down south towards Blackfriars. Hawkins closes his eyes, his body swaying as the cart turns on to Holborn Hill.

'Murderer!'

An old woman's voice pierces the air. His eyes snap open. She screams it again and he sees her, a stranger in the swirling crowds, her face twisted with hatred. Others take up the call, shouting curses down upon him.

'Monster!'

'Burn in Hell!'

How they hate him. Not just for the life they think he took, but for the life he squandered. A young gentleman, given every opportunity. Money, good health, an education – all wasted.

A gang of apprentices leans out of a tavern window, waiting for the cart to pass below them. As it does, they throw a hail of stones at him, laughing at the sport. They are drunk and most of their shots sail wide, but one catches him hard. Blood spurts from his temple. He shields his head with his hands, half-stunned.

A lean, black-clad figure clambers on to the open end of the cart and crawls towards him. The Reverend James Guthrie, the Newgate Ordinary. He holds out a handkerchief. 'They would hate you less if you confessed.'

Hawkins presses the handkerchief to the wound and leans back, staring up into the cold, white sky.

'I'm innocent, Mr Guthrie.'

'Mr Hawkins ...' Guthrie begins, then thinks better of it. He cannot help a man who will not help himself. He jumps down from the cart. 'God have mercy on your soul,' he says loudly, as he strides away. Playing to the crowd.

By the time they reach the edge of St Giles, the bleeding has stopped. St Giles. Drowning in vice, soaking in gin. Shake a house in St Giles and more thieves, whores, and murderers will tumble out than you'll find in the whole of Newgate Prison. It's a fitting place for one last drink. The horses stop outside the Crown tavern without a prompt from their riders. They have taken this road many times before.

The guards help him down from the cart. It is so cold he can see his breath, escaping in clouds from his lips. Someone passes him a cup of mulled wine, pats him on the shoulder. He curls his fingers around the cup, grateful for the warmth. The dark-red wine looks almost like blood, steaming in the freezing air.

The crowds are friendlier here. They shout encouragements and promise to pray for him. They are the lowest of men and the lewdest of women: cutpurses, highwaymen, fraudsters and cheats, only a step from the noose themselves. For the first time in his life he wishes he could linger here, but he has barely finished his wine when he is ordered back on the wagon. As the Crown fades into the distance a thought comes into his mind, hard and certain as prophecy. That was the last time my feet will ever touch the earth.

And now he feels it – the horror that he has fought off for so long. It knocks him reeling, harder than any stone hurled from the crowd.

He is about to die.

No. No! They promised. He will live.

He is a coin, spinning on its edge. Heads or tails. Life or death.

Chapter Six

It was almost a week before I was ready to step into the world again. My jaw was so black and swollen for the first few days that I could only eat light broths and syllabubs. The gouges in my neck worried Kitty so much she insisted on washing them in hot wine twice a day.

'I'll stink like a tavern floor,' I complained, flinching as the wine invaded the cuts.

'Clean wounds mend faster,' she said, dabbing a home-made salve over my throat. Kitty's father Nathaniel had been a renowned physician – and a close friend of Samuel Fleet. When she first moved in to the Cocked Pistol, Kitty had found a cache of his books and journals locked in a chest in the cellar. She would read them avidly when the shop was quiet, or late at night, squinting by the light of the fire.

One morning, a few days after the attack, I was lying in bed when there was a soft tap on the door. I had just propped myself on my pillow when Jenny slipped into the room. She stayed close to the door, fingers on the handle. Her eyes trailed to my bare chest, then darted away. 'May I speak with you, sir?'

'Of course.'

'I'm afraid . . . I'm afraid I must leave your service, sir.'

I hid my dismay. 'Because of Sam? I'll arrange a bolt for your room, Jenny, I promise – it's just that I've been distracted these past days . . .' I gestured to my wounds. 'I will speak with him too, if you wish—'

'It's not that, sir. At least – only in part.' She shielded herself behind the door, half in, half out. 'I've found a position in a house on Leicester Fields. I met the family at church.'

'Ah, I see. Well, Kitty will miss you.' *She'll be furious.* 'D'you need a reference?'

She shook her head, alarmed by the offer. 'It's kind of you, sir, but I'd be grateful if you didn't mention to no one that I worked here. They . . . they say such dreadful things about you in church.'

I chuckled. 'Oh, I can imagine.'

'No, sir.'

Her words stilled the room. *No, sir.* An interruption and a contradiction. This was not how Jenny spoke to me. A chill crept over me; a premonition that whatever she said next would destroy everything. I wanted to jump from the bed and cup a hand to her mouth. Instead, I waited, and a silence stole up between us.

Jenny twisted her fingers together in an anxious fashion. Her hands were red and chafed from her work and there was a small burn at the base of her thumb, where it had brushed against a hot pan. She too seemed reluctant to continue. Her lips were pressed together and she was breathing hard through her nose. *She's scared. Scared of me.*

Don't ask. Don't ask her.

'What do they say of me, Jenny?' The fear made my voice turn cold. The question had sounded almost like a threat, even to my ears.

She swallowed. 'They say you killed a man, sir. In the Marshalsea.'

There was a long pause. She began to shake.

'You must know that is a lie,' I said.

She nodded, without conviction.

'Who is it, who tells such foul lies about me?' But I knew the answer even as I asked. 'Mr Burden?'

Another nod. She took half a step on to the landing. 'He said Mr Gonson will prove it.'

'And people believe him?' Jenny attended St Paul's church at the west end of the piazza. Half the neighbourhood worshipped there of a Sunday.

'No ... at least ... not so much, sir. But then you was seen coming home all beaten and covered in blood and people began to wonder. Sir – I must think of my own reputation, you see? This new position, it's most respectable ...'

'I understand,' I said, and relief washed over her face. 'I would be grateful, Jenny, if you did not speak of this to Miss Sparks.'

'No, sir. I won't say nothing. I promise.'

'You do not believe I am a killer, Jenny?'

'No, sir!' she said. But oh – the pause before she answered. It near broke my heart.

'Very good.' I dismissed her with a nod.

She dipped a curtsey and closed the door. Packed her few belongings and left within the hour.

Damn Joseph Burden, spewing his poison. Rumours spread like the pox in this town – before long half of London would know me as a murderous villain. Heaven knows, I looked the part with my black eye and swollen jaw. I dared not venture out or even downstairs into the shop in such a dreadful state – that would only complete the portrait and set our neighbours gossiping afresh. And so I brooded alone in my room, prowling up and down as if I were back in prison.

I didn't tell Kitty about Jenny's confession. Kitty's love was fierce and volatile as wildfire and it would only bring more trouble. At best she would worry. At worst she would confront Burden. So I kept quiet and prayed for the rumours to die away.

But Kitty was no fool, and she soon grew suspicious of my behaviour. I have always preferred to be out and in company. It was not in my nature to hide away in my room, not even for the sake of vanity.

One night I dreamed that I was trapped once more in the Marshalsea. The guards came for me in my cell and dragged me through the yard towards the wall. They were taking me to the Common Side, to the Strong Room. I began to scream, but I had no voice. They laughed and pushed me inside, locking the door behind me. I was alone. Breathing in the stench of death. The rats, writhing and squealing about my feet. I took a step forward and cold, dank fingers wrapped about my ankles. More hands, fleshless skeleton hands pulling me down. A pile of rotting corpses. I staggered and fell among them. They were holding me down, wrapping me in a tight embrace as the rats swarmed over us, claws scrabbling at my face. The more I struggled, the deeper I sank into the pile, until I couldn't breathe and there was earth in my mouth and I would never be free, I was trapped in here for ever . . .

'*Tom!*' Kitty shook me awake.

I sat up, heart racing. My shirt was soaked with sweat.

She reached for my hand in the dark. 'You were screaming.'

'Gaol.' But it had been more than that. I could still taste the soil in my mouth. And there was a tinge in the air – the high, sweet scent of putrid meat. I had dreamed of Death and it clung to me still, even though I was awake.

'It's no wonder you're dreaming of prison,' Kitty said. 'You've been trapped in this room for too long. You must go out, Tom.'

She was right. The longer I stayed locked in the house the

more I would feel like a prisoner. And the more old dreams would return to haunt me. I lay back down against the pillow.

Kitty curled up beside me, stroking my chest. 'Your heart is beating so hard . . . Are you in trouble, still?'

We both are, my love, if I can't stop Burden from spreading his lies. I kissed the top of her head. 'No.'

She sighed, her breath warm against my skin. 'I *hate* it when you lie to me.'

The next evening Kitty decided to visit the Eliots. She tried to persuade me to join her but I refused, insisting she take Sam instead. I didn't like her walking the dark streets alone and it would do Sam good to spend some time in decent company.

'Stay close to Miss Sparks,' I said, as he wound my best cravat around his neck. 'And remember what I taught you about good conversation.'

He looked at me in the mirror. 'Sentences.'

'Yes, indeed. Sentences.' I paused. 'That wasn't one, for example.'

He tied up his hair with a black ribbon. I had still not persuaded him to shave his head. He would never pass as a gentleman without a wig. Then I tried to imagine Sam in a wig, bowing to ladies and exchanging idle banter with other gents – and was struck once again by the folly of my endeavours. Sam would never be a gentleman – counterfeit or otherwise. He might as well keep his curls if he loved them so much.

I waited until he and Kitty had left, then dressed and strode out into Covent Garden. My jaw was still a little swollen, but my eye was much better. The night would hide the worst of it.

Moll's coffeehouse was as rowdy as ever – the din carried halfway down Russell Street. The customers I knew well, the girls even better, flashing glances at me through the yellow haze of pipe smoke. *Another life*, I reminded myself, with a twinge of regret. I had not come here for sport but for information. This was the best place to discover how far Burden's lies about me had spread. And how much trouble I was in.

Moll King was winning a game of cards, surrounded by drunken admirers. No one knew Moll's real age – middling thirties, I guessed. She was no longer in her prime, but she had a wicked charm, more alluring than the sweet complexion and slim ankles of her freshest girls. Once, her husband Tom had ruled the coffeehouse and the marriage – and Moll had the scars to prove it. But she had worked and waited over the years – always sober, always clever – as the drink weakened him. Now he sat by the fire, bloated and gouty, with half his teeth rotted from his head, while his wife flirted and schemed and ran the place as if he were already in his grave. His name remained above the door, but this was Moll's place and the world knew it. I had been one of her favourites for a while, but she had lost interest now I shared my life with Kitty. I gave her the odd secret from the gaming tables to keep her friendly, but there were so many other young men in town, willing to spend money on her and on her girls. She blew me a kiss across the room and returned to her game.

It was Betty I needed, Moll's black serving maid. I found her making a pot of coffee by the fire. She tilted her chin to a corner table away from the main company. After a few minutes she brought me a bowl of punch, taking a glass for herself and settling down across the table.

People underestimated Betty. They ignored her, in fact. There was always one black serving maid at Moll's – it was a tradition. And she was always called Betty – no matter her real name. Two years ago *this* Betty had replaced another girl. Some customers hadn't even noticed the change – she was just the black maid pouring their coffee. The first time I saw her, it was a quiet evening. I was pretending to read a newspaper while listening to a conversation at the next bench. I'd glanced up to find Betty watching me from a corner, a half-smile on her lips. I grinned back. She'd caught me eavesdropping on the customers and I'd caught her spying on me. Kindred spirits.

I liked Betty – I liked the way she watched the world from beneath her thick black lashes. I think she liked me too. There was something unfinished between us – some path I had missed too long ago to trace again. A secret heat I felt in her gaze. *Another life, indeed.*

She sipped her punch. 'Gonson paid us a visit last night.'

This was not surprising news. Gonson seemed to spend half his days raiding the Cocked Pistol, and the other half searching the coffeehouses for thieving whores to punish. For a man who hated vice so much, he certainly spent a great deal of time immersed in it.

'Anyone arrested?'

Betty cupped a hand to my cheek and guided my attention towards the next bench. Two of Moll's girls were astride the table, lazily pulling up their skirts for an elderly judge and a fawning band of lawyers. The men watched with glazed expressions as one of the girls knelt down, then ran her tongue up the other girl's thigh and . . . Well. Not everyone shared Gonson's crusading moral spirit, it seemed.

'Mistress King has a lot of *friends*,' Betty said, then sucked in her breath. Her fingers traced the bruises along my jaw. 'I heard you was attacked.'

'Defending a lady.'

Betty looked amused. I raised my hands to protest my innocence.

'Gonson asked about you last night.' She leaned closer. Betty wore a rare perfume, laced with the warm, sweet scent of jasmine. It smelled expensive and intoxicating, an intriguing counterpoint to the rough tang of coal smoke caught in her hair. How could she afford it? Perhaps she had a secret lover; a nobleman, or a rich merchant who traded in exotic scents. And at the thought of this I felt a tinge of jealousy, though I was not entitled to such a feeling. She put her lips to my ear. 'He wanted to know if you'd killed a man. And there was plenty willing to talk.'

I muttered an oath. 'What did they say?'

'Lies. Half-truths. Your neighbour came with him – Burden. Went about the room, offering to pay good coin to any man who'd tell the magistrate what a foul villain you were. He's set upon chasing you from your home.'

Or worse. I covered my mouth with my hand. A few months ago I would have laughed at such nonsense and dismissed it. But I had learned not to be so careless. Gonson was persistent and patient, and Burden hated me. A dangerous combination.

Across the room, Moll was calling for more wine. She would not drink it – but she was playing cards with a gang who would. Easier to win against drunken fools. Her table cheered their approval and it seemed to raise the din throughout the coffee-house, as men shouted to be heard over their neighbours. But Betty's voice was soft against my ear. 'Gonson knows about the murder on Snows Fields.'

And for a moment, that dark night enveloped me once more. The desperate fight to survive. An open grave and the taste of dirt in my mouth. The smell of gun smoke and blood. Kitty. 'It wasn't murder.'

'Was it not?' Betty asked, softly.

I drank my punch while Betty watched me, worried. 'Gonson

follows the law,' I said, as much to reassure myself as her. 'There is no evidence. Nothing for him to discover.'

'Then you should stay in your fox hole, Mr Hawkins. Let the hounds pass you by. There'll be someone fresh for them to chase soon enough.'

It was good advice, as ever. Betty had tried to help me once before, and I hadn't listened. A few minutes later I had been arrested and thrown in gaol. 'I just want to be left in peace, Betty.'

She rolled her eyes. 'Of course. That's why you've been working for *James Fleet.*'

Ah. That was the unfortunate thing about Betty. She really did know everything.

Betty returned to her work while I lit a pipe, thinking about Burden and Gonson, and about Betty's advice. I supposed it *would* be wise to leave London for a time. I could visit my father in Suffolk. That would require leaving Kitty alone, which I did not like. Or taking her with me to meet my father, which I did not like still more.

I had no desire to leave the city. Why the devil should I? Why should I be chased from my home by Joseph Burden? Perhaps I should spread a few rumours about him, the blasted hypocrite. Perhaps I should tell the world that the man who lectured his neighbours on their manners all day was fucking his housekeeper at night?

I took a draw upon my pipe and settled back in my chair, breathing smoke in a lazy stream to the ceiling. I felt comfortable at Moll's, especially here on the fringes with a bowl of warm winter punch at hand. Disgraceful things were happening in dark corners, half-glimpsed in the fluttering candlelight. I relaxed – feeling more at ease than I had in days – and poured another glass. How many rumours had I heard and dismissed in this coffeehouse in the last three years? The punch sent a golden glow through my veins, bestowing a false contentment.

The men at the next table were discussing the latest rift between the king and the Prince of Wales. 'All that gold. All that power, and they still can't muddle along together,' one of them said, shaking his head, as if the gold and the power weren't the problem in the first place. It's a trifle hard to find your son agreeable when he's tapping his toe behind you, waiting impatiently for you to snuff it.

Bored by the conversation, I let my gaze drift across the coffeehouse. Then sat up straighter, craning my neck to look over the crowds. Was that . . .? So it was. Ned Weaver, Burden's apprentice. I hadn't spoken with him since the night of the invisible thief. And I had never seen him at Moll's before. Burden would not allow it, surely. How curious. He was sitting on his own at the edge of a rowdy bench, head slumped in his hand. I knew the other men at his table – a foul bunch of villains and drunks who had prompted many of the worst fights at Moll's. Regular customers had learned to keep their distance.

Their leader – a short fellow, all sinew and sneer – muttered something to his companions. They shifted as one and glowered at Ned. He stared into his bowl of coffee, oblivious.

What the devil was he doing here? In the three months I'd lived on Russell Street I had never once seen him out in the taverns and coffeehouses of Covent Garden. The men were whispering to each other now, scowling openly at the foreigner washed up upon their land. Ned was a strong, solid lad with powerful muscles from his years of labour. I'd seen him run down the street carrying an oak table twice his size on his back. But these men were ferocious bastards in a fight – and there were six of them.

I should mind my own business. I had my bowl of punch and

a fresh pipe – and troubles of my own. *Stay in your fox hole, Mr Hawkins.*

Ned rubbed his hands over his face. His clothes were in disarray, his waistcoat unbuttoned, his shirt loose. He looked close to tears.

Damn it. If he were only a bully like his master, someone I could despise and ignore. I should not trouble myself . . . And yet here I was, rising to my feet and pushing through the crowds. Might a few coins settle this? I arrived at the bench just as one of the gang shoved Ned hard in the ribs. He started as if from a dream, then leaped to his feet, fists raised. Oh, God – not another fight. Pain stabbed through my jaw at the thought. If someone hit me again tonight my head would probably fall off.

'Gentlemen,' I said, putting a hand on Ned's shoulder and pulling him back.

Six men scowled up at me. There was a moment's tense silence. I kept my shoulders back. Ned was tall and strong and so was I. Between us we could . . . run very fast for the street, God help us.

And then, to my astonishment, all six men drew back, nervous. After a moment's pause, the leader dipped his chin at me. 'Mr Hawkins.' The rest of the gang followed, nodding sharply and turning back to their punch.

I looked from face to face, amazed by my good fortune and not quite sure I believed in it. But no – it seemed they had no appetite for a fight this evening, possibly for the first time in their lives. Half faint with relief, I grabbed Ned and led him away, back to my table. 'That was a piece of luck,' I muttered, leaning across to borrow a glass for him from the next table.

Ned stole a glance across the room as I poured him some punch. 'There was no luck to it, sir. They was afraid of you.'

'Nonsense.' I relit my pipe.

Ned took a mouthful of punch, then coughed half of it back on to the table. He wiped his mouth with a smile of embarrassment. 'Mr Burden don't allow liquor in the house.'

'So I hear.' I took a long draw on my pipe. 'But he allows Alice in his bed.'

Ned's handsome, open face flashed with anger. 'That . . . that is not true,' he floundered. He was a terrible liar.

'The walls are very thin, Ned.'

He struggled for a moment, loyal to his master. But I could see the desire to confide in someone playing through him, and there was anger there too. His fists, resting on the table, were clenched tight. 'It's wicked, sir,' he said at last. 'Alice Dunn is a respectable woman. But if she doesn't . . . If she refused him . . . She's nowhere to go. She'd end up like *them*.' His eyes flickered to the girls at the lawyers' table, gowns pulled down to their waist. Hands working under loosened breeches.

I laid down my pipe. 'He's taking her against her will?'

'It started a few weeks ago, in secret. We didn't know. Then Alice cried thief the other night – *from his bed*. We all heard her.' He hung his head. 'Now he don't bother to keep quiet. I scolded Alice for it, told her it was a sin. She swore Mr Burden made her do it. She said he makes her cry out so we can hear. I don't know. I suppose . . . perhaps she lies . . .'

But I could tell he did not believe that. There were tears in his eyes, as if the shame were his and not his master's. And in truth how could he stand to lie abed at night and listen to it? We had laughed, Kitty and I, when we heard Burden and Alice together. It made me sick to think of it.

And what of Burden's children, Judith and Stephen? Did they know the truth – did they understand? I hoped to God they did not. I thought of Judith crouched on the stairs that night, spitting Alice's name as if it tasted foul upon her tongue. And

Stephen, threatening to tell Gonson what he saw. What he *truly* saw that night.

I felt a terrible rage growing inside me. This was the man who was spreading foul lies about me? The man who dared to judge me a villain? I closed my eyes. How I hated him in that moment. And the thought came to me before I could stop myself. *I wish that he were dead.* 'That is terrible, Ned. How can you bear it?'

Ned rolled his empty glass around and around in a despondent fashion. He had the hands of a busy carpenter – battered and grazed, quick and clever. 'There's something wrong with him. He ain't himself. I've been his apprentice for seven years. Six days a week working at his side. He promised me a paid position once I'd finished my apprenticeship. And now it's done . . .' His voice fractured. 'He's ordered me to leave by the end of the week.'

'My God!' To promise a position for seven years, to benefit from Ned's labour for all that time – and then withdraw the offer when the apprenticeship was over? It was nothing more than slavery. 'Can he not afford to pay you?'

'Ten times over! There's no sense to it. How will he manage without me? The old fool can't survive on his own, not at his age.'

'Perhaps he expects to hand the business to Stephen?'

'*Stephen?* He couldn't lift a hammer.' Ned's face crinkled in amusement and I was struck once again by his kind nature. I would have felt bitter and resentful in his place. Ned seemed more *perplexed*. As if his master had been replaced with a stranger. It was the puzzle of it all that seemed to trouble him the most. 'What am I to do, Mr Hawkins?'

'I shouldn't worry, Ned. You're an honest man with a good trade. Strong and healthy . . .' I patted his arm. My God, strong was right. His muscles were hard as iron. 'You'll have no trouble finding a position.'

'But it's my *home*, sir.' He paused, eyes filled with tears once more. 'I thought he was proud of me. But he doesn't care if I starve in the street. Seven years. Seven years for *nothing*.'

I frowned in sympathy. Poured him another glass.

By the time we'd reached the bottom of a second punch bowl – of which Ned had drunk half a glass – I had boiled myself into a drunken fury. How dare Burden use Ned in such a cruel fashion? And how dare he blacken *my* reputation in the neighbourhood? Leaving the coffeehouse, I stumbled out into the piazza, Ned trailing anxiously at my heels. The cold night air slapped at my face and the cobbles buckled at my feet. I had not felt this drunk for a long time. I had barely touched a drop since my fight in St James's Park, and I had forgotten to eat supper.

When I reached Burden's house, I pounded my fist against the door.

'Burden! Come out and face me, you son of a cunt!' What had I just said? Son of a . . . what did that mean? I shook my head, clearing it a little.

Ned put a hand on my shoulder. 'Mr Hawkins, sir . . .'

He was strong, but there is no one stronger than an outraged drunk. I wrested myself free and kicked the door, slamming my heel into the wood. When no one came, I kicked it again. I kicked and pounded at it until the blood ran from my knuckles. And then I drew my sword and slammed the pommel into the wood.

At last the bolts swung back and Burden stood in the doorway, angry and defiant – until he saw the sword in my fist. 'What is this?'

I slotted the sword back in my belt – after several failed attempts. It is a hard procedure when there is more punch in one's veins than blood. 'You have been spreading lies. Vile, scoundralous lies.' I paused. One of those words was not, necessarily, a word.

'Ned,' Burden called, beckoning him inside.

Ned shouldered his way past, looking sheepish. As Burden moved to close the door I pushed back, glaring at him through the crack. 'How dare you judge me,' I hissed. 'When you're fucking Alice Dunn against her will?'

Burden looked stunned at this – but he recovered fast enough. He grinned, baring his teeth. 'Mr Gonson visited the Marshalsea today. One of the turnkeys swears you killed a man.'

And of a sudden, I was sober.

'They'll hang you for it,' he crowed. 'That is a promise, Hawkins.'

He closed the door in my face.

Fear washed through me. It wasn't true. It wasn't possible. I was innocent. But I had made enough enemies in gaol – and I could think of several turnkeys who would be happy to perjure themselves for a price. Or worse – tell Gonson what had really happened. Oh, God – no. The ground pitched beneath my feet and I had to clutch the wall to steady myself.

Now the heat of fury had left me I felt exhausted. My hands were throbbing. I stared down in confusion and saw to my horror that my knuckles were raw and bloody from pounding at Burden's door. Oh God. What had I done? The street was alive behind me, summoned by the drumming of my fists. The girls in the brothel across the road grinned and waved as I caught their eye while our more respectable neighbours stood frozen on their doorsteps, mouths open in shock. They hadn't heard Burden's accusation, but they'd seen me beat down his door, raving like a lunatic. *With a sword in my hand.*

I hurried home, closing the door on the world. Collapsed on the stairs. Tore off my hat and wig and loosened my cravat, thinking hard. I should flee to the continent – set off tonight before Gonson could arrange a warrant. I leaped up the stairs, then stopped on the landing. Leave without Kitty? Impossible. If Gonson spoke to the wrong people she would be in just as much danger.

Eliot would help us if we told him the truth. Perhaps he had guessed some of it. Yes – that was the best course of action, at least it seemed to be. My head was still muddled by the drink. I collected a few things for Kitty – some clothes, her father's papers, her jewellery – and all the money I could find in the house. I had just begun on my own clothes when there was a sharp rap at the door.

I cursed and moved to the window. A carriage stood outside the shop, guarded by two men with clubs. My heart swooped like a hawk. I was too late. Another guard stood at the door, a musket at his shoulder. He glanced up and saw me at the window. 'Mr Hawkins. Open up, sir!'

With a rush of relief, I recognised him as the guard I'd saved in St James's Park. These must be Henrietta Howard's men.

I hurried downstairs, gathering my wig and hat from the floor. As I opened the door, the guard gave a short bow and beckoned me to the carriage.

I gestured inside. 'I will leave a note for—'

'—no time,' he interrupted.

I hesitated, suddenly suspicious. 'Where are we going?'

The guard signalled to the others. In a second they had seized me and slung me into the carriage. I tumbled to the floor, a pile of clothes and a jumble of limbs. I struggled up on to the bench while the guard settled back on the opposite seat and slammed the door tight. With a soft cry, the driver urged the horses forward and we raced away, down Drury Lane towards the Strand. I held on to my seat with my bruised hands, feeling somewhat dizzy from the swaying carriage and the speed of my capture.

The guard tapped his swollen jaw. 'Yours is healing well. But you're a young man.' He grinned, revealing a fresh gap in his teeth. With his flattened nose and old smallpox scars, his face was a brutal sight, but he seemed friendly enough. 'Budge,' he said, holding out his hand.

I shook it. 'Am I in trouble, Mr Budge?'

He threw his head back and laughed. 'Up to your neck, Mr Hawkins.'

Chapter Seven

As we reached the entrance to St James's Palace, Budge ordered me to lie on the floor and threw a coarse wool blanket over me. It stank of horse. There was a short exchange with the guards, and then the carriage rolled forward again, rattling across a large courtyard. The horses made a sharp turn and we rolled to a halt. I felt a tap on my shoulder. 'Wait here.' I began to sit up, but Budge pushed me back with a sharp prod.

I lay cramped in the dark, trying my best to prepare myself for my unexpected appointment with the king's mistress. What in heaven was Mrs Howard thinking, to smuggle me into the palace in such a fashion? She must be quite desperate. The thought made me uneasy. She may not have the power to help Mr Gay find a suitable court position, but I had no doubt she could make my life uncomfortable if she chose. As if it were not uncomfortable enough, lying beneath a horse blanket in the freezing cold.

I shifted position, then winced as the hilt of my sword poked against my hip. Deep in my pocket, my silver fob watch ticked softly. It had been a gift from Samuel Fleet. What would my old cell mate make of all this business? Why, he'd be delighted of course – perfectly thrilled. Fleet had lived for trouble. Died for it too.

How late was it? How much time had passed? It was too dark to read my watch. I couldn't risk waiting much longer – I must reach Kitty and flee the city with her tonight. Perhaps I should leave now, escape into the dark city streets. But how would I explain myself to the guards at the gate house? How would they react if they discovered me creeping through the king's palace with a sword at my hip? Knowing my luck, they'd charge me with treason and burn me at the stake.

Footsteps. I shrank beneath my blanket, but it was only a groom, come to free the horses and lower the shafts. The carriage tilted and I slid along the floor, cracking my ankle bone against the seat. I uttered a low curse. The footsteps drew closer. A lantern flared at the window, flooding the carriage with light. I lay still, holding my breath for a long, tense minute. Then the carriage darkened and I was alone again.

Another hour passed before Budge returned. By now I was quite sober and my head was pounding. I threw off the blanket and stumbled from the carriage, stretching my aching limbs and back.

'Too tall,' Budge observed, as if I might want to rectify the problem. 'Apologies for the wait. The king. Speechifying.'

We moved quickly through the stables, the horses stamping and snuffling in the dark. The courtyard beyond was lit with lanterns and torches, bright after my long vigil in the dark. I blinked up at the rambling maze of red brick buildings that formed the palace, marvelling at it all. In spite of my misgivings, I could not help but feel a flicker of excitement.

We crossed the yard, pausing in the shadows as a couple of footmen rushed by with lanterns. When all was still again we turned towards a discreet, unguarded side door. Budge unlocked it and beckoned me forward.

'Quiet now,' he breathed, though we had not spoken a word since I left the carriage.

The corridor beyond was very dark and we had no light, so we were forced to stretch out our hands and brush the walls with our fingertips to guide the way. The walls were smooth and dry. I'd heard St James' was a crumbling, dank old place but it seemed solid enough to me.

My foot grazed against something in the dark and I scuffled forward, almost colliding with Budge. He gave a tiny hiss of annoyance. *Sam would be silent down here*, I thought. All this time I'd been giving him lessons – I should have asked him to teach me some of his own tricks. After a few moments I caught a dim light ahead. We had reached an old back staircase, bowed from the heavy tread of servants labouring up and down. Candles flickered low in their sconces.

On the first landing we passed a fine porcelain chamber pot, the lid left carelessly askew. I wrinkled my nose at the stench. We must have reached the living quarters. So – I was to meet Mrs Howard in her private rooms, with a pounding headache and stinking of horse blanket. Excellent.

At the top of the stairs, Budge relieved me of my sword and dagger, then led me into a small antechamber. The walls were covered with tapestries and silk hangings that shone softly in the candlelight. Silk rugs covered the burnished oak floors. A tall cabinet held a collection of books bound in green leather and embossed with gold. The room was so rich and opulent – and such a contrast from the back stairs we'd just climbed – that it took me a moment to breathe. And all this for the king's mistress. Perhaps Mrs Howard was in better favour than Eliot thought.

Budge knocked on a door at the far end of the room and disappeared into a second chamber, leaving me alone. I took the opportunity to practise my speech, pacing the rug with a soft tread. 'Lady Howard – I trust you are recovered from your ordeal. I was honoured to come to your aid, my lady – but I regret that I am now caught in troubles of my own . . .' I faltered, and stood still, a question forming in my mind.

How had she found me?

I had not given her my name. She had scarcely seen my face in the dark. Enough to say, what? That I was a young gentleman. Long-limbed. Dressed in a black suit and red waistcoat.

So. *How had she found me?*

James Fleet. It was the only possible answer. Mrs Howard had hired him, after all – using Budge as her messenger, no doubt. Fleet must have given my name to Budge and told him where to find me. That was *unsettling*.

And now I began to suspect that there was a deeper game being played here. My task had been to meet with Mrs Howard that night and hear her story, no more. So how was it that I found myself being smuggled into the king's palace in the middle of the night?

I had no time to think further on the matter. Budge reappeared, followed by Mrs Howard. She was dressed in a rose-pink gown fitted close to her waist, a short strand of pearls at her throat. Her thick chestnut hair was tied in a simple knot and decorated with a piece of lace. She must be nearing forty, but she seemed much younger – blessed with a fresh complexion and a graceful figure. And very pretty indeed.

I bowed low. 'My lady.'

She inclined her head. The terror of the attack in the park was long buried – her expression was mild, her blue eyes steady. I'd heard that her nickname at court was 'The Swiss' because she remained always calm and neutral, both in her appearance and her opinions. *The Swiss*. It suited her.

'Mr Hawkins. How kind of you to come.' Her voice soft and seemingly quite sincere. But she was a lady of the court. She must have had a good deal of practice, *seeming* sincere. She held out a slim, gloved hand. I bowed again and kissed it. As I stepped back, I searched for the woman I had seen in the park. But *this* Henrietta was quite composed, her smooth features set in a polite mask. Was this what pleased King George? A pretty bauble, bland and sweet. Well, he was said to be a dull sort of fellow.

'How brave you were,' she said, eyes brightening with admiration.

I decided she was not quite as bland as I had first thought. 'It was an honour to serve you, madam.'

'There are few men fearless enough to stand against my husband in his rage.'

'Your *husband*!' I cried, before I could stop myself. That monster was her *husband*? I could scarce believe it. I tried to remember what I knew of Charles Howard. He'd been a servant to the old king, I thought. A drunken rake by all accounts, with a cruel temper . . . but I had not realised how cruel. The man I had met in the park had been half-wild.

'I thank you, sir, for saving me from him. I was sure he meant to kill me. He has threatened it before.' Her voice was quite steady, but as she spoke she folded her hands together. A subtle sign, but one I had seen at the gaming tables. She was afraid, and fighting with every breath to conceal it. So terribly afraid – even here in the palace.

She drifted towards a tapestry on the wall. I put my hands behind my back and followed her, playing the gentleman. She had taken so much trouble to hide her feelings, it would be ungallant to expose them. 'A fine piece,' I nodded, though I did not care a fig for tapestries. Could I dare hope she had summoned me here solely to thank me? That would suit me very well, if she might hurry it along. Although payment would not go amiss.

I thought of Gonson, gathering his evidence. I did not have time to admire old needlework, even with someone as pretty and intriguing as Henrietta Howard.

'Madam, I am glad you are recovered. But I am not sure how I may assist you?'

Her lips parted in surprise. 'Oh! I have not summoned you here, sir. It is my mistress who wishes to speak with you.'

'Mr Hawkins,' Budge called across the room. 'Her Majesty the Queen is waiting.'

The queen. I knew of course that Mrs Howard was a Woman of the Bedchamber, but had not thought for a moment that it was her *mistress* who had ordered me to the palace, and under such strange circumstances. I stared from Budge to Mrs Howard in bewilderment. What the devil did the Queen of England want of me? Perhaps I was dreaming. Asleep, dead drunk at Moll's, with my head upon the table.

'Mr Hawkins,' Budge prompted.

There was no time to compose myself. Brushing the horse hair from my coat, I followed Mrs Howard through the door into a larger room.

Queen Caroline sat on a red damask sofa, knitting. Her pale, straight brows were drawn in concentration as she bent over her work. A heaped plate of candied fruit rested on a table at her elbow. Behind her lay two long sash windows, velvet curtains pulled back. They would offer a fine view of the park in the day-time. Now, the world outside was black and jewelled with stars.

The Queen of England. This was no dream, but still I could not quite believe my eyes. All the world knew that Queen Caroline of Ansbach was the great power in this family; everyone save her husband. Those famous, mocking lines played about my head. *You may strut, dapper George, but 'twill all be in vain, We all know 'tis Queen Caroline, not you, that reign.*

Mrs Howard glided behind her queen, the modest servant, attentive and silent. Budge stood sentinel by the fire. I glanced at him for instruction, but he gazed ahead, shoulders back. Mrs Howard gave a subtle gesture, bidding me to wait. I stood with one leg half behind the other, poised to bow.

The only sound was the fire crackling in the hearth and the knitting needles clicking back and forth. The queen twirled the wool with her thick fingers and said nothing. There was nothing to do but consider her, and doubtless that was her intent. *Let the speechless fool gawp for a while until he regains his senses.* Her dress was plain and somewhat sombre – a mantua gown in dark-blue silk matched with a black quilted petticoat. There was a prodigious dollop of black lace fixed atop her head, quite mysterious in its design and almost comical.

She had once been as fair as her husband's mistress – fairer, in fact. A quarter-century ago every prince in Europe had wanted her hand. Fragments of her beauty still remained – her thick mane of greying blonde hair bouncing in ringlets down her shoulders, her butter cream complexion. The half-smile that played lazily on her pillow lips. But she had grown stout from childbirth and a sweet tooth. She seemed *inflated* somehow, swollen to twice the size of her rival, standing quietly behind her. No doubt that was why she wore a mantua, the bodice loose and unboned – not a fashionable style, but a good deal more comfortable.

'Howard,' the queen said without looking up. 'Bring me the papers on this boy.' Her voice was warm and rich, laced with a strong Bavarian accent. I felt the hairs on the back of my neck rise.

Mrs Howard crossed to a writing table piled high with books and correspondence. The queen paused in her knitting and began to count the stitches to herself in French, tapping her finger along the needle. The work was very neat. She gave a satisfied grunt and at last fixed me with a look, holding her knitting to her nose like a woollen veil. A deliberate, playful gesture that somehow merely confirmed her power. The world was hers to play in as she chose. She was chuckling to herself as I made my bow, but I could feel her eyes lashing over me like a whip.

'Oh, *mon dieu*. Up! Up!' she said, after I'd bent myself double for a long, back-breaking minute. As if she had not been the one keeping me there. Mrs Howard gave a curtsey and handed a sheaf of papers to her mistress. What a curious, uncomfortable situation for both women. I wondered why the queen allowed it.

'*Thomas Hawkins*,' the queen said, rolling my name around her mouth as if it were one of her sugared confections. She opened up a letter and read the first few lines – or pretended to. She folded the letter and dropped it on the sofa beside her. Settled back against a cushion. 'Well, sir – I hear you fought a great battle in the park. Saved poor Howard from an unhappy reunion with her husband. He is a beast, of course – quite the worst man in England. Mrs Howard has not been as fortunate as I in her choice of husband.' Her eyes gleamed. She had placed emphasis upon the word *choice*. Henrietta had *chosen* to marry Charles Howard.

The queen glanced at her servant, her husband's mistress, her once-friend. 'How long have you been married, Howard? I forget.'

I doubted that very much.

'Two and twenty years, Your Majesty. I was sixteen years old.' Mrs Howard's voice was clear and perfectly composed. But there must be pain somewhere, buried deep. Twenty-two years, married to such a man! How had she survived him all this time?

'Sixteen,' the queen snuffed, as if that were quite old enough to know better. She skewered me with her gaze. '*You* are not married, sir.'

'No, Your Majesty.'

'*No, Your Majesty,*' she mimicked, with surprising skill. '*God forbid, Your Majesty. Why should I marry my red-haired* trull *when she opens her legs and her pocket for free?*' She caught my look of dismay. 'You are surprised I know of this? I surprise myself, sir. I soil my petticoat walking through your sordid little life, hmm?' She lifted the hem of her gown as if in disgust, revealing a pair of exquisite red-heeled slippers, her plump feet bulging over the top.

There followed a short pause, while everyone pretended not to be mesmerised by the queen's feet. And then she dropped her gown, and turned quite serious. 'Well, Howard. Tell Mr Hawkins of your troubles.'

Mrs Howard folded her hands. 'I humbly beg Her Majesty to first permit me to acknowledge the many kindnesses she has bestowed upon her most grateful servant? My pleasing suite of rooms, my position at court, the happy and contented life I lead here full of diverse entertainments and friendships – these are blessings indeed and I am most grateful for Her Majesty's generosity.'

The words were spoken with a grave sincerity – and fell from Mrs Howard's tongue with such fluency I was sure she must have spoken them a thousand times before. To my eye, Mrs Howard did not seem happy nor content, but sometimes words such as these must be spoken, by rote and ritual, to appease those with power over us.

The queen's eyes were hooded. 'You are indeed most

fortunate, Howard,' she acknowledged, 'in your *diverse* friendships.' She waved at her most grateful servant to continue.

'My husband and I are estranged,' Mrs Howard began.

'Estranged! Aye, as a wolf is estranged from a rabbit,' the
queen interrupted. 'You must know of course, sir, that Mr
Howard was servant to the late king.'

I nodded. And how extraordinary this was, that such a turbu-
lent, ill-tempered man should fawn about the court when it
served him. I knew also – as the whole world knew – that the old
king had fallen out violently with his son some years ago and the
two courts had been torn in half as a consequence. Some had
remained loyal to the king, others had followed the Prince of
Wales into exile – a short stroll away in Leicester Fields. Mrs
Howard had been an integral part of that secondary court. Had
it been loyalty on her part to leave the old court behind? Or had
she simply seized the chance to escape her husband?

'Now he serves no one save himself,' the queen said. 'And has
no income of his own. He has squandered it all – all of his inheritance, and his wife's too. Every last penny.' She dropped a
macaroon in her mouth and bit down, closing her eyes in
pleasure. Waved again at Mrs Howard to return to her story.

'Mr Howard has made certain demands of His Majesty. And
violent threats against me.'

The queen swallowed the confection, sucking the sugar from
her teeth. 'Demands and threats! Insolent rogue – he is *abomin-
able*. D'you know, Mr Hawkins, when Mrs Howard was a young
woman he abandoned her in some hovel in . . . I fear I cannot
even pronounce it. Holl-born?'

'Holborn, Your Majesty,' Mrs Howard offered.

The queen threw me a mock-baffled look, as if Holborn might
be somewhere upon the moon. 'Abandoned her to starve along
with their baby son, while he rollicked about the town with

whores and scoundrels. Mrs Howard grew so desperate she even thought to sell her own hair. But you could not get a fair price for it, could you, Howard?' She leaned forward, conspiratorial. 'Mrs Howard is quite famed for her fine chestnut hair.'

I could not think what to say to this and so said nothing, glancing instead towards Mrs Howard in the hope I might offer some silent expression of sympathy. But her head was tilted in mild contemplation, her eyes cast softly to her feet – as if she were listening to a piece of light chamber music and not the horror that was her marriage.

And still I wondered: what did the queen want of me? I was beginning to suspect it involved Charles Howard – his *certain demands* and *violent threats*. In fact, I seemed to have blundered into a rather devious trap. Easy to miss in such a room, with its velvet curtains, its fine old portraits of grave old men covering the walls. The blazing fire and towering heaps of confectionery.

'The truth is,' the queen said, 'I am concerned for my poor Howard. Her husband has always loathed her with a demonic passion but he has kept his temper and his distance for years – I never could fathom why. Now it transpires he was harbouring certain expectations, following His Majesty's coronation. A position. An income. He has been *disappointed* in those expectations.'

'He blames Mrs Howard for this,' I guessed.

The queen bridled. 'No, sir – fie! I should think not! Mr Howard knows full well – *as the world knows full well* – that his wife has no influence upon His Majesty. Not this much!' She pinched her finger and thumb together, allowing no space between them.

I gave a hurried bow of understanding.

'Mr Howard is determined to create scandal and disruption. He demands that his wife is returned to his . . . shall we say into his custody?' She nodded grimly to herself. Custody. That seemed a fitting word for it.

'But, forgive me – he cannot crave such a reunion.'

The queen slid her gaze towards Mrs Howard, and I thought I caught a flicker of fellow feeling. 'No indeed. Mr Howard is more cunning than he seems. He was a soldier for many years, and a good soldier relies upon strategy more than brute strength. Mr Howard does not want his wife, but in law he may insist that she is returned to him. He has persuaded the Archbishop of Canterbury to write in support of his suit.' She gave a sour look that made me very glad, in that moment, that I was not the Archbishop of Canterbury. 'It is all a game, naturally: to cause his wife distress and to force the king's hand.'

She paused, quite furious. Half the world knew that Henrietta Howard was the king's mistress – but it was an unspoken fact that could be ignored by the court and parliament. Charles Howard's threats to expose the affair in such a public and sordid manner, and to involve the Church, could not be dismissed lightly. At the very least the king would appear ridiculous, at worst, weak and vulnerable. Not a favourable situation, barely six months into his reign.

The queen, meanwhile, seemed to have recovered herself. 'Now. I shall tell you a fine tale, sir. It will shock you. A few weeks ago I was working alone, there at my desk, when the door was flung open *boof!* and Mr Howard burst in, snarling and snapping like a rabid dog. Raving drunk of course – the man is seldom sober. He *must* have his wife back. He *insists* upon it. If I do not give her up at once he will *drag* her from my carriage by her hair the next time we venture out. "Well, sir," I said. "Do it if you dare."' She squared her shoulders at the memory. 'He stormed up and down, *comme ça,*' she pointed with her finger, whisking it back and forth, 'raving and cursing and threatening to throw *me* out of the window if I did not oblige him. *Well.* I informed him that he should do no such thing. But he is in truth so brutal, as well as a little mad, and always so *very drunk.* And the sash was open. I did half expect to find myself sailing out of the window at any moment.' She crinkled her lips, amused by the thought.

'Your Majesty! Was he not arrested?'

She shrugged. This was a private matter. 'I said, "Why, Mr Howard, we are both rational beings." I flattered him there, did I not? "Mrs Howard is a loyal and obedient servant and I could not bear to part with her. Let us settle this as reasonable people, sir. Tell me what you desire and be plain about it." Well, once he had recovered from being called rational and reasonable he presented his demands.' She took another candied fruit. 'Three thousand pounds per annum to compensate for his prodigious loss. Else he will seize his wife at the first opportunity and in a most violent and outrageous fashion.' There was a pause while she ate. 'The King is not inclined to pay.'

So much for gallantry. Mrs Howard had been the king's mistress for ten years. Three thousand pounds was a great fortune – but the king could afford to pay it if he wished. Instead he was prepared to let her live in constant terror, trapped in the palace. I'd heard the king was a miserly man – but this was cruel.

'Poor *Swiss* has not left her rooms for weeks,' the queen added, unmoved. 'And His Majesty is quite furious. He describes his fury to me at great length, every evening. It is an intolerable situation.' She closed her eyes. When she opened them again, she stared directly into mine with a fierce, unblinking gaze. 'You will resolve it for us, Mr Hawkins.'

'Your Majesty . . .?' Sweat trickled down my back as the room closed in on me.

'Come now, sir – I did not summon you here to admire your calves, handsome as they are.' She gave Henrietta a sidelong glance. 'My dear Howard, you have entertained us with your celebrated wit long enough. Pray leave us.' She flicked her hand to the door.

Mrs Howard gave a low curtsey, then two more, and backed from the room without a murmur of protest. I had to struggle not to run after her – flee the room, the palace, the city, without turning my head once. I knew what this audience had become – an interview for a position I did not want and could not refuse.

'You are a trifle pale, Mr Hawkins,' the queen said. 'Is it your mother's Scots complexion, or are you palpitating in my glorious presence?'

'Both, Your Majesty.'

She smirked. 'A glass of claret for the boy, Mr Budge.'

Budge brought me the claret in a crystal glass that sparkled in the candlelight. I drank it gratefully.

'You were a friend of Samuel Fleet,' the queen said.

'He was my cell mate.'

'He was *my* servant. Odious, treacherous little man. I was quite fond of him. He resolved a few trifling situations on my behalf.'

My heart thudded hard against my chest. Fleet had confessed to me – shortly before he died – that he had been a spy and an assassin for many years. He'd also told me that he had collected too many secrets along the way – that he had thus become too useful to kill and too dangerous to keep alive. So he had been thrown in gaol to rot. I'd guessed his master was powerful, that much had been plain. I'd never suspected his master was the queen.

'It is a great pity Fleet died in gaol.' Her lips tightened at the inconvenience. 'He must be replaced. His brother believes you might serve.'

Fuck James Fleet to hell – I should have guessed this was

his doing. 'Your Majesty, I fear I would be a grave disappointment—'

'—Come now, sir. I cannot abide false modesty. You discovered Mr Fleet's killer, did you not? And you fought off Mr Howard unaided. Have you not realised you were being tested that night? Well. Perhaps that *is* disappointing.'

'Forgive me, Your Majesty ...' I fell silent, gathering my thoughts. Mrs Howard had not arranged the meeting? No – of course not. It had been a bold move to engage James Fleet and organise a secret assignation in the middle of the night. Mrs Howard was not a bold woman. The queen, on the other hand ...

She smiled. 'I was curious to see if Mr Howard's threats were genuine. So we fixed his wife to a hook and dangled her in front of him. Fleet's brother ensured that Howard learned of the meeting. I must say we did not expect events to turn quite so violent. Poor Budge lost a tooth. And he had such a charming face.'

Budge gave a lopsided grin.

'I have grown tired of Mr Howard's insolence. Samuel Fleet would have resolved the matter in a heartbeat.'

I thought of the deal I'd made with James Fleet – his promise of one simple meeting, a chance to earn my own money. He had known all along that Charles Howard would attack Henrietta's carriage. Had known too that I was being tested to replace his late brother as the queen's private spy.

'I am not Samuel Fleet, Your Majesty.'

'No indeed,' she laughed. 'Let us be kind and call Mr Fleet an *eccentric*.' She arched an eyebrow. 'And a little *too* clever. You, Mr Hawkins, are just clever enough.'

It was not the finest compliment I had ever received. But under the circumstances, I had to agree with her. If anything, she was being generous.

The queen picked up a sheet of paper. 'Mr Howard must be stopped. Here is a list of his favourite taverns. Gaming houses. Brothels.' She handed the list to Budge, who handed it to me.

A hollow feeling grew in my chest. 'Your Majesty. I cannot . . . I am not an assassin . . .'

The queen looked astonished. 'For *shame*, sir! I am not asking you to murder the man – what an extraordinary notion. He's the brother of the Earl of *Suffolk*. You must befriend him, Mr Hawkins.'

Befriend him? I thought of Howard tearing at my throat, snarling in fury. Upon reflection, perhaps murdering him was preferable.

'Once you are on friendly terms, he may let down his guard. You must learn his secrets. Some weakness we might use against him. Seek him out, Mr Hawkins. Apologise for your encounter in the park. Earn his trust. Encourage him in his most bestial behaviour. He knows you are a violent man – he'll appreciate that.'

'Your Majesty, I am not in the least violent.'

She plucked another letter from the pile. 'From Sir Philip Meadows. You stayed at his lodge last autumn, I believe. He says you were a charming guest . . . until you broke a man's nose.'

I gritted my teeth. 'I was provoked, Your Majesty.'

The queen's eyes glittered. 'And were you provoked when you shot a man dead, out in Snows Fields?'

She held my gaze. There was a dark, almost eager smile on her lips. The smile of a woman who has just slid a blade between a man's ribs – softly and with great precision.

'That . . . I was forced to defend myself.'

'The first shot saved your life, of course. But the second?' She tapped the spot between her brows. Where Kitty had aimed and fired. 'What do you think, Budge?'

'He must have stood over him, Your Majesty. Reloaded his pistol. Shot him right between the eyes.'

'Murder, then.'

Budge threw me an apologetic glance. 'Your Majesty.'

The blood was pounding in my ears. I stayed silent, breathing hard. I couldn't trust myself to speak. Any word could be a betrayal.

The queen leaned forward. 'Do you deny this story? That you shot and killed a man last autumn, out on Snows Fields?' Her voice was soft – almost tender.

I swallowed, mouth dry. The fire crackled and sparked. On the mantelpiece, a gilded clock struck the quarter hour. 'No, Your Majesty. I do not deny it.'

There was a long, heavy pause. And then she smiled. Somehow – miraculously – I had given the right answer. The queen studied me closely, as if I were some new addition to the royal zoo. Then she lifted a final paper from the pile – a short note clearly written in haste. 'Budge has been gathering information on you for some time. This message came to us two hours ago. There is a warrant planned for your arrest at dawn tomorrow, for murder. There is a witness. A disreputable one,' she conceded. 'But your neighbour swears he heard you confess to it.'

Burden. 'Damn him!' I cried, forgetting myself. 'That is a *lie!*'

'I should hope so,' the queen replied, amused by my outburst. 'I should hope you are a good deal more discreet than that, Mr Hawkins. We shall send word to the magistrate to destroy the warrant; Budge will arrange that tonight.'

I bowed deeply. 'Your Majesty. I am in your debt.'

'You are *indeed.*' The queen pinched her lips. 'Be sure to repay it, Mr Hawkins. His Majesty is vexed by this tiresome business. And when my husband is vexed we all suffer. You will find something for us, to stop Mr Howard's threats. Within the week.'

I bowed again in understanding. She did not say it, but the implication was perfectly clear. If I did not solve the king's *vexing* problem in the next few days, I could expect no further protection from Gonson and his arrest warrants. There was just one thing I couldn't fathom. I hesitated, afraid I would cause offense. 'Your Majesty. Mrs Howard . . .'

'You wish to know why I go to this trouble to protect her? Why not let her vile husband drag her from the palace by her fine chestnut hair, hmm?' She looked away towards the fire. In profile she was suddenly more striking, with her long neck and strong features. I could see it now, how beautiful she had once been. 'I have grown accustomed . . .' she began. Paused. 'It is a *comfortable* arrangement. Howard is discreet. Modest. And as I say – quite without influence.' A small, satisfied smile.

I remembered what Eliot had said about Mrs Howard – how friends such as John Gay had hoped for preferment when the king came to power last autumn. And how it had transpired that she had no sway with her lover at all – after all those years of *service*. It must have been a humiliating blow. And a triumph for her rival. How many hours had the queen devoted to securing such a complete victory?

The queen was a pragmatic woman. If her husband must take a mistress, let it be someone as passive and powerless as Henrietta Howard. She was beautiful, yes, and charming. But the king would never turn to her for advice, and that suited the queen very well.

'It would be tiresome to train a new servant.'

The queen agreed, pleased by the careful dance we had taken about the subject. She gathered up all the papers she had collected on me and handed them to Budge, who threw them on the fire. She rose slowly to her feet and held out her hand. I knelt and kissed it. She bent down, closer to my ear. 'I know it was your little trull who fired the pistol,' she murmured. 'You must love her very much, to take the blame for murder. *To lie to your queen.*'

I kept my head down. 'Your Majesty.'

'I believe you would do anything to protect her.' She paused – smiled as I met her gaze. 'I am glad you have come to my attention, Mr Hawkins. I think you will be a most loyal servant.'

She waved her hand. I was dismissed.

Chapter Eight

Home. I locked the door and leaned against it, closing my eyes with relief. Here in the dark I untied my cravat and slipped a hand beneath my shirt, reaching for my mother's cross. I was safe – for now. No need to fear a visit from Gonson. No need for a moonlight dash from the city. But for how long – and at what cost?

'Tom . . .?' Kitty stood at the top of the stairs. She was dressed in an emerald wrapping gown embroidered with silver thread that twinkled softly in the candlelight. 'You went out at last,' she cheered, skipping lightly down the stairs. 'I'm so glad! Have you been drinking at Moll's all evening? You must—'

I pulled her into my arms and kissed her, long and deep. A moment's surprise and then she flung her arms about my neck. I pushed her gently against the wall and kissed her throat, her jaw. 'Angel,' I murmured, cupping her face as I kissed her again.

She snatched off my wig, my coat, unbuttoned my waistcoat. Drew me closer. My sword clattered to the floor. I ran a hand under her gown to find her naked beneath. Felt myself grow hard. I moved my hand higher and she moaned softly, guiding me. There. No. *There.* 'Tonight,' she whispered, biting my ear. 'Tonight, Tom.'

Yes, yes, tonight – why not, damn it? After all that had

happened, why wait another moment? I was tempted to take her there in the hallway, but I wanted her in bed, the first time. I gathered her up and carried her to our room, while she giggled with surprise. Dropped her down on the bed and knelt over her, unwrapped the gown so she lay naked beneath me. Just her necklace, with Fleet's gold poesy ring hung upon it. I paused, just for a moment. Then I pulled off my shirt and lowered myself over her. I traced my tongue across her breasts and then lower, lower. She shuddered and arched her back, gasping with pleasure. She was mine, she was mine – and no one would ever take her from me.

She pulled me back up the bed, eyes heavy with desire. Slid her fingers down and unbuttoned my breeches. Hesitated. 'My hands are cold,' she said, blowing on them.

I took them between mine and chafed them together roughly. 'There.'

She stared down at my knuckles, bruised and bloodied from pummelling Burden's door. I had almost forgotten. And I had told the queen I was not a violent man. Kitty sat up slowly. 'What's this? You were in another fight?'

'With a door.' I reached to kiss her.

She pushed me away.

'Sweetheart . . . it means nothing. Come here.'

She drew her legs up to her chest, wrapped her arms around her knees. The cold chill of disappointment seeped over the bed. Again.

'Oh, for God's sake,' I sighed. 'I drank too much punch and scraped my knuckles, that is all. There's no need to make such a damnable *fuss*.'

Kitty, it is fair to say, did not agree with this assertion.

Exile, then. Cast out of my own warm bed. Most certainly *not* tonight, Tom. I stamped upstairs, shirt and blanket under my arm, scowling to myself as if I were the injured party. As if I had not in fact kicked and beaten at our neighbour's door and waved my sword in his face in front of the entire street. Damn Kitty. Damn her stubbornness and her temper. Damn the world and everyone in it.

At least there was a spare bed at the top of the house, in Jenny's old room. I placed the candle on the chair by the bed, threw on my shirt and huddled beneath the covers, seething to myself. There had been no fire lit in this room for days and the walls felt damp to the touch. A crack in the window let in a thin draught, sharp as a blade. Even with an extra blanket, I couldn't stop myself from shivering.

Anger boiled through me. I should leave – storm from the house to the nearest bagnio. Find myself a wench who wouldn't ask anything of me, wouldn't *expect* anything of me save a coin or two. A merry, easy jade who would be grateful to share a bed, skin against skin in the night.

The candle fluttered then righted itself. Oh, God help me. I was coupled to the most infuriating girl in the kingdom. And I loved every damned inch of her. I closed my eyes, imagining her in the room below, pacing the floor and cursing my name. *And crying*, I thought, with a heavy heart. *You've made her cry, again.*

What if tonight were the night she grew tired of me? The night she realised that I'd only brought trouble to her door? Trouble and an empty pocket. I'd thought I'd lost her once before, and the grief had been intolerable. I would apologise tomorrow. We would begin afresh.

The candle burned low and flickered out.

I dreamed of Howard, drunk and raving in the moonlight. He screamed at me to fetch his wife, his lips flecked with saliva. 'You are my friend,' he cried. 'You must help me.' His lips pulled back into a snarl, his teeth yellow fangs sliding from his gums, his breath like rotting meat. He clawed at my shirt, shaking me, shaking me . . .

'Mr Hawkins. Wake up.' Sam's voice, low and urgent. His hand was on my shoulder.

I sat up, squinting as he held a candle to my face. 'Sam. What on earth . . .?'

Orange flame reflected in his coal-black eyes. '*Murder.*'

Kitty. I tore the blankets from the bed and sprang to my feet. Sam blocked my path. 'Sleeping,' he whispered, putting a hand to my chest as I tried to pass him. He pressed a finger to his lips then led me stealthily across the landing to his own room, unlocked the door.

The room was still, and black as ink.

A rustle in the darkness. The low creak of floorboards by the window. And someone's breath, sharp and ragged. I backed away, thinking of my blade, so far beyond reach in the hallway, two floors below.

Sam raised the candle higher and the room came to life. A bed, a table covered in books of medicine and anatomy, the charcoal sketches pinned to the wall, a mirror . . . and a young woman cowering in a corner, blonde hair hanging wild about her face. Alice Dunn – Burden's housekeeper. How the devil did she come to be in Sam's room?

She stumbled into the light. I cursed and drew back in shock. She was covered head to foot in blood. Dark stains spread across her pale-blue gown. Thin streaks clung to her tangled hair. Her apron was smeared with gory trails where she had tried to wipe her hands clean. She looked as if she had walked through hell.

'Dear God!' I cried. 'Are you hurt?'

She said nothing, too terrified to speak. Her eyes were wild. And fixed upon Sam.

He took a step towards her and her hand flew up. She was holding a dagger. The blade was thick with blood from tip to hilt.

Sam moved back, hands raised. Alice's shoulders dipped, the knife wavering in her hand.

'Sam,' I murmured, keeping a close eye upon the knife. 'Fetch some brandy.'

As soon as he'd left the room, Alice gave a sob and dropped the dagger as if it were burning her hand. It clattered onto the floor between us. It was as I'd guessed and feared. She was afraid of Sam. 'What's happened?'

'He's dead,' she answered in a numb voice. 'Mr Burden. He's dead.'

Oh … this was ill news indeed. I reached down, slowly, and picked up the knife. My hand was shaking. It was a fine weapon, with a turned ivory handle chased in gold. The steel blade was sharp, six inches long. A handsome, vicious thing. 'Did you kill him?'

She shook her head. She kept her hands stretched out away from her body, away from all the blood and gore.

'How did you come here? Did Sam let you in?'

Even his name made her flinch. 'It was him,' she cried. 'It was *him*. Oh, Lord. He'll kill me too, I know it.' Her body buckled and she sank to the floor.

'Sit down here,' I said, taking her arm and leading her gently to the bed. She clung to me, weeping silently. I studied her as the tears streamed down her face, searching for any signs of a fight. Burden was a mountain of a man – if Alice had attacked him surely there would be marks upon her body. Her wrists were circled with small bruises, a few days old, and there were more across her neck – four upon the left and one larger one on the right, just under her chin. Four fingers and a thumb. Someone had seized her roughly by the throat. Burden, forcing himself on her. Holding her down. I felt a sharp desire to find the bastard and knock him to the ground. And then I remembered – he was dead. Murdered.

Alice had no fresh wounds upon her that I could see – not even a scratch. The blood was all his.

Dread shivered through me. My neighbour – the man I had threatened only hours before, who had promised to testify against me in court – lay dead next door. And here was his servant hiding in my house, covered in his blood. If Gonson heard of this he would hang us both on the spot.

'Alice – I know what Burden did to you . . . I'm sorry . . .'

She bowed her head for a moment, as if shamed. 'What will they say of me?' she asked, in a raw, broken voice. 'He made me . . . I had to *visit* him every night. I had no choice. But it was different tonight. The room was dark. I was glad of it. Glad I didn't have to look at him for once. He never let me close my eyes. He made me pretend that I liked it, or else . . .' She shuddered, then drew a deep breath. 'I felt my way across the room and climbed onto the bed. It was soaking wet. So I lit a candle. I had to grope for it in the dark. I could feel the sheets, wet beneath my hands and then the flame caught and . . . He was lying there with that knife in his heart. The sheets were red. Thick pools of blood. Oh, God! I'd lain across it in the dark, in all that blood . . . My dress . . . my hands. It was all . . . it was everywhere. I had to stop myself from screaming.' She held out the underside of her right arm to reveal a ring of teeth marks cut deep in the flesh. 'They'd say I done it. Look at me! Look at me!' She began to sob.

'Why do you think it was Sam?'

'He was the thief. I *saw him*. Nasty little rat, creeping about at night. I told them, but they wouldn't listen. Judith said I was mad. Stephen was the only one who believed me.' Her face softened. 'I knew I'd hang for it if they found me like this. And I couldn't run away.' She gestured helplessly at the blood. 'Please, sir. If you tell them it was Sam they'll believe you. You're a *gentleman*.'

'But, Alice, it couldn't possibly be Sam. He can't walk through walls.'

She stared up at me. 'Yes he can, sir. Oh yes he can. And so can I.'

I blinked, confused. Perhaps Judith was right. Perhaps Alice *was* mad.

'He planned it all, Mr Hawkins. He's *evil*, sir. That's why Jenny left. She said—'

The door opened, silently. Sam, returning with the brandy. In a flash Alice grabbed the knife and scurried to the corner again, bare feet crackling dried flakes of blood across the floor.

Sam seemed more amused than offended. He poured a glass of brandy and offered it to her. She shrank back. I took the glass instead and knocked it down. Not as good as the queen's claret, but it helped.

'She thinks I done it,' Sam snorted.

'I *know* you did!' Alice cried. She pointed to a wall hanging fixed in the far corner of the room – faded green silk, embroidered with a white cherry tree design. I had never once given it a moment's thought. If asked, I would have guessed it covered a patch of damp or a hole in the plaster. I crossed the room, growing more troubled with each step. I knew what I would find behind the hanging, even before I drew it back.

Alice really *had* walked through the wall. Or, at least, through a hidden door. Small, discreet, painted the same pale green as the rest of the room. I ran my fingers along its edges. It must have been sealed shut at some point, because there were cracks and splinters around the frame – clear signs that it had been chiselled open again. There was no handle, just a lock. The key was missing.

'The windows and doors were barred, the night I saw him,' Alice said, still holding the knife tight. 'So I knew there must be a hidden passage. I've spent the last week hunting for it, every spare second.' She pulled a hairpin from her apron and fiddled with the lock. There was a soft click, and the door swung free into the room.

The entrance opened into the back of a huge oak armoire filled with fine but old-fashioned gowns in dark silks. The smell of must wafted through the air, and for a moment I was transported home to my father's house, to a forbidden room filled with my mother's dresses, fading slowly.

'They belonged to Mrs Burden,' Alice murmured. She trailed her fingers across a petticoat with deep flounces – a style I had not seen since I was a child. 'I'd planned to show this to Mr Burden, to prove I wasn't lying, or dreaming. Too late now, isn't it?' She glared at Sam.

I pushed the dresses aside, but it was too dark to see into the room beyond. It was an ingenious idea, I had to admit. From Burden's side, the door would appear to be the back of the large cabinet, unless one examined it very closely. This was the work of Sam's late uncle, without question. Samuel Fleet had lived a complicated, dangerous life – one that needed as many escape routes as possible. I could see how it would have been irresistible to Sam. Had he discovered it by chance? Or was it a Fleet family secret?

'You were the thief.'

'Didn't steal nothing.'

'Didn't steal *anything*,' I corrected, before I could stop myself. Yes, of course, that was the boy's great crime in all this – his use of double negatives. 'What were you doing over there, if you weren't thieving?'

'*Practising.*'

'Oh!' Alice cried, horrified. 'Oh, I told you, sir!'

I put a finger to my lips. If anyone woke next door we would be in grave trouble. Sam was not confessing to Burden's murder, he was not so foolish. He meant only that he'd been testing his skills; prowling about just as he had stolen into Jenny's room in the middle of the night. He'd wanted to see how quiet he could be. Not quiet enough, by this account. It was disturbing behaviour, but not proof of murder. I rubbed a hand across my face. It had been a long, wretched night. 'Did you kill Mr Burden, Alice?'

'*Me?*' Alice gaped.

I gestured at her clothes, drenched in blood. She stank of it.

'I *told* you – I never touched him.' She put a hand on her heart. 'I swear on my *life.*'

I glanced at Sam, raised an eyebrow. *Truth?* He tilted his head. *Maybe.*

It would have to do. 'Very well. Hand me the knife.'

She hesitated, then handed it over. I picked up the candle and put a foot through the door into the cabinet, brushing aside a damson-coloured mantua. These were expensive dresses for the wife of a carpenter. Alice gripped my sleeve. 'What are you doing, sir?'

'Saving you from the gallows.'

She put a bloodstained hand to her throat. 'I won't stay here with him. Not without the knife.'

Sam gave me an eager look. If he could not stay here, reason insisted he must come with me. I sighed, and handed him the candle. Viewing murdered corpses was not usually part of a gentleman's education, but what choice did I have? And I suppose he did have experience of moving about the place in darkness. Let him play link boy again, just for the night.

He slipped through, shielding the flame so it didn't catch on the dusty clothes. I turned back to Alice. 'Don't leave this room. And don't make a sound. Your life depends upon it.'

She gave me a frightened nod.

I pushed my way through the oak cabinet, praying that she was sensible enough to keep quiet. Sam was waiting for me on the other side, candle casting shadows across his face. Below us, the rest of the house slept on, oblivious. I glanced back at the armoire, a dark, solid presence that took up most of the wall. As solid as the man who had made it. I tiptoed towards the light in my stockinged feet, wincing at every groan in the floorboards. Something brushed across my face and I flinched. Cobwebs. I scrubbed them away.

'No one on this floor,' Sam whispered. There was almost no breath behind the words and yet somehow they were clear enough to understand. Another trick he'd learned from his father, no doubt.

We crept down the stairs to the second floor, my heart thumping so hard I feared it would wake the whole house. If we were discovered now, all was lost. I could hear the deep *tick tock* of a grandfather clock from the drawing room below, the steady snores of someone sleeping well and deeply. Stephen, I guessed, dreaming happily while his father lay murdered across the landing.

Sam cracked open a door, muffling the sound of the latch beneath a handkerchief. The door swung silently on its hinges; Burden must have oiled them so Alice could slip in at night without being heard. All that talk of sin and he was fucking a young girl against her will. Was his spirit watching us now, mute and helpless in the dark? Was he in heaven? In hell?

I took a slow, steadying breath and crossed the threshold, the dagger in my hand. It must be discovered with the body. If it were missing, everyone would assume that the murderer had crept into the house and taken it with him when he left. And who would everyone suspect . . .?

The bed was hidden beneath thick, red velvet drapes. Sam waited until I'd closed the door then drew them back in one fluid movement.

Burden lay naked on his back, his eyes open and turned to the ceiling. His flabby white chest had been butchered; flesh ripped open, flaps of skin hanging loose. I shuddered. He looked more flayed than stabbed. The violence of it made my stomach turn. His face was frozen, mouth contorted in a final grimace of shock. The bed linen was soaked in blood and smelled of piss and shit. I put a hand to my mouth.

Sam skirted to the other side of the bed, careful to keep the blood from smearing on his clothes. He placed a hand on Burden's cheek. 'Cold.'

I forced myself to look closer. Burden's lips were blue. The blood had begun to dry on the sheets. He could have been killed hours ago. And then his murderer had walked calmly from the room and continued about his business. *Ned, Judith, or Stephen.* The names rose unbidden in my mind. If Alice hadn't killed Burden, it must be one of them. I narrowed my eyes, looking for any trace of a clue, but there was nothing except for the blood and the blade. Reason told me Ned was the most likely suspect – he had the strength and the grievance – but reason had no place here. I couldn't believe it. I couldn't believe any of it. 'Strange,' I whispered. 'To think of them all sleeping soundly so close by.'

'All but one,' Sam replied, moving the candle down Burden's body.

I placed the dagger at the end of the bed.

Sam glanced at it. Raised an eyebrow. Pointed at the wound in Burden's chest.

I gave a low groan. He was right. To protect Alice, to protect *ourselves*, we had to put it back where she had found it. Right back in the heart wound. I picked up the dagger. It was a handsome thing, save for the blood. I hesitated. Could I do this? Push a blade into a dead man's heart?

Sam plucked it from my grasp and with a quick turn of the wrist plunged the steel blade back into the wound. It made a vile, slurping sound as it travelled deep into Burden's chest. I turned away. When I looked back, Sam was examining the rest of the stab wounds.

'Sam. Enough. Come away.' The ground was tilting beneath my feet. I could taste blood in the air – a heavy iron tang. I still couldn't believe that Burden was truly dead. I half expected his corpse to sit up of a sudden and laugh, as if this were all some macabre jest at my expense.

Ned, Judith, Stephen ... There was one other possibility of course. 'Did you do this, Sam?'

He did not seem in the least put out by the question. Had seemed more offended, in fact, when I had accused him of thieving. 'Why would I kill him?' he asked, putting a hand to Burden's ruined chest.

'That's not an answer ... Oh, good God! *Stop that.*'

He ignored me, probing each wound with deft fingers. 'Not gentlemanly?'

'This is not a *game*, Sam.'

He gave a soft, secret smile, as if this were the best game in the world. 'Nine stab wounds.'

I stared at the savage gouges in his chest, the glistening clots of blood. *Nine stab wounds.* This was not the work of a cool-tempered assassin. Whoever murdered Joseph Burden had acted in a frenzy of hate and fury. He would have been covered head to foot in blood when he was done.

Who had more reason to hate Burden than Alice? And I had left her alone next door while Kitty slept downstairs, with no warning or protection.

It was time to leave.

I took one last look at Burden's bloody and butchered corpse. He'd wanted me dead – had been prepared to lie on oath to see me hang. My enemy in life – and he still had the power to destroy me in death. God damn it. I would not hang for this. Wherever Burden was now – heaven or hell – I would not give him the satisfaction.

Chapter Nine

I need not have worried about Kitty. When Sam and I returned to his room, she was standing over Alice – with a pistol in her hand.

'And when did you plan to explain *this*, Tom?' Kitty asked, tilting the barrel towards Alice's bloodstained clothes. 'Is it true? Is the old bastard dead?'

'Stabbed through the heart.'

Kitty tapped Alice's shoulder with the pistol. 'D'you kill him? If that bloated hog tried to force himself on me, reckon I'd stab him.'

'I never *touched* him.'

I closed the door between the attic rooms. Sam slid the hanging back in place.

'He was stabbed many times,' I said.

'Nine,' Sam clarified.

'Whoever killed him would be covered in blood . . .'

We all looked at Alice.

'I told you, it was dark. I didn't see the blood until . . .' She put her face in her hands and rocked softly. Kitty gritted her teeth, frustrated, while Sam watched them both, unblinking. No doubt he would sketch this, later. The maidservant drenched in her master's blood and the girl with a pistol in her hand.

'You must see, Alice, how this seems. You have the very best reason for wanting Burden dead.'

Alice dropped her hands. 'Save for *you*, sir.'

There was a short, cold silence. And then a sharp *click*, as Kitty cocked the pistol. 'Look at yourself, Alice! Tell me why we should not drag you at once to the magistrate?'

'*I didn't do it!*' Alice howled, desperate. 'You must believe me! There'd be no sense in it.'

'Why not?'

Her shoulders slumped. 'He was going to marry me.'

We stared at each other in consternation.

'He announced it while I was serving dinner yesterday. Didn't bother to ask me first. No warning. No argument. Judith ran outside and puked in the yard. Imagine. Her maid was now her *mother*.'

Kitty lowered the pistol. 'You consented?'

'What choice did I have?' Alice looked utterly exhausted. 'At least I'd have some protection. Why – do you think I wanted his rough hands all over me? His fat, sweating belly pressing down so I could scarce breathe? He made me *sick*. I fought him off the first time. But he said he'd tell the world I'd thieved from him. Who would hire me after that? I'd be on the street and on my *back* for every pox-ridden bastard with a halfpenny to spend. Mr Hawkins, sir – you know he'd have done it. He told all those lies about you in church.'

'What's this?' Kitty asked sharply.

I frowned, but there was no value in shielding her any more. 'He was spreading rumours about me. He said that I killed a man, down in Southwark . . .'

'He swore an oath to Mr Gonson,' Alice said. 'Said he heard you through the wall, confessing to it. He was lying, I know. He hated you both. Because you was happy, I think. Happy and young.' She paused. 'I'm glad he's dead. Bastard. I'd have liked to marry him first, though, just for the money. And the look on Judith's face. She'll throw me out on the street now ....'

Kitty paid her no mind. She was staring at me from across the room with a stunned expression, as if the house had collapsed around her. 'Why did you not tell me? What possessed you ...' She trailed away, staring at the pistol in her hand. 'Oh, *Tom* ...'

I couldn't explain my actions in front of Sam and Alice, but I didn't need to. Kitty understood. If she had known that Burden planned to testify against me, she would have confessed to the murder in a flash, in order to protect me. Just as I had lied to the queen to protect her. The difference was that Kitty had indeed pulled the trigger. One bullet for defence. The other for revenge.

She crossed the room and put her arms around me, her head pressed hard against my chest. I drew her close and held her for a long, perfect moment. There. I was forgiven. And all I'd had to do was prove myself willing to die for her. How simple and charming love is.

She stood on tiptoes and pressed her lips to my ear. 'I would never let you hang on my account,' she whispered. '*Never*. Do you understand?'

It was almost dawn. We needed to send Alice back before the household woke and somebody discovered Burden's corpse. Kitty took Alice downstairs to dress her in a clean gown. We would have to take her innocence on trust – and a fair degree of common sense. Alice clearly had little to gain from Burden's death, save for a moment's revenge. Yesterday she had been set to become his wife and share his fortune. Today she had nothing. Who would hire a servant whose previous master had been murdered in his bed?

Whoever had killed Burden had been perfectly content to let

Alice take the blame. Ned, Stephen, Judith – they all knew of Alice's nightly visits to Burden's bed. Alice had screamed like a banshee when she caught Sam in the room that night. Burden's killer must have counted upon her screaming again, when she found the body. The household would have rushed to her aid . . . and discovered her upon the bed, crouched over the corpse. Covered in his blood.

A brutal murder, fuelled by a burning rage. But this attempt to turn suspicion upon Alice had been cold and clever.

Ned. Stephen. Or Judith.

Impossible.

I told myself it was none of my business who killed Burden. Gonson might suspect me, but as long as he did not discover the attic door I was safe enough. And yet . . . and yet . . . It was not a comfortable thought, knowing I was the most obvious suspect. It would be better to learn the truth – in case I needed to prove my innocence.

Sam drew a candle over his bed. Pinched his lips. 'She's left blood on the sheets.'

'If Alice had married Burden, she might easily have borne a child. Several, in fact. How old is Alice? Nineteen? Twenty?'

Sam dipped a neck cloth in a jug of water and began to scrub hard. 'Five and twenty,' he suggested, with a fair degree of malice.

If Alice had a child, Stephen might lose his inheritance, or at least part of it. And then there was Judith, sickened by the idea of Alice becoming her stepmother. Loss of money, loss of pride. Either could have led to murder. But then . . . surely they would have killed *Alice*, not their father?

Ned Weaver was angry with Burden, but angry enough to plunge a blade into his heart? If I were forced to gamble on it, I supposed I would bet on Burden's apprentice – cheated and betrayed. He had the strength for it – but not the heart, surely. Truth was, I would not risk money on any of them. 'Are you sure you didn't kill him, Sam?'

He paused in his scrubbing. 'With a *knife?*' He picked up a pillow, gripped it tightly in both hands. 'Best way – smother them. Looks natural.'

'That's . . . rather sinister.'

'Bad man. Bad death. Deserved it.' He plumped the pillow and dropped it back upon the bed. 'Blood on your shirt.'

I glanced down. There were smudges all down the front from where Alice had clung to me. On purpose, to incriminate me? No, surely not . . . Damn it. It would have to go on the fire – it was too badly stained and I couldn't risk it being discovered. Gonson was sure to pay me a visit before the morning was over.

'Why're we helping Alice?' Sam asked.

'She'll hang if we don't.'

He stared up at me, peat-black eyes filled with frustration. 'They'll blame you instead.'

'Gonson won't arrest me without proof.'

He tossed the bloodstained neckerchief on the fire. It sizzled and spat, damp against the flames, sending grey smoke into the room. He coughed against his sleeve. 'Give her money, Mr Hawkins. Enough to run away.'

I hesitated. I had not considered the idea. It was tempting. Why should I place myself in danger for a girl I barely knew? If Alice left tonight she could begin a new life with a new identity. Sam's father could hide her for a few weeks, then send her wherever she pleased. True, everyone would assume she had killed Burden, but she'd said herself that the best she could hope for now was a ruined life on the street. Was this not the kindest choice, for everyone?

I opened my mouth to speak. *Very well. Let's send a message to your father*. But there was a lump in my throat and I couldn't say the words. My conscience. My damned conscience. If I sent Alice away now she would be named a murderer for ever. She would live a life of fear while the real killer escaped punishment. And what if she were caught and brought back home to be hanged? What then?

Alice appeared in the doorway in the plain, coarse wool dress Kitty used to wear in the Marshalsea. The one she'd been wearing the first time I saw her in Sarah Bradshaw's coffeehouse. It was tight on Alice, especially about the chest, but it would pass.

Sam was not happy. 'What if she tells them about the door? What if she blames one of us?'

'Then we show them this,' Kitty said, holding up Alice's bloody gown. She threw it to him. 'Hide it somewhere safe, away from the house.'

Satisfied at last, Sam grinned and hurried from the room.

Kitty patted Alice on the shoulder. 'Insurance,' she said, sweetly. 'In case you planned to mention the door. Or tried to place suspicion upon Mr Hawkins in some other fashion.'

'I wouldn't do that.'

'No. You won't, will you?' Kitty agreed with a touch of menace. She drew back the wall hanging and ushered Alice through the door, whispering orders in her ear. Start the day as usual. Light the fire and sweep the floor. And wait for someone else to scream *murder*.

Kitty built a fire in our room while I pulled off my ruined shirt, shivering in the cold dawn air. My head was spinning, my eyes raw and dry. I glanced mournfully at the bed, wishing I could bury myself beneath the blankets and escape the world for a few hours. But I could not have slept – my mind was too restless and alert. I thought of Burden lying dead on the other side of the wall. Murdered, just a few inches from where Kitty had lain sleeping. A thought struck me.

'Did you hear anything in the night, Kitty? A struggle? A cry for help?'

'Nothing.' She ripped up my shirt and dropped the pieces on to the fire. 'Perhaps he took a sleeping draught.' She brushed the soot from her hands, eyes cast down. She was thinking of another murder, back in the Marshalsea. I crossed the room and held her.

'When things have settled down, let's leave London for a while. We could go to Paris, or Italy.' I rubbed the goosebumps on her arms. 'Somewhere warm.'

Kitty handed me a fresh shirt. 'Italy.' She smiled. 'I'm sure we'll find new books for you to translate there.'

I had been thinking of travel and adventure, not months cramped over a desk, scratching imaginary lust on to blank pages. But I smiled too, and kissed her forehead. A promise.

I was buttoning my shirt when a scream pierced through the wall. Judith. The screams turned into a low howl of grief. And then Stephen's voice, muffled through the walls.

'No! Oh, Father, no! Murder! *Murder!*'

It had begun.

By the time we joined our neighbours on the street, Ned Weaver was standing guard at the door, his face drained white. He held a large wrench in his hand, turning it in his palm as I approached to play my part. I must appear as curious and ignorant as the rest of the street.

'My God, Ned, what's happened?'

He pushed me back with his free hand. 'Keep away from here, sir.'

'Is it true? Mr Burden has been killed?'

He studied my face for a long moment. 'Aye,' he breathed, at last. There was grief in his eyes and a kind of dull shock. But if he'd killed Burden he'd had hours to prepare his reaction. It told me nothing.

Judith emerged from the hallway and stood at Ned's shoulder, her dark hair in a tangle down her back. She was dressed in a straw-coloured wrapping gown, the bottom stained with her father's blood. Not as much as there had been on Alice's dress. She had discovered him in daylight and must have drawn back at once.

'Miss Burden,' I said, bowing my head. 'I have just heard—'

'You killed him,' she said, her voice hoarse. 'You killed my father.'

'That is not true . . .'

'*Murderer!*' she cried, throwing the word high into the air. I felt the street fall silent at my back.

Ned leaned down and whispered in her ear. Judith savaged me with a contemptuous look, then retreated back into the house. Ned tapped the wrench at my chest. 'I've sent for Mr Gonson. I'll tell him how you threatened Mr Burden last night.' He tilted his chin over my shoulder, to the street beyond. 'We *all* heard it.'

I glanced around. Our neighbours were huddled in groups, whispering and staring as if Ned and I were actors in a play. And judging by their black looks, they had cast me as the villain. I turned back to Ned. 'Did you kill him, Ned? You'd have cause enough.'

Ned wanted to punch me – I could see it in his eyes – but he was no fool. Judith had accused me of murder, but the house had been locked tight last night. An apprentice with a hot temper, betrayed by his master? Aye, that would play well enough in court. 'Go to hell,' he barked, loud enough to be heard halfway down the street. But he kept his fists lowered.

As I returned to the shop, I heard hisses at my back. Even the brothel girls seemed wary, muttering to one another and refusing to meet my eye. When I reached the shop, Kitty was scuffing away tears of frustration and rage. I sat down at the table to fix myself a pipe. My hands were trembling. I stretched them out in front of me, willing them to stop shaking before Gonson arrived.

Kitty sat down opposite me and tucked her knees under her chin. 'If it comes to it, I'll confess to Snows Fields. You are not a murderer, Tom.'

'No more are you, Kitty.'

She looked down at the table, a tear sliding slowly down her cheek. We had never spoken of what had happened out in Snows Fields that terrible night last September. What could be said? She had saved my life – and risked her soul for it. I reached over and brushed the tear away. Passed her my pipe to steady her nerves. She took a long pull, closing her eyes as she breathed out a stream of smoke. 'Italy.'

I covered her hand with mine.

It was a strange, tense hour waiting for the knock upon the door. We heard Gonson arrive at Burden's house and hurry upstairs with his men to view the body. Judith's voice, high and trembling with distress, carried through the walls, though we couldn't make out the words. Then Gonson, slow and measured, asking questions.

It began to rain, a strong wind hurling fistfuls against the window. The room darkened as grey clouds blocked the light. Kitty stoked the fire and held her hands to the flame. 'I can't bear this,' she muttered.

I took off my wig, rubbed my hands over my scalp. And still the puzzle of it turned in my mind, around and around like a clockwork spit. Ned. Stephen. Judith. One of them had stabbed Burden nine times in the chest, then calmly waited for Alice to find the body. And now, just as calmly, waited for the suspicion to fall upon me. How obliging I had been, threatening Burden last night. Well. Let Gonson arrive and have done with it. Let him make his accusations – he had no evidence to support them, unless he discovered the passage between Sam's room and Burden's attic.

A pounding at the door. A wooden club, not a fist. I rose as if in a trance and opened it. Gonson stood in the doorway in a dark-grey cloak, surrounded by his men. He was unshaven and had clearly dressed in a rush, his cravat askew and the buttons of his waistcoat matched to the wrong buttonholes. So eager to stake a claim upon the murder. I bowed. 'Sir.'

He leaned upon his stick, studying me closely. His hat and the ends of his long wig were sodden with rain. 'Mr Burden is dead.'

'So I hear. If you have come to accuse me, sir—'

'No, Mr Hawkins. I've come to arrest you.'

Before I could respond, two of the guards thrust themselves through the door and grabbed me by the arms. I struggled against them, digging my heels as they tried to drag me outside. 'Let me go, damn you!' I cried. 'I'm innocent.'

'You are *guilty*, sir!' Gonson thundered. He shoved his face an inch from mine. 'Do not think me a fool! Burden was set to testify against you this very morning and now he lies murdered in his bed – at your hand. He was a good man. A brave man.'

'He was a hypocrite,' I spat. 'And a liar.'

Gonson gave a nod and one of his men punched me hard in the gut. I doubled over, knees buckling. The next moment Kitty was at my side, screaming curses at them all. A guard struck her with his fist, dashing her to the floor. I leaped at him, but there were too many of them. They took hold of my arms and legs and pulled me outside into the pouring rain. As I fought to free myself, someone knocked me to the ground with a cuff to the head. By the time I'd come to my senses, my wrists were fixed in iron. The guard captain swaggered closer, pulling a thick riding whip from his belt. He pressed it against my throat. 'Attack me again,' he sneered. 'I'll flay the skin off your back.'

I held still, eyes cast down as the rain soaked my bare scalp. I had seen men flogged before, heard their screams echoing through the streets. The captain chuckled, pushed the whip harder against my throat until I began to choke. 'Your slut has more fight in her. I think I'll pay her a visit while you're locked up. I like a whore with spirit.'

I had felt anger like this before and had lashed out, my temper flaring before I could stop myself. My first day in gaol I had been mocked by the head turnkey and smashed my fists into his jaw before I could stop to think of the consequences. But I had been a boy then. I had survived torture and gaol fever and betrayal. Now I was a man, and my rage burned as ice, not fire. I lifted my chin. This guard, this *ape* with his whip was nothing. Nothing. I looked him deep in the eyes. 'If you touch her, I will kill you.'

The guard's grin faded.

'Mr Crowder!' Gonson called, irritably. He was standing a few paces from us and had not heard his captain's threats. He pulled his heavy wool cloak close around his shoulders. 'Enough chatter.'

Crowder and his men dragged me towards Covent Garden. One of them stayed behind to hold Kitty back, but I could hear her shouts and curses all the way down Russell Street. As we reached the piazza, I spied Sam returning from the market. I called out to him as we passed and he ran alongside us, eyes wide with shock.

'Take Kitty to your father,' I said as the guards jostled me away. 'Keep her safe, Sam!'

He nodded and raced off at once.

I felt a moment's relief. Crowder couldn't touch Kitty now

– not unless he fancied a battle with the most powerful gang in London. He pushed his club deep into my back, pressing me forward.

'Mr Gonson!' I called out to the magistrate, striding proudly at the head of the procession. 'Where is your evidence? Where is your *warrant*? You cannot . . .'

Crowder struck me hard across the back of the head. Pain flashed through my skull and I staggered, half-blinded. The guards dragged me on through the streets. I kept my mouth shut.

Chapter Ten

'So, Mr Hawkins – are you ready to confess?'

Gonson paced the cell, hands clasped behind his back. He wore the satisfied air of a man unburdened with doubt; a man who walked in the light, oblivious of his own shadow. He had removed his hat and cloak; I supposed they must be drying by a fire somewhere. Here, in this room, there was no fire. He was warm enough in his frock coat, though his brown wool stockings were damp and spattered with mud. His long, full-bottomed grey wig smelled like wet goat.

Crowder guarded the door, thick arms folded high upon a belly grown fat with ale.

I shifted a little, chains clinking against the wall. I was barefoot and sore, hoisted almost on tiptoes on the ice-cold stone floor. My wrists were raised above my head, iron links fixed to a hook in the ceiling. I had thought when Gonson arrested me I would be slung in the Westminster lock-up, but instead I'd been dragged to a private house in a quiet courtyard. The guards had ripped off my stockings and waistcoat out of spite, and brought me down to the basement. Then they had left me alone for an hour, until my legs were shaking and my arms and shoulders burned. My fingers were numb; when I looked up I could see them blue-white and bloodless.

I had not expected this of Gonson. He was a man of the law. Why bring me here to this private place, except to hide what he was about? This was not lawful. Now he had returned, expecting to find me cowed and terrified, ready to confess.

Did he know what had happened to me in the Marshalsea? Did he look at me and think I was so easily broken? I glared at his smooth, bland face. 'You have no right to keep me here, sir.'

Gonson paused in his pacing, fiddling with the fraying cuffs of his soil-coloured coat. Unlike most city magistrates, he was proud to say that he was incorruptible, which would explain his drab clothes and the outmoded square toes of his scuffed shoes. Or perhaps he thought good clothes were the devil's work. 'My guards have searched your rooms. They found bags packed with clothes and money – enough for a long journey. It is quite clear that your intention was to flee.'

I cursed silently. I'd packed those bags before my visit to the palace last night – and clean forgot them. 'You have no proof I killed Burden. I thought better of you, Mr Gonson. You have a reputation for being a fair man. This is not lawful—'

'No, sir!' Gonson roared. 'Do not dare lecture me on the law! Do not dare!' He clenched his gloved fist, and for a second I thought he would strike me. Then he pulled away. 'I should have listened to Mr Burden, but I refused to act without proof. Now he lies dead – at your hand.'

'For God's sake! How do you propose I murdered him? The doors and windows were locked and bolted. It must have been someone in the household, don't you see? What if one of the children—'

Gonson signalled to Crowder. He strode across the cell and placed his hands upon my shoulders. Then he pressed down hard, wrenching my arms in their sockets. I screamed, and he grinned, pushing so fiercely that I thought my body would be torn apart. I screamed again, the pain ripping through me like fire.

At last, I was released. I sank back against the wall, my body shuddering with the shock. 'I thought better of you, sir.' I rasped.

Gonson frowned, stung by the insult. 'No fault but yours, Hawkins. You force me to use these methods.' He reached into his waistcoat pocket and drew out an arrest warrant, my name scratched upon it. *Thomas Hawkins, for the charge of murder.* Beneath it lay Gonson's signature. I drew away, as if I might be damned by reading it. No man wishes to see such a thing. This was the arrest the queen had spoken of – the one she had overturned in exchange for my help with Charles Howard.

Gonson folded up the warrant and tucked it away. 'I had planned to arrest you this morning. I have a witness swears you shot a man last September, in Southwark. Mr Burden had promised to testify. He heard you discuss the murder with your whore.'

'He lied. They both lied—'

'Quite enough to bring you to justice at last,' Gonson said, refusing to hear me. 'And yet the ink was barely dry upon the warrant when I was summoned to the Marshal's house. He ordered me to cease my enquiries.' He paused, lips pressed into a tight, bitter line. 'He said he had been given no choice. The *City Marshal*, corrupted and threatened on your behalf, sir. I thought you were merely a foolish, whoring fellow – but I see now that you are a devil. I have examined Burden's corpse, sir. You butchered the man. Who is it protects you, Hawkins? My Lord Walpole? The king?' He grimaced at the thought. 'I doubt your *benefactor* will feel as generous when he learns how you used your freedom.' He patted his pocket. 'I'll wager this warrant will be granted before the sun sets tonight. And until then you will remain here, safe from the reach of your *friends*.'

They left me then, my arms still raised and pinned to the wall.

The room was dark as night without a candle. I stared unseeing into the shadows, stunned and exhausted. I hadn't expected this from Gonson. It was a cunning move on his part. He had no proof that I had killed Burden, but by arresting me in such a public way he had sent a challenge to the queen, my secret benefactor. Was I truly worth protecting now?

The hours passed. No one came. I had no food, no water. My mind began to wander, then fracture. I would never confess to Burden's murder, not in a thousand years. But as I stood chained to the wall, freezing and crippled with pain, I began to wonder if I should confess to the murder on Snows Fields. If I told the whole story – if I explained that I was defending myself, there was a chance I would be spared. Transported for a few years perhaps, rather than hanged. Surely I could survive that.

And with that decision, the weight lifted from my heart. There was nothing more to be done. By rights I should have died that night in September. Instead I had been granted a few months of happiness with Kitty – a reprieve I had done little to deserve, God help me. So let Gonson charge me, and Fate would decide the rest. One last gamble. If the world were just, I would be spared.

Yes, I am aware how foolish this all sounds – gambling upon a just world, indeed. In my defence, I had been standing on tiptoes with my arms pinned above my head for God knows how long. I invite you to try it and see how soon your common sense flies out of the window. Something Gonson had been counting upon, no doubt.

The cell door slammed open. Crowder strode into the room with his club held high. I braced myself for another beating. He came closer, wheezing softly. Then he pulled out a set of keys and unlocked my chains.

I collapsed to the floor with a groan of relief. Moments later I was seized in agony as the cramps ripped through my shoulders and arms and along my bare, frozen calves. My fingers began to throb as the blood returned, but when I tried to bend them it felt as though someone was slamming red-hot needles into my knuckles. I lay upon the floor while Crowder tried to kick me to my feet.

At last, when the cramping stopped, I dragged myself up and hobbled from the cell in a daze of pain, Crowder snorting with impatience. After a few limping steps he put his arm beneath my shoulder and half-carried me up the stairs towards a room at the front of the house. Light spilled out from the open door and I could hear a woman's voice, high and wavering. Kitty? No, please God – she would confess to anything to save me. I staggered forward, using the walls for balance. After the freezing cellar, the heat of the room hit me like a furnace. A fire blazed in the hearth, a thick stew bubbling away on the range. Gonson's men sat together at a table, drinking small beer. Gonson himself stood by the fire, wearing a look of mild revulsion as a young woman knelt at his feet, sobbing into her apron. Not Kitty, I realised with astonishment. *Betty.*

'Oh, sir, please!' she shrieked, her voice muffled by the cloth. 'I ain't done nothing. Don't hurt me!'

'Calm yourself, hussy!' Gonson snapped. He leaned down and pulled her hands roughly from her face. 'How did you hear of the Marshal's order? Tell me quick before I throw you in a cell for obstructing my work.'

'I'm not obstructioning, I swear!' she whimpered, wiping her eyes. 'Oh, I think I shall faint, sir – please don't lock me away!'

Gonson huffed in frustration. 'Hawkins. D'you know this foolish creature?'

I rubbed my ruined shoulders. 'There is an order from the Marshal, sir?'

He coloured and said nothing.

'I should like to see it, Mr Gonson.'

He hesitated for as long as he could – as if he wished he might give me anything else in the world. At last he took a letter from a drawer and held it out to me. I grabbed it and read it quickly, heart leaping as I understood its purpose.

The letter was from the City Marshal, requesting my immediate release. More than that, it demanded that Gonson apologise for questioning my good character and that ... I blinked, and read the line again, to be sure I had not dreamed it. It said that I had been charged by the Marshal himself with investigating Joseph Burden's murder. And that Gonson must give me every assistance in my search for the murderer.

'When did this arrive?'

Gonson's blush deepened. He must have held on to the letter for hours, hoping I might confess, or at least give him some new information in the meanwhile. And I almost had. I almost had.

I glowered at him. 'And you speak to me, sir, of corruption.'

Oh, what he wished to say to me then! The fury and frustration throbbing through his veins. But he could not accuse me now, not without risking his own position. Instead he took his annoyance out upon Betty, shouting at her to get to her feet and to stop her mewling. 'How did you learn of the Marshal's letter? Answer me, hussy!'

Betty just shook her head, whimpering with fright.

'Leave her be, Gonson,' I said. 'She's only a coffee maid. She works at Moll's – half the town spills its secrets in there.'

Gonson was disgusted – by Betty, by the thought of Moll's, by the whole world he was forced to inhabit. 'And what business is this of yours, woman? Why should you hurry over here and cause all this fuss? Are you a spy—'

Betty wailed in horror, drowning out his question. 'No, no sir! I only come here because . . . Oh, Mr Hawkins, you must tell him the truth! You know I'd do anything for you, sir!' And with that she scurried across the room and flung her arms about my neck. Before I could reply she pressed her lips to mine, warm and sweet. I had just begun to enjoy myself when she broke away.

'Silly slut.' Gonson shuddered, scandalised.

I spied my waistcoat and stockings piled in a corner. I sat down and put them on, then slipped on my shoes. 'I believe I am owed an apology, Mr Gonson. By order of the City Marshal.'

'Get out.' Gonson's face had turned a remarkable shade of purple. 'Get out, you devil.' He spun back to the fire, unable to bear the sight of me leaving, a free man with my order in hand. He pretended he was warming his hands by the fire, but his shoulders were shaking with rage.

We hurried as fast as we could up King Street. Betty wore pattens over her shoes to save them from the muddy streets, metal soles tinking along the pavement. My own feet throbbed after long hours stretched out upon the cold basement floor, and my legs were trembling. I was exhausted and anxious, but I was free – and the rain had stopped, the sun shining through soft grey clouds. I narrowed my eyes, dazzled by the light.

We walked in silence for a short while, Betty leading the way north past White Hall. My bare scalp and missing frock coat drew a few curious glances until we reached the fringes of Soho, where men chose to mind their own business. We crossed into a quiet backstreet, Betty's feet tip-tapping to a halt.

'Well,' I said. 'That was—'

Betty pushed me violently against the wall. My back and shoulders sang with pain, still sore from my punishment.

'God in heaven,' she spat, amber eyes blazing. 'D'you know the trouble you've caused?'

I glared back at her. 'What? And how is this my fault?'

She spat out an oath and stepped back, hands on her hips. The frightened, wailing hussy had vanished. I rubbed my tender shoulders. Now I thought of it, Betty had never once struck me as the frightened, wailing hussy sort. She had played her part to perfection – presenting herself just as Gonson would expect. A silly strumpet without the wit to know anything of value. He had let a diamond fall from his grasp without even realising his mistake.

'I warned Budge you weren't ready,' she muttered. 'They never listen to me.' She strode off again towards Soho, pattens raised high above the filth. *Tink, tink, tink.*

'You work for the queen?' I called, catching up with her.

She didn't miss a stride. 'Who *doesn't*? And Mr Hawkins,' she added, after a short pause, 'the next time I kiss you as a distraction, *mind where you put your hands.*'

'Next time?'

Betty gave me a look that could wilt flowers. But when I glanced down a moment later she was smiling, just a little.

'How did you find me?' I asked. Gonson hadn't taken me to his own lock-up, but to private rooms. He'd wanted time to sweat the truth from me without interruption, away from the reach of my *benefactor*.

'Damned fool dragged you through the streets in chains. Half the city saw you.'

I frowned. What one half of the city saw, the other half would know of by nightfall. I had been paraded through the middle of London like a criminal. Put a fine coat on a man and he is halfway to a gentleman. Wrap him in chains and he must be a rogue. The town would not forget it.

I had never visited Betty's home before. In truth, if I'd been asked, I would have guessed she slept in the wooden shack next to the coffeehouse. I was surprised she could afford to rent a room of her own – even on a gloomy yard off Wardour Street. She made me wait until all was quiet, walking ahead to open the door. Once she was inside and the yard was clear, I strolled past the house as instructed, then doubled back, keeping to the shadows. When I was sure no one was looking, I tiptoed down the cellar steps and slipped inside.

The room was tiny – no more than six paces wide and five long – but clean and pleasant nonetheless. The floor had been freshly swept, and sprigs of lavender hung from the ceiling, scenting the air along with the jasmine perfume Betty always wore. It was, in fact, the sweetest-smelling room I had ever visited in the city, including the queen's chamber. Betty's scant belongings were stacked neatly on shelves. There were only a few pieces of furniture – a narrow bed, a cane-backed chair, and a small table with a wash bowl and jug. Her pattens and shoes were lined neatly by the door. Betty walked barefoot in her own home.

She closed the shutters and knelt in front of the hearth, striking sparks from a tinderbox. The kindling under the coals took flame, bringing more light and a touch of heat to the room. She put her finger to her lips. 'No visitors allowed. Especially gentlemen.' Her gaze flickered to the ceiling. 'Landlord would throw me out if he found you here.'

I stood over her, warming my hands by the fire. 'That must be inconvenient.'

'Perhaps I prefer it this way.' She settled a pan on its trivet and stood up, clapping the soot from her hands. 'Lie down and rest while I cook this broth. You look half dead.'

I opened my mouth to protest, then realised I was indeed half dead with fatigue. There were no marks upon my skin, but my muscles were bruised and sore from being fixed for so long in one position. I lowered myself down upon the bed, wincing with the pain, and removed my shoes. There was a short passage pinned to the wall, written in a rough hand.

> *I waited patiently for the Lord;*
> *and he inclined unto me,*
> *and heard my cry.*

The fortieth psalm. My father had stamped them into my brain, indelible as a mariner's tattoo. I stretched out upon the bed, but my feet dangled from the edge, so I rolled upon my side and drew my knees to my chest. I sighed into the pillow. I was free, thank God – at least for now – and safe here in my temporary sanctuary.

So much had happened in the last few hours that my head could not rest upon one thought, never mind plan what I should do next. One moment I would think of the queen, and then of Mrs Howard. And then Burden. The sound of the dagger sliding back into his chest. Sam's face as he examined the body, cool and curious. And Howard – I must find him . . . must . . . and then it would all whirl about again, a dance I had never learned, where each step was misplaced, each partner unwanted. Well . . . had I not grown tired of my quiet, cramped existence? Had I not craved this? But for the life of me, I could not remember why. I closed my eyes . . . and in an instant had dropped into a deep, dreamless sleep.

*

I woke to the sound of broth bubbling in the pot. I sat up slowly, rubbing my face. Betty gestured to the table, where hot water was steaming in the jug. I poured it into the bowl and washed my face, neck and hands. It felt so good that I tore off my shirt and soaked my chest and back, rinsing away the grime of the lock-up. Betty glanced up then away hurriedly, stirring the broth with her back to the bed.

When I was dressed again, I settled back in the chair by the fire and ate a bowl of the broth with a coarse chunk of bread and a mug of beer. Betty ate her own dinner standing up, studying me under long black lashes. She had fixed me a fresh pipe which I smoked gratefully, stem clamped to my lips. Slowly, I was returning to myself. I rubbed my wrists, where the iron had chafed the skin.

'You think you are free,' Betty said.

I held up my unchained hands.

'You are not free.'

I took another draw on my pipe, breathed out the smoke in a soft cloud. 'This sounds like the beginning of a lecture.'

She threw a shawl about her shoulders. 'It is too late for that. You are the queen's man now, Mr Hawkins. Those chains are stronger than iron.'

'I didn't think she would save me again.'

'Howard stormed into the palace last night. He stood in the courtyard screaming about his wife and the king and demanding justice. He has lost all sense. The queen saved you because she is desperate. There's no time to find someone else.'

'I do not understand why they tolerate it. Why do they not lock him up? Or . . .' I trailed away. *Or have him killed.* I knew why. Because he was a nobleman. 'And what if I can't resolve the matter?'

'You know what will happen. Don't look for comfort from

me.' She pinned her cap, tucking her tight black curls beneath the cloth. Her face was stronger and more severe with her hair scraped back, but still handsome. Almost regal, in fact. 'I'm late for work. Here.' She tossed me a wig and hat. 'Some *drunken fool* left these at Moll's the other night.'

'D'you know . . .' I squinted at them. 'I think these are mine. Oh! You didn't find a shoe, I suppose?'

Betty muttered something to herself. 'Put out the fire once I'm gone. Don't let a soul see you leave. Takes a long time for someone of my complexion to find somewhere respectable to live.' She fastened the ribbons on her gown, until her chest rose high and firm. She caught me staring and pursed her lips. 'Budge sent a message. Mr Howard will be in Southwark tonight, at the cockfight.'

I cursed into the fire. After all I had endured today, I had no desire to spend the night with that beast. 'Damn it. Well. I suppose I have no choice in the matter.'

'You had a choice!' Betty hissed, rounding on me. She kept her voice low, but there was a force to her words, even so. 'I told you months ago! Go home! Honour your father's wishes and join the Church. Become his heir again. Become his *son* again. All that good fortune and you threw it away. For *what?*'

I frowned at her. 'For a *life*.'

'A life that will kill you.' She shook her head. 'I've watched you, Mr Hawkins. You throw yourself at the world – so sure it will catch you every time. But one day you will fall.'

'My father would adore you,' I muttered, slapping on my hat. I crossed the room and wrapped my hand about her slim wrist. 'This is my nature, Betty. I can't be what I'm not.'

Her pulse thudded against my fingers. 'Perhaps.' She hesitated, then drew away. 'But you could be so much more than you are.'

*

Back on Russell Street, my neighbours greeted my return with worried glances and sharp intakes of breath. The monster had returned. When I stepped into the chandler's on the corner to purchase some fresh quills and paper, the mistress of the shop informed me – in a high, trembling voice – that my credit was revoked. I was no longer welcome. I found the same reception in the grocer's.

As I trudged defeated towards home, a flat, nasal voice called out behind me. 'Quite the leper, Mr Hawkins.'

Mr Felblade, the apothecary, matched his step with mine. He was a most peculiar old man – *eccentric*, to use the queen's charitable term – and a very poor advertisement indeed for his various lotions and tinctures, with their promise of good health and prolonged youth. He was excessively lean, with a long, narrow face, made longer by a towering wig that rose in twin horns upon either side of his head. His clothes – unfashionable since Queen Anne's day – hung from his bony frame as if embarrassed to be seen with him.

'And do you have a cure for leprosy, Mr Felblade?'

He chuckled, then ran his tongue across his wooden dentures. They had a tendency to stick against the inside of his lips, and his mouth was in constant motion, licking and spitting to moisten them.

'It's not wise to walk with me, sir,' I said, hoping he might leave me in peace. 'Bad for business.'

'What do I care if you killed Burden?' he scoffed. 'Couldn't stand the man. No one could. Hypocrites!' He wheeled about and waved his fist at the rest of the street.

He was not the most comfortable ally.

'You'll need a draught for your nerves,' he declared, rummaging in his bag. 'I have a packet.'

The thought of taking anything prepared by Felblade made

my stomach turn. I wouldn't use his powders to dust my wig. 'I'm quite well, sir. But thank you.'

'Sanguine nature,' he said, crinkling his lips in disapproval. He halted outside Burden's house, glancing at me in surprise when I joined him. 'They won't let you in the house, sir. Not in a thousand years.'

I tugged the Marshal's order from my pocket. 'Care to make a bet, Mr Felblade?'

Felblade's eyes danced, anticipating trouble. He knocked on the door with his cane and shouted his name. After a long wait, Ned Weaver opened the door. When he saw me standing behind Felblade his jaw dropped.

'Where is Miss Burden?' Felblade elbowed his way into the hallway. 'Lead me to her, sir.'

Ned hurried to close the door behind him. I stopped it with my foot and poked the note through the gap. 'I'm ordered to speak with you, Ned.'

There was a short pause as he read the Marshal's order, cursing as he began to understand its meaning.

'Well, Ned?' I'd given him quite enough time to read the order. 'Let me in.'

He opened the door, the note dangling loose from his hand. But he didn't move, and I couldn't pass. He might as well be another door, he was so solid. 'For pity's sake. Judith and Stephen . . . we are all grieving, sir. Have the decency to leave us in peace at least until the morrow.'

I snatched the order from his hand, all patience gone. 'I have just spent the day chained to a wall because of this damned family. I will speak with them *now*.'

Chapter Eleven

Ned refused to answer my questions, stamping down to his workshop and bolting the door behind him. There was a loud crash as a table was overturned, followed by something splintering hard against a wall. I left him to his rage and went in search of Burden's children. Orphans, now. God forgive me, but I could not help but think they were better off. And wondered, indeed, if one of them had been harbouring the same thought.

The drawing room was empty, the grandfather clock tocking like a beating heart in one corner. It was a cheerless space with bare walls, lacking the trinkets and soft touches a wife might have brought to the home. The furniture was well made, but very plain – more suited to a Quakers' meeting house than a family room. There was only one comfortable chair, matched with a plump footstool and drawn close to the hearth. I would have bet ten guineas this was Burden's chair. I could just imagine the old sod stretched out by the fire with a pot of ale, while his children shivered together on the hard bench opposite, night after empty night.

And yet I was supposed to believe they were all in deep mourning. Deep shock, perhaps – I would grant them that much. But mourning? Stephen and Judith, trapped and bullied by their father all their lives; and Ned, betrayed after seven long years of service. Rebellious son, cowed daughter, and bitter apprentice. They all had good reason to plunge a knife in Burden's heart.

A voice drifted through the ceiling, toneless as an old bagpipe. Felblade. As I ventured upstairs, my skin prickled with a kind of mournful dread. I had walked this floor only a few hours before, examining Burden's corpse by candlelight while his family lay sleeping. I opened the door to Burden's room and stepped inside. The curtains to the bed were drawn back, but the body had gone and the sheets had been stripped – burned, most likely. The mattress was propped against a wall, waiting to be thrown away. A dark stain had spread through it. Someone had endeavoured to clean the floor by the bed. Alice? If so, she had done a poor job of it, only half-finished. The blood had smeared into the grain of the wood, wiped carelessly. Burden's heart blood.

Motes of dust danced in the late afternoon sun. I felt a moment's pity for Burden, lumbering upstairs last night with no idea that he would never wake again. Then I remembered how he had forced himself upon Alice each night in that bed, and my pity vanished.

A hand touched my shoulder. I jumped back in alarm. 'Damn it, boy!' I snapped without thinking, to cover my surprise.

Stephen stood in the doorway, dressed in his father's black coat. The cuffs covered his hands almost to his fingertips. It would have been comical at another time, but the boy's face was marked with pain, eyes red and swollen. He was also holding a dagger: a six-inch steel blade with a gold and ivory handle. The same dagger I had seen a few hours ago, in Alice's hand. The same dagger Sam had pushed back into Burden's chest.

I took a careful step away from it. 'Stephen. I'm glad to have found you. I have been asked to investigate your father's death.' I drew out the note and held it out to him.

He didn't look at it. 'Mr Burden.'

'I'm sorry . . .?'

'My father is dead. You must call me Mr Burden now.' He squared his shoulders, puffing out his chest in a weak imitation of his father.

'Of course.' I smiled politely, eyeing the blade.

'You will leave my house at once.'

I tilted my head in agreement. I doubted he had the nerve to use a dagger, but *someone* had thrust a blade in Burden's chest last night. I had no desire to be gutted by a fifteen-year-old schoolboy. 'Very well.'

Stephen was pleased with himself. He moved aside to let me pass, lowering the blade. A mistake. I launched into him, slamming him so hard against the wall the air was punched from his lungs. It was easy enough; the boy was little more than clothes and bones. Before he could rally, I ripped the dagger from his hand and spun him around, pushing his face against the wall and dragging his arm behind his back. He yelped in pain – then fell silent as I placed the blade against his throat.

'Did you kill your father?'

'No!'

I twisted his arm higher.

'No! I swear!'

'You'll inherit a fortune now he's dead. Now he can't marry Alice Dunn.'

'I didn't kill him,' he sobbed into the wall. 'Please, sir! Don't hurt me.' His narrow shoulders trembled beneath his father's coat.

I sighed and stepped back. Damn it – what was wrong with me, torturing a grieving boy? And yes – despite expectation, I could see a deep and honest grief in Stephen's eyes. But that did not preclude his guilt. 'I've no wish to harm you, Stephen. I am not your father.'

He cringed, ducking his head away.

'He beat you quite savagely, did he not?'

'I deserved it,' he whispered, miserable. He would not meet my eye.

'That is not what I heard.'

Ned had told me the story the night before, over those two bowls of punch. So much had happened since then I had near forgotten it. He told me that Stephen had been desperate to leave Covent Garden. His father was building three houses near Grosvenor Square. Why not settle the family there? It was a fashionable and respectable part of town, and Burden was always grumbling about the decline of Russell Street: the brothels, the gin shops ... the disreputable bookshops. There would be no need to lock and bar the house so early in a better neighbour-hood. Judith would be able to walk the streets in safety.

Burden had refused – he claimed it was more Christian to stay in the Garden and work to restore its reputation. The Society for the Reformation of Manners relied upon decent citizens to live amidst all this vice, and inform on those breaking the law.

Stephen had persisted. He was a gentleman and this was not a gentleman's address. His school friends mocked him for living amidst the lowest wretches on earth. They made lewd comments about his sister and the *experience* she must have gained just from looking out of her window each day. For the sake of the family's reputation – could his father not see that they *must* leave?

Burden had grown angry. He would not be lectured to by a mewling child. He knew what was best for this family. He seized the terrified boy by the neck and pushed him downstairs into the workshop – threw him across the bench and ordered Ned to hold him down. Then he'd taken a leather belt and thrashed his son without mercy. When it was over, and Stephen crawled weeping across the floor, Burden grabbed him and pushed his face into a pile of sawdust.

'This is what pays for your schooling,' he snarled, as his son choked in the dust. 'My hard sweat. All those years and what do they send back to me? A primping fop with porridge for brains. Well that's an end to it. I shan't pay another farthing. You will stay here and learn how to be a man, like Ned.'

That night Stephen had lain awake whimpering on his bed, battered and bruised, unable to sleep from the pain. And so he had been the first to hear Alice scream *thief*. The first to hobble out on to the landing. The first to enter his father's room and discover Burden in bed with Alice. The hypocrisy. The *injustice*. No wonder he'd taken his revenge the next day in front of Gonson. *'Are you sure I should tell them what I saw, Father? What I truly saw last night?'*

And now I wondered: why had Joseph Burden been so determined to stay on Russell Street? There was something disproportionate in Stephen's punishment – even for a father as stern as Burden. Ned had told me that Burden had never beaten his son so cruelly before. And for what? Asking for something perfectly natural – a decent home for himself and his sister. A chance for improvement.

Why had the thought of leaving Russell Street provoked such fury in Burden? Had he feared they would mock him – his new neighbours on Grosvenor Square? While his son had been transformed into a gentleman, Burden was still a craftsman, with battered hands and a rough demeanour. Was it that simple? Was he afraid of being humiliated by his betters? Here on Russell Street he was free to look down upon his neighbours. Out west they would look down upon him.

The story made me uneasy, even so – the old bear snapping and snarling and refusing to leave his cage. I wondered if he were concealing a darker truth – some pressing reason why the family had to stay on Russell Street. Perhaps the cage was locked.

I looked down at Stephen, weeping in his father's clothes, and felt wretched for the boy. Wretched for myself too – there was no honour or decency in this. And I would gain no more from him now. I left him, crossing the landing to Judith's room. I could hear Felblade speaking with an older woman: Mrs Jenkins, who ran the bakery across the street. Of course. She would have scurried here as soon as the news reached her, eager to offer comfort and lap up the drama. A foul-weather friend, Kitty called her.

I tapped lightly upon the door and entered unobserved save for Felblade, who offered me a dry, mirthless grin. Judith lay beneath the sheets, face to the wall. Mrs Jenkins sat beside her, murmuring the usual platitudes. *Your father was a good man. He's at peace now, my dear.*

'Twice a day, Mrs Jenkins,' Felblade creaked, holding up a bottle filled with a viscous brown liquid. Opiates, I supposed, mixed with molasses. Or coal tar, knowing Felblade.

'I must speak with Miss Burden before she drinks that,' I said from the doorway.

Mrs Jenkins gasped as she saw me. 'Oh! You devil! Have you come to murder us?'

It was only then that I realised I was still clutching the dagger. Unfortunate. I slipped it in my coat pocket. 'No indeed, Mrs Jenkins.'

'My heart! I shall die of shock!' she declared, clutching her bosom and looking sturdy as a carthorse.

Judith sat up as if waking from a dream. Her dark hair hung lifeless about her face, falling into her soft grey eyes. She seemed shocked and frightened – just as she had the night Sam had stolen into the house. The night she'd discovered her father was sharing a bed with Alice.

I gave a short bow. 'Miss Burden. My deepest condolences.'

Her brows furrowed. 'You were arrested.'

'A misunderstanding. I have been charged with investigating your father's death.'

'But you hated my father. No ... no ... do not deny it.' A desolate look crossed her face. 'I hated him too sometimes. There were times when ... When I wished him dead.' She began to shiver. 'Wicked,' she murmured under her breath. 'Such a wicked girl.'

I sat down upon the bed, in the warm dent left by Mrs Jenkins. Judith cast me a timid look, pushing the hair from her face. Her left eye was bruised and swollen.

'Who did this?'

She twisted the sheets beneath her hands. 'It was my fault. I couldn't stop crying. Stephen had to strike me, to calm me down ...'

'Stephen's a good boy,' Mrs Jenkins interrupted. 'I'm sure he feared you might have another fit.' She gave me a sharp look. 'Judith is a delicate girl. We must all be very gentle.'

'Unbalanced. Melancholic,' Felblade agreed, packing away his bag. He slurped his tongue across his teeth. 'A bleeding will restore her. I shall return tomorrow ...'

'No ... no!' Judith cried in alarm. 'No more blood. No more blood.' She closed her eyes and began to shake.

'Shame on you, Mr Felblade,' Mrs Jenkins tutted. 'We will have no more talk of blood and knives, or corpses butchered like pigs in a market. We must not speak of such things! Murderers creeping about the place in the dead of night. Poor Mr Burden stabbed and stabbed again with a vicious blade. Murdered in his own bed while everyone slept! Where is your sensitivity, Mr Felblade? Miss Burden is not sick – she's tired and frightened. And who can blame her after what she saw this morning? Oh!

It makes me dizzy to think of all that blood ... You've been very brave, my dear,' she called across to Judith. 'I'm sure *I* should have fainted clean away if I had seen my father with a blade plunged in his heart. Warm broth and bed rest, that's what's needed.'

'Quite right, Mrs Jenkins,' I said. There had been quite enough blood spilt in this house.

Mrs Jenkins' face scrunched. 'I'm sure I don't need *his* approval,' she huffed, and began scolding Felblade over the price of his opiates.

'I'm sorry I accused you before, sir,' Judith whispered. 'I was ... not myself. I am quite certain that you are innocent.'

I smiled thinly. Easy enough to whisper my innocence in a private room. She had already shouted my guilt to the whole street. I leaned closer. 'Miss Burden. Who do you think killed your father?'

Judith stared at me in surprise. 'Alice Dunn, of course.'

'I see ... But ... I believe your father planned to marry her?'

'Never!' she snapped. She sat up very straight, her eyes fierce and dark as storm clouds. 'My father would never marry that filthy whore. It was a jest – a silly jest. Alice Dunn – mistress of this house? No, fie – not in a thousand years! She killed my father, I am quite certain. And may she burn in hell for it!'

Silence, as Felblade and Mrs Jenkins stared at each other in surprise, and then at me. Mrs Jenkins rubbed her palms together. 'Warm broth,' she trilled, in an anxious voice. 'And rest.'

I rose from the bed, shocked by Judith's outburst. For a moment I had seen pure rage burning beneath her dazed, dreamy surface. Had that rage erupted last night? Could *Judith* have murdered Burden?

'Alice ran away, Mr Hawkins,' Judith called as I left. 'Did you not know? She left this morning. So she must be guilty, don't you see? She *must* be.'

In the workshop, Ned was sanding a stool, running his fingers softly against the wood to check for imperfections. There was no sign of his earlier outburst, save for a broken chair propped in one corner. I stood in the doorway, studying the tools hung neatly upon the back wall. They reminded me of the implements of torture hanging in the Marshalsea gaol. My throat constricted and I felt the iron collar fastened about my neck, biting deep into my skin. I put my hand to the door frame to steady myself, forcing myself back to the present.

Ned knew I was there, but he continued working, keeping his back to me. Stephen had been reckless and confused, muddled with grief and fear. Judith was dazed, and fixed upon her hatred of Alice. Ned's anger was contained, focused.

There were only a few pieces of work on the benches – a half-finished side table, an oak tallboy. These were small projects, made for practice not profit. Burden had been a master carpenter and joiner, his business construction. The grand new squares west of Bond Street were built of brick, but they still needed joists and rafters, wainscots and doors. Ned had talked about his work with pride and passion at Moll's the night before: the need for both strength and precision, an eye for a pleasing design, an under-standing of geometry when building wall partitions and staircases. 'An occupation for the body and the mind,' he'd said, eyes bright. I'd envied him then, for finding a vocation that gave him so much satisfaction. I was – without question – not cut out for the clergy. Nor was I created to sit at a desk, translating whores' dialogues. What would make *my* eyes shine, I wondered. Punch. Kitty.

I had no doubt that Ned would find a good position with another master. If not, surely the Carpenters' Company would help him set up his own business. Assuming he had not killed his old master, of course.

'I must speak with you, Ned,' I said at last.

His back stiffened. 'There is nothing to be said.'

'I did not kill Mr Burden.'

Ned lifted the stool from the bench and turned slowly. 'Those men at the coffeehouse. None of 'em dared look you in the eye. They was afraid of you.'

I leaned against the door frame, bone weary. 'Because they were fool enough to listen to your master's lies. I am not a murderer, Ned.'

'Gonson arrested you.'

'What – is that proof of my guilt, then? He hates me – you know that! He confuses a disreputable life with a wicked one. They are not *precisely* the same.'

'If you had lead a decent life you would not be in trouble now.'

'Oh indeed – *that* is how the world works. You were a model apprentice for seven years. How were you rewarded?'

Ned frowned. He thought I was taunting him. 'Ask what you want and leave. Before I lose patience.'

Ned's years of hard labour had left him strong and fit and solid as a Roman statue. There was also a wall of heavy tools at his back. I took a step back towards the workroom stairs, ready for a hasty retreat. 'Did you kill Mr Burden?'

I asked only to watch his reaction. But I had asked him before, and this time he was not even angry. He resented the question, of course, but beyond that I saw only sorrow and a bone weariness.

'You had good cause to hate him.'

He glanced away. 'I have good cause to hate you, sir.'

'Do you think I wish to be here, troubling you with these questions? I must prove my innocence, Ned.'

'Aye – by placing the guilt upon my shoulders. Tell me, sir – how many gentlemen have you seen hang at Tyburn?'

'I am not—'

'*None.* That is the truth of the matter. Not one. And how many apprentices? Ten? *Twenty?* If I had been arrested this morning instead of you – would I have been set free again within a few hours? Would I have been granted permission to trouble a grieving family? Well damn you, sir – I will *not* go to the gallows in your place.'

I folded my arms. 'Nor should you – if you're innocent.'

'Oh indeed,' he laughed, throwing my own words in my face. '*That* is how the world works.' He moved across to the back wall and plucked a hammer from its hook. Oh, fuck the world – Ned Weaver and his damned carpentry tools. 'Do you know how long Mr Burden lived in this house? Twenty years.' He gestured about the room. 'Built it with his own hands. Twenty years without a moment's trouble. Then you arrived, and within three months he's murdered in his bed.' He slammed the hammer against his work table. The sound cracked the air between us. 'That is not chance, sir.'

'No trouble? For God's sake, Ned – he was fucking Alice against her will every night. He—'

Ned raised the hammer and moved closer. I pulled the dagger from my coat. Ned gasped as he recognised the ivory handle. 'Where did you find that?'

'I wrested it from Stephen. He attacked me, unprovoked. This damned house, Ned!'

Ned looked a little shamefaced. He slung the hammer into a corner and sat down, broad hands clasped on his knees. 'If not you ... If not me ...'

I didn't reply. He knew the answer. Stephen. Or Judith.

He groaned and put his head in his hands.

'I'm sorry, Ned. I know they must seem like family . . .'

'Seem?' He gave a hollow laugh. 'There is no *seeming* about it. I'm their *brother*.'

Ned would not speak for a long time after that, dismissing my questions with a wave of his scarred hand. I settled down on the steps into the workshop and waited. Patience – patience was the key. The best confessions come unforced.

'Mr Burden was a good man,' he said at last. 'He lived a sober, Christian life. But . . .'

Ah, there it was. *But*. We are all good men save for that one short word. I leaned forward. 'But?'

'He was led astray by ill company, when he was young. Lewd women. Low sorts. They encouraged him to swear and drink strong liquors. To visit bawdy houses.' He paused, disgusted. 'He abandoned his apprenticeship. Fell into debt, and was forced . . . Mr Hawkins, you must swear not to repeat this story to a soul. I only wish to explain . . .' He stood up and began prowling the workshop, straightening tools and brushing dust from the table. A tidy room for an untidy story. 'He found work as a brothel bully.'

I began to laugh, covering it with a cough when I saw Ned's agonised expression. Well, well, well. Here was a rich story. Joseph Burden, guarding the door of a whorehouse for a living. And that sanctimonious prick had judged *me*. The gall of the man! My God, if he were still alive I would have enjoyed throwing *that* in his bloated old mug.

'It was only for a few months, you understand,' Ned added hurriedly. 'He grew ashamed of what he saw. What he *did*. He joined the Society as an informer. He began attending church again and met Mrs Burden. Her dowry gave him the capital to build this house and start his business. She was a pious, devoted lady. Mr Burden often spoke of how she saved him.'

How her money saved him, more like. 'But you are not her son.'

'No, sir.' He bowed his head, ashamed. 'I was born in Newgate. My mother was a whore and a thief. She pled her belly to escape the gallows. After I was born she was transported. Died of a fever on the boat.'

'I'm sorry.'

He brushed a rough hand across his eyes. 'Never knew her. I was raised by my aunt and uncle down in Surrey. Good, honest folk – farmers. But they had seven children of their own. My uncle couldn't provide for me so they wrote to Mr Burden. My mother always swore he was the father . . .'

I raised an eyebrow. Given her occupation, that would be hard to prove one way or the other.

'Mr Burden didn't believe I was his son – not at first. He took me on as his apprentice to atone for his past vices. He felt responsible for my mother's death, because he had once . . . in a weak moment . . .' He blushed.

Only once? I doubted that very much. And if Ned hadn't lived such a buttoned-down life, he would see it too. A man such as Burden wouldn't take a bastard into his home to atone for one brief episode of lust – not without proof or some other inducement. 'But you are *truly* his son? You are certain?'

Ned smiled. 'I worked with him in this room for seven years. He began to notice things. Not just my appearance, but the way I moved. My way with the tools. A hundred tiny things that no one else would ever notice. Look at me, sir. Now you know the truth – can you not see the resemblance?'

I tilted my head. It was true, Ned was as broad and strong as Burden, if not as tall. His brows were pale and his complexion fairer too, but that could have been an inheritance from his mother. Yes, there was a resemblance; a greater one than Stephen shared with his father, in fact – but then Stephen had spent the last seven years at his school desk instead of fixing roofs and nailing down floorboards. There was no way to prove it for certain, but Burden had clearly believed Ned was his son. And given it must have been a reluctant admission on his part, I was inclined to believe it too. He must have stared at the boy for hours, wishing away the likeness until he could deny it no longer.

'If all this is true, why did he break his word to you, Ned?'

'That was *my* fault! I wanted him to recognise me as his son. I vowed I would leave unless he told Stephen and Judith the truth. Ah – how I wish I had not pressed him so hard! My father was fair with me, Mr Hawkins, but he had a strong temper. I should have been patient and obedient, as he taught me. I do think . . . I do *truly believe* he would have changed his mind in time. If only for Judith's sake.'

'Judith?'

He coughed with embarrassment. 'She has grown fond of me.'

Fond? Ah. 'Oh dear.'

'I didn't dare tell Mr Burden, but . . . it was an uncomfortable situation.'

I winced, thinking of my own sister. Uncomfortable? Excruciating, I should say. Neither of us spoke after that, for quite a while.

The more I considered Ned's story, the more I doubted he was the killer. With Burden dead, he'd lost any hope of being recognised as his son. Stephen might be weeping in his room, and Judith was swigging opiates to dull her senses, but it seemed to me that Ned was the most affected by Burden's murder. No chance for reconciliation. No chance to make his father proud. Strange, that of all Burden's children, it was Ned – his bastard – who loved him the most.

'I'm afraid for his soul, Mr Hawkins,' he said, as he escorted me to the door. 'The manner of his death – it gave him no chance to repent his sins. He was not himself, these past few weeks. His treatment of Alice . . .'

I could hear Mrs Jenkins fussing over Stephen upstairs. They would never winkle her out of the house now – not unless someone more interesting was murdered. The queen should have hired Mrs Jenkins to investigate Charles Howard instead of me – the woman was a walking newspaper, crammed with gossip. *The Daily Jenkins*. Still, she would be a help too, with Alice gone. 'Is it true that Alice has run away?'

Ned glanced up the stairs. 'Judith threw her out. I warned her not to be so rash. And now you are released . . . *Alice*.' He laughed without humour, marvelling at the thought. 'I can scarce believe it, but she had most cause . . .'

I shook my head. Burden had been torturing Alice for weeks in secret. Why kill him now, when he had promised to marry her? Kill him after the ceremony, perhaps, when the ink upon his will was dry. But not before. I took the knife from my pocket. 'Your father was stabbed nine times in the chest. That was rage. Revenge.'

His eyes widened. He tore the blade from my hand. 'How d'you know that? *How d'you know he was stabbed nine times?*'

I shrank back, realising my mistake. How could I know, indeed, if I had not seen the corpse? 'Half the town knows it!' I protested, feigning indignation. But I sounded nervous, even to my own ears – and Ned was suspicious once more.

'You were angry with him last night. And very drunk.'

So, we were back to this. Damn it. 'The doors and windows were barred. I'm not a ghost, Ned. I cannot walk through walls.'

'Perhaps there's another way in.' He paused, narrowing his eyes. 'Alice said she thought there must be a passage between the houses . . .'

Thank God I played cards for profit. My face was a mask, but my heart was thudding so hard against my chest I was sure he must see it beating through my coat. Heaven help me – if Ned found the passage between the two attic rooms, I was lost without a hope. I clamped my hat to my head. 'There are no doors and no passages. Whoever killed your father is still here in this house, Ned. If I were you, I should sleep with that blade beneath your pillow.'

Chapter Twelve

The Cocked Pistol was open for business. I watched from the street for a time, recovering my wits and savouring the last thin light of a long, cruel day. Business was steady, despite my ignominious arrest, customers entering with their usual furtive slide. Sam had taken charge of the shop. He was well suited to the task, swift and discreet – and the customers didn't notice him studying them closely beneath lowered lids. Perhaps later in his room he would sketch that young servant, come to collect a fresh parcel of books. One of Lord Hervey's men, I thought. His lordship was a great friend of the Prince of Wales. As he often ordered two copies of the same volume, we'd begun to suspect that one set was being smuggled to Prince Frederick for his pleasure and education. What would his mother think of that? Perhaps she would be pleased. It was vital the boy knew how to breed, after all.

Sam handed over the parcel and pocketed the small tip. For all the trouble he had caused with his moonlight skulks about Burden's house, I had grown oddly fond of the boy. Fond enough to dismiss the notion that he could have killed Burden. Reason told me I should not discount him – the son of a murderous gang captain, the nephew of a master assassin. But I could not believe him capable of such a violent, bloody murder. And for what purpose – sport? No, Burden's killer had been seeking revenge or justice. I doubted Sam had much time for either.

Burden's children were another matter entirely. The more I considered the life they had endured, the more certain I was that one of them was guilty. Burden had kept Judith a prisoner all her life; she rarely left the house save for church. Well – she was free now. I glanced up at the windows, shuttered in mourning. I had seen her sitting there countless times, pale and drawn, watching hungrily as life passed beneath her gaze. 'Poor Judith', the gossips had called her, while Felblade delivered another draught for her nerves.

Stephen must have dreaded a similar fate, once his father refused to send him back to school. He'd been given a sharp taste of his new life – beaten half to death for daring to question his father's authority. And then, bitterest of all, he had discovered his father was not only a violent bully, but a liar and a hypocrite. Had this been enough to kindle a murderous fury in the boy? That thin-limbed, trembling colt? Rage could give the weakest soul the strength of ten men. Cut off from his school and his friends, with his inheritance in peril, Stephen had powerful reasons to murder Burden. Money, justice, revenge. Of the three children, he would gain the most from his father's death. Now *he* was master of the house – and free to live as he pleased.

Freedom for Judith, freedom for Stephen. In another world I would have walked away from the whole damned business – let God stand in judgement when all was done. But I had my own freedom to consider. My own precious neck.

I must press a confession from one of them, or at least discover some clear proof of guilt. The blade had been found with the corpse, but what of the killer's ruined, bloody clothes? There would have been no chance to destroy them today, not with half the neighbourhood trailing through the house offering condolences. The clothes must still be hidden somewhere inside, and would remain there unless one of the children attempted to smuggle them out. One could hardly drop them upon the drawing-room fire.

I rolled my aching shoulders, glad to have found one small thread of hope. I would seek permission to search the house thoroughly tomorrow. In the meantime ... A couple of tattered street boys stood outside the baker's shop. Doubtless they might keep watch for a few halfpennies and a couple of Mrs Jenkins's rolls. I crossed the street towards them, but they squealed as I approached, scampering away before I could explain myself. It was a melancholy moment. I was a monster now, was that it? And I felt a shiver in my soul, some pre-sentiment that more trouble lay ahead. Once a man was named a monster, the mob was rarely far behind.

Sam, at least, seemed pleased to see me returned safe from the lock-up – in his fashion. He clambered over the counter and took my hand, shaking it without a word. I showed him the order and his face took on an expression of awe. 'The City Marshal's hand,' he murmured, brushing the paper as if it were the finest silk.

I plucked it back. He liked to practise different hands when it was quiet in the shop. 'What's the sentence for counterfeiting a Marshal's note?'

Sam looped an imaginary rope about his neck and pretended to hang, swaying on the spot with his tongue hanging out. It was a little too convincing for comfort.

'How many hangings have you seen, Sam?'

'Hundreds. Saw Jack Sheppard nubbed. Stood beneath the cart.'

I'd seen Sheppard swing too – my first winter in London. The mob had loved him, pulling on his legs to help speed his passing. It had ended in a riot, his friends fighting to keep his body from the chirurgeons. Thousands upon thousands streaming through the streets, trampling everything in their path. I'd thought I would die in all that madness and had wished myself safe at home in Suffolk. When I survived, pulled clear by strangers into the nearest tavern, my shirt torn and my lip bloodied, I knew I never wanted to leave.

'Thomas Hawkins. Oh, you wretch.' The door slammed back upon its hinges. Kitty: face smudged, clothes damp with sweat despite the cold. 'Look at you! Look at you here without a care in the world when I am half *dead*. I've trudged the streets all day searching for you. Every gaol, every lock-up. They laughed at me, Tom. They laughed and jeered and groped ... How long have you been free? Oh! You cannot even *guess* how much I hate you, you thoughtless prick.'

'I thought you were safe. *Sam*. You were supposed to take her to St Giles.'

He lifted a shoulder. 'She weren't inclined.'

'*She*,' Kitty said, whisking up and down the shop in a blind fury, 'has just returned from Gonson's house. That fucking guard who did this,' she pointed at a bruise on her cheek. 'He kept me waiting half an *age*, then said you were set free hours ago. Said you'd left with your *black whore*.' She kicked over a stool. 'He said you kissed her, in front of the *whole world*. Did you ...? Oh, you villain – you *did* kiss her!'

'Well, no, not precisely,' I flustered. 'She did somewhat *rather* ... but she only kissed me to distraction. *For* distraction, that is. *For* distraction. A slip of the tongue.'

'*A slip of the tongue*,' Kitty mimicked nastily. 'And I suppose your tongue just *slipped* into Betty's mouth?'

'Oh damn it, Kitty – it was an act, that is all. If you would let me explain ...' I reached for her, but she evaded my grasp, leaving the shop and running up the stairs.

I glanced up at the ceiling. 'Well, Sam. I suppose I had better meet my fate.'

He grinned. Wrapped the rope around his neck and swung back and forth.

Kitty was lighting a fire in our room. She heard me enter and sit down upon the bed, but she didn't turn around until the hearth was blazing. She took off her cap and unpinned her hair, tossing her head so the curls bounced down her back. She knew I loved that.

'Am I forgiven?' I took off my wig and slung it in a corner. I was too tired to argue. Too tired to move. My limbs ached from the lock-up, and my mind was distracted, bouncing from thought to thought like a racket ball.

'*Betty.*' She loosened the ribbons to her gown and pulled out the stomacher beneath, exposing the soft parting of her high, round breasts.

And suddenly, my mind was still.

'D'you want her, Tom?' She slipped off her shoes and balanced a foot upon my thigh. Slid it higher. *Ahh* . . . She rolled down her stocking. 'I've seen the way she looks at you. Like this.' She parted her lips and stared down at me from lowered lids. *Need. Desire.*

'Oh, fie – plenty of women look at me like that. That is—'

Kitty snorted and rolled down another stocking, flinging it at my face. 'No, no – true enough. Half the town wants to fuck you and the other half wants to hang you.'

I kicked off my shoes. 'And you would like to do both, I suppose.'

She clambered on to the bed, unfastening the buttons on my breeches. And then she kissed me, a kiss of possession. She slipped her hand lower, pulled my cock free. 'Say you are mine,' she murmured. 'Mine alone.'

'I'm yours.'

She smiled. Oh, I wanted her. I wanted her now. No more waiting. I rolled her beneath me, pushing her gown high above her hips. *Yes, yes, yes.* I lay over her, placed all my weight upon my shoulders.

Fuck! The pain ripped through my muscles and I fell back against the bed, panting hard.

'Tom?' Kitty sat over me. 'You're hurt?'

'Gonson chained me to a wall.' I flung an arm across my eyes. *Damn it.*

She lifted my arm away. 'Lie back.' She undid my shirt and touched my bruised and aching shoulders. Ran her hands down to my wrists, chafed by the iron cuffs. 'My love,' she sighed, and unhooked her petticoat.

I sat up beneath her, kissed her neck. 'I can't lie on top of you. My shoulders . . .'

She pushed me gently back to the pillow and slid off my breeches. Wriggled free of her skirts. And then she sat astride me, leaning down to kiss my lips as she tilted her hips.

I reached down, skimming my hand up her long, smooth thigh. Silk. Perfect silk. 'This is not—' I began, then gasped as she pressed against me. ' . . .how I imagined . . .'

'Indeed?' Kitty's green eyes shone bright as she pushed back her hair. 'It's *precisely* how I imagined . . .'

Afterwards we lay quietly, Kitty resting her head upon my chest. For all the time we had spent in bed together this was different. We talked for a while, drifting. Some good had come from the day after all. If I had become a parson, this would be my sermon. Take pleasure in these quiet, sweet moments of contentment. They are few – and they are everything. I smiled, and closed my eyes . . .

'Oh! You've fallen asleep, damn you.'

I woke with a jolt. 'I wasn't sleeping!'

Kitty pecked my cheek. 'You snore when you're awake? Fix yourself a pipe, Tom – we have a great deal to discuss. At least, I will talk and you must listen for a while – and you listen far better with a pipe between your teeth.' She crossed her legs beneath her, still naked, still beautiful.

'I do not snore,' I grumbled, groping for my watch. A quarter past eight. Fuck the stars. I must effect a meeting with Charles Howard tonight, and that meant crossing the river to Southwark. I slipped from the bed. 'Forgive me, sweetheart. I have an appointment. We'll speak tomorrow.' I searched through my closet, shivering as the air nipped my skin. Howard was a nobleman – I would need to dress well to join his company. But the Southwark streets were filthy and the benches at the cock-fight would be rough and splintered. Hmm. I rejected a pair of velvet breeches in favour of a brown silk knit, and had just selected a satin-fronted waistcoat when I realised that the room was deathly still.

Had she fallen asleep? Or was she glaring at my back, seething with annoyance? I glanced around. Ah, yes.

'We will speak *tonight*,' Kitty said, from the bed. She threw my shirt over her head and padded across the room, half coquette, half tiger. 'The last time you had an *appointment* you were attacked by a madman. Tell me what's happened. Tell me *everything.*'

And so I did. *Almost* everything. We sat by the fire and shared a pipe while I told her about the deal I'd made with James Fleet to meet Henrietta Howard, and the terrible fight that had ensued in St James's Park.

'Was it thrilling?'

'No.' Good God, no.

'But you *hoped* it would be,' she murmured, sadly. 'You were bored.'

It was true. And now she spoke that truth aloud, how petty and foolish it sounded. 'Not with you.'

She climbed on to my lap and took the pipe from my lips. 'So what now? What tangle of trouble have you fallen into?'

I told her about my visit to the palace.

'The *queen*.' She laughed in amazement. 'Tom I could kick you – why did you not tell me of this before? So. We are to meet with Howard tonight?'

I stared at her in alarm. The thought of Howard meeting Kitty, those mad, blazing eyes raking over her . . . 'No, no. He's a monster, Kitty – truly. You cannot come with me.'

'Why – do you forbid it? Do you think you can command my obedience now that you've stolen my maidenhood?' She pressed a hand to her forehead and mock-swooned.

'Stolen? You flung it at me with both hands.'

She giggled, burying her nose in my neck. 'Let me help you, Tom. I've saved your life before.'

Yes – and killed a man to do it. What would she say, I wondered, if I told her that the Queen of England knew what she had done? That she was holding that secret over me like a blade pressed to my heart? 'It will be a bloody, dreadful night,' I said, trying a different tack. 'I'm to meet him at a cockfight in Southwark.'

'A cockfight? Perfect!' She jumped to her feet. 'I haven't been to one in *months*.'

As we dressed I told Kitty about my visit to the Burden house that afternoon.

'Ned is Burden's *son*,' she murmured, lacing her boot. She knew the streets of Southwark of old and wouldn't waste a good shoe on all that filth. 'There is a resemblance, now I think on it. His mouth. The shape of his jaw.'

'I believe Ned is innocent, at least. More than anything, he wanted to be recognised as his father's son. Burden cannot acknowledge him from the grave.'

'Judith murdered him,' Kitty said, gesturing for me to tie her corset. 'I'm sure of it. She hated her father.'

And wished him dead – she had confessed that much herself. And yet . . . I frowned, pulling the strings of Kitty's corset. If only I could tie up Burden's murder so neatly. Kitty swept up her hair and began to pin up her curls. I leaned down and kissed the nape of her neck, breathing in her scent. Rose water and the soft trace of sweat. I was glad to have confided in her – it helped to talk through my ideas. 'I favour Stephen for it. Judith is too . . .' I struggled for the best word and landed upon Mrs Jenkins' description. 'Delicate.'

'Delicate?' Kitty stabbed another pin into her hair. '*Honestly*. Did she swoon at you, Tom? Did you grasp her trembling hand? *Oh dear Miss Burden, don't be afraid, I shall protect you, you poor delicate daisy. Puh.* All that *lisping* and *whimpering* – I don't believe a word of . . . *ow*, not so *tight*,' she gasped, loosening the corset a breath. 'Leave room for pie. I'm half starved from traipsing about town all day . . . No – can you not see it, Tom? Judith with the blade, taking revenge upon her father at last? All those years playing the dutiful, obedient daughter, locked away in her room like a nun. And not one of your *French nuns*, Tom, stop drifting.'

'You do not like Judith.'

'I do not like Judith,' she agreed. 'I should not mind so much if she murdered her father. What – why should I mind? He wanted you dead! But she was cruel to Alice, and sneaking with it. She was always so meek and mild in front of her father. But she treated Alice like a dog as soon as they were alone. Slapping and pinching her for the slightest mistake.'

I shook my head – but it was not so hard to believe. Judith was not the first mistress to take out her frustrations upon her servant. No wonder she was so furious about the marriage. Ned may have spent seven years as Burden's apprentice, but Judith had served eighteen years' hard labour as his daughter – and in the end had as little to show for it. And now Alice – the only member of the household over whom she had the slightest power – would rise to mistress of the household.

It should have been enough to convince me of Judith's guilt – but still the same question remained unanswered in my mind. If it were the marriage that made her so angry, why did she not kill *Alice*?

I slung my sword low upon my hip, hoping I would not need to draw it tonight. The impossibility of the evening's task pressed hard upon my aching shoulders. How the devil was I supposed to befriend the man I'd bludgeoned unconscious only a week before? *Oh, I say – good evening, sir. Do you recall our meeting upon St James's Park where I beat out your brains with your own pistol? How delightful to make your acquaintance again. Now, would you be obliging and reveal some scandalous details of your life that I might sell to the Queen of England?*

Perhaps Kitty might coax something useful out of the brute. She knew how to tease out secrets, how to listen in the shadows. Men underestimated Kitty, and she played upon it. Women too, for that matter. Which made me wonder . . . 'Kitty – how did you come by all this gossip about Judith and Alice?'

Kitty skimmed away, pulled out a gingham shawl. 'Alice told me.'

'Alice has run away. Judith threw her out.'

'I know. She's upstairs. I've hired her to replace Jenny.' She drew the shawl over her shoulders. Caught my horrified expression. 'We do need a maid, Tom. Unless you would like to scrub the floors and wash the dishes and darn your stockings and—'

'—I do not question the need for a servant, Kitty. I just question the need to hire the one who crawled into our house last night covered in blood and waving a knife.'

'Which I was able to use in negotiations. She'll cost a shilling less than Jenny each month.'

'That will be a great comfort when we are murdered in our bed.'

'We must keep her hidden for now. Alice is afraid that Judith will accuse her now that you have been set free.'

'She already has. There is still a chance Alice is guilty,' I whispered, glancing anxiously at the ceiling.

'No. It was Judith. I am decided, Tom.'

Sam was downstairs, dismantling the old, broken printing press that lay gathering dust at the back of the shop. He liked mechanical objects – he enjoyed pulling them apart and putting them back together. I'd known boys like him at school – boys who wanted to peel back the skin of the world and see how it all worked. There was no mystery that could not be solved by close and careful study, preferably beneath a microscope.

I told Sam to hire a couple of street boys to watch the Burdens' house in case anyone tried to smuggle out a set of bloody clothes. Then I wrote a brief note to Gonson asking him to send one of his guards over tomorrow to help me search the house for evidence. My God he would hate that – but for all his faults, Gonson was a dutiful magistrate. He would do as he was bid – albeit through gritted teeth. 'Deliver this to his home, Sam,' I said, and gave him a couple of shillings. 'And treat yourself to a good supper and a bowl of punch when you're done.'

He pocketed the coins. He would probably buy a cheap bowl of stew at some fleapit, and save the rest. After all, what was a body but another machine? Food was fuel, and nothing more.

I took Kitty's hand and we set off for Southwark. She wore her grey riding cloak with the hood lowered. She smiled up at me as we walked, a little shyly. No longer a maid. I squeezed her hand and grinned back. *I'm yours.*

If I close my eyes now I can see us strolling through the town towards the Thames, feet slipping on the damp cobbles, talking about what we would do once our troubles were over. Our lives stretching ahead of us, so many paths to take.

And then I open my eyes and all I see is the thick grey wall of my cell. I am in the condemned hold at Newgate, sentenced to hang. And Kitty is gone for ever.

PART THREE

As they ride west down the Tyburn Road, the handsome new houses of Marylebone make way for rolling fields, dull brown and muddy. Black crows strut over the ridged ground, wings clasped behind their backs. Beneath the hedgerows, hard banks of snow thaw slowly in the pale spring sunshine. It has been a cruel winter. The air is fresher here, the sky more open. It makes him think of the Suffolk coast where he grew up. I will never go there again. I will never see my father or my sister again. I will never . . . I will never . . .

'*Oh, God!*' *he breathes. Only his guards hear him. They watch and listen closely, memorising every detail. People will pay good money to hear of Thomas Hawkins' last moments.*

And now, there is no road left. He can hear the roar of the crowds gathered up ahead. Tens of thousands have congregated on Tyburn Hill to see the spectacle, stretching far out into the fields beyond. Scores more have come to pick their pockets. Best place to thieve a watch, a hanging.

The constables fight a path through the throng, beat the surging crowds back with clubs. People are climbing trees, hanging from ladders, balancing on the tops of roofs and walls and carriages. A father lifts his little boy on to his shoulders. The rich and fashionable folk sit in raised galleries next to the gallows, wrapped in greatcoats and scarves, chattering idly over the latest court gossip. Hawkers weave through them all, selling fruit and bowls of warm buttered barley. He can smell hot wine and sweet nutmeg in the air. His stomach rumbles. He has eaten poorly since the trial, his fine clothes hanging loose from his shoulders. And now, of all times, his appetite has returned – his body in protest, shouting its desire to live.

The carts turn in a wide circuit to the left, and he sees the gallows at last. Tyburn's triple tree. Three solid posts knocked deep into the earth, topped with three cross beams to form a triangle. Big enough to hang a dozen men. The hangman, John Hooper, lies along one of the cross beams, a pipe clamped between his lips, fixing the ropes with strong, deft fingers. As the carts approach, he flips one over. It tumbles down, swinging lightly.

If the pardon comes, it must be now.

The guards prod him to his feet. The Marshal is leaning down in his saddle, talking with his constables. He glances at the four carts, then gives a sharp nod and rides up to the gallows. 'Friends,' he bellows over the din. On his third try, the crowd quietens a little. 'Good Christians.' Someone shouts something from the back and a whole patch of spectators laugh.

Hawkins' heart is pounding so hard he can barely breathe.

The Marshal waits for silence. He slips his fingers into his saddlebag. Tugs out a scroll of paper, sealed with bright red wax. A royal pardon.

Chapter Thirteen

I am told that evenings at the Whitehall cockpit are a genteel affair, where peers lose their fortunes with quiet dignity and ladies are barred entrance for fear of fainting. Southwark cockpits, by contrast, are a grand tour of hell. Howard, true to his nature, had chosen the very worst.

The pit was hidden in a maze of back alleys off Deadman's Place – a series of twists and turns I have no care to remember now. Kitty knew it well from her time working in the Marshalsea, and kept her cape and gown bunched high above the filth as she led the way. I walked a step behind with my hand upon the hilt of my sword, watching the shadows. We were too close to the gaol for my liking – I had earned myself a mean set of enemies in that damned hole, and a cockfight was precisely the place to find them again. I had conceived a bitter hatred of Southwark since my stay in prison, and this was the first time I had returned to the Borough in months.

Another twist, and we arrived at the mouth of an alley blacker than a parson's coat, rats scuttling and squealing in the darkness. A torch flickered at the dead end, beckoning us forward. A tavern without a name, hidden for a reason. I thought I glimpsed a movement up ahead, and touched Kitty's shoulder, but there was nothing there. I had come to expect danger from every shadow in this city. As we paused, I heard footsteps behind us and a short, tough-looking rogue hurried past without a glance, hood covering his face, long cloak flapping at his heels as he ran. Not Howard, but a similar build – strong and solid – and fearless in a place bristling with danger.

The windows of the tavern were boarded with thick planks, but we could hear the rabble inside, rowdy and violent. A guard stood at the entrance – a dark-skinned man with a grubby hat shoved onto his bald scalp. His face was a hideous mess of old scars, puckered and seamed like poorly stitched leather. A face to haunt nightmares, but for his eyes, which were clear and in this moment, at least – merry. He was laughing with the man who'd pushed past us, but his smile faded as we joined them.

'No wenches,' he said, barring our way. 'Not tonight.'

His companion pulled back his hood. 'Sure and what am I, Jed?'

Jed spat a wet clod of tobacco at his feet and chuckled. 'Fuck knows what *you* are, Neala Maguire.'

Neala . . .? The torch caught the man's face and revealed that *he* was, in fact, a woman – shorter than me by a head, but by God she was as broad and solid as an oak tree. Her black hair was cut short to her nape, framing a strong face and a square jaw. She spoke with an Irish accent, her voice low and rough as a man's.

Kitty stepped forward, the torch turning her red hair to spun gold. 'Have you forgotten me so soon, Jed?'

'Kitty!' He grinned in surprise, then grabbed her in a tight hug, lifting her half off the ground. 'Didn't know you in them rum togs. Heard you was left a round sum.' He jerked his chin towards me. 'He come after?'

She put an arm about my waist. '*Before.* Loves me for my sweet temper not my purse, ain't that right, Tom?'

Jed near pissed himself laughing. 'Go on,' he said, gesturing inside. 'Never saw you.'

The tavern was packed, the air thick with pipe smoke, sweat and liquor. The noise alone almost knocked me from my feet – men yelling to be heard as they clustered around the ring in the centre of the room. I stood dazed, battered by the sound, the stink, the roiling mess of it all. I'd fought in riots quieter than this. If a man found himself in trouble here, then God help him – no one else would. I craned my neck, searching for Howard, but couldn't see him in the crowds. There must have been two hundred men in there at least.

Kitty grabbed my hand and pressed eagerly to the front, kicking ankles and treading on toes to carve a way through as spectators fell back in shock, open-mouthed. There were no other women that I could see. Some fellows grinned at me as if I were the luckiest devil alive, while others spat oaths and frowned in disapproval.

We pressed forward to the edge of the ring, leaning over the fence. The cocks were being paraded before the fights began, smart and proud of their silver spurs. Kitty studied them all keenly, as if she were choosing one to marry. 'I like the look of him,' she muttered in my ear as one strutted by with its chest puffed. She elbowed the man on her left – an old gent in bent spectacles. 'Hey, there. What's his pedigree?'

His eyes swivelled behind his thick lenses, then widened in dismay. He tugged at my cuff. 'Sir, this is not proper! The entertainment tonight ... It is not suitable for a lady ...'

Kitty laughed at him. 'Do I look like a fucking lady?'

The man opened and shut his mouth like a panicked fish. Damned with a 'yay' and damned with a 'nay'. By God, I knew that feeling.

Two of the cocks began to squabble, pecking and clawing the air. The room goaded them on until they began to fight in earnest, turned savage by the crowd. The owners shouted and waded into the fray, but it was too late. The larger cock jumped upon its opponent, and with one vicious slash of its spur, ripped open the other bird's belly. It was still pecking and jabbing furiously when its owner pulled it free. The injured bird lay bleeding and calling piteously, guts spilling out onto the sawdust. Its owner cursed and wrung its neck. The cock's legs scrabbled and danced, then fell still.

The parade over, the tavern owner lumbered into the ring to announce the start of the night's entertainment. A gladiatorial fight with swords . . . he skidded to a halt as he spied Kitty. 'Out!' he yelled over the din. 'Take that strumpet *out*!'

Two hundred men craned their necks to stare at us. There was a woman in the crowd! For some reason I couldn't fathom, this was an outrage beyond measure. True, most cockfights were meant for men alone, but there were always a few women allowed in the room – women of the town, in the main . . . but tonight there were none, save for Kitty.

A fat, sweaty man in a waterman's doublet cupped his hands to his mouth. 'Have you come to see a handsome cock, slut?' He grabbed his breeches.

'Aye, but I'll take the last one standing,' Kitty yelled back. 'Not the first one spent in the ring.'

The waterman's jaw dropped, and then he guffawed with laughter, raising his fists in approval. Nothing a Thames boatman appreciates more than a filthy mouth. The crowd roared with him, but there were as many protests as cheers. I drew Kitty closer. 'You might be safer outside with Jed,' I whispered in her ear. Scenes such as this could turn ugly very fast.

The landlord grabbed me by the coat. 'Out. Both of you. Unless you want a blade in the ribs . . .'

A shot rang out. There was a moment of shocked silence, and then chaos, as men ducked beneath tables or pulled out their own daggers and pistols.

'Fuck,' the landlord breathed, lifting his gaze to a bench at the back of the room. A man in a dark velvet coat stood on the bench with a pistol in his hand, smoke trailing from the barrel. A gentleman with a mad man's face, lips twisted in a humourless grin. *Howard*.

The men who had drawn their own weapons groaned or sat back down upon seeing him. Perhaps because he was a nobleman – or perhaps because his reputation was well known in such a place. Either way, no one had the appetite for a fight.

He stared at me for a long, terrifying moment, as if he might eat me alive. Then he relaxed, and tucked his pistol back into his coat. 'Let 'em through, Smith,' he barked at the landlord. His manner was rough, but his voice had the clear, irresistible authority of a courtier. Smith obeyed at once, cursing under his breath as he led us across the room.

Howard was sitting above the ring on a raised platform, attended by a gang of five men. Two I recognised as his chairmen, the rest were gentlemen – of a fashion. Howard watched me without a word as I clambered up to meet him, his face curiously blank. I tensed as he stepped forward, jaw aching at the memory of his last punch. At least there was no powder left in his pistol. If he attacked us I could pull Kitty back into the crowds and out of the tavern in a flash. I was sure she knew the back alleys around here better than Charles Howard.

'You're a brave man ...' he said, taking a long swig from a bottle of claret.

I said nothing, watching him closely. Ready to run.

' ...bringing such a fine jade here.' He bowed towards Kitty, then returned his gaze to me. His eyes seemed to glow in the candlelight – the gleam of a man standing on a precipice for the sheer hell of it. 'What's your name, sir?'

I stared at him. Was it possible? Did he not recognise me? 'Thomas Hawkins,' I replied, too astonished and relieved to lie. I gave a short bow.

'A gentleman,' he said, voice thick with sarcasm. 'Well then, sir – join us.' He gestured to his chairmen to leave the bench. As they rose, the young rake propped between them slid boneless to the floor and lay still. Howard put a foot beneath the boy's ribs and rolled him out of the way.

The rest of the party was drunk too, bottles littered beneath the bench, but Howard seemed steady enough. Well, he had enjoyed years of practice – he was in his early fifties now, though he looked much older. I thought he must have been a handsome man in his youth, but he had ruined himself by decades of wild living. His face was bloated and sallow, with burst veins across his nose and cheeks.

'My thanks for your help, sir,' I said, nodding at the bulge of his pistol beneath his coat. 'You must permit me to buy another bottle or two ...' A debauch would be a good way to extract useful information from Howard – if I could remain sober myself.

'Put a guinea on the Irish bitch when she comes on and we're even,' he said, grabbing my shoulder and giving it a mighty squeeze. I buckled a little, and let out a silent whimper. I still ached from the morning's torture. I smiled and nodded through the pain, though I hadn't the faintest idea what he meant. He welcomed Kitty with a surprisingly charming bow, while I set-tled down upon the bench, marvelling at my good fortune. He truly didn't remember me from the fight in the park. Well – it had been dark and he had been fearsome drunk. And I *had* knocked him senseless. There was still a cut upon his brow even now, scabbed and bruised. With luck I'd knocked the memory clean out of him.

He took another swig, studying me closely. 'I feel I know you from somewhere, Hawkins . . .'

The blood drained to my toes. 'The gaming tables, perhaps . . .?'

He scratched his jaw. 'Perhaps.' He took Kitty's arm and escorted her to the bench, settling her beside him. I gritted my teeth as he patted her hand, forcing myself to hide my revulsion. And yet there was some ghost of gallantry in his behaviour – some echo of a younger man more able to dissemble and present a gentlemanly appearance. *There* was the actor who had fooled Henrietta into marriage – the dashing captain wooing a sheltered young girl half his age. An orphan from a noble family with a fair fortune. He must have been licking his chops behind his hand. How long had he waited to reveal his true nature? A few days after the wedding at most, I wagered. A few days before the beast ripped its way into the open. Poor Henrietta. Only sixteen. She must have been terrified.

'D'you know, it's strange,' Howard frowned. 'You *both* seem familiar. Are you an actress, madam?'

'No, sir,' Kitty smiled. 'We own a bookshop, on Russell Street . . .'

He swayed, thinking. 'Hah! Cocked Pistol! Best damned shop in London!' Howard punched one of his companions in the arm. 'D'ye hear that, Drummond?' And soon the entire company fell to discussing the shop and what a great, civic service it performed. I could scarce believe my luck. Not only did Howard not remember our fight, it transpired he was one of our best customers. He sent a boy for most of his purchases, but was sure he had met us both on his own brief visits. I confess I did not remember him, but then I spent most of my time upstairs at my desk.

'Was there not a murder on Russell Street last night?' Howard asked. 'Some old bore was talking of it at White's . . .'

'Joseph Burden. Carpenter. He lived next door.'

Howard gave a jolt of surprise, then began to laugh, clapping a hand to his knee. 'Joseph *Burden* . . .' he chuckled. 'Haven't heard that name for a while. Now there was a vicious, godless rogue. He'll be roasting in hell tonight, on my word.'

Kitty stared at him. 'Godless?'

'He was a brothel bully when I knew him,' Howard said. 'Bawdy house off Seven Dials. Twenty years back, now . . . Blackest, meanest place in the city. Not for simpering boys, you understand. Rooms for every vice.' His eyes glinted. 'Whipping. Pissing. Dogs if you fancied.' He laughed and the rest of the company laughed with him. 'Burden was paid to stop the worst of it. If a man took a knife to a girl, or beat her too hard. But he had debts. One could always pay him to look the other way.' He laughed again. 'My God. The things Joseph Burden *didn't* see . . .'

Fresh cheering brought our attention back to the ring. Someone had entered the pit – in a state of near undress. 'Neala!' Kitty gasped. I leaned forward. My God, so it was – the Irish girl we'd met outside. She had removed her long riding cloak to reveal a tightly laced bodice and a short petticoat of white linen, her solid legs bare. She was holding a two-handed sword, the blade a good three inches broad. She raised it high, drawing another roar from the crowd. A second girl joined her in the ring dressed in the same uniform, though she wore red ribbons on her sleeve where Neala wore blue. Her blonde hair was tightly plaited close to her head, to keep it from her eyes.

'A guinea on the blue,' Howard ordered, pushing me towards the pit. 'First to draw blood.'

'And a pie!' Kitty called after me.

I found a man near the front of the tumult willing to take my bet – the same waterman who had traded insults with Kitty. Neala was striding about the ring, calling out the many fights she had won. She spoke of her eight brothers back in Ennistymon, who'd taught her how to use a sword like a warrior. I was near enough to catch her eye as she passed. She gave a curt nod before turning to shake her opponent's hand.

I had never seen a female gladiatorial battle before. I'd heard of them being used to entertain the crowds before the men came out to fight – a little sport with no real danger. This was different. The point of Neala's sword was blunt, but the edge was sharp as a razor. I tapped the waterman's shoulder. 'How many rounds?'

He shrugged. 'They're fighting for coin. Depends how desperate they are.'

Neala was down on one knee, praying with her head bowed. As she rose she crossed herself, then bounced on the balls of her feet.

'Papish bitch,' someone muttered beside me.

I suppressed a frown. My mother had been raised in the Catholic faith. I bet him a crown the *bitch* would win. Touched the gold crucifix hidden beneath my shirt for luck.

The fighters circled one another slowly as the men shouted encouragement. They both held daggers in their left hand to ward off blows, keeping the swords away from their bodies. The English girl was taller than Neala and moved fast. She was the first to attack, her sword crashing down hard enough to ring out through the tavern. Neala bowed her legs beneath the blow and sprang back.

It was a hard, brutal fight, and the packed room was hot as the centre of hell. The girls were soon drenched in sweat, their skin glistening and their white petticoats clinging to their thighs. As I glanced over the seething crowd of men, I understood why Kitty had been so unwelcome tonight. It was not just a lust for blood that had them baying at the girls. Several spectators had shoved a furtive hand in their breeches.

I leaned over to the waterman, pointed to a gang of apprentices across the ring rubbing themselves with vigour. 'Side bet on who spends first?'

The waterman snorted. 'Young puppies. They'll be spent before I'm done speak—' He stopped. Pulled a face. 'Told you.'

Howard squeezed in next to me and put an arm around my shoulder. 'Some sport, eh?'

I had to admit it was a great spectacle. The other girl was a pretty creature and knew how to play to her audience, flashing them smiles as she hacked hard and fast with her blade. With a quick dart she sliced open Neala's arm, blood spurting from the wound. First blood to England. The crowd cheered. Howard had lost his bet.

'Bad luck,' I said, but he didn't seem to care. But then, it wasn't his guinea.

He leaned closer and pointed at Neala's blood, spattered on to the sawdust. 'Nothing better, eh, Hawkins?'

A hundred thousand things.

'I'd like to see your scarlet whore in the ring. She's a wild slut, no doubt. How d'you keep her to heel?' I shook my head, not able to trust my tongue. He laughed. 'You're not sick for her, are you? Damned fool.' He pushed back into the crowds to talk with the landlord.

There was a pause as Neala's wound was stitched and a bandage applied. She took a large glass of spirits to steady her nerves and returned to the ring, blade high.

'Game girl,' the waterman said at my side.

The fight continued. After half an hour Neala had suffered another cut across her chest and was bleeding heavily, but her opponent was staggering with exhaustion now, barely able to raise her sword to protect herself. Neala could have moved in ten minutes before and chanced an attack, but she took her time, prodding and thrusting and falling back until the crowd grew restless.

'*Finish her off for fuck's sake!*'

'*Use your blade, damn it!*'

She ignored them, parrying a final, weak attack. Her opponent crashed to the floor and dropped her sword, hands raised in defeat as Neala approached. Neala threw her fist in the air and grinned as the few of us who had bet on her to win shouted our approval. Hah! I was up one crown! And down a guinea, but there was no need to think of that.

The loser was now walking through the crowds selling herself for the night to the highest bidder. No one seemed interested in buying Neala and she did not seem interested in selling, either. She took her winnings from the fight and crossed the ring to greet me. I congratulated her and invited her to join us for supper. Her eyes flickered up to Howard's bench where he was seated again, talking with Kitty. A guarded look crossed Neala's face. 'That's your woman up there? I would take better care of her, if I were you.'

I watched with a sinking heart as Howard laughed and smiled, the mask back in place. Neala was right to scold me – but I could not send Kitty home on her own. The dark streets were just as dangerous as Howard – and at least I could keep my eye upon him. I sighed to myself. So much for my pretty dream of my first full night with Kitty. So much for a blazing fire, a warm bed, and the finest wine I could afford. I bought her a wretched-looking pie and returned to the bench. The first pair of cocks were out in the ring now, parading in their silver spurs once more as the landlord called out their pedigrees. Kitty broke off her conversation with Howard to take the pie.

'We should bet on that one, on the left,' she said, taking a huge bite. 'Saw his grandfather fight like a fucking demon in Clerkenwell.' She nudged her shoulder against mine. 'Is this not fun, Tom? We should come here every week.'

I knocked back some claret, grimacing as the fight began and the cocks tore at each other. The truth was, I hated cockfighting. I know I am alone with the Quakers, but I can't bear to watch two innocent animals ripping each other apart for sport. It's a shame, as there is good money to be made if one knows the birds' pedigrees and fighting history – but I cannot help my squeamish nature. I tried to explain this to Kitty as her favourite gouged a wide hole in its rival's neck then stood on its lifeless body, crowing in triumph.

She wiped the grease from her fingers. 'You wish me to feel pity for a chicken?' She kissed my cheek. 'Dear Tom.'

The night drew on and Howard grew restless. He had won a few bets in the first matches, but was now down almost three pounds – all of it borrowed from the pockets of the young sot under the bench, who had barely stirred all evening. I asked the most sober companion left standing who the boy was – a nobleman, I thought, judging from his clothes.

'That he is, Hawkins,' Howard interrupted. He dragged the boy to a seated position, leaning him against the bench. The boy's head rolled back. 'He's my son. Henry – wake up, damn you.'

Henry Howard. Henrietta's son – her only child. I stared at the young rake sprawled in a drunken heap, a sloppy string of drool sliding down his chin. Then thought of his mother, gracious and composed, her face cool and still as a portrait. And yet the resemblance was there, beneath the debauchery. He shared Henrietta's high forehead and clear complexion, and the contours of his face were remarkably similar. I saw little of Howard in him, save for the drunkenness, of course.

Henry hiccoughed, then spewed a thin stream of vomit at our feet.

'*Gah . . .*' Howard cursed. At his signal, one of the chairmen threw the boy over his shoulder, pushing his way through the crowds. Hopefully the fresh air would revive him. 'Can't take his liquor,' Howard scowled after them both. 'It's his mother's fault, damn her.'

I smiled, playing my part. I couldn't risk the night ending here, although I wanted it to with all my heart. Howard could tell a good story at the start of an evening, before the liquor scoured away the thin veneer of charm. There were old war stories, and wicked court scandals from his years attending the old king. He had lived a free, rakish life, and there must have been a time, long ago, when he had been entertaining company. But now he was an old, ruined man, on the turn like spoiled milk, sour and sickening.

Worst of all was his hatred of his wife, a poison running through his veins. He had spent much of the night regaling me with sordid tales of his marriage, before Henrietta had found sanctuary at court. I sensed that he told these stories often, to anyone who might listen. He took the part of the villain with a strange sort of glee, as if his life's great purpose had been to torture and degrade his wife in every conceivable fashion. He'd squandered her inheritance, roaming the town while she starved in filthy lodgings. And when he did come home, he brought back whores to torment her, fucking them in front of her.

'One son, that's all she gave me,' he sneered, as Henry was carried lifeless through the tavern. 'What use is a wife if she can't keep a baby in her belly?'

Somehow, I kept my composure. How would it serve

Henrietta if I punched Howard, or stormed away in disgust? I must find something useful to bring back to the queen. 'You are separated now, I believe?'

'Not in law,' he snapped. 'She is still *mine* – and always will be. She can hide in her rooms, but I'm still here, in her head.' He tapped his temple with his fingers. 'For ever.' And then he started upon another loathsome story, of some small rebellion punished with a savage beating. How it had left her deaf in one ear and why that was not his fault. How she should thank him now, as it spared her from listening to the king's tedious conversation.

It was not the first time I'd heard a man speak of beating his wife of course, nor would it be the last. Take a walk through the Garden and there are plenty of women with black eyes and split lips. But Howard spoke of it with a boastful pride I had never heard before, as if it were his duty and his pleasure.

It made me all the more determined to find *something* to stop him, for Henrietta's sake as well as my own. But what could I tell the queen that she did not already know? The gambling, the drinking, the whoring, the debts, the violence, the cruelty. What news could ever be enough, given Howard's position? Ned Weaver resented me because I was the son of a gentleman, and so favoured by the law. Charles Howard was a nobleman. If his brother died without an heir, he would become Earl of Suffolk . . .

. . .Unless someone ran him through with a blade first. I confess, the thought did cross my mind. One quick stab in the back, in some dark alleyway. If I were a different man, how easily I could resolve the matter. If I were Samuel Fleet, in fact – the man the queen expected me to replace.

'You hold your drink well,' Howard said, slapping my back.

I took the compliment, but in fact I had only sipped at my wine. It had been easy enough to pass my bottle on to one of

Howard's companions, or spill a few glugs upon the floor. Kitty had spent most of the night at the ring, betting on the fights without drinking. We had both kept our wits sharp.

Howard leaned closer. 'I've hired a boat,' he shouted, his breath hot and wet in my ear. 'You must join me. Both of you. Plenty of drinking hours before dawn.'

I nodded and told him I would find Kitty, though I had no intention of bringing her with me. I took a slow circuit about the tavern, and found her at last at the door, talking to Jed. I drew her to a shadowed spot beyond the reach of the torchlight and explained about the boat trip.

'You must go home now,' I whispered, reaching for her hand in the gloom. 'Would Jed escort you home, d'you think – for a fee? Or that Irish girl, perhaps?'

'Neala. She left some time ago.'

'It won't be safe on the boat, Kitty. There's nowhere to escape on the river, and I can't protect you from six men, even if they're half-dead with drink.'

She squeezed my hand. 'He doesn't remember you, Tom. And you need something to give to the queen.'

The cockfighting was over and the tavern was emptying, men streaming out into the chill air. Some of the winning cocks were being carried through in wooden cages, squawking and crowing and flapping furiously. I called over to Jed and asked if he would guide Kitty home for a fee. 'I have business with Charles Howard.'

'Howard? Keep away from that bastard. Take her home yourself.'

Kitty prodded me in the ribs. 'I am not a sack of potatoes to be carted about the city. I shall go where I please.'

'Kitty . . .'

'Now, now – what's this?' Howard cried, clapping his hands as he stepped into the night. 'A lovers' quarrel?'

'Miss Sparks is a little tired. I'm arranging a safe passage home.'

'Home? What the devil are you mewling about, Hawkins? No, no – I will not part with my new friends. You must come with me.' He put his arms around our shoulders and dragged us away. 'I *insist*.'

The boat was waiting for us at St Saviour's Dock, bobbing and swaying against its mooring. It was a barge fit for a nobleman, with a broad cabin in the stern and a smaller one at the bow. How this particular nobleman had paid for the trip I could only guess – he had lost a fortune in the tavern, and yet he tipped the head oarsman a crown as we boarded. His son must have deep pockets. Henry was still with us – in a manner of speaking. He had puked several times along the way and had to be carried on to the barge by Howard's chairmen. The rest of our party we had lost to another tavern behind the cathedral. Praise the Lord.

As the boat pushed off I cautioned myself to remain calm. Howard had invited us as his guests. He had no memory of our fight and no reason to believe our meeting had been anything but pure chance. I had my sword at my side and was more sober than I'd been in years. And still ... it wouldn't be wise to trust him. While he headed to the stern in search of more wine, I slipped a coin into the head oarsman's pocket. 'If I tap your shoulder, row us to the nearest steps,' I murmured.

The Thames was quiet, with only a handful of boats upon the water. And no surprise – it was late, and the air was biting. A gang of revellers called out cheerfully as we passed, and Kitty waved at them. A hard wind blew across the water and she shivered. 'Let's go inside. I think there's supper laid out.'

I touched her hand. 'Stay close to me.'

Howard emerged from the cabin with a fur blanket under his arm. 'Here you are, my dear,' he said, draping the blanket over Kitty's shoulders. She smiled and wrapped it tighter against the wind. A touching moment, if he had not spent the evening counseling me to beat her into obedience. He balanced his way over to his son, who was slumped at the edge of the boat, heaving bile into the water.

Howard knelt down next to him. 'You drink like a woman, Henry. It's a damned disgrace. Your mother has ruined you.'

'My mother is a *whore*,' Henry slurred into his father's face. They were the only words he'd spoken all evening.

Howard patted his shoulder. 'Good lad.'

Henry swivelled around and vomited into the river.

'Shall we go inside, Mr Howard?' Kitty said.

He smiled.

The world seemed to slow. Howard, smiling. The oars slicing the water. And Kitty, heading for the cabin. Out of my reach. I knew we were in danger, knew with that one smile that the evening had turned upside down. I touched the oarsman's shoulder. He kept on rowing. 'Sorry, sir,' he said, from the corner of his mouth.

'They're in my pay, not yours,' Howard said, pulling his pistol from his coat. He laughed, and tapped the cut on his brow as I stumbled back. 'Did you think I'd forgotten you, Sir *Nobody*? My wife's *champion*?'

He had known all along. Lured me here to the river with Kitty.

'Mr Howard,' I said, keeping my voice steady. 'Turn this boat to shore.'

'Did you plan to kill me? Did she pay you?'

'Mr Howard—'

I heard a scuffle and a soft cry behind me. Howard's chairmen were dragging Kitty into the cabin, a blade at her throat. One of them whispered something in her ear and her eyes widened in fright. *No, no, no.* I ran after them, reaching for my sword.

A sharp crack on the back of my skull. Then nothing.

Chapter Fourteen

I came to in an empty cabin, lying on the floor. My hands were bound roughly with rope and my sword was gone. I lay in the dark, half-senseless. Then I remembered. *Kitty*. I staggered to my feet, shaking my head to clear it. Pain stabbed my skull.

I'd been thrown in the small cabin at the bow. I lurched to the door, but it was barred from the outside. I threw my weight against it, but it wouldn't give. I pounded with my fists, screaming for help. She was alone with Howard. I'd let him take her. That monster. I kicked and yelled, but the door stood firm.

Then suddenly there was a heavy thud as the bar was raised and dropped to the ground. I pushed open the door and almost fell into Henry.

'What the deuce ...?' he slurred, with a lopsided grin. 'A game?'

I held up my wrists. 'Aye, aye, a game. Untie me, Henry.'

But he was too foolish with drink, giggling and stumbling over the knots. I cursed and pushed him away, wheeling around to the head oarsman.

'For pity's sake help me.'

He hesitated, glancing over his shoulder, doubt in his eyes.

'On your conscience, sir. Say the boy freed me. *Please.*'

He leaned across and untied the knot. 'Stern. Hurry. I'll row closer to shore.'

They had taken my sword, but my dagger was still tucked somewhere in my coat. I searched for it in a panic until my hands caught the hilt. I seized Henry by the scruff of his neck and pushed him towards the stern.

He flailed in a panic. 'What's this? What's happening?'

I pressed the blade against his throat and he held still, sober enough at last to realise that this was no game. I kicked open the door to the larger cabin.

Kitty was crouched on a bench at the far end of the room, a broken bottle in her hand. There were scratches on her face and her sleeves were torn. How long had I been unconscious – a few minutes? She had fought off three men in the meantime – three men staggering with drink perhaps, but still, it was a miracle. One of the chairmen lay unmoving under the table, and the other was holding a handkerchief to a deep cut on his forehead.

Howard dragged the table to one side to reach Kitty, his hat and wig knocked free in the fight.

'Let her go!' I cried.

Howard turned and cursed. His soldier's training held him still while he assessed the odds. 'You are not a killer,' he decided.

'I am for her.' I pressed the point deeper into his son's neck. A trickle of blood spilled over the blade.

Howard reached into his jacket and took out his pistol. He aimed it at Kitty, who shrank back. 'Why, did you think you were winning this little scrape?' He laughed at her. 'It was a game, no more.'

My head whirled. Howard was mad enough to shoot her and powerful enough to get away with it. The risk was too high. I lowered the blade and Howard's chairman snatched it from my hand. He pushed Henry out of the way and wrapped an arm about my throat.

'Now then, Kitty,' Howard said. Her name on his foul lips. I couldn't bear it. 'Put down the bottle.'

She hesitated.

He cocked the pistol.

Kitty dashed the bottle to the ground, the glass smashing into a dozen sharp pieces.

Howard began to unbutton his breeches, one-handed. 'Are you fucking my wife, Hawkins?' He glanced at me. 'Well, sir?'

I shook my head.

'Liar. Why else would you fight for her?'

My heart was burning in my chest. What could I say to him? How could I talk of honour to such a man? He planned to rape Kitty in front of me, in front of his son. I would not let that happen. I must not.

Howard put a hand in Kitty's hair and pulled sharply. He called out to Henry. 'D'you see now, boy? This is how you train the wild ones. Let them play. Let them think they're strong. And then you—'

Kitty flung herself back at him, tumbling them both to the ground. As they fell she turned and drew her knee up, forcing it hard between his legs. Howard screamed and dropped the pistol; it span away beneath the bench as he curled into a tight ball, rolling in agony in the broken glass. It spiked his skin, blood-stains blooming on his white shirt. 'I'll kill you,' he whimpered. 'I will *kill you*.'

Kitty stood up, swaying as the boat rode over a wave. Then she raised her heel and stamped down upon on his free hand, grinding it against a thick shard of glass. He screamed, still clutching himself with the other hand. Screamed until there was no breath left.

The chairman ran to help his master. I grabbed my blade, snatched Kitty's hand and we lurched from the cabin out on to the deck. The Thames rolled black and deep, the moon shining on its surface. The oarsmen had brought us close to Somerset House on the north side of the river, but we were still a good twenty yards from shore.

The cabin door crashed open and Howard raged on to the deck, bent double in agony, his pistol raised in his bloody fist.

There was no time to think. I jumped from the boat, still holding Kitty's hand.

I heard the crack of the pistol and then the river closed over my head, filthy and ice cold. I flailed to the surface, gasping in shock as the freezing water knifed my skin. A couple of watermen waiting for custom at the steps stood up in their boat and began to shout in alarm. I could hear Kitty floundering a few feet away, her gown dragging her down. I swam over to her, battling the pull of the water. As I grabbed her arm, a wave knocked me back and I slipped under, still holding her close.

I surfaced, spitting out a mouthful of rank river water – and saw the barge looming towards us. Howard stood at the prow, screaming at the oarsmen to row faster, his face twisted with fury. In a few moments, the boat would smash straight into us. I swam desperately towards the watermen, calling out for help as I held on to Kitty's waist. The water was weighing us both down now, turning our clothes to lead. The watermen rowed out to meet us and we clung to the side in terror as they turned back to shore. When we reached the steps I dragged Kitty out to safety.

'You there!' Howard shouted at the watermen from the river. 'Hold them both for me. I'll pay you!'

Our rescuers discussed the offer as I pulled myself on to the steps, coughing up the foul-tasting water. I reached into my sodden clothes and threw a shower of coins at their feet. 'Please,' I said, crawling up the steps on my hands and knees.

One of the men held up a lantern, squinted at the barge. 'Is that Charles Howard?'

'Gah!' The other one spat into the water. 'I fucking hate that nob.' He pulled me to my feet. 'G'on with you. Run.'

I couldn't run. I could barely walk. My skull was pounding from the blow to my head, and I was shaking from the cold. But somehow I staggered up the Somerset steps and found Kitty, collapsed at the top and shivering. She looked half dead. The sight of her brought me back to my senses. With my last strength I gathered her up and half-dragged, half-carried her away, heading back towards Covent Garden in a desperate, lurching run. I would have picked her up and slung her over my shoulder, but I had lost my strength that morning, chained to Gonson's wall. Somehow, I must find a way to press on. I could still hear Howard shouting furiously as he reached the steps. We were not free of him yet.

I stumbled forward, trying not to panic. It was very late now, the streets dark and quiet. We could not go home, that much was certain. Howard was in such a state of fury I was afraid he would break down the door and murder us all.

I looked over my shoulder and spied him in the distance with one of his chairmen. I hurried on to Russell Street.

'Home,' Kitty mumbled, tottering against me. She felt bone cold.

'We can't go home,' I whispered.

She slumped, knees sagging, senseless. And somehow, with the last of my strength, I picked her up and slid her over my shoulder. My muscles screamed, but I felt them only dimly through the fear and urgency. I lumbered on to Drury Lane, winning curious looks from the few street whores still out searching for business. I could hear Howard cursing my name as he followed, narrowing the gap between us. I turned left on to St Giles.

Now, Howard, you son of a bitch – follow us if you dare. For all your mad rage let's see if you are a match for the rookeries of St Giles. I took the first alley I could find and plunged in, the darkness swallowing us whole.

I could go no further. As I reached the end of the alley I sank to my knees, shuddering with the cold. I lowered Kitty to the ground and gazed up at the ropes and walkways high above our heads. Everything was still.

'My name is Thomas Hawkins,' I called up through numb, frozen lips. 'I work for James Fleet. We need his help.'

Nothing.

Or the merest whisper of something on the wind. The softest creak of feet along a walkway.

I slumped in the mud, clutching Kitty for warmth, but she was cold as death. Why had I let her come with me tonight? Why had I not stopped her? 'I'm so sorry,' I whispered. 'I'm so sorry.'

I heard footsteps behind us. Howard was striding down the alleyway, clutching a bottle, his chairman holding a torch to light his way. My God, he was truly a lunatic to enter St Giles in the middle of the night. I rolled to my knees and raised my hand, panting heavily. 'For pity's sake, Howard. *Enough.*' But he did not know the meaning of the word.

'On the ground, in the filth. How fitting. D'you know, I think I shall piss on you both before I kill you.' He took a swig from the bottle and began to pull at his breeches. Blood streamed from a wide gash in his hand, where Kitty had ground it into the broken glass.

I was shaking with the cold now, my wet clothes burning like ice in the winter night. My teeth began to chatter. I clamped my jaw shut. I didn't want him to mistake me – to think I was afraid. I was far beyond fear now, or anger. All that mattered was to keep Kitty safe. I pulled myself to my feet. One last fight.

Howard leaped at my throat, pushing me hard against a brick wall. I tried to throw him off but I was too weak. I tore at his injured hand, scraping my nails into the wound. He howled in pain and let go. I barrelled into him, shoulder pressed into his stomach. He staggered but didn't fall, wrapping his hands about my throat again. I choked as he pressed his thumbs into my windpipe, crumpling to my knees . . .

. . . and then I was free, gasping air into my lungs. I could sense a struggle around me, some brief fight. By the time I was recovered we were surrounded by a ring of men in plain, patched clothing. Plain but clean. One of them held a blade to Howard's throat. Another held his chairman.

A short, powerful figure slipped noiselessly into the torch-light, hat worn low, his nose and mouth covered in a black cloth. James Fleet. He reached down and touched the pulse in Kitty's neck. 'Inside,' he said to one of his men, who picked her up and carried her away. She didn't even stir. Why was she not moving? I wanted to speak, but I couldn't find my tongue. Everything had taken on a strange, muffled feeling, like a dream. My teeth were chattering again. Someone threw a cloak over my shoulders.

Howard turned to Fleet. He was a soldier once more – and he recognised a fellow captain. 'I am Charles Howard, brother of the Earl of Suffolk. That man is mine.'

Fleet smiled. He gestured to his man to lower the blade away from Howard's throat. 'And how much is he worth to you, my lord?'

Howard grinned, stepping away from his captor. 'A guinea.'

'A *guinea* . . .' Fleet murmured. 'D'you hear that Mr Hawkins? How much you are valued?' His men laughed softly.

Howard scowled. The madness was returning, now he was free again. No one laughed at him, especially not a gang of low thieves.

'No deal, Mr Howard,' Fleet said. 'Now leave.'

Howard's eyes bulged in fury. 'How dare you! How *dare* you bark orders as if I were some common footman! I will—'

Fleet tipped his chin – a silent command. A moment later Howard's chairman fell to his knees, his throat cut. Blood gushed from the wound, spurting in a thick stream. He choked for a few seconds, then slumped to the ground, dead.

Fleet stepped back from the pool of blood spreading out into the dirt.

Howard gaped at the body. And then he ran.

I must have collapsed after that as I remember nothing more until we reached Fleet's den. The blow to my head and the freezing cold of the river had left me dazed and tired to the marrow. As to what happened to the chairman, poor devil, I never learned. Every man pays a price for entering St Giles in the dead of night. His price was harsh indeed – and all the crueller when his master had escaped without a scratch. So the world turns – kill a nobleman and the rookery would be razed to the ground, the gang hunted down and hanged without mercy. Slit a chairman's throat and no one would notice or care.

When I woke I was being carried up the stairs to the large room at the top of the house. Some of Fleet's gang stood about, smoking and talking in soft voices. 'Strip those wet duds off him, Connie,' someone said, and an old woman hobbled over, her hair a wispy cloud of white beneath a quilted cap. She removed my clothes, batting my hands away when I tried to help, then wrapped me in a linen sheet and several thick blankets. I was so weak I had to lean on her as she led me to Fleet's chair by the fire. '*Muito rápido . . .*' she scolded when I tried to pull it nearer the flames. She rapped her heart with her fist. 'It stops.' She pressed a bowl of hot chocolate into my hands and ordered me to drink. I tried to ask her about Kitty, but either she couldn't understand or I had lost my wits with the cold – my words felt jumbled and heavy on my tongue, my thoughts slow and confused. I drank the chocolate through chattering teeth and slowly returned to my senses.

At some signal Fleet's men gathered themselves and headed out again. Best not to think of the business they planned. One of them paused at my chair, shrugging on his coat. 'She's with Gabriela.'

I tumbled down the stairs, drunk with exhaustion, clinging to the walls as I searched each room. At last, I found her.

She was lying in a small cot, buried under several blankets, red hair wrapped in a velvet cap for warmth. A dark-haired woman was sitting by her side, singing softly in Portuguese. Gabriela, Fleet's wife. Sam's mother. There was beauty in her features, her smooth complexion, her black curls streaked with silver. A great, grave beauty – save for the long scar on her face. It curved from temple to jaw, puckering her cheek and dragging down the corner of her right eye.

She beckoned me forward. 'For one moment.'

I stumbled to the bed. A lantern cast an amber light across the blankets, but Kitty's skin was white as marble and her lips were tinged blue. I took her hand, pressed my face to hers to be sure she was still breathing. 'She's so cold.'

Gabriela put a hand on my shoulder. 'You must rest.'

I shook my head, and the room spun around me. I had to stay awake and look after Kitty. But I couldn't keep my eyes open. I lay down next to her. She didn't move. It was as if I were lying next to a stone statue on a tomb.

Fleet entered the room and spoke quietly with Gabriela by the fire. They sounded worried.

Strong arms pulled me from the bed and lifted me away. I was too weak to protest. Another room, men asleep on the floor. A bed, warmed with a bed pan. Blankets thrown over my shaking body. In my fevered state I thought I was back in the river – that our escape had all been a dream. The blankets were waves and I was sinking down, the icy river closing above my head. The water roared in my ears. I reached for Kitty but I couldn't find her. I was alone in an empty ocean. I slipped away beneath the waves, drowning in darkness.

Chapter Fifteen

A warm dry bed. Sunlight on my closed eyes. Shouts and drunken curses rising from the streets, the rumble of carts and the scrape of a fiddle. A dog barking. It had all been there at the edge of my senses, seeping into my dreams. I swallowed, mouth dry, and rolled over. Groaned as pain bounced about my skull.

'*Awake!*' a voice yelled, delighted. '*Awake, awake, awake!*'

I opened my eyes a crack. A tiny, dark-eyed child was leaning over me, her face inches from mine. Three more girls lined the bed, whispering and watching me with keen interest. Sam's sisters, without question – all variations upon the same theme, with dark, clever eyes and raven hair, and all dressed in drab, faded gowns, restitched to fit. The oldest girl had tucked a wisp of gauze about her neck, bright scarlet flecked with gold. It burned in the morning sun like a jewel, or a warning. She lifted her baby sister from the bed and kissed her curls. 'Run and tell Pa, Bia.'

I was desperate to leave the room and find Kitty, but a light shuffle beneath my blankets revealed that I was quite naked. Exposing myself in front of James Fleet's daughters did not seem wise.

After some whispering and giggles, the eldest girl introduced herself as Eva. 'Becky. Sofia,' she added, indicating her sisters.

'You snore,' Becky informed me.

Eva hushed her. 'You're teaching Sam to be a gent.'

Becky and Sofia sniggered at the thought of such an impossible task. I sat up, as much as was decent, holding the blankets to my chest. 'In a fashion . . .'

Eva touched her neckerchief. 'Might I make a lady d'you think, sir? I should like to wear fine clothes and—'

'Out. All of you. Damned hussies.' Fleet stood in the doorway, holding Bia in the crook of one arm. From his hot, crabbed expression I guessed that he had not asked his daughters to stand sentinel over my bed. As they ran laughing from the room, he blocked Eva's path. 'What's this?' he snapped, tugging a handful of the scarlet gauze. 'Take it off, child.'

'I'm *indoors*, Pa,' she wailed, clutching it back to her chest. 'No one can see.'

As father and daughter argued, Bia struggled free and clambered back on to the bed. She scrunched her way up to my shoulder and put a dimpled hand to my face, dark eyes sombre. 'Bad man gone?'

I thought of Howard, backing away into the shadows. 'Yes, little one. All gone. Your papa chased him away.' For ever, I hoped.

'Bad man all gone,' she said, satisfied, and traced a grubby finger down my cheek. Then she slid from the bed and toddled after her sisters.

Fleet watched her go, shaking his head. 'Five girls. God help me. Sore head?'

I lowered my feet slowly to the ground, wrapping a blanket around my hips. The room tilted and I had to breathe hard to steady myself. 'I'm well enough,' I said, touching the back of my skull. There was a small bump, but not as bad as I'd feared. 'Kitty?'

'Upstairs.'

I rose and hobbled across the room, each step jolting my head.

'*Clothes*, Hawkins. This ain't a brothel.' He pointed to a bundle on the floor and left. My dagger rested on top of the pile.

Scratchy woollen breeches, an old waistcoat for a much fatter man, a tattered cravat. A wig, too – but it looked so lousy I dared not touch it, never mind place it upon my aching head. I wondered who these clothes had belonged to and how they had come here – then decided it was best not to be too curious in Fleet's house.

Out upon the landing I heard the murmur of conversation on the floor above. I limped barefoot up to the room at the top of the stairs, drawn by the voices and the scent of warm spiced food that hugged the air.

And there she was, sitting by the fire, her feet tucked up under her skirts. She was still pale, but a thousand times better than the night before. We looked at each other across the room, safe now after the dark horrors of the night. Then she slid to her feet to greet me. I put my hands to her face. Her skin was warm. 'You're well?'

She nodded and I kissed her, wrapping my arms about her waist as if she might disappear.

'Oh Lord, Tom,' she gasped, breaking away. 'You will squeeze me to death.'

I loosened my grip. Slowly recalled that Fleet was in the room, and his wife Gabriela, holding a baby in her arms. Daughter number five, I supposed. Eva, Becky and Sofia, grinning and nudging each other. Little Bia, watching us wide-eyed on the table, chewing her fist. And Sam, leaning against a wall in the corner, hands in his pockets. Mute, as ever.

I gave Gabriela a short bow. 'Thank you, madam.'

She smiled at the courtesy, her eyes tired. 'Lucky. Both of you.'

Her accent was a complicated mix of Portuguese and St Giles. She crooked a finger into her baby's fist and jiggled it up and down. 'No jumping in river no more. Yes?'

'I swear it – upon my life,' Kitty said. 'I feel as if I've been run down by a wagon.'

Fleet put his hand on my shoulder. 'Come with me.'

Phoenix Street was crowded and chaotic, and everyone was selling – food, gin, bodies. A tinker stood in a doorway, clanging an iron pot, his nose caved in from the pox. He stank of piss, the bottom of his coat sodden with it. I looked away, my head pounding in time to his noise.

There was a frost in the air this morning and I was grateful for it – it woke me up, and freshened the streets a little. A man ran past us, dragging a hand cart filled with clothes. For a brief moment I thought I saw the chairman's coat buried in the heap, stained with blood. But the wheel almost ran over my toe and I was forced to leap back. By the time I'd recovered, the cart had vanished.

Fleet strode through the ragged stream of life, squinting at the winter sun with eyes more accustomed to the dark. A cluster of men nodded as he passed, but most minded their own business. We turned into a sunless alley and Fleet sighed, as if coming home. Turned and twisted again until we reached a ruined courtyard, overlooked by gloomy, tumbledown houses. No carts rolled down here, no hawkers called their trade. Windows were shuttered tight against the day, and all was still. The ropes and walkways of the rookery loomed high above our heads, blocking the light. Here we were both in shade, the world dyed grey.

He tapped his toe against the cobbles, hands in pockets. 'D'you know this place?'

I looked about me. The press of broken houses, the narrow balconies hung with tattered sheets. This was where I had stopped last night, when I could run no further. This was where I had called Fleet's name – and he'd answered.

He held out his hand. Two guineas glinted in his palm.

My payment for meeting with Mrs Howard in St James's Park. He had known all along that her husband would attack the carriage. He had sent me there without warning and I had almost died as a consequence. No doubt he thought last night had squared the matter. But if he had not lied to me when we shook hands upon the deal, then I would never have met Charles Howard in the first place. Kitty would never have been hurt and threatened and half drowned.

He pressed the coins into my hand with a smile. 'Take them, sir. Don't forget, your life is worth only half that.'

'You betrayed me.'

'Mr Hawkins,' he said heavily. Wearily. 'You knew the dangers. You betrayed yourself, sir.'

'What – I should have guessed you worked for the queen?'

'I work for myself.' He snuffed back a laugh. '*Gentlemen*. All that schooling . . . I forget what fools you are. You ain't equipped to live in the world. You strut about, so sure you're the cleverest souls in England. D'you think your wits are sharper than mine, sir?'

'I—'

'Of course you do. Even now. Tell me – what was it you studied at Oxford?'

I scowled at him. He knew the answer full well.

'*Divinity*.' He chuckled, as if this were some great joke. 'Three years wasted upon the next world. Well – I have spent eight and thirty studying *this* one. Who has the best of it, d'you think?'

'What do you want of me, damn you?'

'You know, sir, you know.'

Aye – I did. He had made a great deal of money working with

his brother. Samuel had been a spy for the queen – and for others, no doubt. Now I was to replace him – with Sam to assist me, I supposed. A fine and lucrative deal, with very little risk for James Fleet. 'I will not work for you.'

He laughed and shook his head. Laughed again. 'It's not an offer, Hawkins. It's an order.'

A knot tightened in my throat. Now I understood why Betty had been so furious with me. She had realised at once what I had lost, in that fatal moment when I had shook James Fleet's hand. I thought of the Marshalsea – of the tortures I'd endured to secure my freedom. Now – a scant three months later – I was a prisoner again. And for what? A brief dazzle of excitement. How could I have been so reckless? It was not enough to shrug and say it was my nature, not enough to rail at God or Fortune. I could have prevented this.

No wonder Fleet mocked me as a fool. He clapped me on the shoulder, and the weight of his hand felt like an iron chain. 'Breakfast,' he said.

'I'm not hungry.'

'Course you are.'

Of course I was. *It's not an offer, Hawkins.* I was Fleet's man now – and the queen's. God help me – I'd be lucky to survive the week.

As we headed back up Phoenix Street, Fleet plucked Eva's gauze neck cloth from his pocket and threw it into the gutter. For a moment it fluttered there in the filth, gold thread glinting in the sun. Then a street boy snatched it and ran, scampering up a wall on to the rooftops and away.

Sam had brought a letter from Gonson – a reply to my request to search Burden's house. Gonson railed at my insolence, though he had no choice but to comply. *It will prove nothing, sir,* he wrote, *save your black-hearted cruelty and the innocence of Burden's children. You will be judged for this one day, Hawkins. Such devilish behaviour does not go unpunished.* There followed more sermonising, which I did not read. All that mattered was his promise to send a constable to the house later that afternoon. In the meantime, Sam told me that the street boys had watched the house all night. No one had come and no one had gone – the house had remained barred and silent, as if Burden were still alive, ruling the family with the Bible and his fist.

Gabriela served a late breakfast of plum porridge, richly spiced and delicious. I ate three bowls of it, much to her satisfaction. 'This how a man eat, Samuel,' she scolded her son, who had picked out all the currants and dotted them along the rim like dead flies. Then she bowed him to her breast and kissed his head, running her hand through his curls. '*Belo*,' she smiled, her long scar puckering her face. Sam said nothing. But he closed his eyes for a brief moment, and smiled too.

A quick pipe and a pot of strong coffee, and I was eager to return home. Fleet had already thrown off his boots and was snoring softly in a hammock, recovering from the night's work. Kitty kissed Gabriela goodbye and we headed down the stairs.

'Could I not go with them, Ma?' Eva begged her mother. 'Mr Hawkins promised to make me a lady.'

What the devil . . .? Kitty and Gabriela stabbed me with a look. I raised my hands in protest.

'I would make a fine gentlewoman,' Eva trilled, swishing her gown and fanning herself with her hand.

'A fine *strumpet*,' Sam muttered, dodging a slap as he ran for the stairs.

'You stay here with me, Eva,' Gabriela said firmly. 'We put you out in the world, I think you break it.'

*

I kept my borrowed hat low over my eyes as we reached Covent Garden. Most of the passersby did not recognise me in such mean clothes. Those who did seemed wary and puzzled. How simple it had been yesterday when I was the monster, arrested and dragged to gaol by Gonson's men. They did not like me any better today, walking free about the streets in my eccentric suit of ill-matched clothes. No doubt the news of my enquiries had spread, creating even more confusion. What should they make of me? Was I to be pitied? Reviled? Feared? No one knew. And so they kept their distance, until they had an answer on which they could all agree. And God help me, I had best find Burden's killer before then. This was how mobs were born. Confusion and fear, and then a swift, angry decision. *That one. He's to blame.*

It struck me that both Fleet and the queen would be interested to see how I resolved my troubles with Burden's family. I had proved my reckless courage, protecting Henrietta Howard from her husband. Now my skills of reasoning would be tested as I searched for the killer. If I was successful, I would have proved myself useful to them. If I failed, I would most likely hang. It was a provoking thought.

I followed Kitty into the shop to hunt for paper. She was standing in the middle of the room with her hands on her hips, staring up at the shelves. She picked up a pamphlet, dropped it back on its neat pile. 'Someone has been in here ...' she murmured. She ran through the shop to the barren printing press, walking around it and frowning.

'Is anything stolen?' I asked, puzzled. 'Everything seems in order ...'

'*Perfectly* in order.' She trailed a finger over the press, looking for dust. 'I have never seen it so clean and tidy.'

'Thank you, miss.' Alice appeared from the back storeroom

carrying a mop and bucket, her gown hoicked up to her knees. Her face was hot, and stuck with straggles of blonde hair that had escaped from her cap. She gave a jump when she saw me and quickly untucked her gown, swishing it back below her ankles. 'I've cleaned the whole house, top to bottom. Walls, floors, windows . . . Jenny was a good girl, but I must say . . .' she sniffed, not saying. 'That . . . *boy* wouldn't let me in his room.' Her eyes flickered to the door, where Sam was leaning against the frame. 'Not that I care. As if I have any interest in touching anything of *his*.' She scrubbed the mop back and forth with some violence, though the floor was clean enough to host a ball.

Kitty stared about her in astonishment. 'You must have worked all night.'

'I work hard, miss,' Alice said, pleased. 'Always have. And it was either that or lie in bed and wait to be *murdered* by *someone*. So I lit some candles and, well. As you see.'

I asked Alice to heat a few buckets of water. Kitty had bathed back in St Giles, but I could still smell the river stink on my skin. I found a sheaf of paper and took it upstairs to my desk. Sam trailed after me like a shadow. He seemed confused.

'Mr Hawkins. If I'd wanted to kill her . . .'

'That is not a happy way to begin a sentence, Sam.'

'Why would she feel safer washing the floor?'

'I've no idea,' I sighed, dipping my quill. 'But we have a clean house for it, so my thanks for that.'

'But . . .,' Sam looked bewildered. 'It would be *easier*, with the mop and bucket. I could use them to wash the blood after and . . .'

I fixed him with a look.

'There's no *reason* to it,' he muttered and slunk up to his room.

I wrote a note to Budge, explaining that my meeting with Howard had not gone as hoped. I must find some other way to defeat him, given I could no longer attempt to befriend the devil.

My only consolation was that he had not guessed I was working on the queen's behalf. I asked Budge to supply the names of Howard's cronies and enemies, old neighbours and creditors. And then I sat back, despondent. Howard's murderous attack on the barge should have been more than enough to hook the bastard, but he was a nobleman. He could not be shamed or blackmailed by such behaviour. A light skirmish with a disgraced gentleman and his whore, no doubt that is how he would describe the matter. The court would shrug its shoulders and return to its card game.

I closed my eyes, transported back to the cabin, Kitty's torn sleeves and terrified expression. Howard's eyes, cold and mocking. I could tear out his throat for it. At least she had fought free. Perhaps he would think twice before threatening a woman again; but I doubted it. It seemed to be his greatest pleasure in life.

I sealed the letter and called up to Sam to collect it. By the time I was done, Alice had filled the tub by the fire with steaming water, adding a few splashes of milk to soften it. 'Thank you, Alice,' I said, but she'd fled before I'd even loosened my cravat. It amused me for a moment, until I remembered what her last master had forced her to do.

I eased myself into the water and gave a soft moan of relief. My body ached from head to foot: my shoulders still stiff from Gonson's chains, the bump on my head throbbing softly. I lay dozing in the water until it turned cool, then soaked the last of the filth from my skin. I would have scrubbed the entire night from my bones if I could.

After a hasty shave I reached for Samuel Fleet's old banyan. Kitty had liberated the old red dressing gown from the Marshalsea, along with Fleet's indecipherable papers and the poesy ring, which she wore always on a chain about her neck. The banyan had been too large for him; he'd had to wear the sleeves rolled. I didn't have the heart to turn them back down to my wrists.

I built a pipe and trailed to the window, shivering in the cool air. Stephen Burden was walking up towards his home in his father's suit, a sword dangling about his legs and tripping his ankles. No one had taught him to fix it well; it needed tightening. I thought of my own sword, lost on the river. I must buy a new one.

Once Stephen was inside I opened the window and called to the street boys watching the house. One hung back, still afraid, but his bolder brother ran through the dusty road and gazed up at me.

'Did he take anything from the house?'

The boy shook his head. Chewed his lip. 'D'you kill Mr Burden, sir?'

'No.'

He shrugged, persuaded. I reached in my banyan pocket and threw down a penny. He caught it neatly and hurried back to his companion. A moment later the younger boy hastened over.

'Sir! I don't think you stabbed him neither.'

I rolled my eyes and threw down another penny for his cheek. All I needed was another six hundred thousand pennies and I could buy the rest of the town. I poured myself a glass of wine. There was nothing to be done now except think, and wait for Gonson to send an order for the house to be searched. He did not appear to be in a great hurry to help.

I heard footsteps and smiled. Kitty. She moved up behind me and tucked her chin on my shoulder.

'Alice is cleaning the cellar. She says we need rat traps. Or a cat.'

'We could have died last night.'

She stole my pipe and took a long draw. 'I think I should speak with Judith, Tom. Alone. You are too soft-hearted when it comes to ladies in distress. Remember *poor* Mrs Roberts?'

I snatched back the pipe. 'I am perfectly able to see past a woman's trickery.'

'Of *course* you are,' she conceded, nuzzling the back of my neck. 'But there's no harm in my having a little try . . .' She trailed her hand beneath my shirt. 'Do you not think?'

'I suppose not,' I said, closing my eyes as her hand moved lower.

An hour later, Gonson's man, Crowder, arrived with the order to search Burden's house. I caught him leering at Kitty and had to will myself to uncurl my fists. After Howard's attack on the river, any glance, any perceived insult, was enough to heat my blood.

Ned opened the door. He read the order several times over, shaking his head in disbelief.

'Mr Gonson wishes the family to know, this was not *his* choice,' Crowder said slyly. 'The *gentleman* has friends.'

Ned gave me a sour look. 'Pray tell Mr Gonson he may send a dozen constables,' he said, raising his voice so the whole street might hear. '*We* are innocent.'

I pushed my way past, losing patience. 'We will begin with your workshop, Ned. And Miss Sparks wishes to speak with Miss Burden. Pray call her down.'

'No, for pity's sake!' Ned cried in dismay. 'She is still sick with grief.'

Kitty squeezed past him, her gown brushing against the wall with a soft rustle. 'And so Mr Hawkins should hang, Ned? To spare Miss Burden's nerves?'

'Wait!' Ned called, his hands spread wide in appeal. 'Wait, Miss Sparks, I beg of you. I will send for her.'

It transpired that Judith was still abed and needed time to dress, so Kitty helped search the workshop. We opened cupboards, hunted beneath loose floorboards, tipped back furniture.

All we found was a bloodstained bandage that had slipped behind a cabinet, but it was coated with dust and had clearly lain undisturbed for months. Given Ned's battered hands, the blood could have come from any number of old injuries.

Ned seemed eager to join in the search, helping Crowder to move back the heavier furniture, and holding a lantern up to inspect the darker corners. I was surprised by this at first, until I noticed that he was most interested in the walls connecting the house with the Cocked Pistol.

'He's looking for a passageway,' Kitty murmured, as Ned tapped the brickwork.

I nodded, anxious. Watching Ned rap his knuckles against the plaster, testing for hollow spots, I had to fight to seem unconcerned. It had taken Alice a week to find the hidden passage in the attic, but she could only search in secret, in stolen moments. Ned might spend all day hunting if he wished. If he discovered the door in the armoire, I was lost. My only defence rested upon the fact that the house had been barred and locked on the night of the murder.

We searched the parlour next, with no luck. The room was stark and cold, no fire lit in the hearth. The grandfather clock tocked its dull heartbeat. I opened the casing. The pendulum paced slowly back and forth. No time. No time. No time.

Kitty put a hand on my slumped shoulder. 'We'll find something.'

Crowder snorted.

The door opened and Judith entered with Mrs Jenkins, her black-gloved hands crossed solemnly in front of her. She was dressed in mourning clothes – a black crêpe mantua with a long train that picked up clumps of grey dust as it trailed along the floor. Her dark hair was swept into a tight bun. It made her face seem sharp and much older. A black lace shawl covered her head and fell across her shoulders to her waist, where it was pinned with an ebony brooch. The gown and the shawl were of an antique style not worn in years – she must have found them in her mother's armoire. It was an unsettling thought, Judith searching through all those old gowns, so close to the hidden door.

Judith's appearance was so eccentric that even Crowder seemed baffled, bowing to her as if she were some old dowager duchess and not an attractive young woman. She ignored him, her grey eyes fixed on Kitty.

'Miss Sparks. You wished to speak with me.' The wandering, dreamy voice she had used upon me had vanished. She was clipped, imperious.

Kitty stiffened, but held her temper. 'Indeed, Miss Burden. Alone.'

'Impossible!' Mrs Jenkins cried. 'Poor Miss Burden, as if she is not weighed down enough with grief and sorrow. It is not to be endured—'

'—Oh *you* must stay, Mrs Jenkins,' Kitty interrupted. 'I insist. I meant only that the *gentlemen* must leave us in peace. We must be allowed to speak freely. As women.' She gave a delicate cough that she must have learned at the theatre.

Mrs Jenkins bit back a smile of pure joy. She patted Burden's chair – the only comfortable seat in the room. 'Well, then. Come Judith, you must sit here. I insist. I shall be quite content on that charming . . . stool.'

'This has always been my seat,' Judith said, sitting straight-backed upon the wooden stool furthest from the fire. She gestured to Burden's chair. 'That was my father's chair. I could not bear to sit on it.'

Mrs Jenkins gave the chair a nervous glance, as if Burden's ghost might be sprawled there. Comfort won out. She settled herself down, fanning her skirts as Kitty pushed the men from the room.

We stood outside the firmly closed door, excluded.

'What could Judith have to say in private?' Ned asked, mystified.

Laughter drifted from the drawing room. 'Oh, my dear!' Mrs Jenkins chuckled. 'Well, we cannot blame you for *that*!' The three women burst into fits of giggles.

Ned flushed. They were speaking of him, of course.

'They're all whores beneath their frilly gowns,' Crowder sneered.

Ned curled his fist. I put a restraining hand on his arm. *Let it be.* 'We'll leave you to your work, Ned.'

The kitchen brought no fresh clues. It was not as full-stocked as I would have expected, but that might simply be an indication of Burden's puritanical mania. The Society for the Reformation of Manners had a good deal to say about rich food and hard liquor. No doubt it also had a good deal to say about fucking your housekeeper against her will. Perhaps he hadn't attended that meeting.

Beyond the kitchen lay a backyard, rather desolate. The yards on this side of Russell Street faced due north and rarely caught the sun. Burden's yard was neat and well-tended, with winter herbs growing in pots and a small plot raked out for vegetables. I remembered something Kitty had told me when I had first moved in to the Cocked Pistol. She had been describing the *peculiar* family next door and how rarely she had seen the daughter out in the neighbourhood.

'She comes out into the yard each day for an hour to tend the garden. Always the same time each morning. I think it's the only time her father allows her out, save for church. Can you imagine, Tom? I could not stand it.'

Nor I. I stepped back so I might see the house better. Judith's room lay at the back. One hour a day. I'd had more freedom in gaol. Eighteen years looking down upon the same view, the same little plot.

Crowder stood on the yard step, spat in the soil. 'Nothing here.'

I pointed towards the privy in the corner. The stench leaked out across the yard – there had been no one to tend to it since Alice had left.

Crowder's lips puckered. 'I'm not searching in there. I'll catch the plague.'

We argued for a time until at last I agreed to pay him a couple of shillings. He searched with such ill grace I was tempted to kick him in. But there was nothing to find – not in the corners, nor in the hole. He picked up an old plank of wood and pushed it into the filth below. It slopped and sucked against the wood, releasing an even thicker stench. As he pulled it back out there was a sharp squeal and a fat rat leaped from the hole.

I jumped back as Crowder raised the plank and dashed it hard over the rat's body, knocking it senseless. He drew out a knife before it could recover and skewered it in the neck. The rat screamed and writhed under the blade as its blood squirted up Crowder's sleeve. Crowder twisted the blade, gouging a hole until the rat's head was half-severed from its body. At last, it lay still.

I staggered away, light-headed. The rat, the blood, the stench. I put my hand against the wall and bent double, heaving out a mouthful of acid bile.

Crowder found this hilarious. He kicked the dead rat back into the privy hole where it landed with a soft splat. I took a deep, steadying breath and stood up straight.

Ned was watching from the yard step. He looked puzzled.

'The blood,' I explained, pleased he had witnessed this.

Perhaps now he would not be so ready to believe I could murder his father in such a brutal fashion.

I paid Crowder his fee and sent him off to the Turk's Tavern. I had no further need of him. I would search the rest of the house alone.

In the drawing room the women were still talking. Ned waited outside, pacing. 'I cannot make you out, Mr Hawkins. My father said you were a wicked devil. And yet . . . I cannot tell.'

Glints of gold thread in the mud. Quite a concession. Ned had been raised to believe in absolutes. Weak or strong. Friend or foe. Pious or damned. That a man could be *half* a rogue was an uncomfortable discovery.

The voices in the drawing room had grown louder of a sudden – and sharp with it. There was a shout, followed by the sound of crockery smashing to the floor. Mrs Jenkins gave a cry of dismay. '*Miss Burden!*' she scolded.

Judith ran from the room, her face contorted with misery.

'Judith . . .?' Ned asked, astonished. He reached to take her arm.

'Do not touch me,' she cried, dragging herself free. 'Don't . . . don't . . .' She broke into a sob, covering her mouth with a black-gloved hand as she stumbled up the stairs.

Mrs Jenkins clutched the door frame. She looked as though she might levitate with excitement. 'She called Miss Sparks a—' She stopped herself. 'Well. I am almost *dead* with shock.' She ran upstairs after Judith, thrilled.

Kitty swished her gown through the door with a triumphant smirk.

'What have you done?' Ned cried. 'What did you say to her?'

'I told her you once groped me, in the shop.' Kitty flexed her fingers, and grinned.

Ned was aghast. 'I did no such thing.'

'Of course not. I'd chop your hand off. I was curious to see how she would react.'

'That was cruel of you – tormenting a young lady in mourning.'

'In *mourning*? Celebrating, I should say. Why would she mourn the man who kept her prisoner for eighteen years? Who wouldn't let her marry her *beloved* Ned Weaver?'

Ned stared at her, horrified. 'Did you ... you did not tell her ... that I am ...'

Kitty stepped closer. 'Her brother?' she whispered, holding his gaze for a long, dangerous moment. Then she drew back. 'No, I held my tongue. For now. Was that not kind of me? Are you not most grateful that I kept your secret?'

'It would kill her,' he whispered. 'I'm sure of it. Felblade says she is unbalanced. Her humours ... We must be kind, Miss Sparks. It is only a passing attachment.'

'She's in love with you, Ned. She is sure you will marry her, now her father is dead.'

An unhappy silence settled in the hallway. This was where we had seen Judith collapse upon the stairs, after she had seen Alice in her father's bed. Whatever she had said in that moment, Burden had struck her for it. Struck the words from her mouth.

Ned shook his head. 'Miss Burden would never hurt her father. I will not believe it.'

He walked away, back to the sanctuary of his workshop.

'It was Judith,' Kitty said as we headed upstairs to find Stephen. 'I'm sure of it. That *temper*.'

'It's not proof, Kitty.'

When we reached the landing, she paused to loosen the ribbons across her stomacher. She untied the handkerchief covering her chest and released a few stray locks from her cap. 'How do I look?'

I stared longingly down her gown.

'Perfect,' she grinned. 'I shall have Stephen spilling his secrets in a heartbeat.'

'He'll spill something.'

But Stephen's room was empty. His bed had been stripped, his closet was bare. I pulled back the furniture to search for any hiding places or discarded clothes, but found nothing save for a miniature, lying in the middle of the floor, of his sister as a young girl. The surface was cracked and the frame bent. It looked as though Stephen had deliberately crushed it under his shoe.

The mystery of Stephen's disappearance was quickly solved: he had moved into his father's room. We found him slumped in a chair by the fire, dressed in a loose chemise and velvet breeches, a pipe dangling from his fingers. Strange, that he should move so swiftly to the room where his father had been brutally killed. The floor by the bed was still stained with blood.

Stephen barely stirred as we entered. Drunk, I realised – and my thoughts flew to Henry Howard, Henrietta's son. Another boy pretending to be a man, pretending to be his father. Stephen had struck his sister yesterday. From rage? Grief? Or the desire to fill his father's boots?

Kitty knelt by his bare feet, offering him a generous view of her chest. He blinked and rallied a little.

'I am sorry about your father,' she breathed, touching his hand.

He swayed in his seat and brought his pipe to his lips. Missed, and poked his nose. Once he'd found his mouth he took a tentative draw. Coughed out the smoke, eyes watering.

Kitty attempted a few questions, but the boy was fuddled with drink – and grief, perhaps. Let us be generous. I searched through all the garments I could find – Burden's rough work wear and sober suits, Stephen's fine-tailored clothes. It must have cost Burden a great deal of money to send his son to school and dress him as a gentleman. And yet at the end of his life he seemed to have regretted the decision.

What a strange and sombre household. There had been so much at work beneath the surface that it was a struggle to make sense of it. That is true of all families, I suppose, but this one was ... *peculiar*, as Kitty said. Three children, all now orphans, and yet they seemed locked in their own private gaols, barely conscious of each other's presence. Judith trapped behind her veil, muted by Felblade's opium. Stephen stupefied with brandy. And Ned in his workshop, brooding. Each wondering if the other were guilty. One of them knowing the truth.

This was how Burden had raised his children – isolated from the world, breathing in a noxious atmosphere of threat and mistrust. Who did they have, save for Mrs Jenkins? No family that I could tell. Where was their lawyer? Where were their friends from church, their uncles and aunts? They had no one but each other – and yet they had rejected even this small comfort. Each one a fortress, guarded and alone.

Stephen was burbling about his plans to leave Russell Street. *It was not suitable, not fashionable. This eastern side – filled with lower sorts, disgusting. One must move west, west, west. He would hire Ned to build a grand new house on Grosvenor Square. I am not my father, Miss Sparks. Scrimping old fool. Wouldn't spend a farthing and see how he's rewarded. Dead at three and forty. I will have new clothes, new furniture, new everything. I want nothing of this place. Nothing. Let them tear it down. Burn it to the ground for all I care. Burn it all.*

He began to weep.

'And your sister?' Kitty asked softly. 'She approves this plan?'

'Damn my sister. Damn her!' Flecks of spit showered from his lips. 'What do I care of Judith? She may starve in the street if she wishes. Or ... let her marry Ned Weaver and ruin herself.'

Kitty rose to her feet, brushing dust from her gown. 'Well, I'm sure your father would have approved.' She smiled down at Stephen. 'He was most fond of Ned, I hear.'

Stephen gave what he hoped was a scornful laugh, but it came out shrill and piping. 'My father had promised to throw Ned out on to the street. Why does he stay here? I shall send him away.'

Kitty tightened the ribbons on her gown, tucked the lock of hair back beneath her cap. 'But your father loved Ned, did he not? Much more than he loved you?'

'No!' Stephen cried. He leaped from his chair with his fist raised, but he was too drunk. He swung wide and slipped, crashing to the ground. 'No ...' he sobbed. 'It's not true. It's not true.' He clutched the bottom of her gown.

Kitty pulled away and left the room. Stephen curled himself into a ball, tears streaming down his face. It was the drink in part, turning him maudlin. But there was grief, too. Kitty's talk had struck his heart. I looked down at him, wondering what words of comfort I could give. 'Your father loved you, Stephen.'

He glared up at me. 'What business is it of yours?' he snarled, hating my pity. 'Get out! Get out of my house!'

Kitty waited for me on the landing, tucking her handkerchief back over her chest.

'That was ill-done, Kitty.'

'I wrung some truth from him, didn't I? You could hang for this, Tom. If we cannot prove it was Judith or Stephen ...' She lowered her voice. 'If they find the passage. We can be gentle and honourable if you wish. And you will *die*.'

We searched the rest of the house for another hour, breaking our nails as we dragged up floorboards and pulled at loose bricks.

I found a few spatters of blood on the staircase leading up to the attic, but guessed that these had come from Alice's flight back to her room after she found Burden's body.

'Why did you hire Alice, Kitty?'

We were in the abandoned attic room where Burden stored his wife's old gowns. I had not seen the armoire in daylight – it was a huge, ugly thing, but it served its purpose. Kitty had thrown the contents to the floor, searching for any bloodstained clothes buried at the back. My God, so close to the hidden door ... it made me sweat just to think of it. I was glad Ned had returned to his workshop sanctuary.

Kitty shook out an old gown and held it to the light. 'I told you. We lost Jenny, and Alice needed somewhere safe to stay.'

Somewhere safe, right under our noses. 'You're keeping her prisoner.'

Kitty gave me a sly look. 'She wants to work for us, Tom. And you must admit it's rather clever, keeping her close by. And the house has never been so clean.'

Not for the first time, I thanked God Kitty fought on my side. 'You would sacrifice her, if it came to it? You know she's innocent.'

'Do I?' She rummaged through the rest of the late Mrs Burden's dresses, black and heavy. The stiff material rustled as it fell to the floor. 'She appeared in our house in the middle of the night, covered head to foot in blood. I am not saying she's guilty, Tom. I am only stating the facts. It would be for a *jury* to decide.'

'They would damn her in a second.'

'Then we must discover the real killer.'

Ned, Stephen, or Judith. We had returned to that old conundrum. It must be one of them – and still we had no proof.

We finished the search with nothing. I couldn't understand it. There should be something – some fragment to help us. We returned home in gloomy silence. Alice had laid out an excellent supper, which I picked at with my head in my hand, feeling sick with fear. I had been so sure of discovering *something*.

* * *

I know now why we failed in our search. It had all been based upon a false assumption.

Ned, Stephen, or Judith. Which was guilty?

The answer? None of them. They were innocent, every one.

Sitting here in my prison cell with the promise of a noose just a few days away, I could curse myself for my mistake. But I have been cursed enough these past weeks. I need all the luck left in the world. So I say nothing – just bow my head and pray.

PART FOUR

Saved. Thank God. His knees almost give way with the relief. Damn them to hell for torturing him all the way from Newgate to Tyburn. Bastards.

The Marshal breaks the seal and unscrolls the pardon, holding it above his head. The wind tugs at the paper, almost pulling it from his hand. 'His Most Gracious Majesty George II has granted his royal pardon to one of those condemned here today.' He pauses and the crowd cheers. This is better than the opera.

The Marshal smiles. 'His Majesty pardons . . .' Another pause.

Hawkins growls quietly between clenched teeth. He grips the edge of the cart, knuckles white with tension.

' . . . Mary Green.'

A deafening roar. Mary's friends pull her from her cart and carry her along on their shoulders, shoving the constables out of their path. Strangers reach out to touch her gown. Lucky, lucky. She passes close to his cart. Her face is dazed with shock at the sudden reprieve.

His throat closes with fear. There must be another one. There must be a second pardon.

But the Marshal has jumped down from his horse. He is arguing with a surgeon's assistant, a stringy lad with pale brows and bulging eyes. His master is expecting four bodies for anatomising, not three. There are costs to consider. The transportation. The guards. The coffins.

'You will be compensated, sir,' the Marshal assures him, patting the air with his hands. 'You will be compensated.'

Hawkins collapses to his knees. He is lost. Now, at the end, he knows it. He will hang, marked for all eternity as a murderer. His family will be forced to bear the shame – his poor sister and his father, already sick and weary of life. The strain upon his heart – it will kill him for certain.

What a fool he'd been, to believe their promises. He curses them all as the constables guide his cart beneath the gallows. And he curses himself too. He should have listened to Kitty. She'd warned him.

Kitty. He stands quickly, searching the crowds for a flash of red hair. Pale freckled skin. She's not there. Of course not. How could she be?

Chapter Sixteen

I had begun the day in the slums of St Giles. Now it was night and I was being smuggled back into St James's Palace. A horse blanket again, and deserted back corridors. Up the servants' stairs by torchlight to the queen's antechamber.

Budge had sent a note in response to my request for more information on Howard. '*No time. Mtng tonight. Await carriage.*'

I paced the floor alone for a few minutes, longing for a pipe. It was not satisfactory, pacing a floor so heavily covered with thick silk rugs. I wanted to hear the stamp of my feet, to feel the jolt of it through my body. I would suffocate in this warm, quiet room with its tapestries and terracotta busts and marble furniture. I should pick up a gold-legged footstool and throw it through a window. At least the cold air would help me to think.

Damnation, I needed that pipe.

What was I supposed to tell the queen? My encounter with Howard had ended in disaster. Perhaps she would dismiss me and find another poor fool to resolve the matter. Yes, yes – and perhaps she would knight me and shower me with diamonds.

'Mr Hawkins. How pleased I am to see you, sir.' Henrietta Howard glided into the room in a dove-coloured damask gown, embroidered with a burst of silver flowers. The gown creaked a little as she moved, stiffened beneath with glue to push out the skirts. Her expression was serene, her lips parted in a half-smile of welcome. What did it cost to bury one's feelings so deep? Was she not afraid she might lose them one day? Treasure sinking slowly to the ocean floor and nothing left but the surface, becalmed for ever. 'You met my husband last night.'

I bowed my head.

'He spoke of me.' A statement, not a question. She must know the foul stories he spread about her around the town.

'Nothing of consequence.'

She did not believe the lie, but seemed grateful for it. She paused, then added, 'My son?' Somehow she made the question sound quite casual, though no doubt she longed for news of Henry.

I bowed again, thinking of the young rake spewing vomit into the Thames. His dumb astonishment when I put a blade to his throat. 'A good-natured young gentleman.'

She smiled. This she chose to believe. 'He was always a merry child – and quite devoted to me. It infuriated Charles. He would abandon us for months in our tiny hovel. Henry and I muddled along together well enough, I suppose. It's strange – I thought myself quite wretched, then. But perhaps I was happy.' Her brow furrowed, as if trying to remember an old acquaintance.

'It is very cruel of Mr Howard to keep your son from you.'

'He is a cruel man,' she agreed with a shrug. 'D'you know, Mr Hawkins, I have not seen Henry since he was ten years old.'

I stared at her, aghast.

'We were separated when the two courts split. I was forced to make a decision – to remain with Her Majesty, under her protection – or return to live with my husband. I couldn't . . .' she trailed away. 'I had to leave Henry behind, with Charles. I couldn't save him.'

And Howard had spent the next eleven years poisoning the

boy against his mother. He had shaped Henry in his own image: a drunken brat with a fathomless, sprawling hatred of Henrietta.

'I've always hoped that one day Henry would understand why I had to leave him,' she added. 'Surely reason would prevail and he would be released from his father's spell. Even now – I still hope. But the reports I receive of him, his wild behaviour . . . I fear Charles has taught him too well.'

'He's just a boy – one and twenty. I'm sure I was just as wicked at his age.'

'And now?'

'Oh – much worse.'

'I do not doubt it.' She laughed, and I caught a glimpse of how she might look stripped of all her burdens – light and happy. A soul made for sunshine but lost in shadow.

There was a soft clunk as the door to the queen's chamber opened. Budge peeped through the narrow gap, like Mr Punch peering around the curtain. He beckoned me with a crook of his finger, then opened the door wider.

I stepped back to allow Mrs Howard through first, but Budge stopped her with a subtle shake of the head.

'I am not required?' Four words, laced with meaning. This meeting was of great significance to Henrietta. For weeks she had been held under siege, a prisoner in the palace – all because of the man who had tormented her for more than twenty years. Was she not entitled to hear my report on the matter? But no – *she was not required.* The queen and her games of power and revenge, played out in small denials, countless cruelties, day after day.

The room was stifling; thick, tasselled drapes sealing in the heat from the fire. Behind them the windows rattled in their casements, under attack from a violent rain storm. The queen sat at her desk, dressed in a loose green velvet gown – a curtain in human form. She dropped her quill as I entered and pushed herself slowly to her feet. I bowed and she held out a gloved hand to kiss.

She settled down on her sofa, lifting her feet onto an ottoman. She picked up an ivory fan pocked with jewels and flapped it about her bosom in a gay fashion. I'd heard the queen described as a grave, devout woman, but in private she and Budge shared a mischievous, pantomime humour. It sat strangely upon them both tonight – a merry jig played over a battle scene. An enormous plate of confectionery rested just within her grasp – a jumble of sugar biscuits, macaroons and candied ginger too large even for her prodigious appetite. Presented for comical effect again, I was sure – a parody of her own gluttony emphasised to grotesque proportions. A joke only she was entitled to make.

A pretty girl of about seventeen was playing a game of chess against herself at a small table. One of the queen's daughters – Princess Caroline or Amelia I guessed, from her age. Her blonde hair was powdered white and decorated with silk flowers, her lithe figure robed in a lavender gown fringed with pearls. She bore a close resemblance to her mother – a beguiling hint of Caroline's own youth, when her beauty matched her wit. But, whereas the queen's expression settled naturally into bright interest and amusement, her daughter appeared sullen, slapping the chess pieces down upon the board as if she might like to crush them beneath her fingers. She caught my glance and frowned at the impertinence. I took a hurried interest in the ceiling.

'He is not at all handsome, Mama,' she complained, as if she had been sold a ruined bolt of silk. 'I do not like his arms, and his feet are too big. His legs are tolerable.'

The queen chuckled. 'Emily, *ma chérie*, opinions are vulgar.

You must be more like Mrs Howard. She has said nothing of consequence since ...' she fluttered her fan, considering, '...1715?'

'I would rather *die* than be like Mrs Howard.'

'Of course you would. Life is wretched. The world is hateful. How uncharitable of God to make you a princess.'

Princess Amelia rolled her eyes. 'He should have made me a prince.'

The queen grunted in agreement. 'And poor Fritzy a princess. *Laissez-nous maintenant, chérie.* I must speak with Mr Hawkins about something of tremendous interest.'

'*Oh!*' the princess exclaimed, sweeping the chess pieces to the floor. 'Order him to tell *me* something interesting, Mama. Or I swear I shall die of boredom, right here on this horrid rug.'

The queen's lips twitched. 'Well, Mr Hawkins. Something interesting for the princess. Not *too* interesting,' she added hastily.

I thought for a moment, then smiled. 'Has Her Royal Highness ever heard of a female gladiator?'

Princess Amelia had not. I described Neala and her fight at the cockpit, how she had used her strength and stamina to defeat her opponent – in very few clothes. The princess sat with her large blue eyes fixed on mine, enraptured.

'I should like to meet this Irish woman,' she said, when I was finished.

The queen removed her glove and reached for a bonbon. 'And you never shall,' she promised. She dismissed her daughter with a wave, but then called her back and kissed her on both cheeks. When Amelia had left, she turned her gaze on me. 'A shrewd choice of story, Mr Hawkins. Rather too shrewd, I think. And now you have one for me, I believe.'

'Your Majesty,' I said, and began to describe my meeting with Mr Howard. She stopped me mid-breath. 'No, no. I wish to hear first about your neighbour. Mr . . .' she pretended to reach for the name. 'Beadle? Boodle?'

'Burden, ma'am.' She remembered the name well enough. Teasing again. I told her as much as I could, given that I could not mention Alice's bloodstained arrival through the wall, or Sam's midnight prowl around the house. Burden was murdered and I was suspected – that was the crux of the matter.

'You threatened him with a sword? In front of witnesses? A little rash, sir.'

'It won't happen again, Your Majesty.'

'Clearly. No need to threaten a dead man.'

'I only mean—'

'Yes, yes. Don't be dull.'

I paused before speaking again. It was not enough to be useful to Queen Caroline: one must be entertaining as well. I supposed this was to counteract the many hours she spent in the king's tedious company. He had – I believe – only two topics of conversation: either detailed discussion of historic military campaigns or the wonders of his beloved Hanover and how it eclipsed England in every respect. So I must make up for her husband's failings. Gratitude might do the trick. 'I must thank you, ma'am, for securing my release from custody yesterday.'

The queen glanced at Budge, sweating by the fire. 'Did I deign to do that, Budge?'

'Either that or find a new recruit, ma'am. And that would have been diff—'

'—tedious. And now here Mr Hawkins stands on his *tolerable* legs, expressing his gratitude. *Mon dieu.* We have indeed been generous. He might be languishing in gaol were it not for our generosity. He might be sentenced to *hang.*' She wiggled her fingers over the teetering pile of confections and selected another macaroon, smiling in triumph when the rest stayed miraculously in place. 'So I'm sure he has discovered something tremendously helpful about Mr Howard.'

'Your Majesty. Forgive me, I—'

'—You have heard, I'm sure that Howard caused a grave disturbance just two nights ago? Stood in the courtyard screaming that his wife is a whore and insisting that we give her up to him? His Majesty was furious – he cannot bear to have his sleep disturbed. Poor Mrs Howard must have been mortified.'

'Your Majesty, could Mr Howard not be arrested, or at least—'

'The law is with the husband, Mr Hawkins!' the queen snapped, for a moment truly angry. 'He has every right to claim his wife, and by force if he wishes. What – d'you think the king should have him arrested? And then I suppose you would like to see a public trial about the matter?' Her blue eyes – so like her daughter's – blazed so hard I feared I might be scorched by them. 'You were released in order to resolve this matter. Was I too generous, Mr Hawkins? Perhaps you *did* murder your neighbour. Perhaps Mr Budge should speak again with the City Marshal.'

I placed my hands behind my back, planted my legs. I had suffered such cruel blackmail before, in prison. I would not buckle beneath her threats. 'I am innocent, Your Majesty.'

'That is hardly relevant. Tell me what happened last night and we shall see if we can sift something of value from the dirt together. As you are too dim-witted to discover it alone.'

I described how I met with Howard at the cockpit in Southwark, the disgraceful stories he had spewed up about his wife, and indeed the king – some treasonous. Might that help? The queen looked bored and contemptuous. So I continued with our trip along the Thames, Howard's assault on me and his attempted rape of Kitty.

For the first time, the queen seemed interested. 'She fought him off? Without your aid?'

'Yes, Your Majesty.' I described how Howard had fired a pistol at us as we plunged into the river. Attempted murder – might that be of use? No, apparently it would not. I finished my story, from our freezing, desperate swim to the steps, to our escape through the city to St Giles and our rescue at the hands of James Fleet. I did not mention the poor chairman, his throat cut solely to encourage his master to run. And so my story ended, as it must, and we reached the part I had dreaded.

The queen rinsed her fingers in a pretty porcelain bowl. 'Your little trull is a spirited creature, is she not? So. How do you propose we stop the brute?'

I had no answer. Howard was a nobleman, the heir to an earldom. There were different rules for such men. I knew it. The queen most certainly knew it. The whole *world* knew it. What did it matter if he threatened a young woman with no family and no reputation? Who the devil cared if he vowed to murder me? Who was I? A disgraced gentleman from an obscure family, living above a notorious print shop, translating whores' dialogues for money.

'Sir?' the queen prompted, watching me twist and turn on her rope. Watching with a gleam of interest – encouragement, even. Another test for her new servant.

I must think of something. If I left this room without giving her what she needed, I might as well hang myself tonight and save everyone the trouble. I had been released from Gonson's custody solely on this promise – that I would provide the queen with *something* she could use against Howard. But what?

I forced myself to think calmly. Howard held the winning hand, and I could not change that. What, then? When a man held all the cards, what could one do?

Let him win.

And there it was. So neat. So simple. Let him win. Blackmail would never have worked upon Howard – he was too powerful and too volatile. One did not back a wild animal into a corner. Coax him out. Bribe him. But with what? Not money. The king had refused his demands of three thousand a year. A title? I dismissed the thought – that would be more complicated and costly still.

The room was silent. I could feel the queen and Budge watching, waiting. *Concentrate.* What did Howard want? Henrietta. No – that I would not do. And he didn't want her, not really. He just wanted to make her life as wretched as possible. He wanted to torture her for making that one terrible mistake of loving him, a very long time ago.

And then I knew the answer. There was one very simple way to satisfy Howard. It would cost the queen nothing. But poor Henrietta . . . It would cost her everything.

I wouldn't say it. I wouldn't ruin a woman's life solely to save my own. I would conjure something better. Something kinder.

'His son.' The words slid from my tongue and the betrayal was done.

A look of puzzlement crossed the queen's plump face. And then she understood. Already her clever mind was turning, turning.

'Henry Howard was on the boat last night.'

She grunted. '*Henry.* I remember the child. A sweet, foolish thing. What age is he now, Budge? Fourteen? Fifteen?'

'Twenty-one, ma'am,' Budge replied softly. His expression was sombre, all the play and mischief drained from his face.

'Twenty-one.' And now she too seemed to have caught the melancholy mood. She reached for a sugared almond.

'He was very drunk,' I said. 'Asleep under the table most of the night, and vomiting the rest of it. Forgive me, ma'am . . .'

She waved away the apology.

'...Howard takes great pleasure in corrupting the boy. Henry doesn't have his father's cruelty—'

'—Not yet. Hard liquor makes a hard man.'

True enough in most cases. But I had to believe Henry had enough of Henrietta's sweet temperament to counteract Howard's influence. There must be hope in all this. After all, I had spent the last few years drinking and whoring and gaming like a fiend, and my own heart had emerged intact. Hadn't it?

'Howard is determined to turn Henry against his mother. He has convinced Henry that she's a whore.'

'That must have taken considerable effort,' the queen said, rattling the sugared almond against her teeth.

'He wants revenge upon Mrs Howard. He wants her to suffer. More than anything. He would not refuse three thousand pounds a year, of course ... but it is his hatred of his wife that propels him.' I stopped, unwilling to speak further.

The queen continued to suck her confection, *snick, snick, snick* against the top of her mouth. She glanced at Budge, raised an eyebrow. 'Mr Hawkins has dragged a sacrificial calf into the room. But he does not have the courage to slit her throat.' She played with a diamond ring on her little finger. 'Why, Mr Hawkins – would you have me wield the knife for you? Are you afraid to look in the poor, trembling calf's eyes? Are you worried her blood will spoil your clothes ...?'

My mouth was dry. The queen spoke the truth, and I was sickened by it. I had condemned both Henry and his mother tonight in this room. I had ruined both their lives to save my own. Not to say the words now, at the end, was mere cowardice. 'Mrs Howard must write to her son. In detail. She must tell Henry that everything his father claims of her is true.'

The queen slid her gaze from mine, thinking. 'Yes,' she said at last. 'Howard will like that. He always enjoyed humiliating his wife.' And to her credit, she looked disgusted. 'Is it enough? No,' she answered herself. 'Continue, sir.'

Somehow, I forced the words from my lips. 'She must promise never to contact her son – to relinquish all claims upon him.'

'Your Majesty,' Budge interrupted. 'I doubt she will agree to that. She fights a case at present in secret. She is seeking a legal separation from Howard.'

My heart sank. The Howards had lived apart for many years, but to pursue an official, legally binding separation – it was almost unprecedented. For a judge even to consider the case, there must have been the most devastating evidence of Howard's cruelty. And here I was, delivering Henry into that monster's hands for ever.

The queen was looking away into the fire with a soft expression. 'We will give him his son. And the letter. And twelve hundred a year. Control, humiliation and a fat fee. It will suffice. In return he will not fight the separation. Yes. I believe this will work. Blackmail would have enraged Howard. He might have lashed out in spite. This way, he will believe he has won. He will like that.' Her lips pressed into a tight line. 'Men do.'

Aye, he will believe he's won. Because he has. I cleared my throat. 'Should we not consult with Mrs Howard, ma'am?'

'With Mistress Switzerland?' The queen fanned herself slowly. 'What might she possibly contribute to the matter? She is neutral in all things.'

'Not on *this* matter, surely, Your Majesty?' I pressed. I owed Henrietta this much at least. 'Not over her only child? She might prefer to leave the court? Should she not be granted the choice . . .' I stopped abruptly. The queen's cheeks had tinged bright pink.

'*Choice?* No indeed, Mr Hawkins. Howard is my servant. She will do *precisely* as she is told.'

There was a long, angry silence. There was something deeper here – old wounds of betrayal. Henrietta had been the queen's servant long before she became the king's mistress. They had been allies and confidantes once, when they were young women. When the queen was still the Princess of Wales, just a few years married. Still beautiful and still adored, by all accounts.

'It is a hard thing to lose a son,' the queen said at length. Her gaze slid to mine.

She knew I must have heard the stories – the prince and princess banished from court in disgrace, their children held hostage. The King had given Caroline a devastating choice: stay at court with her children or leave with her husband. Her youngest boy had been just a few weeks old and very sick. He had died before the family had reconciled.

And then there was her oldest son, Frederick, raised alone at the court in Hanover – a stranger to the entire family, including his mother.

The queen understood the agony of losing a son – through death and through estrangement. Now she would inflict that torture upon Henrietta. It was pragmatic, necessary – and cruel. But who was I to judge her now?

'Twelve hundred a year,' she said. 'The king will accept that. He will rail and kick his hat about the room for a few days. In a few weeks he will be pleased that we have saved him eighteen hundred pounds per annum. In a few *months* he will believe it was all his idea.' She tapped her fingers playfully against the arm of the sofa. 'Adequate, Mr Hawkins. Adequate. You will do.'

A clear dismissal. I was released – at least for one night – and at no great cost, save to my conscience. I bowed low, feeling ashamed and relieved in equal measure.

On a whim, she tugged the diamond ring from her finger and

dropped it into my palm. 'For your little trull. For her courage. I am glad she left a mark on the brute.'

Mrs Howard waited in the antechamber. If she were anxious she didn't show it. Small wonder that her face was so smooth and unlined. An even temper made for an even countenance. Given all that she had endured, her equanimity was nothing short of miraculous. But maybe that was why she had survived for so long, through all those years of torture at her husband's hands. And now she would suffer again, because of me.

'You look pale, sir,' she said. 'Was Her Majesty not pleased with your news?'

I stared at my shoe. I had polished the silver buckle so hard that I could see my face in it, distorted. 'She was satisfied, I believe.'

She drew closer, tilting her head so that she could look into my downcast eyes. 'The queen lays her traps very well,' she said, softly. 'We only see them when they bite down upon us. Whatever you have done, whatever she has made you do . . . you must not blame yourself, sir.'

I couldn't answer her. She meant to be kind, but her words shamed me. The truth was, I had seen the trap and I had thrown her upon it, to save myself. Little comfort that Howard would now retreat and leave her in peace. Henrietta would never see her son again.

I was saved by Budge. 'My lady. Her Majesty wishes to speak with you.'

She curtsied and went to see her mistress. Now at last I could look at her; her straight back, her smooth, graceful step. Would the queen enjoy telling her husband's mistress she had lost her son for ever? Or would she choose to be kind? And there lay her power. There lay the motive for all Queen Caroline's plots and schemes. The power to choose.

Budge led me back through the winding passageways and on to Pall Mall. It was very cold and clear, and the sky was blazing with stars. I lit a pipe and found that my hands were trembling.

'Her Majesty has an effect,' Budge observed. He tucked a wad of tobacco into his cheek and began to chew. 'How go your enquiries?'

'Very ill.'

'Unfortunate. I hear reports. The town's against you, Hawkins.'

'The town can fuck itself.'

He spat a thin stream of brown liquid onto the ground. 'Joseph Burden was an arsehole by all accounts. But he lived in that house for twenty years without trouble. Then you arrive next door. Rumours of violence. Rumours of murder. Rumours you can't seem to shake …' He held up a hand, refusing my objections. 'Burden says he has proof you killed a man. You threaten him. He dies the same night. I'm struggling to see this as a coincidence, Hawkins. And I like you.'

'It's not a coincidence, I'm sure. The whole street saw me fight with Burden – including the killer.' I held out my arms. 'I am the perfect scapegoat.'

'That is,' Budge said, 'the problem with waggling a sword in a man's face.'

'True enough. But even had I *not* threatened Burden, everyone knew he planned to testify against me.' I paused. 'I have been thinking upon this matter a great deal.'

Budge rolled the tobacco around his cheek. 'No doubt.'

'You said it yourself, sir. Burden lived on Russell Street for twenty years without trouble. He ruled his house as if he were the keeper of a gaol, not the head of a family. Lectured them from the Bible each night. Punished every act of defiance, no matter how frivolous. No mother to soften the blows, to offer any warmth or kindness.' I paused. Budge was watching me, curious. I wondered if he had guessed the truth – that my own childhood had not been so very different. Well, well. Nor ten thousand more, no doubt. 'Judith and Stephen obeyed him all their lives. Ned lived under his yoke for seven years and never once rebelled.'

'First apprentice in history.'

'It was not fear alone that made them obedient. I believe . . . it gives me pain to say it, but I believe they *respected* him. Ned said that for all Burden's faults, he was a fair master. He lived by his own strict rules. That would have meant a great deal I think, in such a closed, private household. That he was an honourable, Christian man.'

'Then they found out he was fucking his housekeeper.'

'Precisely. The night that . . .' I stopped. I had almost said Sam's name. 'The night Alice cried "thief". They'd obeyed him without question year after year – and this was their reward. Ned was to be thrown out of the house without a farthing. Stephen was to be removed from school. Judith must watch as her servant became her stepmother.'

Budge pondered this. 'I'd say the apprentice had the most to lose.'

'True. But I shared a bowl of punch with Ned the night of the murder. He wasn't angry with Burden because of the money. He was angry because Burden had broken his word. All those years of lectures, teaching them how to be good, honourable souls. He taught them too well.'

Budge snorted. 'He was killed for his sins?'

'No, not that. Think on it for a moment. Once Judith found him with Alice, he gave up the pretence. We heard him through the walls, Budge. He forced Alice to cry out so that everyone might hear. *Gah* . . .' I dashed my spent pipe to the floor and broke it beneath my heel. 'But still he expected them to obey him, as though nothing had changed. *That* is why the attack was so ferocious. It was not the beatings and the lectures that drove one of them to stab Burden to death. It was his *hypocrisy*. It *wasn't fair.*'

Budge touched my arm, a subtle warning. I stopped, chest heaving. I must have been shouting. A couple of young beaux strolled past, smirking at one another. I knew one of them from the gaming houses, the youngest son of some lesser nobleman. Did he recognise me? Oh, very good. Another piece of gossip for the coffeehouses. *I say, did you hear about Hawkins, shouting like a lunatic on the Mall? The fellow's gone half-mad with guilt, no doubt . . .*

I feared I was pouring my own feelings too deep into this story. My own father was a strict and sober man. He had lectured me on my wilfulness and wickedness on countless occasions, made me feel as though I were a sinful child . . . and then later I'd discovered I had a half-brother, Edward. Younger than my sister and me, but born while our mother was still alive. While she lay dying of a long illness, in fact. Even now, I could summon the anger in a moment. The furious sense of injustice. That said, I had never felt the urge to pick up a dagger and stab my father through the chest for it.

'*Why* did he become so reckless? After all those years?'

Budge had no answer. And I was back at the start again, running about in circles. *Ned, Judith, Stephen.*

We had reached Charing Cross. This was where I'd had my first encounter with Charles Howard, when he'd almost run me down in his sedan. Now one of his chairmen was dead. A memory surfaced from the night before. The blade ripping fast across his throat, blood spurting from the sudden gash. His expression, puzzled, then terrified. A terrible noise in his throat, a choking wet sound as he tried to breathe.

Had he been the one holding the back of the chair? The one who had nodded his apology as he passed, and smiled at me? God help me, I couldn't even picture his face. Only his eyes, at the very end. Pleading. *I'm dying. I'm dying – help me.*

I rubbed my face. And Howard survived. Worse. The bastard had *won*. 'Did you know that Burden was a brothel bully, twenty years ago?'

Budge was amused, but not surprised. No doubt he had heard of a thousand such secret hypocrisies.

'Ned told me he worked there to pay off his debts.'

Budge closed one eye, searching his memory. 'Don't remember him. And I visited a fair few brothels back then ...'

I cast my mind back. Howard had talked about the place last night, had he not? What *had* he said about it ...? It had unsettled me at the time. 'Seven Dials, I think. Devilish place, by the sound of it.'

Budge came to a sudden halt. 'Aunt Doxy's.'

I shrugged. Howard hadn't mentioned the name. 'He said there was a room for every vice.'

Budge spat the last of his tobacco to the ground. '*Fuck*. Burden was the bully at *Aunt Doxy*'s ... That was ... have you not heard the stories?'

'Only what Howard told me last night. He said that if a girl was badly beaten or cut, Burden would keep quiet – for a price ...'

Budge gripped my arm, shaken. Budge was not the sort of man who allowed himself to look shaken. 'Wicked things happened in that place, Hawkins. There was rumours ... A man could ask for anything he wished. *Anything*. More of a club than a brothel. Invitation only. Then one night, it burned down to the ground. All the whores escaped, and the customers too. They stood on the street and watched the flames tearing up the place.

Then they heard the screams. Man and a woman. Aunt Doxy, for certain. The man ... No one knows. They was burned alive, Hawkins, slowly. Bad way to die. *Very* bad. You could hear 'em screaming way over on Castle Street. They found the bodies later, what was left of them. Chained together in death.'

'They never found who did it?'

'The whores knew, but they was too scared to say. Or too glad, maybe. I heard it was revenge. Some young jade, got her face all cut. Foreign girl – Spaniard, I think.'

My heart dipped. The truth began to circle about me, wheeling like a bird of prey. 'What happened to her?'

'Don't know. She died, maybe. Maybe not.' A shrug.

Maybe not. Maybe I had seen her just this morning. Maybe she had saved my life last night.

Gabriela.

I made a hurried excuse and abandoned Budge in the middle of the street. He must have guessed from my countenance that something was troubling me – I was too disturbed to hide it. I wandered the streets for a long, wretched hour, scarcely noticing where I was headed. Surely I must be mistaken. There must be countless women with scars upon their faces.

And then I thought of little Bia, clambering on to the bed this morning. Tracing a pudgy finger down my face. *Bad man gone.* I'd thought she meant Howard. But she'd been tracing a scar. Her mother's scar. Bad man. Burden. They did not sound so very different.

Somehow I found myself outside the familiar green door of the Cocked Pistol. I opened my watch. Not yet ten o'clock. I must speak with Gabriela – but not now. Not until I could be sure that her husband was out on his own business.

A night visit to St Giles, God help me. I would be damned lucky to survive it.

Sam was sitting on the stairs, sharp chin resting on his knees. He grabbed my coat as I passed him. 'Mr Hawkins—'

'Not now, Sam.' Not now. And if my darkest thoughts were true – not ever.

Kitty waited for me by the fire in our room, her father's journals in a stack by her arm. I was struck by the sharp hinge of her life. Nathaniel Sparks had been a distinguished physician and a gentleman, and the family had lived in great comfort. But he had died, and Kitty's mother had lost herself to grief. Lost herself to gin too in the end, falling further and further until she was selling herself for it. Kitty had escaped, or had been abandoned – it was hard to say as she refused to speak of her mother. She might even be alive yet, though I doubted it. Half the town knew that Kitty had inherited a fortune when Samuel Fleet died, and from what I'd heard, Emma Sparks would have been the first in line demanding a hand-out. It was five years at least since Kitty had seen her mother. How she had survived on her own was a mystery. All I knew for certain was that she had somehow remained a maid, and could fight like a demon. No doubt these two facts were connected. I had tried to coax the truth from her, and she had bitten and snapped like a vixen until I gave up.

I had thought there would be time. We had only met last autumn and there had been no rush. And now I had more pressing concerns. Seeing Nathaniel's medical papers reminded me how little I knew about Kitty Sparks. I knew her heart, at least – and I suppose that in the end that was all that mattered.

Alice brought us a late supper and then we retired to bed, exhausted by another troubling day. I held Kitty in my arms and we talked drowsily of small things. She had slipped the queen's ring onto her wedding finger, where it twinkled softly against the sheets. I was tempted to ask her again to marry me, but I knew she would refuse. Tomorrow. I would ask her again tomorrow.

Chapter Seventeen

A soft pressure on my shoulder. 'Sir. It's time.'
I opened my eyes. Alice tiptoed out of the room and downstairs while I dressed haphazardly in the dark. I could hear Kitty breathing deeply against her pillow, quite still. I leaned as close as I dared and touched my lips to her hair.

I had asked Alice to wake me at four o'clock. She had stayed awake down in the kitchen, cleaning by candlelight. She poured me a bowl of coffee, which I drank quickly, feeling it sharpen my senses. She didn't ask where I was going. It was not her place.

Sometimes, when I looked at Alice, I saw her as she had first arrived in this house, covered in blood. Red smears on a ghost-white face, and blue eyes staring fixed in terror. A gruesome palimpsest, the Alice of that night placed in front of the one she had become. *Our* Alice, always scrubbing and mopping and sweeping as if there were layers of dirt that only she could see.

Some part of me had always wondered if we had accepted her story too readily, but now I knew she was innocent and was glad Kitty had brought her here.

'Keep the doors locked and the windows shuttered. Don't let anyone in until I return. And don't let Miss Sparks out.'

If Kitty knew where I was going tonight, she would insist on coming with me. I would not risk it, not after Howard's attack on the boat. Let her curse my name and tear out her hair in fury, I didn't care.

'How will I stop her?'

A good question. 'Just try your best, Alice.'

She nodded, frightened. I was sorry for it – Alice had suffered enough these past weeks – but it could not be helped. At least she did not know where I was going.

St Giles – in the dead of night. A short stroll into hell. But first I needed a guide.

The previous morning, Fleet had told his men that I worked under his protection. The word was passed about the gang. One small benefit of our agreement and one I had not expected to need so soon.

Fleet had said that if I needed to speak with him, I should leave a message at the Coach and Horses on Wellington Street. I headed there now through the ink-black streets. The tavern was empty, but a message was sent. Ten minutes later, one of Fleet's men arrived and motioned me towards a dark corner of the room.

'The Captain's working.'

I nodded. In fact, I had depended on it. 'It's urgent.'

'He won't come here tonight, Hawkins.'

I lowered my voice, though there was no one to hear us. 'Then take me to Phoenix Street. I can wait for him there.'

He chewed his cheek, thinking. 'What's this about?'

'Not your business.'

He frowned at that, but it was the right thing to say. He wouldn't trust a man who spilled his secrets so easily. Thought some more. 'I'll take your pistol.'

I feigned reluctance, then handed it over. I had kept my

dagger, hidden in the lining of my coat. Fleet's man gave my pistol to the landlord for safekeeping and said I would collect it later. *Later.* An imagined time, when the night was over and I was safely home again. We would see.

We carved a straight route through St Giles; none of Sam's scampering back and forth. I knew where Fleet lived and there was no need to hide it now. We sauntered down streets that would have throbbed with danger had I walked through them on my own. I still felt fierce eyes watching us, heard the whispers in the walkways above our heads, but I had been granted safe passage into the heart of the stews. How I would come out again I wasn't sure. I never was very good at planning ahead.

We came into Fleet's house through the square this time, instead of Sam's preferred route over the rooftops. Ducked into a mean timber house and then out again through a narrow passageway to the back yard. We had reached the centre of the hidden square. Candles burned at the top of Fleet's home, but otherwise all was still. It was four-thirty in the morning. Most of the gang would not return until dawn.

A few men stood guard inside, drinking and playing cards to pass the time. They nodded as I passed them. The message had reached them long before we had.

Gabriela sat by the fire, in the room at the top of the house. Her hair was loose around her shoulders and she looked very tired. Another night keeping vigil for her husband. How could she stand such a life?

I bowed quickly and rubbed my hands to warm them. It was a bitterly cold night. There were a few flakes of snow sparkling on my coat. It had begun falling as we entered St Giles and now the world beyond the windows was a blizzard, bright white and silent.

Her lips puckered in amusement. 'You blue with cold again,

sir?' She drew up another chair close to the fire. 'We wait here. James will be home soon.'

Not too soon, please God. 'I was hoping we might speak, Mrs Fleet.'

'Gabriela. Sit. They have taken your weapons, yes? I am sorry, I must ask. We are alone.'

She poured me a cup of hot wine. We were not alone, of course. Fleet's men were close by. Did she guess that I might have a dagger, hidden about me? It would be a mistake indeed to underestimate her: James Fleet's wife. No doubt she too had a blade somewhere, tucked beneath her skirts. I let my gaze wander across her gown. It was plain and grey, but it fitted neatly to her figure. If it had been stolen, someone had restitched it very well. Her waist was thick from bearing her six children, but she was still a fine, handsome woman, save for the scar. And even that seemed to suit her, now I had grown more used to it.

A golden brooch glinted at the centre of her chest and I thought of Eva's red gauze scarf, threaded with gold. Her mother, it seemed, allowed herself at least one small trinket.

I had been studying Gabriela, but she was watching me too, her eyes a warm, coffee brown, fringed with thick lashes. She looked very much like Sam, but she was less awkward, more comfortable in company. 'The wine is good?'

'Yes. Thank you.'

'Is what they give on the road to Tyburn.' She drained her cup, sucked the wine from her lips. 'Last drink of the damned. You stare at my scar, Mr Hawkins. *Calma, calma,*' she laughed as I flustered my apologies. 'I know why you have come. I am not *bird-witted.*' The last word was pure St Giles, the *tt* lost somewhere in the back of her throat. She leaned forward. 'There are men downstairs. I call them, they slit your throat. So we speak quiet and you leave. Yes?'

I stared at her. I had not ventured a single word about Joseph Burden, or the brothel in Seven Dials.

She touched a finger to her scar, traced the line down her ruined cheek. 'This is my life. My story. I know when a man want to hear it.' She tucked her bare feet beneath her gown. 'I am a Jewess, you know this? My family lives in Portugal for hundreds of years. We convert,' she fluttered her hand, showing the shallow extent of that conversion. 'The Inquisition does not trust we are faithful. You know what they do to such people? Burn. Torture. So we run – sail for England and freedom. My mother and father, my two brothers. My sister. This is . . . twenty-one years ago. I am thirteen.' She gazed into the fire, eyes hollow. 'There is a storm. They die.'

She stopped. It had taken a great deal of strength to say those few stark words. Her loss hung between us, unspoken. After a moment, she continued.

'I am thirteen and alone in London. Pretty. No one to care for me. I have only a few words of English. What do you think happens to such a girl?' She shrugged at the ways of the world. 'I am starving and afraid. A kind woman take me in. "Poor little Gabby. Call me Auntie". She gives me clothes and food, a bed. And then she make me work for them.'

'Aunt Doxie.'

She poured us both another glass of hot wine, blood-red liquid splashing from the jug. 'You hear of Joseph Burden, I think?'

So much venom in her voice when she spoke his name. 'Ned Weaver told me . . .'

A sharp tilt of the chin. 'His son. *Yes.* I know this.'

'He said Burden worked at a brothel in Seven Dials. Charles Howard told me the same story last night.' I frowned at the memory, and reached for my pipe.

'I remember *him*. He used to visit.'

'He said it was different from other brothels. Nothing was forbidden.'

She curled her lip, mimicked her old bawd. *'Whatever you want, sir. If you can pay. Whatever you want*. And Mr Burden standing out on the front step, so tall, his arms like *this*.' She clutched her own slim arm and gripped hard, as if it were solid oak. 'A bully should protect the whores, you understand? He is paid to stop the customers when they grow too wild. Mr Burden, though – he takes money from the customers and he lets them do whatever they wish. Sometimes he watches. Sometimes he joins them.'

'He cut you.'

'This?' Gabriela touched her scar again. 'No, sir – let me tell you what Mr Burden did.'

But then she stopped and said nothing for a long while. Her breath was shallow and very fast. A slick of sweat shone on her face, though it was still snowing. She pressed her palms together and held her hands to her face as if in prayer. When she looked up once more, she had returned to herself. *Calma*. 'There was a man. I will not say his name; he does not deserve to be remembered. He was old, very ugly. Very cruel. All the girls are afraid of him. He likes to frighten them, you understand?

'One day he ask for me for the first time. Points at me as if I am some animal at Smithfield. *That one*. Aunt Doxie does not want to sell her little Gabby – some time he leaves marks and I am so pretty, worth so much to her. But ... *Whatever you want, sir. If you can pay*. She names a fee – enough to buy every whore in the brothel. He laughs and pays double. It is a game to him. He likes to play games.' She closes her eyes for a second. 'He takes my hand. He feels that I am shaking all over and he laughs again. He likes that I am afraid. He knows I have heard the stories.

'Aunt Doxie leads us to this man's favourite room. It is high up, very high at the back of the brothel, very quiet. She tells to Mr Burden – stand outside the door and call if there is trouble. Then she leaves and we are alone. The man gives Mr Burden half a guinea. He says, keep your mouth shut.'

She picked up the poker and pushed it deep into the fire, turning over the coals and building the flames higher. She did not turn back to look at me, but kept her eyes always on the light. 'This man. He ties my hands. He ties a cloth over my eyes. I stand like this for a long time, so afraid, waiting in the darkness. Then I feel a blade, here.' She touched her throat. 'He whispers in my ear, tells me all the things he will do with it. I start to cry. He strikes me so hard I fall to my knees.

'I shall not tell you, sir, what he did to me then. Only ... Before him, I would fly from my body, you see? Always. Like a bird, until it was done. But I cannot escape him. The pain and the fear, I think he will kill me. I dare not fly away. I am trapped. And I begin to think no, Gabriela, no. You are strong. You are not a child. Your family drown but you survive. You live. And I take my fists like this, still bound, and I push him away. I kick and shove until I am free. I pull off the blindfold and I run to the door, screaming, screaming.

'Mr Burden stands there. He looks angry. He tells me I am a stupid whore, that I must not make trouble. I run past him towards the stairs, towards life. I am bleeding but I am free. Then I feel his arms about my waist, pulling me back. I try to fight, but he is too strong, like a nightmare. He carries me back up the stairs to the room. He throws me down on the bed. He puts his weight upon my back, pushes my head into the pillow and I can barely breathe. He says, "Be quiet, slut. Earn your keep."

The other man thanks him. He points to his face – there is a small cut on his brow, just a light scratch. He takes his knife and says, "Hold her down. The bitch will pay for this."'

Gabriela pulled her knees up beneath her chin, wrapped her arms around her legs.

'When it was done they left me to bleed. I was too weak to move, too shocked. One of the maids found me. When Aunt Doxie saw, she cursed me. Cursed *me*. I was ruined, close to death. *Worthless*. She pushed me out on to the street. I don't remember no more. I must have staggered into St Giles – I don't know how. I should have died in the gutter. I think I wanted this. But see, here I am.' She turned to me at last. 'I survive.'

'How?'

She smiled, like an angel – her eyes shining. 'James. He found me. He carried me to his brother's friend, Dr Sparks. He saved my life.'

Nathaniel Sparks – Samuel Fleet's great friend. *Kitty's father* had saved Gabriela. 'Gabriela . . . you know that Kitty . . .'

'His daughter. Of course! I know Kitty, when she was very tiny. My God the noise. She cry, cry, cry. I think I go deaf. That's why we save you last night. For Kitty. What – you think I fall in love with your legs?' She smiled again. A light had returned to her face, now the worst of her story was over.

If I were a wise man, I would have left her then. Everything I had feared was true. *So leave, now – and quickly. Run from this world of butchery, murder and revenge. Grab Kitty's hand and flee the city and let this tragedy play to its end without you.* But I didn't move. I stayed quite still, pressed into the chair. I must know it all.

'The brothel burned down.'

Gabriela's eyelids grew heavy. 'Yes.'

'Two people, burned alive.' Aunt Doxie, and the man she would not name. Who did not deserve a name. Lost and unmourned for ever. 'James did this for you?'

'*Yes.*' And there was love in her voice.

'But he spared Joseph Burden.'

'No, sir. We did not spare him.' She hugged her knees to her chest. 'I still dream of that night. So many times. I had *escaped* that room, you understand? But *he* dragged me back there. *He* held me down. You think to kill him was enough? A few moments of pain?

'The night James burned down the brothel we could not find him. He'd fucked one of the new country girls. A fresh maid. Worth good money. Aunt Doxie found out and she have him kicked from the door. James and Samuel, they search the town and at last they find him. On his knees in church, sobbing like a child. He knows why the brothel burns down. He knows that now is his turn. James was going to slit his throat, but Samuel . . . Well. You knew Samuel, sir.'

Oh, yes. I knew Samuel Fleet. Never once chose a straight path if a crooked one were on offer. Or better yet, a maze of his own devising, full of twists and turns and general confusion.

'Samuel said, "Think, Brother, is it not better to let the man live and suffer? Why should he escape the miseries of existence?" You remember, this is how he talks?'

'I remember.'

'He says, "Mr Burden – you train as a carpenter, yes? So you will take up your trade once more. You will become a respectable citizen, go to church, read the Bible. You will marry and have children. All that you earn, you will pay to us. And one day we will come back and we will finish what was begun today. We will take your life. But not today. And perhaps not tomorrow. If you run, we will find you. If you try to speak of this, we take you and we kill you slowly. So you think that burning alive is a mercy."'

Only Samuel Fleet could have dreamed up such a plan. It was

so elegant, so cruel. So *profitable*. How he must have enjoyed watching Burden, trapped all those years in a dull, virtuous life. I doubted Fleet could imagine a worse torture for any man.

'Twenty years, we let him live. He works like a dog and we take his money. Twenty years – always afraid one night my husband will come for him. I wonder sometimes if his heart burst from fear. But he lives. He marries and has children.'

'Ned said his mother was a whore.'

'His mother was a *young girl*. The country girl that Joseph Burden took for himself. Aunt Doxie threw her out too. She have nothing, so she steals. And she is caught.'

I sighed at the thought of another broken life. Ned's mother had pled her belly at Newgate. Her son had saved her for that short while, but then she had died on her way to the colonies. 'You made Burden take Ned in.'

Gabriela drained her glass. She was tired, of a sudden. 'So. There is my story.'

'But it is not finished.'

'No.' A long pause. 'Samuel was killed in gaol. Of course he had lived next door to Burden for several years. He found it amusing. He would say, "Good morrow, neighbour, what – has my brother not killed you yet?" He said to Burden, "you must thank me". That he was the only one who could persuade James to spare his life. And this was true. Samuel said to James, let the children grow up first. I agreed with this; they are innocent. When Samuel died, Burden knew his own death was coming.'

And now I understood Burden's strange behaviour in the weeks preceding his murder. He knew he could be killed at any moment. He brought his son home from school to be close to him in his last days. He refused to move house, knowing that all the profits from his business had drained into James Fleet's pocket. He refused to give Ned a position for the same reason. And – my God, of course. He forced himself on Alice. Ned couldn't understand Burden's behaviour in the last weeks of his life – it had seemed so out of character. The truth was quite the reverse. It was the previous twenty years that had been out of character for Burden. He may have gained some bullying satisfaction from his work with Gonson and the Society, but his natural inclination was very different. Why not fuck his maid, when Death lurked around every corner? When Gabriela's son moved in next door, silent and watchful?

Sam Fleet, with his mother's curls, his father's black-eyed stare, and his uncle's name. Sam Fleet, who crept into Burden's house in the middle of the night. *Practising*.

Sam had grown up looking into his mother's scarred face every day. He must have heard her screaming at night, when the dreams came. I had rejected him as the killer because he had no reason for it and because of the ferocity of the attack. In fact he had the strongest motive to kill Joseph Burden. Beneath that still surface he must have been in turmoil for weeks.

I must accept the truth, much as it pained me. Sam was Burden's killer. Hadn't I asked the boy that night, when we stood over the butchered, bloody corpse?

Did you do this, Sam?

And he had answered with his own question.

Why would I kill him?

Gabriela's story had woven a spell upon me, while the snow storm blew through the town. Or perhaps it was just that I was exhausted, and sickened to my soul. I understood why she and James would seek revenge upon Burden. I could almost applaud them for the way they had extracted that revenge over the past twenty years, as long as I did not think upon Burden's children and the dismal effect it had had on their own, blameless lives.

But to send Sam to live next door . . . they must have known what would happen.

'Did you order your son to kill Burden?'

Gabriela untucked her feet and stretched. 'I think he is too young. But James say, "He cannot be apprentice all his life", and I understand. It is a mother's wish to keep her children always young, and safe. But Sam is fourteen. He is not a boy.'

So it was as I had feared. Sam had been sent to live at the Cocked Pistol in order to murder Joseph Burden. James Fleet had never wanted a gentleman for a son – he'd wanted a killer. It was, after all, a family business.

We both fell silent. Downstairs, Fleet's men were still caught in a rowdy game of cards. Someone was playing a tune on a penny whistle, shrill and jaunty. My head was throbbing from the wine, and the heat of the fire. I should leave. Fleet would return home soon. If he knew that I suspected Sam, I was sure he would kill me. I had begun to wonder about Gabriela, too. Had she kept me here all this time, waiting for her husband to arrive?

'You wonder how to leave,' Gabriela said, toying with the gold brooch at her chest. 'You are afraid.'

'Foolish not to be.'

'Foolish.' A half-smile. 'You are clever in your own world. A gentleman's world. But here . . . Ahh, sir. How I wish you had not come here. I wished it from the first moment you walked into this room. I am thinking, thinking . . .' She tapped her forehead. 'How to save you. I should like to save you, Mr Hawkins. A shame for you to die.'

I shifted slowly in my seat, thinking of the dagger tucked in my coat. I could reach for it in a heartbeat. And, what? Stab her? Could I really do such a thing?

'I must protect Sam,' she said. 'And you are fond of him too, I think.'

'Yes.'

Her smile deepened. 'You are a good man.'

'Sometimes.' And what splendid rewards it brought me. 'You shouldn't have sent him to me. I thought I was helping him. I knew he was the thief, that night. In my heart I knew it. I should have stopped him.'

'You cannot stop a tiger, Mr Hawkins.'

I stared at her, speechless. Is that how she saw her son? As a *tiger*? He was not a predator, for God's sake. He was a boy. And between her pride and my neglect, we had lost him.

'I have a suggestion, Mr Hawkins. Kitty tells me this morning about Alice. About her dress. Covered in blood . . .' She raised an eyebrow.

I nodded, struggling to keep an even expression. I understood her meaning. If I was willing to accuse Alice of Burden's death and use the dress as evidence, I would be free to leave. Otherwise – I would not escape St Giles with my life. I pretended to consider the proposition. Rubbed my face wearily. 'Yes. Very well.'

I rose to my feet, turning to the window. It was still dark, but the roofs were covered in snow that glowed in the moonlight. Gabriela rose too. She was very beautiful in this strange half-light. I had been watching her for so long that I hardly noticed the scar any more, though it cut so deep through her brow, and down to her jaw. She leaned closer, and for a strange, fluttering moment I thought she meant to kiss me. But no, no – I caught the tightening around her eyes. The sudden set to her mouth. I leaped back just as she sprang forward, pulling the brooch from her chest. Not a brooch but the hidden top of a dagger, slid between her breasts.

I was a *good man*. And she had not believed me.

She swiped again with the blade, and I threw myself back,

stumbling towards the balcony. The dagger sliced along my arm. I felt a sharp sting and then warmth as the blood began to flow. She was shouting now too, calling for aid.

I barrelled through the door out onto the balcony, groping desperately for the ladder. And now the household was in uproar – I could hear cries from below as Fleet's men responded. The first footsteps upon the stairs. A moment later Eva ran into the room.

'Ma!' she gasped, her face white. 'Ma, no!'

Gabriela spun around, distracted. I grabbed the ladder and flung it across the gap. It hit the roof opposite with a dull thud, knocking away a patch of fresh snow. I had to clamber up – it was the only way across to safety. But all Gabriela had to do was snatch the ladder from this side and I would fall. I hesitated, clutching my wounded arm. And suddenly Eva pushed her way past her mother, throwing herself between us.

'*Eva!*' Gabriela snapped, furious.

'*Go!*' Eva hissed.

Without another thought, I clambered on to the ladder. It bowed under my weight, rocking a little with no one to hold it steady. I inched my way along, terrified that Gabriela would shove Eva aside and I would be tipped from the ladder to my death. But no, here was the rooftop ahead of me. I flung myself up on to the icy timber. The ladder scraped from the roof and crashed to the ground.

I lay on my back, the sky spinning above me as the cold air caught my breath. Snow melted through my clothes. *Stand up, stand up.* I rose carefully to my feet. Rooftops, stretching out far into the distance. *Frosted* rooftops, ice sparkling in the halflight. I put one foot out and it skated ahead of me. One careless step and I could break my neck.

On the balcony below, Gabriela was pointing up at me. One

of Fleet's men clambered down to collect the ladder, rested it against the house below me. He began to climb up to meet me.

I slid carefully to the other side of the roof. There was a balcony below. I jumped down, then dropped from there to the street, landing heavily on my hands and knees. I pulled the dagger from my coat and ran down Phoenix Street. If I could reach the Garden, the market traders would be filling the piazza. Fleet's men would not risk attacking me in such a public fashion – it was not their way.

The streets were quiet and I must have seemed half-crazed, even for St Giles, with my dagger in hand. Who would risk attacking a man under James Fleet's protection? And then, as I turned a corner he was there, in front of me. I ran straight into him.

We stared at each other, the one as surprised as the other. And I thought of the man behind me, only a few paces away.

Fleet recovered first. 'Hawkins. What the devil . . .'

'Gabriela. Sir, you must go to her now. She's in danger. Run, sir, run!'

A tumble of words that made no sense. Only that I knew now his one weakness. How much he loved his wife, and the lengths to which he would go to protect her. *Gabriela. Danger.* It was enough. He didn't stop to wonder why I was in St Giles. Why I was running in the opposite direction. He thought only of his wife. He ran towards her, and I fled through the streets, faster than I had ever run in my life.

As I reached the turning to Long Acre, I was almost crushed beneath the wheels of a vegetable cart. I leaped to the pavement, panting hard, my heart hammering against my chest.

'You stupid arsehole!' the cartman yelled over his shoulder. 'Almost killed you!'

I waved my apologies. People were staring. My stockings were soaked and ripped from my scrabble across the rooftop, my wig and hat lost in the chase.

I didn't care. I was safe – and I had the truth. Now I must decide how to use it.

Chapter Eighteen

'You must leave the city. At once.'

I leaned over the hot punch and breathed in its steam. 'I know, Betty. I know.'

We were hidden in a quiet corner at Moll's. I'd sat at this table many times before, nursing a sore head after another night's debauch. But it was not liquor that made my head pound now, or my hands shake. I reached for my tobacco and built another pipe, conscious of Betty studying me hard under those thick black lashes. She knew that I had run foul of Fleet's gang, nothing more. Anyone who knew Gabriela's story would be in danger, and I had no wish to put Betty's life at risk.

I drank a glass of punch in silence. After the exhilaration and relief of my escape, here was the crash back down to earth. I should go home, pack my belongings and leave within the hour. But home meant Sam. I couldn't face him, not yet. I couldn't bear to look into those black eyes and see the truth staring back at me.

I had never felt so angry before. My body was shaking with it. I had witnessed cruelty before – even murder. But James Fleet's crime, and Gabriela's . . . surely even God couldn't forgive it. They had corrupted their only son beyond all hope of return. A boy of fourteen. If I reached out and told this story to the man at the next table, his head bent low over his *Daily Courant*, he would shrug his shoulders. Some black-hearted villain from St Giles raises his son to be a killer. What of it? What news was this? Sam had lived among thieves and murderers all his life. Why should any of this matter? Son of a whore, son of a cut-throat gang captain. If any boy had been born and raised to kill, it was Sam.

But there were other paths he could have taken, with that sharp, inquisitive mind. He could have been a lawyer or a stock-broker or a physician or an anything he damned well chose, given time. And now? Even if he escaped the rope, those paths were closed to him for ever. He had stolen into a house and stabbed a man to death. It would shape the rest of his life. How could it not?

How could a father want this for his son? Even a killer such as James Fleet – did he not dream of better for his only boy? And I wondered – did he send Sam to me with an order to kill Burden? Or had he simply placed him next door and waited for the inevitable act? Did he think that absolved him of the sin? No – Fleet would care nothing of absolution. He was a murderer many times over. He *must* have ordered the boy to do it.

I thought of Sam creeping around the Burdens' home at night, knife in hand. *Practising*. He'd confessed in that one word, but I'd refused to hear it. He'd tiptoed into Burden's bedroom, ready to strike . . . only to find Alice Dunn curled up next to her master. An unexpected complication. He couldn't kill Burden in front of a witness – she would have woken the whole house. So he'd waited for another night, when Burden was alone – then thrown suspicion on poor Alice.

I thought back to the night of Burden's murder. Sam had been most anxious to let Alice take the blame. If she had run, as Sam had suggested, everyone would have believed she was the killer, instead of me. Had he pressed for this out of some twinge of loyalty, or guilt for placing me in danger? Or was Alice simply a more suitable scapegoat? Gentlemen don't hang, as a rule. But a lowly servant, with no friends and no capital . . .?

I could no longer trust my feelings in the matter. What did I know of Sam, truly? This was the little moon-curser who just a few months ago had led me to his father's gang to be robbed and beaten. And still I had trusted him. I'd followed that flickering torch without question through his narrow, twisted maze – and it had brought me here.

I didn't blame Sam. If anything, I blamed myself. All this time he had spent under my roof and I did not have the wit to see he was in trouble. Jenny had warned me there was something wrong with the boy. He had sneaked into her room while she was sleeping, for God's sake! If I had only paid more attention. If I had *listened*. Instead I had landed on some fool notion that Sam and I shared some unspoken affinity. I too had suffocated beneath my father's expectations. The difference was, my father was a country parson. Sam's father was a murderer.

I should have helped the boy, not colluded with him. Now it was too late and Sam was set upon a path that led only to more death, including his own. How many boys from St Giles had begun this way and ended up swinging from a rope before they even reached their twenties? I could be kind to myself and say that Sam's fate was sealed the day he was born into that family of thieves and murderers, but I knew better. I was furious with James Fleet and with Gabriela – a white-hot anger pouring like burning metal through my veins. But I saved a portion of that anger for myself. Somehow, surely, I could have prevented this.

Betty touched my wrist, fingers brushing lightly against my skin. I blinked. How long had I been staring out across the coffeehouse, lost in thought? My pipe lay upon the table, burned-out. The man at the next bench had left, and a group of lawyers' clerks had gathered by the fire, stamping their feet to thaw out their toes.

I took a last swig of punch. It had turned cold. 'I must return home.'

Betty's hand tightened about my wrist. 'Fleet will be watching the Pistol. Mr Hawkins – you *must* leave London now. I can send a message to Miss Sparks.' She leaned forward, forcing me to look her in the eye. 'Go to my lodgings now and hide there. I can bring you clothes, food, coin – everything you need within the hour. There is a coach to the coast that leaves from the George . . .'

I scarce heard her. *Kitty.* I rose from the table, struck with a sudden fear. Kitty was at home, oblivious to the danger we were in. What if Fleet had sent his men to the shop? She wouldn't know to bar the door to them. They could be there even now as I sat witlessly over a bowl of punch.

Betty gazed up at me as I stood, her lips pursed. 'No one ever listens . . .'

'One half-hour, that is all. I must fetch Kitty.' I smiled. 'Thank you, Betty.' And on a whim I leaned down and kissed the disapproval from her lips.

She let me, just for a moment, then pushed me away. 'Fool,' she muttered.

The bells of Covent Garden were striking seven as I left Moll's. Light had begun to build in the sky. The market on the piazza was still busy, the scent of ripe fruit and warm barley mingling with the pungent but not unpleasant smell of livestock. A knife sharpener had placed his cart beneath the sundial in the middle of the square. I winced as I passed, the high shriek of metal scraping along stone almost unbearable on the ear.

So – it was resolved. Farewell to London and the life I'd built here. My flight would convince the whole world of my guilt, but I would live and keep Kitty safe. The career of a gang captain was a short one. I had never seen a man hang at Tyburn older than forty.

Perhaps when James Fleet was dead, we might return and resolve matters. The taverns were full of villains who'd been transported and stolen home again to live in secret.

As I hurried through the square, I began to sense a crowd gathering at my back. More choice gossip for the scandalmongers of the Garden. I searched the crowds and rooftops for Fleet's men but found only sullen glares from old neighbours who had once smiled and nodded in friendship. Was there something more sinister about their behaviour today? There was a boldness in their stares that unnerved me. I sensed a brewing anger, as if they had decided, en masse, that they had reached the end of their patience. A ripple of fear ran through me as I crossed briskly on to Russell Street. Anger of this kind could turn a crowd into a mob very fast – and a London mob showed no mercy.

The knife sharpener's wheel turned again, grinding the steel.

I reached Mr Felblade's shop. The apothecary stood on his step, pounding something into powder with a pestle and mortar. He grinned, lips stretched over his assortment of rotten teeth and wooden plugs. 'Disciples, Mr Hawkins?'

I glanced back over my shoulder. A dozen or so men were indeed following me at a short distance, clumping through the grey slush of melting snow. They were led by Joshua Purchase, who ran the gaming shop on the other side of the Pistol. I cursed them all under my breath. How was I supposed to escape the town in secret now?

I turned and confronted them, feigning nonchalance. 'May I help you, sirs?' I asked in an imperious tone. It held them back for a heartbeat, men so used to deferring to their betters . . . but my clothes were in tatters, my wig and hat lost in my desperate flight from St Giles. How thin a line between a gentleman and a low rogue. Clothes and confidence. I drew myself as tall as I could manage. 'Well?'

They glanced at one another, then nudged Purchase. He had always struck me as a sneaking, cowardly fellow, but he seemed to have drawn courage from his elevation to mob leader. He pointed a finger at my chest. 'Murderer.'

My heart skipped. *Murderer.* Accused in the street for all to hear. Flung like a gauntlet at my feet. Something had changed – some invisible boundary had been crossed. What now? Did they want to take that final step into riot? Did they want to turn on me and tear me to pieces? I could see the uncertainty in their faces – to act or to back down. The wrong word, the wrong gesture and I was lost. No one would come to my aid.

Purchase leered at me. He was so close I could smell the gin on his breath. He must have been drinking all night.

I took a step back – and made a short, mocking bow. As if I were amused. Indifferent. And then I turned my back upon them all. It was a risk, and I feared that they would jump upon me and drag me down. But to show fear to the mob would only give them courage and an unspoken permission to attack. To walk away with my back straight and my head high was my only chance.

As I turned, a slight figure emerged from the shadows. Sam. He tilted his head up the street, towards the shop.

'Trap,' he mouthed. 'Run.'

I hesitated. It could be true. Or *this* could be the trap. Perhaps James Fleet was in the Pistol with Kitty. Would he hurt her? Kitty's father had saved Gabriela . . . but Fleet was a practical man. He would do whatever was necessary.

A mob at my back. A gang up ahead. The blood pounded in my ears as I walked faster towards the Pistol. Sam's eyes widened in panic. 'Mr Hawkins!' He shook my arm, as if I might need waking. 'Run!'

There was a shout up ahead, and a group of men spilled from the Cocked Pistol. I gave a sharp intake of breath. Those were not Fleet's men. Gonson's constables were gathered at the shop door, armed with staves. The magistrate stood in their midst in his ridiculous long wig, peering down the street. Our eyes met and he gave a start, then beamed in triumph.

'There he is! Seize him!'

Before I could run, the mob at my back surged forward, pushing me to the ground. I bucked and fought, but it was no use; it felt as if the whole damned street were holding me down.

Gonson approached, surrounded by his men. I raised my head as best I could, sun glinting in my face. Crowder placed his boot on my face and pushed it into the mud. The dust and filth filled my mouth and nostrils and I began to choke, eyes streaming.

'Lift him up,' Gonson ordered. Rough hands brought me to my feet. I spat the dirt away. My ribs ached from my neighbours' boots.

I struggled against the guards. 'What is this? You have no right . . .' Crowder cuffed me across the jaw.

Gonson had begun to address the growing crowd. The news had escaped into the streets, and people were running from the shops and taverns and coffeehouses to witness the spectacle. 'My friends,' Gonson cried and pointed his stick at my chest. 'Witness this wretched villain. Guilty of every foul sin known to man. My Society has warned you of rogues such as this, polluting our great city. We good citizens have been silent for too long. We have avoided our *duty* for too long. And in our complacency we have allowed evil to flourish. Let this be a lesson to us all. It is our responsibility to rid these streets of such vermin.'

It was a long speech, delivered as if he were some high minister of government. No doubt he had practised it in the glass this morning. He paused as the crowd cheered its approval, his chest swollen with satisfaction. No matter that half the crowd was comprised of the *vermin* he was railing against. Take away the sinners and who would be left? The honourable Mr John Gonson alone, striding about the empty town, shouting valedictory speeches to himself. Perhaps that was his great dream.

He pulled out an arrest warrant and held it up to the crowd. 'Thomas Hawkins. This morning Edward Weaver discovered a hidden passage between your attic and the home of Mr Joseph Burden. I knew Mr Burden. He was a good man. An honourable, blameless man. And you killed him.'

'That's a lie!' I cried, struggling beneath the guards' grip. 'I'm innocent.'

Crowder struck me another blow, splitting my lip. I tasted blood, hot and metallic on my tongue. Another guard clapped my wrists in iron. People were cursing my name, shouting 'Murderer!' and pressing forward, snatching at my clothes. In the chaos, they began to fight with the guards to reach me. Gonson was shoved in the back, his hat and wig slipping askew. 'Good people!' he cried, struggling to be heard over the din. Someone kicked him in the shin as they clambered past, and he fell to the pavement, sprawling in the freezing mud. Two of the guards ran to his aid.

'Move,' Crowder hissed in my ear, shoving me forward with his club. We stumbled along together with a great press of bodies at our backs, Gonson scurrying to the head of the procession with his guards forming a tight band around us. As we reached the Pistol, Kitty flung herself out of the door.

'Tom!' she cried. Then she was bundled back inside. The door slammed and I was dragged away, unable to save her, unable to save myself.

The mob followed us all the way down the Strand and along Fleet Street. The noise was unbearable and terrifying, drowning out the usual cries of the street. People stopped in their business to stare, a few joining the ragged procession as if it were a day at the fair. Gonson had deliberately chosen the most public of streets to ensure my humiliation and disgrace. The whole town would learn the news within hours. Thomas Hawkins – murderer. Dragged in chains through the city with the mob at his back. What jury would believe in my innocence now?

This was Gonson's revenge, I was sure of it. He had been forced to give up his enquiries against me and I had mocked him for it. Now he was vindicated. He was positively radiating with righteous triumph as we reached Old Bailey.

And so we arrived at Newgate. I had entered prison in chains before, but that had been alone save for one bailiff, in a quiet back alley in Southwark. Newgate was a grand palace of villainy and shame, and I was led there with half the town baying at my back. I knew the gatehouse to the prison well – I had passed it many times. But oh – the sight of it now, with its twin turrets and iron portcullis! My arrest had felt like some terrible dream. Now I was awake.

I half stumbled and the crowd jeered. 'Look!' someone cried out. 'The Lord tripped his feet to show His wrath.'

Oh, indeed? Is that how God spends His days? Tripping up sinners with His celestial boot? Madness – but Gonson nodded his approval. I had thought better of him. For all his pride and rigid manners, I did not think him a vain man, to play to the crowds.

The main gate to the prison was closed behind the portcullis.

Crowder banged on a postern door in one of the turrets and it creaked open an inch. A turnkey peered out at the mob, worried. 'Bring him inside. Quickly, damn it!'

The guards pushed me towards the door. 'I'm innocent,' I called out to the crowds. 'I swear it!'

The turnkey shut the postern gate on them all – guards, neighbours, gossips, and villains. My shoulders sagged with relief. They would have thrown a rope around my neck and hanged me from the nearest shop sign, given the chance. I was in prison, but I was safe. For this much at least I could thank Gonson. Everything must be done in the correct manner, with the correct paperwork. He probably wrote a release order for his cock before he pissed from it.

And here indeed were papers to complete, signatures to flourish, seals to press. And one last lecture to give. 'Mr Hawkins,' he murmured, tilting his head to observe me better. 'God has punished you at last. You murdered a good man and tried to throw the blame upon his grieving children. Now you must pay for your monstrous crimes. You had best look to your soul, sir. I doubt you will live above a month.'

He walked away without another word.

The turnkey watched Gonson leave with a sour expression. 'Prick,' he muttered, then turned to me. 'You're a gent,' he said, half statement, half question. 'Governor says you have capital.'

I tapped the purse nestled in my coat pocket. He drew it out and tipped a stream of coins into his hand. I held out my wrists and he unlocked the chains.

'You've been in the clink before,' he guessed.

'For debt.'

'You'll know how to behave then.'

I nodded. I had indeed learned a great deal of gaol etiquette from my time in the Marshalsea. Don't punch the turnkey. Don't accuse the governor of murder. And most of all, mind my own fucking business.

'Governor thinks he can find room for you off the Press Yard. Best cells in the gaol if you can pay.'

'I was expected?'

The turnkey shrugged and led me through the prison to the Condemned Hold. He locked me in, leaving me to grope my way in darkness for a time. When he returned, he pulled back the hatch on the door and offered me a cheap tallow candle, for thrice its value. I took it and did not complain. As I said – I understood gaol etiquette. Let the bastards squeeze you and say nothing.

I settled the candle on the rotten board hammered into the wall. It gave off a wretched, stuttering light that spat shadows around the cell. The tallow added to the stench of the place, the bad air laced with shit and vomit from an overflowing bucket in one corner. Flies buzzed about the rim, feasting on the filth. The reek of it hit me each time I passed by. And yet I could not stop *pacing*, around and around, restless in my confinement, angry at the injustice. And afraid, yes – to my very soul.

As I paced I tried to find a solution to my troubles, but my mind kept wandering back to Kitty. I was worried about her, alone with Gonson's guards. Would they have left by now? But then what of Fleet's men? What if they were waiting for just that opportunity to attack? I kicked the wall in impotent fury. How could I protect her when I could not even protect myself?

The candle died and the room returned to darkness. I felt my way to the small bench and waited.

At last the door opened and Mr Rewse, the governor, stood in the doorway. His twin keys of office hung from a ring attached to his sagging belt. They were huge – over a foot long and at least an inch thick – and clanged together when he moved.

He crinkled his nose. 'Fie, it stinks in here,' he muttered, as if this were nothing to do with him. He waved me out into the corridor and led me to his own private lodgings close by. A chink of hope opened in my heart. Had the queen used her influence again? Was I to be released?

Rewse ushered me into a snug, pleasing room with good furniture, paintings and sketches upon the wall, embroidered cushions. Evidence of a Mrs Rewse, I supposed. 'Call for me when you're done, sirs,' he said, then bowed and left.

John Eliot – Kitty's lawyer – stood with his back to the blazing fire. He smiled briefly, but his eyes were grave. Any dreams I'd had of rescue sputtered and died in that one look.

He clasped my shoulder. 'Hawkins.'

'Kitty—'

He squeezed my shoulder with his pudgy fingers. 'Quite safe.'

'Thank God. I'm innocent, sir. I swear it.'

'Of course.' The kindness and trust in his voice broke me in a way Crowder's club never could. Tears sprang in my eyes. I brushed them away roughly.

We sat down by the fire and I fortified myself with a bottle of burgundy Eliot had brought for the purpose. He asked if I had discovered anything of use during my own investigation, but there was little I could offer without plunging us all into even greater danger. I could scarcely admit that Sam had murdered Joseph Burden. I feared for my life in here as it was, locked up with half of London's villains. One or two must belong to Fleet's gang. If I peached on Sam, or Fleet himself, I would not survive the night, and nor would Kitty.

Nor could I implicate anyone else, not with good conscience. And even if I did, who would believe me? I was the most obvious suspect.

Burden had accused me of murder. I had threatened him the

night before he was killed in front of half the street. My only defence had been that the house was locked, with no way in or out. Now that Ned had found the passage, how could I *possibly* be innocent? Eliot did his best to strengthen my spirits, but I was not a fool. If my case came to trial, I would be convicted and I would hang.

I put my head in my hands, rubbing my scalp. In the tumult of the last few days I had not found the time to visit the barber, and my hair was growing back. I must shave it. There would be lice in this prison, rats in every corner, and fleas in the sheets too, no doubt. Oh, God. I had thought I'd left all this behind. At least I could not catch gaol fever a second time. Yes – what excellent news. There was every chance I would live long enough to be hanged from the neck.

'I've spoken with Rewse,' Eliot said. 'He can offer you a decent room by the Press Yard. It's part of the Keeper's House. For the better sorts of prisoner.' He coughed, embarrassed. 'You will have more privileges than most. Light, good air, the yard for walking. And you will not be chained. That is good news, is it not? It will not be so very bad.'

'How much will this cost?'

Eliot worried at his lip.

'How much, sir?'

'Ten shillings a week,' he confessed. 'But you know, sir – Kitty would spend her last farthing to secure your comfort.'

Ten shillings a week. I could rent half an inn for that. 'How does she fare, sir? Are you *sure* she is safe?'

'I'm sure she is,' Eliot replied, puzzled. 'Why would she not be?'

My stomach knotted. She had been spared so far, but for how long? 'She must be protected, Eliot. You must see to it.'

'Why, is she in danger? My God, what has happened, sir? What is it you are hiding from me?'

I must find a guard to protect Kitty – and Alice for that matter. Someone strong, and skilled with a blade. But how could I trust such a man under my roof, with Kitty? I couldn't. And then I smiled. Not a *man*. But a woman . . .

It took me a while to persuade Eliot that hiring an Irish gladiator called Neala Maguire to guard the house was not some garbled act of lunacy, but I pressed him on it until he capitulated. 'And you must advise Kitty to send Sam home at once. It would not be seemly for him stay now.'

'Seemly . . .?' Eliot raised an eyebrow. Behaving in a *seemly* fashion had never been a great priority of mine. And given that Kitty had been living – unwed – with a man now accused of murder . . . But he saw I was determined, and what did it matter to him if some boy from St Giles was sent home or not?

Once I had persuaded him and he had given me every possible assurance that he would comply, I felt my spirits lift a little. If we could all survive tonight, we might still find a way to resolve this. 'Mr Rewse was kind to lend us this room.'

Eliot sniffed. 'It's not for charity. Not yours, at least. He made a fortune out of Jack Sheppard. Paying visitors. They'd line up to peer through the grate. Rewse hopes you'll prove equally profitable.'

'Sheppard escaped prison four times. The whole town was obsessed with him. No one will pay to see me.'

'Forgive me, sir, but I fear you're mistaken. You're a gentleman. Young. Handsome. The details of your story – the fact that you insisted on investigating the case and interrogating Mr Burden's family. It will cause a sensation.'

My heart sank. I had seen this before. By morning there would be ballads and pamphlets and broadsheets about the murderous gentleman Thomas Hawkins. No matter if I escaped death, I would be branded for ever as an infamous monster.

'I have a message from Kitty,' Eliot said, more quietly. 'Gonson has her under guard at present – he wishes to question her tonight. But she said *she would bring the dress* tomorrow, at first light.' He paused. 'She's not planning to dress you as a woman and smuggle you out, is she? No, no – best not to say a word. It worked for Sheppard that time, I suppose . . .'

I sat back hard against the chair. Alice's dress. Yes – it might still work, we might still be able to swing the suspicion upon Alice. Her bloody clothes. Her appearance through the attic door, holding the knife. Sam and Kitty would bear witness to that. Was it not more believable that Alice had turned to Burden in bed and stabbed him? Given what he had done to her night after night? With the dress and the witnesses, it would make a good case.

A dark shadow settled on my heart.

Chapter Nineteen

There was no choice to be made. I could not send an innocent girl to the gallows just to save my neck. Yet still I didn't sleep that first night in gaol. A sly, insistent thought crawled through my mind, leaving a trail of poison. *Save yourself. Whatever the cost.*

It is a hard thing to hold a key in your hand and not turn the lock. It seemed to me that there were two of us in the cell that night. My true self, pacing the floor, banging my fist against the wall and cursing all the mistakes I had made. And then there was my shadow, who waited for daylight only to betray Alice and free himself. As the slow night hours passed, there were times when I was tempted to become that shadow. I would live. But as what? Not as the man who had entered this cell, that much was certain.

I was mortally afraid. I didn't want to die at the age of six and twenty. I didn't want my name cursed and spat upon, down through the ages. I didn't want my father to think I was a murderer.

My father. I groaned aloud at the thought of him. Three years ago, at our last meeting, we had thrown cruel, bitter accusations at one another and I had vowed never to see him again. Then last autumn, after my release from the Marshalsea, he had astounded me with a letter filled with regret and forgiveness. It had made me wonder if the stern, unyielding man I remembered was just a phantom. I had even contemplated returning home and joining the clergy – but I had been weak from gaol fever at the time. London was my home. *Kitty* was my home.

And so I'd stayed, translating whores' dialogues, drinking and gambling and growing bored with my cramped, narrow life. The same old traps into which I had fallen so many times. I'd written to my father once a week, telling him nothing of substance about my life. I would speak of the books I had read, or news from the court and the town. I would describe the streets and buildings growing up all around me, and the foreign travellers I met, passing through the city. My father would reply in a meandering scrawl I barely recognised, the effort clear in every line. That alone was enough to tell me what he never could put down upon the paper – that he loved me.

How I wished I could speak to him that long, cruel night! Not for counsel – I knew what I must do. Nor for his lectures, heaven help me – I'd heard enough of those over the years. What I yearned for was his comfort and reassurance. My father would understand and approve of my decision to save Alice, though it threatened my own life. And he would pray for me.

Kitty would never understand. She would throw Alice to a pack of starving wolves if she thought it would save me. True, she did not know for certain, as I did, that Alice was innocent. But did I honestly think that would have made a difference to her? The fact that I could ask the question and not know the answer was disturbing.

Alone in my cell I faced the bare truth of the matter at last. I must renounce Kitty, for her own sake. She loved me with a ferocity that made her reckless. It was a dangerous love – one she had risked her life for. One she had killed for.

I could become the shadow crouched waiting at the door. I could walk out of Newgate tomorrow and take up my old life. And an innocent girl would hang.

It had never been a possibility. My old life was gone. It had only ever been a short dream between two prisons. I must awake from that dream and accept my fate. The shadow lifted and dissolved.

Light filtered through the barred window, brightening the room. I could hear the swish and scrape of a broom as a maid swept the floor outside my cell. Morning. Kitty would be hurrying through the streets, a dress covered in thick bloodstains rolled up in her basket. Hurrying to save me, not knowing it was my turn to save her this time – her life and her soul.

I took a deep breath and readied myself, practising the words I must say until they fell easily from my tongue. When the turnkey arrived, I was ready, straight-backed and cool, with a hollow space where my heart had been.

'Are you turned *mad*?' Kitty hissed. She grabbed the edges of my coat as if hoping to shake the sense back into me. 'Tell him the truth, for God's sake.'

We stood in Mr Rewse's private room, a fire glowing in the hearth, tea and slices of pound cake upon the table as if we were visiting an old acquaintance. Kitty had unrolled Alice's gown and thrown it, triumphant, across the desk. It lay there for the governor's inspection, a nightmare of a thing mottled with rust-red stains. The heat of the fire had loosened the faint scent of stale blood into the air.

Rewse bowed over the dress, examining it with a mixture of revulsion and growing excitement. He scraped at a dried scab of blood, crumbling it between his fingers. He could charge visitors extra for this. 'You say this dress belongs to your maid?'

'Alice Dunn,' Kitty said, releasing me. 'We both saw her in it, the night Mr Burden was murdered. She escaped through the attic, holding the knife. Sir, this dress is proof that Mr Hawkins is innocent. You must summon Mr Gonson immediately. We will explain everything.'

She was holding on to his jacket now, pulling and twisting the material in her anguish. Stepping back out of the scene I could see her with the governor's eyes. She looked frantic and desperate and very young. He tugged his coat free and turned to me, not sure what to make of the story. 'Well, sir?'

I hesitated. Kitty began to shake. 'Don't,' she whispered. 'Please, Tom. Don't.'

'Mr Rewse, I wish this were true. But I cannot implicate a blameless young girl. I have never seen this dress before.'

Rewse inhaled sharply. 'Mistress Sparks. This was a wicked act . . .'

'The guilt is mine,' I replied. 'Miss Sparks is a foolish jade, easily duped. The dress was my idea. I grew afraid last night and in my fear I conjured up this story. But in the light of day . . .' I glanced at Kitty. 'I find I cannot throw the blame on to an innocent soul.'

Kitty stared at me, bewildered. 'Why do you say these lies? They will *hang you*, Tom. Please. *Please*. I cannot bear it.'

'You see, sir,' I said, forcing myself to ignore her. 'A pretty, empty-headed bauble. I fear she would do anything to protect me. Indeed I'm sure she would confess to the murder herself if she thought she might save me.'

'I suppose . . .' I could see him pondering his choices. Creating false evidence was a serious matter, but I had owned to it. He did not seem inclined to punish Kitty as well.

I drew him to one side. 'She believes herself in love, poor wretch. Makes fools of us all, does it not?'

His eyes softened. He gave a rueful nod.

I lowered my voice further. 'I would be most *grateful* if you could dismiss the entire matter.'

He sucked his bottom lip, hiding a smile. He had not missed the implicit bribe. Gratitude meant one thing in prison. Payment.

We shook hands – two men of reason who understood the frantic foolishness of young, heartsick girls. It was how Rewse saw the world, and I played upon it. One more lie and then I was done.

Kitty's face was very pale. She knew what I was about – she would have done the same for me if she could. 'I am not a fool. I am not *empty-headed*. I am telling the truth. I have another witness—'

'—Enough,' I snapped. '*Enough*, Kitty. Go home. And do not come here again.' I glanced at Rewse. 'I would be most obliged if you could escort Miss Sparks from the prison. I do not wish to see her again.'

I left the room without another word. Kitty gave a low, hollow moan of grief that echoed off the prison walls. Then silence. I asked the turnkey waiting outside to return me to my cell.

As we walked deeper into the prison, the walls began to press in upon me. I stopped and reached out a hand to steady myself, the stone cool and damp beneath my fingers. I had just destroyed my best – perhaps only – chance of release, but I knew I had made the right decision. If I had confirmed Kitty's story, Alice would have been found guilty. She would hang for it, without question. And then I really would be guilty of murder.

There was a cost, of course there was. That is the secret the priests and bishops never preach from the pulpit. They speak of the cost of sin with great relish, but they never admit there is a cost for virtue, just as painful to bear. I had lost my freedom and I had lost my love. I might even lose my life. And what had I gained in return? The right to look myself in the eye and say, 'I am Thomas Hawkins. I remain myself.'

Only two people could help me now. Queen Caroline was my best hope. She could not prevent the trial from going ahead but she might persuade her husband to grant a king's pardon – if she were so minded. I would not walk free – not from a sentence of death – but it could be commuted to seven years' transportation.

And then there was James Fleet. Dangerous, but not without power and influence. Would he come to my aid after all that had happened? Perhaps – if it were in his interest.

We had reached my cell. I leaned closer to the turnkey and murmured in his ear. 'I must send a message, in secret.'

The turnkey smiled.

How much simpler prison was, with money in one's pocket.

Fleet did not come at once. Let me stew for three days, the bastard. In the meantime, Mr Eliot helped me prepare for my trial. He was brusque with me now, conducting our business with a cold civility that wounded me, though I didn't show it. As I had been charged with murder, I must present my own defence at trial. Eliot could support me solely upon specific points of law. He brought me books and papers as I requested, but added no words of comfort or sympathy. I was the rogue who had broken Kitty's heart – ignored her visits and left her letters unread. He tried only once to speak of her, and I reacted angrily, ordering him from the cell. He never mentioned her again. After that I would sometimes catch him looking at me from the corner of his eyes, wondering and full of doubt. But I could not risk telling him the truth.

He did at least – unknowingly – perform one valuable service. Amidst a pile of letters to be delivered I tucked a short message to Mr Budge, offering my unwavering service to his mistress and begging for her aid. The next day came a response, of sorts. *All in hand. Be patient.* Eliot handed the note to me with the rest of my correspondence, not realising he was acting as messenger to the Queen of England.

It was a Sabbath when James Fleet visited me at last, and I had just returned from chapel. Half a dozen prisoners were condemned to hang on the morrow. They had sat together on a black bench in the middle of the room. The prison Ordinary, the Reverend James Guthrie, gave a tedious, hectoring speech. A few of the condemned wept, and one pissed himself – through fear or drunkenness I couldn't tell. The yellow stream trickled slowly across the flagstones as those nearest lifted their feet out of the way. I decided not to return to chapel.

James Fleet was waiting for me in my cell, smoking a pipe. He stood up as I entered, and we shook hands, warily. He sat back down on the bed while I leaned against the wall. It was a frosty morning and the chill of the wall against my back helped keep my senses sharp. I had slept poorly, these past days.

'I know Sam killed Burden.'

Fleet breathed out a long stream of smoke. Shrugged.

'You ordered him to do it.'

'He botched it. Should've used a pillow. Stifled the bastard. Coroner would have said he died in his sleep. But nine stab wounds . . .' He shook his head. 'No disguising that. He botched it.'

My hands curled into fists. Burden had held Gabriela down while she was cut and tortured. Sam had grown up with the scars of that night – the one on his mother's face and the ones she buried deep inside her. He'd heard her screaming in terror when she dreamed herself back in that room, night after night. And Fleet had used the hatred this had instilled in his son as a weapon.

What did he expect, sending Sam to live next door to Burden? Sam had killed the *bad man* – just not in the way Fleet had intended.

'I misjudged him,' Fleet said. 'But the boy had to start his trade somehow.'

I said nothing. I was struggling to breathe, I was so angry.

Fleet waited. He saw my bunched fists, he knew I despised him. He was not the sort of man to apologise or explain himself. He was not interested in arguing the morality of his actions with me. He had chosen to live his life this way a long time ago and I would not jolt him from it now. And of the two of us, who was faring better? Once this meeting was concluded, which of us would walk through the prison gate a free man?

'I've told no one,' I said at last.

'That's why you're still alive, Hawkins.'

I ignored him. 'I will remain silent on one condition.'

'Kitty,' he guessed.

'She knows nothing about Sam, or Gabriela. What happened at Aunt Doxie's.'

He flinched and looked away for a moment. Still angry after all these years.

'I will say nothing – to my lawyer, to the jury.' I pushed myself from the wall and crossed to the bed, forcing myself to sit down next to him as if we were easy companions. 'You know I would do anything to protect her, just as you protect Gabriela and your family. So let us be plain. As long as Kitty remains untouched, you have my silence.'

Fleet pulled the pipe from his lips and gazed at the tip of the stem. 'Could just kill you.'

'That is true.' I had prepared for this. I'd been waiting three days for him to visit me and had used my time wisely, considering every possible reaction.

'I have a man in here. One word and you'd find a knife between your ribs.'

'You could arrange that,' I agreed. 'But it would seem suspicious. The coroner would investigate.'

'Coroners can be bribed. And my man would die before giving up my name.'

'He would hang for it, though. You'd like to avoid that, I think?'

He took a final draw of his pipe, the tobacco crackling in the bowl. The smoke curled above his head. 'I have no wish to harm you, Hawkins. You're useful to me. I only kill for profit or protection.'

And for revenge.

He tapped my arm. 'Convince me.'

And so I made my case to a jury of one. I told him that I had broken all ties with Kitty – had not spoken or written to her since she'd visited with Alice's dress. She knew nothing – he could be sure of it. If she had even suspected Sam she would have told the world by now. Fleet accepted the truth of this. Kitty was not one to stay quiet, even if her life were at risk.

'I have sent a message to the queen. I have every hope she will arrange my pardon. When it comes, most likely I will be sent away on some service. Or transported, I suppose.'

'Hmm.' Fleet tilted his head from side to side, weighing these possibilities. 'Or you will hang.'

I shifted uneasily. I'd heard no more from Budge or his mistress – but the note had counselled patience. 'If I'm hanged then you will have no need to harm Kitty. You are fond of her, I think. Gabriela says you knew her as a baby.'

'Enough,' Fleet said, holding up a hand. 'Enough. Let me think.' He stared at the ground for a long, agonising pause. Then, with a sudden decisiveness, he tucked away his pipe and held out his hand. I shook it. He rose slowly, hands on his knees. He was getting old for a gang captain. He wouldn't last much longer, surely. That would be my mission in life, should the pardon come – to outlive James Fleet.

He banged on the door to attract the guards' attention. They were playing cards at the far end of the ward and it took a while to rouse them. Fleet, unconcerned, waited with his hands tucked in his pockets. 'You're treated well?'

'Tolerably.'

'Need anything?'

Not from you. Kitty was still paying Eliot's fees and – I presumed – all the other debts I was accruing in here. I doubted my bill came to more than a couple of guineas. I had lost my appetite in the last few days.

'Should have let the maid swing for it.'

'She's innocent.'

'So are you. Can't afford honour in this world, Hawkins. It'll kill you faster than the plague.'

Chapter Twenty

After that the days dragged on inexorably to trial. Gonson helped prepare the case against me and found a long line of outraged citizens to speak against my character. Most of them paid subscription to the Society for the Reformation of Manners.

There was no clear proof that I had murdered Burden. There were no witnesses to the murder. But I had threatened to kill him in front of a dozen neighbours, many of whom were willing to testify against me. Meanwhile, who could I ask to defend my honour? My father was too weak to travel, and my sister must stay with him. They both sent letters to the court, devastated and sorrowful and speaking of my kind and gentle nature. But what else could be said of me? I was a rake and a gambler, thrown out of the Church because of my scandalous behaviour. Most of my respectable friends had abandoned me years ago, and my new ones had vanished the second Gonson slapped the iron cuffs about my wrists.

I had two old friends I might have called on, given more time. One was in Scotland, entangled in business he couldn't leave. He wrote a letter in my defence – at the risk of his own reputation. The other – a friend from Oxford – was travelling on the continent. By the time the news reached him, my troubles would already be over, one way or the other.

And then there was my oldest friend, Charles – but we had not spoken since my time in the Marshalsea. *Charles.* I could not think of him. There was only misery and pain there – a black cloth thrown across our friendship for ever.

Kitty of course remained true, but I could not call upon her.

I was alone – and it did not suit me. I am a man who likes company, the noisier the better. Sitting alone in my cell day after day weakened my spirit and gnawed the hope from my bones. Yet I found I could not bring myself to speak with the other prisoners nor even venture into the press yard save to stretch my limbs. Buried in my narrow cell, I had become almost numb to my surroundings, as if hibernating from all my troubles. I had also lost my appetite, to the point that Mr Rewse grew concerned and sent a message to Eliot to pay me a visit. He looked tired – perhaps the new baby was keeping him awake. Dorothy had given birth the day after my arrest. More likely it was the strain of defending London's most notorious villain.

'Are you sick, sir?' he asked, drawing a chair to my bed. He did not show any signs of pity.

I lay listlessly upon the mattress, hand flung across my brow. How could I explain that I was grieving for Kitty, when I had pushed her so violently from my life? I knew she came to the gaol every day only to be sent away. She wrote to me each day too – bribing the turnkey to smuggle the letters straight into my hand. Each day I threw them into the fire without reading a word. 'Tell her this,' I told the guard as the flames licked the pages. 'Tell her she wastes her time and her money.' She had taken to writing messages upon the envelope, large capitals underlined. *READ THIS, DAMN YOU!* and *TOM – YOU MUST LET ME HELP, YOU STUBBORN BASTARD.* I loved her for it with all my heart. And tossed her words to the flames again.

'The town has turned against you,' Eliot said. He handed me a broadsheet he'd found pinned to the wall at Moll's. It described Burden's death in horrific detail – the nine stab wounds, the knife plunged into his heart, right to the hilt. Judith's desolate cries of 'murder' echoing in the night air, 'sending a chill to the soul of all Christianlike men who heard them'. There were sketches too. One showed my arrest, bare-headed and fighting the guards. Another showed the murder itself. The artist had drawn Burden in his bed, fast asleep. I stood over him, blade held high, about to strike. I looked demonic, lips pulled back in a horrible grin.

I crumpled the paper in my fist and collapsed back upon the bed.

Eliot leaned closer. 'Do you not see the danger you are in, Hawkins? For God's sake, man – what ails you? Why do you not defend yourself?' He lowered his voice. 'Are you guilty?'

I roused myself enough to glare at him. 'No.'

He snuffed in irritation. '*No*. Always *no* and nothing more. It is not enough, sir! Do you wish to hang?'

I covered my face in my hands. And despite my best efforts, I began to weep.

When I was recovered I rubbed my face and sat up. Eliot had not tried to comfort me, or offered any words of kindness, but his expression had softened a little. He picked up the crumpled broadsheet and smoothed it across his knee. 'We *must* counter this. Give me something to tell the town. Let them hear your defence.' He hesitated, cleared his throat. 'Mr Defoe has offered to visit you and write of your story . . .'

Daniel Defoe. Well, he had written Jack Sheppard's story – and made a tidy profit from it too.

'He is inclined to believe in your innocence,' Eliot said. 'The prosecution's case is weak. You are being tried by the town, Hawkins. Defoe could turn them about. Remember how the mob protected him when he was in the pillory? He wishes to speak with you and with Kitty—'

'*No.*' I sprang to my feet. If Fleet suspected that I'd engaged Daniel Defoe to tell the real story of Burden's murder, Kitty's life would be forfeit and so would mine. 'I forbid it,' I said fiercely. 'Do you understand, Eliot? Do not speak further with Mr Defoe, nor to anyone else.'

Eliot rose from the chair, baffled and frustrated. 'What ails you, sir? Kitty is convinced of your innocence, and yet you act as if you are guilty.' He sighed, puffing out his fat cheeks. 'I have practised law for over thirty years. I know when a man is hiding something. I am your lawyer, sir. I am bound to keep your secrets safe. You must trust me. You *must* tell me everything – or else I cannot help you.'

It was tempting. My God, how I longed to unburden myself at last. Holding in the truth was making me ill. My dreams were nightmares and my waking hours were worse. But I couldn't risk it. What if he told Kitty? What if he even hinted at the truth?

'There is nothing to tell. I am innocent. That is all.'

Eliot's shoulders sagged. 'I will visit again in the morning—'

'—No. No more visits, sir. I thank you, but we have no more to discuss.'

'Mr Hawkins! Your trial is set for the day after tomorrow . . .'

'I am quite aware of the date, sir.'

Eliot frowned. 'I think you are determined to hang,' he said, defeated. 'Well. Eat some supper, at least. And call for a barber, for God's sake. The jury expects to see a young gentleman on Thursday, not Robinson Crusoe.'

He left, no doubt cursing me under his breath. And who was I to Eliot, after all? Kitty's idle, drunken beau, a feckless rake who would squander her fortune if he could only get his hands upon it. He didn't know the iron core that ran through me.

Obstinate. Wilful. My father's favoured words for me as a child. I could waft happily through life when it suited me, but when I had set my mind upon something I could not yield – ever.

Still, Eliot's visit had not been without value. I could not risk selling my story to Mr Defoe, but if I might concoct a way to write it myself in secret, with close instructions for its safe-keeping … The thick, dank fog of melancholy that had surrounded me ever since I had arrived at Newgate dissolved a little. My future was no longer mine to shape – it rested in the hands of twelve men and one woman. But the past still belonged to me.

And so the day came for my trial – Thursday 26th February. I took Eliot's advice and called at dawn for the prison barber. He grumbled when he saw the thick black stubble that covered my scalp and face – I had not been shaved since my arrest. It took him a half-hour and three passes with the blade before he was done, and he charged double the usual fee for his trouble. Once he had left I dressed in my sober black waistcoat and breeches. I had no mirror and could only guess at my appearance. Judging from the way the clothes hung from my frame, I supposed I must be an alarming sight, gaunt and haggard. My eyes felt raw from lack of sleep. Well, there was nothing to be done – and indeed it would appear odd if I bounded bright-eyed into court.

My hands began to tremble as I wound my cravat and so I paused and sat down upon the bed. I had never felt so alone as in this hour. All my life I had sought the company of others, happy in a large, boisterous crowd. Now there was only silence and a cold cell. My friends were gone or unable to help. My family were many miles away. My sister had written several let-ters and I had wept over them all, knowing that she if no one else would always believe in my innocence. But how I'd shamed her!

How would she ever find a husband now, with such an infamous brother? My dear sister Jane – always so good to me. And here was her reward. I closed my eyes and imagined myself home, walking the old coastal path, the sea sparkling beneath an endless sky. A taste of salt and clean air on my tongue.

Someone began to play the fiddle in a neighbouring cell and voices filled the air, new words set to an old ballad.

>*Tom Hawkins was a parson's son*
>*With evil in his heart*
>*A deed most wicked he has done*
>*And so he'll ride the cart.*

>*He stabbed Jo Burden with his blade*
>*The blood is on his hands*
>*A noose old Hooper he has made*
>*The gentleman will hang.*

The key rattled in the lock and Mr Rewse stepped into the cell, a set of iron chains slung over his shoulder. He had let me live unfettered these past weeks, but now I must be chained again for all the world to see. I rose and let him fix the manacles to my wrists. *This is a play*, I told myself. *Act the part you have been given and you will be spared.* They led me through the ward, my fellow prisoners shouting and joking to one another as I passed. I had not tried to win friends in Newgate, keeping to my cell as much as possible. I had not repented, nor had I fallen in with the lower sorts who drank and whored their way to the gallows. Worst of all, I had continued to protest my innocence, which infuriated the good and the wicked alike. So there was no fellow-feeling as I walked through the gaol. They sang my ballad again to send me on my way, while the turnkeys chuckled to themselves.

I comforted myself with the knowledge that Budge was still endeavouring to secure my release. He had written again, briefly, to say that his mistress would prefer the matter to be resolved at trial and hoped that I would be set free without her aid. I wished that too, in the way one might wish one could fly or pluck gold coins from the air. Wishing would not make it so.

We took a passage beneath the street, connecting the prison to the Old Bailey. My chains clinked as we walked, the sound echoing through the tunnel. Eliot stood waiting for us at the other end.

'You look ill, sir.'

'You would have me skipping like a spring lamb, I suppose?'

'The King's Council has called Kitty to testify.'

I stared at him in horror. He seemed to draw some comfort from my reaction – proof that I was at least decent enough to care for Kitty's reputation. 'She wishes to speak in your defence. You may call her as a witness.'

I shook my head. God knows what she would be prepared to say in order to save me. Eliot sighed, as if he had expected my response. He seemed so dejected that on impulse I clasped his hands. 'Thank you, sir, for all you have done.'

He gave an exasperated laugh, as if to say – *you have let me do nothing.*

'You are a good man, Mr Eliot. And an excellent lawyer.'

'Aye . . .' He glanced towards the courtroom, where the judge and jury waited. 'But what sort of a man are you, Hawkins? I fear I cannot tell.'

And so we entered the court and the world knows what happened next. I will not write of it here. To place myself in that room again, the sweat pouring down my back, mouth dry, barely able to breathe with fear . . . and all about me the rows of spectators, half of them old acquaintances, all craning to get the best view as if this were the theatre and not my life. James Fleet was there, tucked quietly in the shadows, to be sure I behaved.

And on the front row, Charles Howard, face set throughout in grim, glowering concentration. When at last it was over and the verdict came down, he rose and picked up his hat, pushing past his neighbours to reach the aisle. I passed not two feet from him as the guards led me in chains back to prison. He smiled, teeth bared, but it was his eyes that I remembered, alone in my cell. Those terrible eyes, gleaming in cold triumph.

PART FIVE

THE
TRYAL

OF

THOMAS HAWKINS,

Gent. of SUFFOLK, lately of

Russell STREET

AT THE

OLD BAILEY;

On the 26th of *February* 1728.
Upon an Indictment for the Murder of

JOSEPH BURDEN, a master carpenter of
Covent Garden.

LONDON.
Printed for *E. Curll* near *St. Paul's*;
and Sold by the Booksellers of
London and *Westminster.*
1728. [Price 6*d.*]

. . .the Prisoner was brought to the Bar at 9 in the Morning, a very great and extraordinary Audience present; diverse Gentlemen of Distinction and a Crowd of Ladies. The Prisoner pleaded Not Guilty as at his Arraignment.

The Council for the Crown open'd the Indictment; setting forth, That the said *Thomas Hawkins*, gentleman and former Student of Divinity, being a Person of inhuman and cruel Disposition did Assault and Murder the said *Joseph Burden* in the Unfortunate Victim's own bed; and that the Prisoner did Stab him nine times with a great Dagger. And that the Prisoner did wound the said *Joseph Burden* with a fierce cut to the Heart, plunging the Blade to the very hilt and drawing forth great Geysers of Blood, by which the aforementioned soon died.

The King's Council proceeded to open, That the Prisoner at the Bar was well known to hold a great Loathing and Hatred of his Neighbour, and had been witnessed upon several occasions threatening to Strike and Murder the Unfortunate Deceas'd.

The Council continued, That the Prisoner had every means of entering his neighbour's home, which was upon Russell Street, having constructed a Secret and Ingenious Door between the attics, granting him Access whenever he so Wished. And thus the Prisoner had entered into the home of his Unfortunate Victim and murder'd him in an act most callous and cunning.

Following this Brutal Act the Prisoner compounded his crime and with Great Wickedness sought to place Suspicion upon innocent parties: *Stephen Burden* the son of the Deceas'd, *Judith Burden* who was his Daughter and *Ned Weaver*, his apprentice. That thus, despite a childhood bless'd with good Fortune and the best of Educations, the Prisoner shew'd himself to be not only a Cold and Pitiless murderer but also a Coward and a Liar, having no decency or honour.

To prove the Indictment, the Council for the King called several Witnesses.

The first was *Judith Burden*, daughter of the unfortunate deceas'd, who swore that *Hawkins* had threatened her Father upon several occasions. She depos'd that she had discovered the body of *Joseph Burden* on the morning of the 12th of January.

Being asked by the King's Council, Was he dead? She reply'd Aye, Aye and with a Knife in his Heart. At this she broke down. The Court call'd for a Cordial to ease her Nerves. When she was recover'd the King's Council asked, And what thoughts came to you when you saw your Father dead? And the witness reply'd that she thought *Mr Hawkins* had murder'd him, as he had promis'd. At which she broke down again.

The Prisoner at the Bar ask'd permission to question the Witness but the Court deemed that she was too much Distress'd, and that the Prisoner had question'd her close enough when he was at Liberty, to no avail. This Answer drew great Approval from the Audience gathered.

Stephen Burden, son of the Deceas'd, deposed that he heard the Prisoner threaten his Father on diverse occasions. That his Father held the strong conviction that *Hawkins* was a Violent and Dangerous man who frequent'd Brothels and Gaming Houses and consort'd with base Company, and that he was most Vex'd by his arrival in the neighbourhood. Being asked if his Father was afraid of the Prisoner, the Witness replied that he was, mortally afraid.

Hawkins asked the Witness if he had ever seen him strike his father, or shew any violence towards him. The Witness conceded he had not.

Hawkins. And did your Father not strike you often, and your sister?

The Witness did not answer. When prompt'd by the Court

he replied, Aye, but only for my Instruction and I am glad of it now.

Ned Weaver, a Carpenter and Apprentice to the Deceas'd, confirmed that the Body was discover'd by *Judith Burden*. He testify'd that the Prisoner had threaten'd his Master, but added that he was not himself, having taken a great deal of Liquor. He describ'd the Secret Passage between the Houses and agreed that the Prisoner had both the Wit and the Opportunity to kill *Joseph Burden*. The Witness added he did not believe there was ample Proof, nor did he believe it was in the Prisoner's Nature to Commit such a Foul deed. The Court interject'd that this was for the Jury to decide, and asked the Witness to step down.

The King's Council then call'd upon Diverse members of the Neighbourhood, including *Hannah Jenkins*, a Baker's Wife, *Everett Felblade*, an Apothecary and *Joshua Purchase*, a Gamester. All testified that the Prisoner had threatened great Violence against the Deceas'd and that there was the strongest Animosity between them. *Purchase* deposed that the Prisoner was well known about the Town as a Rake and a Gambler, who consort'd with lewd women and common Whores.

Hawkins asked if the Witness were not describing himself and half the Town with it, which drew much Laughter from the lower sorts in the Gallery. The Court called for Order.

Felblade, ask'd if he agreed with his Neighbour's testimony, said that in his Opinion all men were capable of Murder and *Mr Hawkins* no more than most.

Mrs Jenkins testify'd that after the Murder the Prisoner had impos'd himself upon the Family, Interrogating them in a Cold and Arrogant fashion. The Prisoner also insisted upon searching the House in a most Unseemly manner, causing great Distress to the poor Children of the Deceas'd. The King's

Council asked, Did the Prisoner Discover anything of Note to aid his Investigation?

Mrs Jenkins. He did not, Sir. And I hope he is Asham'd of his Wickedness.

The next Witness called was *Mr Gonson*, Magistrate for the Borough of Westminster and member of the Society for the Reformation of Manners. He testify'd in clear and well-documented terms how he had come to suspect the Prisoner and had indeed Detain'd him and question'd him closely upon the Matter.

Hawkins interjected, asking the Witness if he had not arrested him without just cause and subsequently order'd him chained to a wall and left for many Hours without food or water. The Witness replied that this was Regrettable but that the Prisoner had resisted his Arrest.

Hawkins. And for that I should be tortur'd and left to die of Thirst? To which the Witness acknowledg'd that he should have provided Water, but that the Circumstances had been of such an Extraordinary Nature he hoped the Court would forgive this brief lapse in Duty.

Hawkins. Pray tell me, Sir, upon God's oath, is the Evidence for this Case enough to Judge me?

Gonson. I believe that you are Guilty, sir.

Hawkins. It is not a question of Belief, sir. Is the *Evidence* sound?

After a long pause, the Witness answer'd that in his View, it could not perhaps be termed sound in its entirety. He added that the Prisoner had the Cunning and the Ability to make himself appear Innocent, when the World knew he was Guilty. He Describ'd to the Court how the Prisoner had defy'd the Law, escaping his just Imprisonment by calling upon powerful Friends.

Hawkins. If I have such Friends, why do I stand here Today?

Gonson. Perhaps they have Forsaken you, sir.

The Witness added that the Prisoner had been given Opportunity and Good Fortune and chosen to Squander these gifts. That he was a Man of diverse good parts and that his Disgrace was all the more Shocking for it. He suggest'd that the Prisoner was a stern Lesson for all young Men attract'd to a life of Dissipation and Sin. He counsell'd *Hawkins* to look upon this Trial as preparation for the Greater Trial he must face in the next life, or else risk Damnation. He urged the Prisoner to Confess and Repent and throw himself upon God's infinite Mercy.

The Prisoner stated once more that he was Innocent, and that it was not his Soul nor his Nature that was on trial. That he must be Judged upon the Evidence alone and that, as a man of the Law, the Witness had himself agreed there was no Case to Answer.

Gonson observed that the Prisoner shewed more Industry and Wit in Court than he had in life, and lamented a Life wasted in Gambling, Drinking and Carnal Pleasure.

The Prisoner reply'd with a pert Remark, which the Court struck from the Records.

The Council for the King then called *Alice Dunn*, a maid in the house of the Deceas'd at the time of the Murder. She confirmed that *Judith Burden* discovered the Body, but seemed most Agitated and Reluctant to answer the Questions put to her by the King's Council, which led to a severe Reprimand from the Court. Thus Chasten'd she confessed that the Prisoner knew of the Passage between the houses.

King's Council. Is it true you have since left the Household to act as servant for the Prisoner at the Bar?

Alice Dunn. Sir, I was hired by *Mistress Sparks*, who has treated me with great Kindness.

King's Council. Is it not the Case that you Seduc'd your old Master? Was not that the reason *Miss Burden* ask'd you to leave the household?

Alice Dunn. Sir, my Reputation—

King's Council. —The Witness will answer the Question.

The Prisoner at the Bar interjected, asking what Relevance this was, and that the Witness was not on Trial. He appealed to the Court that he had no wish for a Respectable young woman to be abus'd on his Account. After some Deliberation the Court order'd *Alice Dunn* to step down and the King's Council called its final Witness, *Catherine Sparks*.

Being ask'd how she came to know the Prisoner, the Witness reply'd, We met in the Marshalsea gaol.

King's Council. And you now live under the same Roof, at great Risk to your Reputation?

The Witness reply'd that it was her own house and that she might invite whoever she pleased to live in it with her.

King's Council. Do you share your Bed with the Prisoner at the Bar?

Cath. Sparks. That is no Business of yours, sir.

King's Council. It is well known about the Neighbourhood that you are a Notorious whore.

Cath. Sparks. If it is well known, why do you ask?

King's Council. The Witness will—

Cath. Sparks. —It is *well known* that the King's Council visits the [comment struck from the Record] three times a Week and likes to [comment struck from the Record] while being [comment struck from the Record].

The Court called for Order.

The King's Council moved that the Witness *Catherine*

312

Sparks be arrested following the Trial and Whipped for her Insolence.

The Witness observed that the King's Council was most Preoccupied with Flogging and [comment struck from the Record].

The Court ask'd the Witness if she were a Relative of *Nathaniel Sparks*, the celebrated Physician.

Cath. Sparks. He was my Father, sir.

The Court noted that he was a man of Honour and that it was a great Calamity to see his Daughter in such a Grave and Lamentable situation.

The Witness thanked the Court but declar'd that she was quite Content with her Life, save for her current Woes. She spoke at length of the Prisoner's Kind and Gentle acts towards her and diverse Others and swore that he was Innocent. She insist'd that the Prisoner was not capable of such a Bloody deed and that on the Night of the Murder he was in her Company at all times and Cou'd not have Done it.

The Prisoner interjected, reminding the Witness that she was speaking upon Oath and must not Perjure herself on his Behalf.

The Witness answer'd with great Vehemence that she was right Glad that the Prisoner troubled himself to Speak to her and was it not a Shame that he had not reply'd to her letters, and had refus'd to Meet with her despite her Many and Various requests to do so, giving no Consideration to her own Feelings upon the Matter, and moreover was it not a Folly that it took a Trial at the Old Bailey before he would speak two words to her and only then to Accuse her of Lying and so make further Trouble for them Both, and that she call'd upon the whole Court to Witness that the Prisoner had thus shew'd himself to be a Witless Fool and had indeed no Capacity for Murder not only because he had, she must concede, a Good Heart, but also a Muddled Head, to a Degree that was Vexing beyond all Measure, and it was truly a wonder he had surviv'd this long, and a marvel indeed that she yet cared a great deal for him – God help her – and begged that the Jury would Judge the case by its facts and not by the Prisoner's Behaviour, which was Perplexing and Infuriating in equal Parts. And she ask'd the said Prisoner if he had turn'd mad, and should be locked in Bedlam instead of Newgate, and did he not see that her Heart was Broken? At which point she Wept most Piteously, and the Prisoner seem'd much affected, though he did not Reply.

The King's Council, who had failed to Interrupt this testimony at Several Junctures, took this opportunity to dismiss the Witness, who was led away by *Alice Dunn*.

The Court observ'd that it was a great Pity to see such a spirited young woman ruined by a Black-Hearted villain, and that here was Instruction for any foolish Strumpet who had fallen into evil company. The Court then spoke thus:

Prisoner, you hear the Charge and Evidence against you; now you stand up on your Defence.

Prisoner. My Lord: notwithstanding what has been sworn against me, I am Innocent. I confess I did threaten the deceas'd but this was done in a moment of ill humour and under much provocation and also Liquor. The deceas'd had spread Vile lies about the Town and had threaten'd to Destroy me. I am Guilty of speaking Violence, my Lord, but not of committing it. Indeed I have an abhorrence of Violence. I could no more stab a man than plunge the Blade into my own Heart.

My Lord, the King's Council has offer'd no proof that I committed the Act, only Rumour and Conjecture. I swear upon my Soul that I am Not Guilty and beg that the Jury considers the Facts and does not Judge me upon my Character, for I own that I have not always Behav'd with Good Judgement, and should I be spared will Strive to be a better Man, God help me.

The Court asked if the Prisoner still believed the Murder was committed by one of the children of the Deceas'd, or by *Ned Weaver*, his Apprentice?

The Prisoner reply'd that he did not. He acknowledg'd that in his Desire to prove his Innocence he had caused Distress, and express'd his Apologies to the family. He added that it was his belief that a House breaker had stolen in and disturb'd the Victim, and so murder'd him in cold blood.

Council for the King. And how does the Prisoner account for the Doors and Windows being barred and lock'd?

Hawkins. I cannot account for it, sir. I am at a loss. But I swear I am Innocent.

The Court asked if the Prisoner wished to call upon any witnesses to speak in his defence?

Hawkins. I regret that I have no witnesses to call, my Lord.

The Court observed that a Man with no Friends or Family to speak for him at such an Hour was a pitiable Wretch indeed and the Jury should consider this Fact when they came to Deliberate: that the Prisoner could not find one Soul in the whole Kingdom to speak for him.

And here the Prisoner rested his Defence.

The Court then proceeded to sum up the Evidence to the Jury with great Discernment and Observation. The Guilt or Innocence of the Prisoner was left to the Jury's Determination, who did not leave the Court but agreed after a brief time upon their Verdict, finding Thomas Hawkins Guilty of Murder; and the Verdict was so Recorded.

FINIS

Chapter Twenty-One

The jury found me guilty. Twelve gentlemen, who cared so little for my defence that they did not even deign to leave the courtroom to deliberate. A hurried discussion, curt nods, and it was done. I have sat with friends and agreed supper plans with more care and scrutiny.

Friends. The judge had spoken the truth – what good was a man with no one to speak for him when his life hung in the balance? I had spied a few of my old companions in the crowds, watching me fight as if it were a game of skittles. No doubt they would be placing bets on how soon I would hang. These were the men I had called friends these past few years. Not one had spoken for me.

The guards led me through the courthouse, men jeering at my back. I barely heard them, barely noticed as I was taken deeper into the gaol, back to my cell with its thick stone walls and tiny window. I thought of Kitty, weeping as she left the court, her head buried on Alice's shoulder. I saw Fleet nod his approval as I was dragged away, our business concluded. And I thought of Charles Howard, smirking with satisfaction. Fleet and Howard . . . These are the men who prosper in our age.

I collapsed to the floor, dazed with shock. I had prepared for this moment and still it knocked me reeling. *Guilty.* Condemned for ever as a murderer. My heart felt like a brick lodged in my chest.

I sat unmoving as the day faded and the shadows lengthened. A cold wind blew through the window so I dragged the blanket from the bed and wrapped it about my shoulders, but it was thin and offered little comfort. At some point a voice asked if I wished for supper, but I could not bear the thought of food, not tonight. I rubbed my eyes with the heel of my hand, exhausted beyond all measure but unable to sleep.

My thoughts returned to Kitty, dressed in her emerald gown, her face drawn. She had seemed thinner too, her cheekbones sharp where before they had been soft and plump. She had stared at me, hoping to see beyond the mask of indifference I wore. I had forced myself to stare back, eyes cool, my true feelings buried far beyond reach.

I reached for them now, though. I clung to them in the dark. They were all I had left.

The next day I had a visitor – and she brought hope at last.

Betty appeared at my cell late in the evening, her face hidden beneath a dark riding hood. She must have bribed the turnkey on duty for his silence. He reached to grope her arse as she slipped through the door but his fingers grabbed thin air. Betty had worked at Moll's for two years – she knew how to avoid a man's grasp and make it appear an accident. That, indeed, was Betty's great skill – twisting and turning and dancing out of harm's way, without ever causing offence or bringing attention down upon her head.

The door clanged shut and we were alone. She lowered her hood but wrapped her cloak tightly about her. The air was cold and dank even in this gentlemen's part of the gaol. She took in the limits of my cramped cell, and my ragged appearance, eyes ringed with shadow from another sleepless night. The man in the next cell had been raving all night in some feverish delirium, screaming that he was in hell and begging God to spare him. Then he was quiet. I had lain in the dark with no candle, the silence heavy and oppressive. It was so black and still that I conceived a strange fear that I was already dead and trapped inside my coffin. When dawn came, I felt a moment's relief to know I was alive, before I remembered where I was.

Betty lowered the heavy basket she had brought with her and began to unpack it. Bread and cheese, a bottle of claret. Candles. Paper, quills and ink. A few books. A thick blanket. I snatched this eagerly. 'Thank you.'

She winced and looked away, embarrassed to see me so desperate, but there was nowhere to rest her gaze. A narrow cell, a bed, a table and chair. Names scraped into the thick stone wall by other wretched souls.

VALENTINE CARRICK 1722
L. NUNNEY 20yrs GOD SPARE MY SOUL
ABRAHAM DEVAL – INNOCENT

All hanged.

I looked at Betty and she looked at me, just as we had done the night we'd first met. We had laughed at each other across that crowded room. Now we stood in an empty cell, in silence.

Betty worked long hours at Moll's, but I had never seen her so tired as she was now. Her brown skin was dull and tinged almost grey, as if she had been ill, and her eyes were bloodshot. Had she been crying? For me?

She ran a finger beneath her cap, tidying her curls. 'I have good news.'

This was unexpected. If the news were good, why did she seem so grave?

'Mr Budge has spoken with the queen. You will be pardoned.'

It took me a moment to understand that I was saved. Then I gave a cry and dropped to my knees in joy and relief. I could not think or speak. Betty knelt down next to me, peering into my face. 'Mr Hawkins?'

I clasped her to me, circling my arms about her waist. 'I will live.'

She let me hold her for a time. 'There is a cost.'

My heart dipped. She did not need to explain. The queen could ask anything of me now, and I must obey. And still the verdict would remain. Even with the pardon, I would be named a murderer for the rest of my life. I did not care, not then. I wouldn't hang – and that was all that mattered. 'I will *live*, Betty.'

She tilted her head as if to say, *in a fashion*. She had warned me that this day would come. I had not run when she had begged me to, and now my life was no longer my own. But it was a *life*. There would be a tomorrow and a tomorrow . . . And the chance to wriggle out of the queen's grasp one day.

Betty returned to her basket and laid out a modest supper. She poured us both a glass of claret and we sat down together like an old married couple.

'When will the pardon come?'

'I don't know. Late, I think. Budge said you must be patient.'

I lowered my glass. 'I am sentenced to hang in ten days.'

Tears sparkled in her eyes. She seemed so anxious that I found myself trying to reassure her, acting in a more confident manner than I felt. I lit a pipe and told her of my plans to write a full confession of all that had happened to me, in the hope that one day it would help to clear my name. She did not ask why I did not speak out now and save myself – Betty did not ask questions when she knew there could be no answers. She promised to find a way to smuggle the journal from my cell when it was done, and to keep it hidden. I trusted her to read it and to understand its secrets – to know when it would be safe to pass it on to those who should know the truth.

I took Betty's hand, unable to speak for gratitude. How many nights had she served me my punch and lit my pipe these past two years? Always quiet, always watching, anticipating what I needed. A bowl of strong coffee, most days – and a kick on the arse. She had sent me home more times than I could remember, while I protested I was good for one more drink, one more card game, one more throw of the dice. Now here she was when all my friends had abandoned me.

She slipped her hand from mine.

'Don't leave,' I said, and my voice crumbled. 'Please.'

She hesitated. Shifted closer. It was enough. I gathered her in my arms and held her as if she were a rock in the ocean, the only safe harbour for a thousand miles. Found her lips and kissed her, because I was lost and afraid. Because Kitty was so far beyond reach.

A key rattled in the door. 'Gate's closing,' the turnkey hissed.

Betty took my arm, whispered in my ear. 'If you find another way to escape, take it.'

I nodded, though we both knew the pardon was my only hope.

She raised her hood, masking her face from the turnkey. Her eyes were soft and sad. 'Fare well, Tom.'

I gave a low bow; lower than I would have given the queen. By the time I looked up, she was gone.

*

Tom. Only now, as I write down Betty's last words to me, do I notice it. She had never called me by my Christian name before. I was always *sir*, or *Mr Hawkins*. We might flirt and tease, but I was never *Tom*. I stare at my name on the page and I wonder about her visit. Was it truly a kindness? Or something more devious?

Well, Betty – am I right to doubt you? Nine days I have waited for the king's pardon. Nine sleepless nights. When the waiting became unbearable, I began to write this account as a distraction, from the first moment I heard Alice Dunn scream *Thief!* until this moment here, remembering that final kiss and the look in your eye when you called me by my name. *Fare well.*

Now, on the eve of my hanging, you send word at last – *Be patient*. Always the same message. Will the pardon come on the morrow, as they load me on the cart? Or is this merely a cunning way to keep me quiet until the hangman silences me for ever? Tell me – if I smuggle these pages to you, will you truly keep them safe? Or will you burn them and all the queen's secrets with them?

I hope, my dear, that you have not betrayed me.

I had planned to end my story here. I have spent so much time writing that I have neglected everything else. My hand is cramped from long hours holding a quill, my fingers stained indigo-black with ink. My past is written, but at the expense of my soul. Three others are set to hang with me tomorrow. While I have sat scribbling in my cell, they have spent long hours praying and begging God's mercy for their sins. They are ready for their journey.

In vain the Reverend James Guthrie has visited me each day. He is a pompous man, well-pleased with himself. No, that is not just. He has rescued countless souls from damnation. I only wish he did not brag about it quite so much.

It is Guthrie's duty to write an account of every prisoner hanged at Tyburn. He recounts their short, squalid lives with gleeful disapproval, then casts himself as their saviour. By the time they reach the gallows they are weeping with gratitude. They rejoice at their redemption, eager to leave this world so that their souls might fly to heaven.

These, at least, are the stories Guthrie likes to tell. There are some obstinate sinners who refuse to play his game. They repent in private or not at all – drinking and whoring their way through their final days. He does not like these stories so well, but he can still bend them to his use. Examples of the witless fools who will burn in hell for their ignorance and obstinacy.

But what is he to do with a man such as me? A man who refuses to confess? Who protests his innocence, even as he is led to the gallows? There can be no repentance without guilt. No *salvation* without guilt. Instead there is only doubt, thin but persistent. *What if we are wrong? What if we are hanging an innocent man?*

There are no lessons to be learned from such a story. At least, not the sort of lesson the Reverend James Guthrie wishes to teach.

Guthrie visits my cell not to offer comfort, but to seek resolution. And every day I disappoint him. He tells me I am bound for hell. I correct his quotations from the Bible. He reminds me that Pride is the greatest of all sins, and leaves.

What will he write of me, I wonder?

This afternoon I summoned John Eliot and directed him to write my will. I do not have a great deal of capital – ten pounds at most. It should be enough.

When I named the beneficiary of my meagre fortune, Eliot raised his eyebrows in surprise. 'How will I find the boy? He's disappeared.'

'Aye. He's good at that. He'll magick himself back once I'm gone.'

Eliot scratched the name onto the paper with a reluctant hand. *Sam Fleet of St Giles, nr Phoenix Street.*

Sam has not quite disappeared. I know this because he came to visit me this morning.

I was sitting alone on a bench in the press yard. I had paid Mr Rewse a bribe so that I might have some time to myself in the open air. I think he did it out of kindness as much as profit. Since my conviction, Rewse had allowed dozens of curious souls to tramp past my cell. They'd peered in through the grate, eager to see the gentleman as beast, trapped in his cage. They gossiped about me as if I could not hear or understand them. If I turned away it must be out of shame. If I held their gaze, they swore they saw the devil in my eyes. If I covered my face, or paced about the cell, or stared gloomily at the cold stone floor, then I must be in despair at my guilt, and the wretched state of my soul. Not one of them thought I looked innocent.

Mr Rewse was different. He has met more cut-throat villains than anyone in England. I am no murderer, and he knows it. He also knows the way of the world. He won't help me, but he is courteous, regretful. When I asked if I might sit in the yard for a while on my own he agreed and sent the turnkey to escort me out just before the dawn. I watched the light spread across the sky and felt the early spring sunshine upon my face. I closed my eyes. A few hawkers were calling their wares on the other side of the wall, but otherwise the city was at peace. And for once I liked it better that way.

'Your cousin,' the turnkey said.

I opened my eyes and there was Sam. He looked smaller than I remembered, and younger, more like the link boy who had scampered through the streets than the young man I'd come to know at the Cocked Pistol.

The turnkey strode away, calling over his shoulder. 'One half-hour.'

I had spent a great deal of time wondering what I would say to Sam should I ever see him again. I had ridden the waves of my feelings like a raft upon the ocean. Anger at his betrayal, naturally. Shame too, that I had let a boy of fourteen fool me for the second time. Most of all, I felt a profound sorrow for us both. I would most likely die for Sam's crime tomorrow. But he would have to live with it.

He was a boy – a clever, capable boy. Had he been born into a different family I was sure he would not have killed Joseph Burden – nor anyone else for that matter.

I gestured for him to sit, but could think of nothing to say. And so we sat in silence for a long time.

'Mr Hawkins,' he said at last. He twisted his body so that he could look hard into my eyes. 'I am very sorry.'

To my surprise, it was enough. And a whole sentence, indeed – what progress! I put my hand on his shoulder. 'You still have a choice, Sam. Even now. You do not have to follow your father's path.'

His shoulder sagged beneath my hand. It must seem impossible – a prison he could never escape.

'You know, my father wanted me for the Church. I defied him.'

Sam glanced at me, and then up at the walls around us, and the high windows barred with iron.

'Yes, very well. Perhaps I am not the best example.'

His lips twisted into a half-smile.

I lit a pipe, thinking about Sam and wondering how I might help free him from his father's murderous grip. My own life was ruined, but there was a chance I could save Sam's. Wouldn't that be the greatest revenge upon James Fleet? To turn his only son against him?

'If you could do anything in the world, Sam – any occupation you wished. What would you choose?'

'Surgeon,' he replied, without hesitation.

I was pleased with his answer. It seemed fitting somehow, that he should atone for the life he took by saving others.

'I'd study the body,' Sam added, eyes brightening. 'Every detail. I think it is like . . . like a wondrous machine. Imagine – a corpse, its parts cut free, laid out and—'

'—yes, yes,' I said hurriedly. If I hanged on the morrow, and no one rescued my body from the anatomists, this would be my fate. The very thought left me light-headed. 'A surgeon. Very good.'

'Pa would never allow it.'

I smiled to myself. *Precisely.*

The bells of St Sepulchre sounded across the yard. Sam rose and straightened his jacket, squinting in the sun. 'Mr Hawkins. Did you do it, sir?'

I frowned at him, confused. He could not mean . . .

We stared at each other. As the seconds passed and the bells tolled, confusion turned to horrified understanding. No. *No.* Not possible. 'What do you mean?'

'Did you kill Mr Burden?'

I half rose to my feet, then sat down again, hard. I didn't know what to do or what to say.

Sam saw my consternation. 'You think *I* killed him?'

'You did not?'

'No.' He winced, as if ashamed.

'You swear, upon your soul?'

'I swear, sir.'

I lowered my head, trying to think, but all was confusion. How could this be? It made no sense. It wasn't possible. 'But your mother told me . . . your *father* says you are guilty.'

He bit his lip. 'I know. I told them I done it.'

I sprang to my feet and he leaped back. My God he was fast when he needed to be. There were ten paces between us before I could reach out and grab him. 'Why?' I cried. 'Why in God's name would you say such a thing?'

'I was supposed to kill him. Pa told me I had to. And . . . I *wanted* to . . .'

'For your mother.'

Tears glimmered in his eyes. 'And for Pa. He was proud of me, when I told him. And the gang. They respect me now.'

I think if Fleet had walked into the yard at that moment I would have beaten the life out of him. 'And what – you're content to see me hang, boy? So you might strut about St Giles?'

'No, sir!' he cried. 'Pa swore you'd be safe. He *promised*. Said he'd paid you fifty pounds to stand trial. He said he was going to help you escape tonight, that it was all planned. He said you was angry with me. That I mustn't come here . . .'

'That is not the deal we made, Sam. He threatened Kitty's life.'

He flinched, as if struck.

'That's why I stood trial for murder. To keep Kitty safe.'

He covered his face with his hands. 'No . . . he wouldn't. Pa wouldn't . . .' But of course, he would – and Sam knew it. I reached out and he clung to me, weeping in my arms. 'He lied,' he sobbed. 'He lied to me.'

'This is *good* news, Sam. You are not a murderer.'

He broke free, wiping his eyes. 'But it's my fault you're here.'

No, it is your father's, I thought, but he seemed so dejected I held my tongue. I sat back down upon the bench and he joined me, elbows on his knees, head down.

'If I'd done what I promised. If I'd took the pillow and . . .'

And smothered a man to death. 'But Alice was there.'

He nodded, miserable. 'Tried to practise on Jenny. See how much noise it took to wake a girl. You can get quite close, Mr Hawkins,' he added conversationally, as if describing the best way to approach a nervous horse. 'Tried again, but Alice woke. Sleeps light. Screamed the house down.'

There was more he wanted to say; I could see the struggle in him. I waited, letting him find his way through it. 'Mr Hawkins,' he confessed at last, in a whisper. 'I'm *glad* Alice woke. I'm glad now, that I never killed Mr Burden.'

I squeezed his shoulder.

'I think she done it,' he added. 'Alice.'

I froze. I had not even thought so far. I was still learning to accept the fact that Sam was innocent. But no, please God – not Alice, after all. Not Alice, sleeping under the same roof as Kitty. With her bloodstained gown dismissed as evidence by my own hand.

'Sir,' Sam said, tugging at my sleeve. 'What now?'

What indeed.

'I must tell Pa—'

'No! No. Let me think, Sam.' I shuffled the possibilities in my head. It was too late to accuse Alice. I had told Rewse that the dress was a counterfeit. That Alice's appearance in our house on the night of the murder was a story, nothing more – told to cast doubt on my own guilt.

And how would I explain this sudden change in my confession, to Rewse, to Guthrie or Gonson – to the world? *Ah, yes, sirs – I was led to believe that a young boy called Sam Fleet had murdered*

Mr Burden, at the request of his parents. I then struck a deal with the boy's father – who is, by the way, a murderous gang captain – to stand trial for the murder. I was coerced into this agreement by Mr Fleet, who promised to kill the woman I love if I did not comply with his wishes. So you see – I am quite innocent and I trust you will now release me at once, although I have been convicted of murder and am set to be hanged on the morrow.

They would not believe a word of it. It would sound like the desperate ravings of a mad man. I would be mocked and dismissed as a coward and a lunatic. Nothing worse than a man who cannot go to his death with dignity. And could the queen risk sending a pardon under such circumstances? And of course, for my story to make even a hint of sense, I would have to betray Fleet to the authorities. Such a betrayal would bring swift retaliation.

Kitty.

No, there was nothing to be gained from telling the truth – and a great deal to be lost. I must stay silent, at least for now. But it gave me a glimmer of hope, that she would be safe after tomorrow. If I was hanged, the killer would have no reason to feel threatened by Kitty. If the pardon came, the sentence would still be placed upon my name. And as Sam was innocent, Fleet would have no need to fret about what Kitty might say on the matter.

'You have trapped yourself, sir,' Sam said, when I had explained it all.

'I suppose I have.'

'*Love*,' he said, as if it were some exotic disease. 'Dangerous.'

Yes, indeed. But hopefully not fatal.

From the corner of my eye I saw the turnkey step into the yard. My fellow prisoners edged out through the door, blinking at the sun.

'Don't worry,' I whispered, guiding Sam from the yard. 'I will not hang tomorrow.'

'The queen?'

I halted. Was a man allowed *no* secrets, damn it?

'The walls are thin at the Pistol.'

'Aye, especially with your ear to them.' I cuffed him lightly. I'd only spoken of the queen to Kitty. Alone in our bed. What else had he heard? Little sod.

As we reached the edge of the yard, he hesitated. 'Mr Hawkins, sir,' he said, shyly. 'I think you would have made a good parson.' He gave a short bow and vanished through the door.

Who killed Joseph Burden? I cannot believe I have reached the end of my story and still cannot fathom the answer. Not Sam, after all. Then who? Those old names I had rejected return to haunt me. Ned Weaver. Stephen Burden. Judith Burden. And Alice Dunn – I suppose I must consider her again. Any one of them could have done it. And every one of them had good cause.

I cannot believe it was Ned. He does not strike me as the sort of fellow who could let another man hang for his crime. He does not strike me as the sort of fellow who would murder a man, either.

Kitty had been certain it was Judith. There was enough anger in her, true enough. But was there enough *strength* in her to fight her father? To stab him nine times before he could even call for help?

Stephen had the most to gain. With his father dead he thought he would inherit a fortune. And though in truth he had inherited nothing, at least he was free to live as he chose after years of oppression and cruelty.

Then there was Alice. Was this not the simplest explanation? She had stumbled into Sam's attic room covered in blood and holding a knife in her hand. Burden had raped her, night after night. And yet he had also vowed to marry her, and she had said yes. She would have been mistress of the house. Mistress over Judith.

I have spent the night pacing my cell, turning these thoughts over and over until they have become tangled together in an endless jumble of possibilities. My God, the four of 'em might have done it together for all I know.

I can think on it no more. I can do no more. There is no time left to reflect upon the sins of others. In a few hours they will sling me on a cart and drag me through the streets to Tyburn. I must tend to my own soul.

Even now, on the day of my hanging, I cannot believe that things have come to such a pass. Surely I will wake from this nightmare and find myself at home in the Cocked Pistol, with Kitty beside me. She will roll upon her side and put a hand upon my cheek. And she will say, 'Be still, Tom. You're safe. You were only dreaming.'

Then I press my fingers to the thick walls of my cell. I drum my fists against the stone. This is real. This is real and I must prepare myself for the worst. If the king's pardon does not come, I must be ready.

God forgive me. Father forgive me. My beloved sister Jane: your brother loves you always.

Kitty. If I live, read this and know that I am out in the world somewhere, thinking of you. Maybe you and Sam can discover Burden's killer together. But keep safe, above all. I fear you should not trust Alice. I fear you should not trust anyone.

And if I should die today, know that my last thoughts were of you. Live well, my love, and remember me.

Hooper, the hangman, climbs down from the gallows and pulls the pipe from his lips. He gestures to Hawkins' wig. 'I'll need to take that now, sir.' The air chills his bare scalp. Hooper pats his arm, surreptitiously stroking the blue velvet of his coat. These clothes will be his payment, when it is over.

He ties the rope around Hawkins' neck. The knot presses tight against the back of his neck.

From the cart, Hawkins can see thousands of men and women, stretching out to the horizon. Every eye is turned upon him. The air is hot with sweat and dirt and perfume. The noise is deafening, it rolls over him and thrums beneath his feet. People are singing and shouting. Some are laughing. A few good souls are praying for him. It does not seem real. Even now, some small part of him is sure they will realise their mistake. That they are hanging an innocent man.

'Confess!' someone cries.

A cheer rises up to shake the heavens. This is what they want from him. This is the story they demand of Tyburn. Crime. Confession. Repentance. Death. Salvation. They wait, expectant.

The noose is rough about his throat. It chafes his skin as he cries out. 'I am not guilty!'

Boos. Jeers and catcalls. Mud flung at the cart. Hooper ducks, eyeing the blue velvet tenderly. 'Better confess, Mr Hawkins. It's what they want.'

Hawkins sighs. What does it matter now what the crowd wants from him? But then he thinks of them all, a hundred thousand souls laughing and jeering as he dies slowly on the rope. It could take a man a quarter-hour to die. It would be better, he thinks, to be cheered out of this world than cursed from it.

So – it is a confession they demand of him. Very well. He takes a deep breath and begins to speak. 'My friends. Upon my soul. I confess …' The crowd screams its approval. He shouts to be heard above it. ' … I confess that I have lived a wicked life. Immersed in every vice.'

A few groans, but more laughter. A spattering of applause. The court beauties lean forward in their seats.

'I confess that I am a gambler. I confess that I am over-fond of liquor and low company. I have wasted many nights in taverns and brothels and cannot say that I regret it. I confess that I broke a woman's heart – and that I do regret, more than anything in this world.' He swallows hard. The ladies fan themselves. 'I confess all these things. But I swear upon my soul, I am not guilty of murder.'

A cheer goes up, the loudest of the morning. He has won them over, now at the end, with the rope about his neck. They do not care if he is guilty or innocent. In the face of death, he has conducted himself well, with wit and swagger. This is a good dying. *And in the end, that's all that matters. Beneath him, a few paces from the gallows, he sees the Reverend James Guthrie shaking his head, face tight with disapproval. It is his duty to record the last confessions and dying words of the condemned. He will have to write these words in his own hand.*

This is the first cheerful thought Hawkins has had all day. He looks up at the gallery, at the rows of women. My God, all those women. His lips curve slowly in a wolf's grin. Let them remember that …

And then he sees her. Judith Burden. She is sitting in the middle of the gallery, black-gloved hands in her lap. She holds his gaze. Smiles.

His heart slams into his chest. That dress. That black, widow's gown. Of course.

'Wait!' he cries, but it is too late. Who would believe him now?

'Courage, sir,' Hooper murmurs.

The white hood slips over his head, rolls down until it covers his face. He breathes, and the air sucks the cloth against his lips. Courage. *Yes. That's all he has now. That and a few last, precious breaths. Use them well.*

He closes his eyes and thinks of Kitty. The fresh, sweet scent of her. Powder-white skin, smooth and soft as silk. Her fingers against his chest, her breath hot and urgent on his throat. A soft cry of pleasure.

He had this, at least, before the end.

The noose tightens about his neck.

God forgive my sins.

Someone pulls the horse forward. He feels the cart move beneath his feet. A moment later his body swings free.

THE BALLAD OF THOMAS HAWKINS

Tom Hawkins was a parson's son
With evil in his heart
A deed most wicked he has done
And so he'll ride the cart.

He stabbed Jo Burden with his blade
The blood is on his hands
A noose old Hooper he has made
The gentleman will hang.

They rode him off to Tyburn's tree
They led him to his death
They stretched his neck for all to see
He took his final breath.

All rakes and scoundrels, now I pray
You learn this lesson well
A gentleman was hanged this day
And now he burns in hell.

PART SIX

Chapter Twenty-Two

L ife. It rips through me.

As the air sucks into my lungs.

As the blood pulses through my veins.

Life. How it burns.

I open my eyes and see nothing. My arms are pinned to my sides, my knuckles pushed hard against solid wood. My fingers and toes are numb. I can feel movement beneath me, the roll and sway of a cart. We are travelling at a furious pace, hooves thundering on the cobbles, but I am held tight in the darkness. I try to move, and pain screams through my cramped muscles. I stop. Breathe. Take in the scent of wood, fine grains of sawdust catching my throat.

I am trapped in my coffin.

I kick out at the lid in a frenzy, crying for help. My voice is a thin rasp, my neck swollen and bruised. No one will hear me over the rattle of the cart. The memory of choking, flailing on the rope seizes me. I cannot breathe. I will suffocate alone here in the darkness.

Terror gives me back my strength. I kick harder and the wood splinters against my boot.

'*Quiet, damn you.*' A rough male voice. '*Lie still. If you want to live.*'

I fall back, panting heavily. I feel as if I have lain asleep without moving for a hundred years. I try to stretch, and my legs cramp again. It is torture, but I push through it, gritting my teeth. Sensation returns to my fingers and toes, a throbbing pain laced with a thousand hot needles. As if pain is the only proof of life.

Where am I? Am I safe? I concentrate on the sounds outside my narrow wooden box. I can hear drunken cries, the high squeal of street hogs, ballad singers and hawkers, and a low bell tolling my own death. The cart slows, caught in the crowds, then surges forward again. Someone curses the driver. The cart turns and the noise changes. Whispers, and the sound of a bottle smashing. A baby screaming somewhere high above our heads. The wheels of the cart rattling over broken cobbles. The driver coughs. 'Damned dust.' We roll to a halt, the horses snorting and chewing at their bits.

The coffin begins to move, sliding from the cart. It swings into the air and I roll inside, smashing my knee. What if I am to be thrown into the Thames? I take a deep breath, ready to fight, but the coffin is carried higher, resting on solid shoulders. Boots thump and voices curse as we tilt and turn up the stairs. I count four storeys. The men are grunting now with the effort.

A door opens. The coffin is lowered to the floor with a heavy thump.

'Here he is, then.' Someone kicks the side. 'Ten pounds.'

'We agreed five.'

Kitty.

'Five to bring him here. Another five and I'll keep quiet.'

'A bullet in your throat will do that well enough.' A sharp, metallic click. 'Leave us. Now.'

A pause. The door slams shut. Hurried footsteps back down the stairs.

She starts to prise open the lid with an iron crow, nails groaning against the wood. I push hard from the other side and it starts to give. At last it splits open. I struggle free and roll on to my back, stunned and gasping for air.

Wooden rafters stretch high above my head. Daylight streams through an open window, casting blocks of dazzling light on to the bare floor. Curtains billow in a soft spring breeze. The room smells of gin and unwashed clothes. I sit up slowly, still dazed and uncertain. There are piles of rags stacked against the far wall ready to sell. The floorboards feel rough under my fingers; the breeze chills the sweat on my chest. *Am I truly alive? Where am I?*

Someone coughs loudly on the other side of the wall, hawking up thick phlegm.

Not heaven, then.

Kitty kneels down next to me. She has pulled off her mob cap. Her face is flushed pink from the effort of opening the coffin. It is the most beautiful thing. She is the most beautiful ... The room fades and I begin to slide to the floor. She grabs hold of my shoulders. 'You're safe,' she says. 'Tom – do you understand? You're safe.'

I try to speak through my bruised and swollen throat. '*Kitty.*'

Her bright-green eyes soften in relief. 'Idiot.' She kisses my forehead, my lips. Kisses me as though she is breathing the life back into me. I break away, staring in wonder at the face I have missed so much, touching clumsy, half-numb fingers to her cheek.

I don't know how I came to be here, what magic she has wrought to bring a hanged man back from the dead. All I know is that my heart is beating, my pulse is racing, my skin is warm. I lean against her and weep with joy, like a child.

*

Later, we lie tangled upon the narrow bed, a thin sheet draped at our hips. My need had been wild, more animal than human. I would have devoured her if I could, teeth scraping her skin, fingers digging into her flesh. She had held me tightly, back arched, caught in her own frenzy. I spent inside her and collapsed, only to rise again twice more. My body, rejoicing in the simple truth – *I am alive*.

Only now, half dozing, do I ask how the miracle was accomplished.

She sits up, reaches for her wrapping gown. 'We paid Hooper.'

I think back to the gallows, Hooper lying stretched upon the high beam, smoking a pipe. The last moments as he rolled the cap down over my face. *Courage, sir*. My breath hot and fast against the linen. The roar of the crowd.

'There's ways to tie a knot to finish things fast. Here.' She coils her long red hair and slips it over one shoulder. Presses two fingers against her bare neck, below her ear. 'And ways to make it slow.' She moves her hand to the back of her neck, where Hooper had tied the rope. 'You only *seemed* dead when he cut you down. You were still breathing. A little.'

'You were there?'

She shakes her head. 'I couldn't ...' She glances about the room and I know she is thinking of that long wait, not knowing if I were dead or alive. I reach over and grip her hand. Tears brim beneath her lowered lids. At last, she begins again. 'We paid Skimpy to smuggle you on to the wrong cart.'

I raise an eyebrow.

'He works for the surgeons. Brings the bodies back for anatomising ...'

My stomach turns at the thought – how close I had come. I remember the surgeons' assistant from the gallows – a pale, thin lad with white-blond brows and lashes, arguing with the Marshal.

I wonder if he will be in trouble with his masters for losing a valuable corpse. Most likely not – bodies often disappear on the road back from Tyburn, grieving families dragging the coffins away for a decent burial. Jack Sheppard's body had been taken by his friends and buried.

'Where are we?'

She smiles. 'Phoenix Street.'

I sit up in alarm. *We paid Hooper. We paid Skimpy.* 'Fleet arranged this?'

Her smile fades. 'No. Wouldn't trust that bastard to piss straight.'

It takes me a moment to guess. '*Sam.*'

'He came to see me last night. Told me everything.' She punches me once, very hard, in the arm. 'You promised there'd be no more secrets between us, Tom.'

I rub my arm. 'Fleet threatened to kill you.'

'All the more reason to tell me, you stupid prick!'

I let her rage. She has every right. I had been so proud of my own martyrdom I had never stopped to consider the toll it had taken on Kitty. She had spent the last few weeks broken-hearted and desperate. Behind the arm-punching and curses I can see how much I've hurt her. Her cheeks are hollow, her sweet little belly stretched taut. So much for my noble self-sacrifice: it has almost destroyed her.

'I'm sorry,' I say, when she is done, or has at least run out of breath. I lean in to kiss her and hear a soft, irritable sigh from the doorway. Sam has slipped into the room, God knows when. Best not to ask. Kitty tightens her gown and jumps up from the bed, crossing to him on tiptoes. She pulls him further into the room, clasping his hand in both of hers. The hero of the hour. I must confess I suffer a curious pang of jealousy at that. I'd felt some pride this morning, going bravely to my death. Now here I am, rescued by a boy of fourteen and a surgeon's assistant called Skimpy. I am *grateful*, but . . .

'You're well, Mr Hawkins?'

There is a tremor in Sam's voice, as if I might still be angry with him. I wrap the sheet around my waist and hobble to meet him. Hug him for as long as he will let me, which is not very long at all. He keeps his hands at his side and stays rigid. It is like hugging a short roll of heavy cloth. 'You saved my life.'

He stifles a grin of pride. Better, is it not, to save lives than to end them? He hands me a broadsheet, warm from the press. Guthrie's account of my life and death, curse him, printed fast for profit. 'World thinks you're dead.'

The world thinks I'm a monster.

'We'll stay here for a few days Tom,' Kitty says as I sit back down upon the bed, still reading. 'Let everyone forget all about you.'

'A gentleman, hanged for murder? They won't forget me in a hundred years.'

'We'll go to Italy, just as we planned. Sam will keep looking for the true killer.'

'Alice,' Sam says, as if the thing were settled.

The killer. My God. I had quite forgotten amidst all the drama of *dying*. I crumple up the broadsheet and toss it across the room on to the unlit fire, taking some small pleasure in hitting my target. 'No. It wasn't Alice. You were right Kitty. It was Judith.'

Perhaps it was because I had been so close to death. A flash of revelation as my soul prepared to escape its cage.

I had seen her through the crowds, dressed in her mother's mourning gown. She had been granted a place of honour in the galleries, surrounded by powdered courtiers, a single jet-black stone in a flower bed of colour. She sat forward in her seat, lips parted, gloved hands laced across the folds of her dress, as if she were waiting for her favourite opera singer to take the stage.

She was so young. And beneath her composed expression, so *very* lost. A boat unmoored and drifting on the open ocean. Our eyes met and in that brief communion I had seen how much she wished me dead. Not out of malice, nor for revenge, but to be sure that suspicion would never fall on her. She smiled at me. Gave the tiniest nod of acknowledgement. *Thank you, sir. I am most obliged to you.*

Hooper prepared the cart, and still we'd stared at each other across the crowds; murderer and victim locked in one last deathly gaze. She clutched her gown in anticipation, fingers twisting and turning the black silk. Black for mourning. Black for death. A black so deep no stains of red would show upon it.

Hooper rolled the cap over my face.

'Wait.'

But it had been too late. My feet slid from the cart and the rope pulled taut.

'I'll kill her. I swear it, Tom. I will fucking murder her.' Kitty is prowling the room, all thoughts of exile vanished. 'Turn your back,' she snarls at Sam, and throws off her wrapping gown without waiting to see if he has complied. She tugs on her stockings, garters, petticoat, stomacher, then reties her gown. Decent, then – as decent as she can be. She catches me watching her and grins. 'Beast.' She hunts for her pistol. It takes her a while to realise I am holding it.

She lunges and I lift it high, out of her reach. There is a short tussle, Kitty pulling on my arm.

'Dangerous,' Sam warns, eyeing the cocked and loaded pistol.

I uncock it and throw it over to him. He catches it neatly and tips the powder onto the floor.

Kitty paces the room, annoyed. 'You cannot stop me, Tom. Who saved you today? Do you think it was Fate that cut you down from the scaffold still breathing? Or God?'

'No—'

'No indeed. *We* saved you. Me and Sam. If he hadn't come to me last night – and d'you know he had to *steal* his way in to avoid Alice and Neala . . .'

'He enjoys stealing into places.'

Sam shrugs. This is true.

'How can you jest?' Kitty cries, fresh tears springing in her eyes. 'They let you hang, Tom. *They let you hang.*'

'We must find a way to make Judith confess,' I persist. 'She is the only one who can prove my innocence. She can't very well do that if you shoot her first.'

Kitty wipes her eyes. 'She let them arrest you in her place. She lied under oath in court. She sat in her room swigging poppy juice while I sobbed my heart out every night for you. Six weeks. And she never thought to speak out. She murdered her father and she let you hang for it. She will never confess, Tom.'

'Perhaps. But I must try.'

Chapter Twenty-Three

Midnight on Phoenix Street and the city was alive, pulsing with revellers celebrating my death. It had been a good dying. I had shown pluck and a certain swagger at the end. That was something to admire, especially here in St Giles.

I stood with Sam, shielded behind a wall, waiting for a sprawling crowd to pass. His father was holding a vigil for me at home with all his gang. I'd kept my word and held my tongue – the greatest virtue among thieves. They honoured me tonight, now that I was safely dead. Sam had slipped away while they drank and sang and raised toast after toast to Mr Hawkins. They did not know that Sam had not killed Burden. How disappointed they would all be in him.

A few revellers straggled into a gin shop. When it was quiet enough, we stepped out into the street.

The night was mild and damp, a light rain misting the air. Sam had brought me fresh clothes to replace my suit of blue velvet – we had sent that to Hooper the hangman. A fair price for saving my life, I thought – along with whatever else Kitty had paid him. I had cost her a great deal these past weeks. I pulled the collar of my greatcoat around my ears.

'They won't see you.'

I understood. People only see what they expect to see, and no one expected to see a dead man strolling about the town. But still, I preferred to keep my head down and my collar up. I bent my neck low and felt the bruise around my throat, where the rope had cut deep. For a moment, I couldn't breathe.

Sam held out a torch coated in thick black pitch. I took the tinderbox from my coat pocket and struck the flint, bright sparks flying from the stone. The torch caught fire and Sam raised it high. And of a sudden he was that young boy I'd met last September. The boy who promised to light me home and instead led me into darkness.

'Well, look at you, Sam. A moon-curser once more.'

He smiled a true, broad smile. 'No, sir. Not tonight. Tonight I'll see you home.'

On Long Acre, the pavements were covered in broken glass, sodden broadsheets, and the occasional drunk. I almost tripped over an old watchman, dead to the world and snoring, his lantern burned out. It was always the same the night after a hanging. Tomorrow he would stumble into a coffeehouse, clutching his head and cursing my name.

In the Garden, a few whores limped beneath the arches, clutching themselves for warmth and looking for a fresh customer. Most were busy, on their backs in their meagre rooms, or pushed up against a wall in a back alley. Men needed to fuck after a hanging, to feel the blood pumping in their veins.

At Moll's place, light glowed in the windows. Moll's voice carried across the piazza, sweet and sad. A song of mourning.

'Holding a wake for you,' Sam said.

So, this was how it felt to be a ghost. Some part of me yearned to draw near. Was Betty there, and did she grieve for me? She must have known the pardon would never come, even as she promised it. Her visit had ensured my silence between the trial and the hanging.

Betrayal. Well. I had felt that sting before. I pulled my hat low and kept my eyes on the cobbles.

We were home soon enough. *Home.* My heart rose. I had not dared to dream of coming home again. I tapped softly on the door and it swung free at once, Kitty waiting anxiously behind it. She had hurried back from St Giles under Sam's protection hours before, to prepare and to keep a close eye upon next door. She kissed me in silent welcome as Sam extinguished the torch, grinding it into the iron snuffer fixed to the wall outside.

'Alice is asleep in Jenny's old room,' she whispered. 'Neala's in the kitchen. I slipped a draught in her beer. She sleeps light.'

Alice and Neala had kept Kitty company throughout my imprisonment, Neala standing guard through the nights. There had been threats from some of the neighbours, convinced that Kitty had been involved in the murder. Neala had kept them away. Felblade had spoken out for her too, it seemed. Strange to discover true friends in such times and in such unexpected quarters. I was grateful to them all and did not want them tangled up in tonight's plan. Safer for them to think me dead, maybe for ever. Whatever happened tonight, I had not yet decided what should follow. There was, after all, a freedom in being dead. It could be a welcome chance to begin afresh, with a new name and none of the old ties I'd allowed to bind me. The thought of not being in the service of the queen, or James Fleet – of answering to no one but myself . . . Well, it had its appeal.

Kitty grinned, excited by the fresh drama. Perhaps I should have slipped opiates in *her* beer. No, no. I had learned my lesson. I had chosen Kitty – and she had chosen me. For good or ill, we would face our troubles together.

We tiptoed up the stairs, paying mind to every loose board. When we reached Sam's room, I took out the pistol and handed it to Kitty. 'It's not loaded.'

She scowled, then turned it around in her hand, testing its weight in her palm. Mollified, she tilted her chin towards the secret door, hidden behind the hanging with its white cherry tree design.

Kitty went first, followed by Sam. I stood alone for a few seconds, the candle flickering in my hand, then plunged through to the other side.

Burden's house was very still. Kitty had been studying the household these past weeks, while I languished in my cell. Judith hadn't replaced Alice – perhaps she could not find anyone to join such a cursed household. No one had visited, either, save for one very stern lawyer who came almost every day, clutching a fat bundle of papers. Rumour was the business was in trouble. Even Mrs Jenkins had been banished since she'd served her purpose at the trial. It had left her suspicious, the way she had been used and discarded – and her sharp eye noticed things she had missed before. One of her customers had seen Ned visiting the Carpenters' Company. 'Asking for charity,' she'd guessed, and that guess had been transmuted into fact about the Garden.

I took the candle and examined the gowns hanging in the cabinet, running my hands over the flounces and pleats. They smelled of campion. The heavy black mourning gown was missing.

On the day I searched the house, Judith had dressed herself in that gown. She had thrown a heavy lace shawl over her head that fell all the way to her waist. She had pinned it carefully with an ebony brooch, to cover the fabric beneath. Her appearance had struck me as strange and affected even at the time. Why not order a new gown, or have the older one tailored to a modern cut? No one would have expected her to be in full mourning dress so soon. I'd thought it a sign of her grief, or an unbalanced mind. I had pitied Judith then. I had thought her weak.

And so I had searched every corner of the house looking for bloodstained clothes, while Judith had sat primly in the drawing room, wearing the same dress she'd worn when she killed her father. Smiling on the inside while I searched like a fool for what was right in front of my eyes.

Clever, wicked girl.

Down on the next landing we paused, each drawing strength from the other. The plan we had agreed to on Phoenix Street had seemed simple enough. Kitty and I would coax the truth from Judith. Sam would stand watch. And we must be quiet. Ned would be sleeping downstairs in the workshop, Stephen across the landing in his father's old room. If either woke we were all in trouble.

'No blood,' I whispered, for the hundredth time. I would not have another death on my conscience. Kitty and Sam exchanged guarded looks. I had the distinct impression they had agreed something rather different, out of my hearing. '*Swear it.*'

They complied, eventually, with a good deal of reluctance and head-shaking. I stepped closer to Judith's door; reached for the handle and turned it slowly. The latch clunked and the door opened, creaking softly on its hinges.

The bed stood in the middle of the room, the canopy open to the night. I could hear Judith breathing softly. And this was shameful, was it not – stealing into a young girl's bedchamber while she lay sleeping? I felt a prod in my back – Kitty urging me forward, most likely with the pistol. She was overly fond of that weapon. She closed the door behind us.

'She murdered her father,' Kitty whispered, catching the doubt in my eyes. 'She let you *hang*, Tom.'

Judith stirred, legs swishing under the sheets. Her dark hair fanned out across the pillow, a few damp strands clinging to her cheek. Her pale-blue night gown lay unbuttoned at her throat, revealing a silver cross on a delicate chain. She had let me hang. And now she slept, peaceful and content.

Her eyes fluttered beneath closed lids.

Kitty hurried to the bed and covered Judith's mouth with a folded handkerchief. Judith's brows furrowed, then her eyes opened wide in shock. She tried to scream but the sound was muffled by the cloth.

Kitty clamped it harder to Judith's lips. 'Be still.'

She gave a slight noise in her throat then nodded slowly, watching Kitty.

I stepped forward with the candle held high. 'Judith.'

She flinched at the sound of my voice and saw me at last. For a moment she lay senseless with shock, eyes bulging as she tried to understand what she saw. Then she began to whimper. I moved closer and her eyes rolled back in her head. She slumped back down in a dead faint.

'That was obliging of her,' Kitty said. She pulled out a couple of rags and tied Judith's wrists to the bedpost. She used the handkerchief as a gag.

This did not sit well with me. I shuffled from foot to foot, the floorboards creaking beneath my weight.

Kitty gave me an impatient look. 'Find the dress.'

I searched the closets while Kitty lit more candles about the room. I soon found the mourning gown and matching petticoat. I laid them out across the bed and lowered one of the candles over the skirts, tracing my fingers across the silk. It would have been drenched in blood the night of the murder. Judith must have spent many secret hours sponging it clean. There were still a few faint marks in the fabric. Some, caught in the stitched seams of the quilted petticoat, would be easily covered by an apron. The stains on the bodice were harder to discover, mere faded patches where Judith had scrubbed out the blood. I scratched a fingernail along a seam and a tiny dark brown fragment of blood flaked into my palm. A jury would call it dirt, an old smudge on an old dress, but I was satisfied. Judith had killed her father.

It was not just the stains; it was the defiance with which she had worn the dress during the search. At my trial. At my hanging. The tiny smirk on her face, as she enjoyed her own private joke. It was only now that I began to understand Judith and the depths of her sickness. We had all dismissed her as a poor, timid thing. And perhaps she was – her life smothered and ruined by her father, flinching beneath his hand, his sharp words. But something else had grown beneath that fragile surface. Something strong, formed of anger and bitterness. Alice had known the truth about her mistress – but only Kitty had listened. Kitty had suspected Judith all along.

Judith blinked, waking in confusion. Her face was pallid, her lips almost white. We had frightened her half to death.

Kitty tipped a jug of ice-cold water in Judith's face.

She jolted with the shock, gasping beneath her gag. When she discovered that she was tied to the bed she gave a muffled cry and pulled at the ties, turning her wrists frantically as she tried to slip free.

I sat down upon the bed and she shrank back, terrified.

'Be still,' I whispered. 'I've not come to hurt you.'

Kitty sat down on the other side of the bed, pistol resting in her hand. 'Do not presume the same of me.'

Judith stared at her, then nodded her understanding.

'I wish to speak with you, Judith,' I said. 'If we remove the gag, do you promise not to cry out?'

She nodded again.

I loosened the knot, then lifted the handkerchief free. She was trembling violently.

'Are you a ghost?'

'No, indeed.'

'I saw you hang. I watched you *die*.'

I touched my throat, where the rope burns chafed my skin. 'For your crime.'

For a moment she seemed almost ashamed. Then she pursed her lips and looked away.

I threw the mourning gown across her lap. 'You did a fair job, soaking out the blood. But it's still there.'

A long silence. She knew, now, that she was caught. A tiny, petulant shrug. 'Well, it's a maid's job, is it not? Scrubbing clothes.'

'It was clever of you to wear it. Easier to hide the stains.'

'All those dresses,' she murmured. 'Turning to dust. He never let me touch them. They were for a woman, and *I* was not a woman. I was his daughter. I must never grow up. Have you seen all those fine silk dresses, sir?' she asked, in a slow, dreamlike voice. 'I shall have them unpicked and made anew, cleaned and restitched in the latest fashions. I shall do everything my father denied me. I shall walk about the town. I shall visit the theatre and the shops.' She paused, a light smile playing across her lips. 'I shall marry Ned.'

'Is that why you killed your father? So you could—'

'—So I could *live*. And to see his face. Oh ... his face! He thought I was Alice. His filthy whore come to his bed again. Then he saw the knife. He was so shocked he didn't even cry out. I stabbed him and I stabbed him and all he could say was, *Why, Judith? Why?* Croaking like an old toad. Even as I plunged the blade into his heart.' She laughed. '*Why, Judith? Why?* I told him, when it was over. When he was still. He never let me speak. Always lecturing. But I could talk to him now he was quiet. I could tell him anything I wanted. *I am not a little girl now, am I, Father? A little girl could not kill such a big man so easily*.' Her eyes

356

flickered from mine to Kitty's. She giggled. 'I have shocked you both. The rake and his whore. How funny. You knew my father, how he treated us all. I was *suffocating*.'

'You could have run away,' Kitty said.

'No! No . . . I had to stay here. For Ned.'

She didn't know that Ned was her brother. I'd thought he might have told her by now – but then he had always worried about Judith. She was so *fragile*. I shook my head.

'He loves me,' Judith cried, mistaking me.

'*Quiet*,' Kitty warned.

'Why do you not believe me?' she wailed. 'I told Father and he laughed at me. He called me a silly slut. He said that he would never let me marry Ned or anyone else. He said he would send Ned away. He pinned me down and he beat me. I thought he would kill me.'

Ahh . . . here was the Burden I remembered. And I had almost begun to feel sorry for him.

'Then he announced that he would marry Alice. And I thought, *Oh, no, Father. You shall not. You shall die and everyone will think it was Alice or Mr Hawkins.*' She laughed again.

I rose and walked to the shuttered window, loosening the catch. It would be light soon. I had the truth, from the lips of the murderer, but would she confess it in public, without a pistol to her chest? Of course not. I rested my head against the cool windowpane.

'You let me hang, Judith,' I said, turning back to the bed. 'You knew I was innocent, and you let me die in your place.'

'*Innocent?* You killed a man, when you were in gaol. The world knows it.'

Kitty began to laugh. It was a mean, dangerous laugh.

Judith pulled anxiously on the ties at her wrists. 'Why do you laugh at me?'

Kitty smiled at her. 'I meant to kill you,' she said. 'But this will be much better. To let you live and suffer. I thought I'd lost Tom for ever. It broke my heart. So now, Judith, I shall break yours.'

'Kitty . . .' I said softly, in warning.

She ignored me. 'Has Ned asked for your hand?'

Judith fell still. 'He will. I know he will. He must . . .'

Kitty laughed again. 'Poor Judith. You have no idea, do you? Ned doesn't love you. He *can't* love you. Shall I tell you why?' Kitty pressed her lips to Judith's ear, soft as a kiss. 'He's your brother.'

Three words. Each one a blade.

'*No.*'

'That's why your father refused his permission. Ned Weaver is your brother, Judith. He will *never* be yours.'

'*No!*' Judith screamed – a long, terrible wail. It tore through the room, a sound of desolation and despair.

Kitty slapped a hand across Judith's mouth, but it was too late. There was a thud as a door opened wide, followed by a short scuffle. I jumped from the bed, Kitty still struggling to silence Judith.

Stephen burst into the room holding his father's sword, closely followed by Sam. Stephen's courage fled the instant he saw me, a living spectre standing over his sister's bed. His legs buckled and he collapsed to the floor. The sword clattered from his hand. 'Oh, God!' he cried, hands clasped in prayer. 'Protect me from this devil.'

I kicked the sword over to Sam. 'I am not a devil, Stephen.' I pulled down my collar, so he might see the burns upon my throat.

Stephen stopped praying. He raised his eyes to mine. 'The Lord spared you,' he said, in a dazed wonder. 'He heard my prayers and in His wisdom He spared you. Oh, praise God!'

I frowned at him. Why would Stephen pray for his father's

killer? Why was he so glad to find me alive? I remembered his empty room, the portrait of his sister stamped into the floor. I remembered he had hit Judith that first morning, after she had cried *Murder!* Not to calm her down, after all – but in anger. In shame.

'You knew I was innocent.'

He began to weep.

Stephen had guessed his sister was guilty the moment he saw his father's body. The rage of the attack had convinced him. He'd lived under the same roof in the days leading up to the murder, and had heard them fighting. Watched as his father beat Judith for speaking out. Heard her crying in her room, tears of hatred and frustration. He'd seen her face when Burden announced he would marry Alice, and banish Ned from the house. When Stephen walked into his father's bedroom and saw the blood and the knife, he'd *known*. But then he'd pushed the truth from his mind. It was too painful, too horrifying to accept. 'She's my sister. I couldn't . . .'

'You let me hang for it.'

Stephen dropped his head. 'The jury found you guilty.'

'But you knew, Stephen. In your heart you *knew* it was Judith.'

He began to cry again, great gulps. 'I prayed for you, sir. Over and over in my room. I swear it.'

Judith glared at him from the bed, disgusted. She pulled again at the rags about her wrists, struggling to free herself. 'So. What now, Brother? Will you betray me? Will you let me *burn*?'

A burning. The punishment for petty treason. The king rules his people, and a father rules his family. For a girl to murder her father was the same, in law, as murdering her king. She would be burned at the stake if she were caught. I had not considered this.

'You killed our father, Judith!' Stephen cried.

'Well? What of it? How many times did we dream of it? How many times did we *pray* for it? Do you not remember, the last time he beat you for daring to speak against him? He would have killed you if Ned had not begged him to stop. I had to kill him, Stephen. I had to kill him because you were too weak.'

Stephen jumped up and ran from the room. Kitty ran after him. 'He'll wake Ned,' she hissed.

'Stay here,' I ordered Sam. 'Keep her quiet.'

Stephen had not run far – only back to his father's room across the landing. He was crouched over a chamber pot, puking loudly. Kitty and I stared at one another helplessly. What now?

'Where *is* Ned?' I wondered. We had made enough noise to wake half the street. Surely he must have heard us by now.

'He left us,' Stephen sniffed, wiping his mouth with the back of his hand.

Kitty crinkled her nose. The air now stank of fresh vomit, laced with the usual bedroom smells of a fifteen-year-old boy. 'Where did he go?'

'I don't know. In search of work, I suppose. The business is in ruins. Father spent all the money.' He hung his head. 'There's nothing left but debts.'

Kitty touched my arm. 'Tom. *That's* why Burden planned to marry Alice. The *debts*.'

Of course. It had always puzzled me, why Burden would marry his housekeeper. Even more so once I'd heard Gabriela's story. Now I understood. He had not loved Alice – of course not. But he knew his life was in danger. If he died, then all his debts would pass to his family – to Stephen and Judith. But if he married Alice and named her in his will, she would be forced to take on all the responsibility for repayment. Thank God he had died before Alice married him. She might have spent the rest of her life rotting in a debtors' gaol.

'We owe money to half the town.' Stephen sobbed. 'And my sister. My sister ... What am I to do?'

I glanced at Kitty and could guess what she was thinking. *Learn to fend for yourself, the same as every other wretched soul in this world.* He had let me hang, after all. But I did not have the heart to hate him. He was a boy – older than Sam in years, but younger in so many ways. His father was dead, and all he'd inherited was debt. He might well be thrown in gaol now, instead of Alice.

So I said nothing, and the room fell very quiet. The whole house, indeed, was silent.

And then I thought of Sam and Judith, alone across the landing.

Something dark fluttered in my chest.

The door to Judith's room had been closed. I stood outside it for a moment and prayed to God I was wrong. Then I turned the handle and stepped inside.

God had not listened to my prayers in a very long time.

'Sam.'

Sam removed the pillow from Judith's face and stepped back. Her wrists were still tied to the bed, her eyes staring up at the ceiling, empty of life.

'No blood,' he murmured. 'I promised.'

Sorrow pressed against my throat, like a rope. I couldn't speak.

He cradled her head and slipped the pillow back into place. Delicate. Gentle. Turned to face me.

'Had to be done.'

No. No. Not in a thousand years.

He pulled a letter from his pocket. A confession, forged in Judith's hand. He must have written it earlier, on Phoenix Street. He must have planned it all. And wasn't that Sam's way? He tucked it under the candlestick by the bed. Plucked a bottle of Felblade's opiates from the table and poured the contents out of the window. Smooth and fluid as a dancer, well-trained in his art. 'She couldn't live with the guilt. Your death. Her father's.' He placed the empty bottle next to the note.

I said nothing. My heart was breaking.

Sam brushed a stray lock of hair from Judith's face and stepped back. 'Look. Is this not better? See how peaceful she is.'

I forced myself to look at her. Her dark lashes closed. Her lips tinged blue. The girl who just a few moments before had been so alive. Who had wanted so much to *live*. Poor Judith. Silenced for ever.

I spoke at last, the words heavy on my tongue. 'Your father will be proud of you.'

He smiled up at me, black eyes shining. 'I didn't do it for him, Mr Hawkins.'

EPILOGUE

Dawn in London, but there will be no sun today. A carriage whisks its way through the rain-soaked streets, water hissing beneath the wheels. The windows are closed and covered with thick black curtains. The cushions are of black velvet, trimmed with gold.

And I too wear black; fitting clothes for a dead man. Kitty sits at my side, watching me in that new way she has. Careful. Concerned. I wish she would shout at me instead. I miss it.

Five days have passed since my hanging. The newspapers are filled with stories about Judith's confession and her suicide. The town is horrified and fascinated and can speak of nothing else. Broadsheet writers indulge themselves with lurid fictions of her life and death. They tell of her final moments, imagine her weeping with guilt as she drinks the fatal draught of opium. There are fresh illustrations too, of Judith attacking her father, blade held high. Swooning at the trial. Attending my hanging with a secret smile upon her face.

Poor, tragic Thomas Hawkins, hanged for a crime he did not commit. How quickly I have been transformed from monster to blameless victim. I could walk into any tavern or coffeehouse in London and be declared a miracle. A saint. The thought turns my stomach.

I had declared my innocence for weeks, and no one would listen, even as they put the noose about my neck. Now at last the town believes me. *Now*, when the guilt of Judith's death presses so hard upon my shoulders that I can barely lift my head.

*   *   *

I had walked from that room without a word. Left Judith lifeless upon the bed, her skin turning cold. I found Kitty on the landing, her face pale. She had guessed, too. Her eyes softened with pity as she saw my expression. No need to ask. Dead.

'Leave now, Tom,' she'd said, touching a hand to my bruised throat. 'Let me take care of this.'

And she did. Somehow she convinced Stephen that the note was true, that Judith had suddenly transformed from the fierce, defiant woman who had mocked him from the room, to the weak, fragile girl, too racked with guilt to continue living. He did not ask how she had broken free of her bindings or when she could have written the note. He turned away from the truth, just as he had turned away before when he realised Judith had killed their father. In time the memories of this night would fade, and he would be left clinging to this comfortable lie.

I walked back up into the attic and its smell of dust and camphor. Sam trailed behind me with a candle. I put a hand lightly on his chest and his face dropped.

'Mr Hawkins?'

'Go home, Sam.'

I slipped back through the attic door. I don't suppose I shall ever see him again.

I spent the next few days hiding in our close-shuttered bedroom. Smoking, thinking. Alice and Neala kept the visitors away. Alice thought I was the most wondrous creature in the world. I'd saved her from the gallows and now here I was, alive and well after my own hanging. Neala thought it was God's work. Kitty knew better.

'You shouldn't grieve for Judith.'

I couldn't explain that I was grieving for Sam, too. Everything he might have been. Everything he now *would* be. His father's son.

One slight comfort, that first terrible day – Ned returned home. He came to visit me, squeezing himself through the attic door. He looked haggard and sick with grief, but he shook my hand and smoked a pipe with me, and promised not to tell the world I was alive. We didn't speak of Judith. What could be said, after all? But he promised that he would look after Stephen.

'He's my brother,' he said, simply.

I had begun to think, lying in that darkened room, that I should remain dead. I had no desire to become the city's latest wonder – the hanged man who cheated Death. And then there was the chance to free myself of all those old debts, to James Fleet, to the queen. To invent myself afresh, a new man. We had enough money to live contentedly in another country. Somewhere I could feel the warm sun on my skin, breathe fresh air. Drink the water. Imagine such a marvel.

It was time I paid attention to the lessons I had learned last autumn, in the Marshalsea. The lessons I had learned riding the cart to Tyburn. Life was adventure enough. There was no need to go about prodding the damned thing with a stick.

'Are you sure you would not grow bored?' Kitty asked.

I yawned, stretching out upon the bed. 'I should love to be bored.'

And so it was settled. Alice and Neala would take care of the house and shop. Kitty and I would travel to the continent. I would write to my father and sister to let them know I was alive.

The rest could believe what they wished. Perhaps we would come back one day. Perhaps not. I began to dream of sunlight and orchards instead of graves and gaols.

We gave ourselves a month to plan. Foolish. We should have left at once. I have said it a thousand times before, and one day I shall take the care to listen to myself. There are no secrets in this city.

This morning I heard voices raised in the shop, Kitty cursing and Neala shouting at someone to leave. And then a lazy, drunken drawl I recognised at once. *Charles Howard.* I grabbed my dagger and ran downstairs.

'I thought you should know, Miss Sparks. *I* stopped the royal pardon. D'you understand?' He was standing in the middle of the shop with a bottle in one hand and a sword at his hip. Drunk as ever, and a dangerous look in his eye. 'He is dead because *I* demanded it of the king himself. And who will protect you now, eh?' He sneered at Neala. 'This Irish invert?'

'Mr Howard,' I said, softly.

He spun on his heel. I took some satisfaction in watching his beetroot face drain white.

'Not . . . not possible,' he slurred. 'I watched you hang. What the devil . . . What are you?'

Even as I stepped towards him, he hesitated. The man was wild enough to fight anything, even a demon from hell. But then the soldier's training saved him. He'd fight a ghost, but not a ghost with a dagger, supported by a woman with a double-handed blade. He backed out of the shop and ran up Russell Street, cursing us all.

He was gone, but I had been seen, and the rumours were spreading across the town. We kept the doors closed and I returned to my hiding place upstairs, hoping the story would fade. A few hours later a black carriage drew up outside the house, and a guard with a battered face jumped down. Rapped upon the door until Alice was forced to open it.

'Hear there's been a resurrection,' Budge called up the stairs. 'Hurry down, Mr Hawkins. And bring Miss Sparks with you.'

The carriage slows and turns sharply. I draw back the curtain. We've arrived. I settle back against the seat and reach for Kitty's hand. A squall of rain spatters on the roof and I flinch, remembering the road to Tyburn, the stones clattering about my head.

Budge appears at the window, holding up a large umbrella. He beckons me out of the carriage. Kitty picks up her gown and slides to join us, but Budge shakes his head. 'Just you, Hawkins.'

'You asked for us both.'

'Her Majesty wishes to speak with you alone.'

Kitty slams the carriage door closed and drops back against the seat. Folds her arms. 'Her Majesty can kiss my rain-soaked arse.'

I follow Budge up the back stairs to the queen's rooms, leaving a trail of muddy footsteps behind me. In the antechamber, Henrietta Howard waits in a lilac gown, tightly corseted and hung with jewels. Her expression is light and composed, her hands loose at her side.

I bow. 'Madam.'

Budge glances anxiously at the door to the queen's room. 'My lady,' he warns.

'One moment, only.' She draws me to one side. 'Mr Hawkins. You have survived after all. How remarkable.' She smiles, but she does not seem so very pleased.

Perhaps, indeed, she loathes me with an exquisite passion. It is impossible to guess from her countenance. For eleven years she had dreamed, desperately, that she might see her son again.

She had hoped that as he grew older, Henry might realise the truth about his father, and forgive her for abandoning him. I wonder what she was forced to write in her letter to him, and I feel ashamed, again, for my part in it. 'I am so sorry, madam, about your son.'

A flash of pain crosses her face. It is gone as fast. 'I had a son. For ten years, *I had a son.* That much alone I can say.'

'But you are free now. You may leave your rooms, visit your friends. Walk in the park without fear.'

'Yes, sir.' She folds her hands together. 'These are comforts indeed. I am most grateful.'

'And here you are, Mr Hawkins. Risen from the dead.'

I present a low bow.

'Are you angry with me, sir?'

I look up, still bent in my bow. 'Furious, Your Majesty.'

She laughs, great hiccuping gulps that make her long strands of pearls slide across her vast bosom. 'Princess Amelia is in deep mourning for you. Such a heroic death. She will be most disappointed when she hears you are alive. *Debout, monsieur.*'

I stand. It is many weeks since our last meeting. Since then I have been arrested, put on trial, sentenced to death, hanged, and revived. The queen, meanwhile, does not appear to have moved. Her dress is new – a heavy, dark-blue sack gown – and there is a fresh plate of confectionery at her side. Other than that, the room is precisely as I remember it, and unbearably hot. She holds up a fan embroidered with garden scenes. Fans herself.

'All in black,' she muses. 'How very sober you look. I suppose you wish to know why I chose not to pardon you?'

Chose? And with that word she reveals the truth – that my death was indeed part of her agreement with Howard. The truth is, she had enjoyed very little choice in the matter – and she would rather die than admit it. 'I am sure Your Majesty had a very good reason.'

'Oh, he is sure. What, am I your servant, to solve all your petty troubles? Fold them up *comme ça*?' She snaps the fan closed. 'What a conceited notion. Perhaps the Queen of England had no reason at all. Perhaps she was busy playing cards or embroidering a handkerchief. Budge, pour the boy a glass of claret.'

I sip the wine. It is even better than I remember. The queen decides to rise. This takes some effort and she appears to regret it, wincing as she walks to the fire. A touch of gout, I think. When she first arrived in England she would walk for at least an hour every day and wore out all her ladies-in-waiting.

'Have you ever visited Yorkshire, Mr Hawkins?'

I am too tired to wonder at such an unexpected question. 'No, ma'am.'

'I'm told it has a rugged charm.' She lets her gaze wander over me for a moment, but leaves the jest unspoken. 'We have a friend, in need of assistance. You will set off at once. You may take your little *trull* along, if you wish. You had best marry her somewhere along the way. Your city manners will not be appreciated in the North.'

'Your Majesty . . .' I stop. Why waste breath refusing? This is not an offer, it is a command. I throw back the last of the wine. Bow my obedience.

Budge leads me back down the stairs. When we reach the final landing he hands me a sheaf of papers, bound with a black ribbon. 'For Yorkshire.'

I tuck it beneath my arm. There are many things I wish to say to him. That I feel betrayed. Ill-treated. That I have no desire to travel all the way to Yorkshire, or perform any service for his mistress. But there seems no purpose in arguing, and so I say nothing. I find that I am saying less these days.

Budge is not used to my new, sombre ways. He peers at me, worried. 'You hoped for an apology.'

'No.' I am not so foolish.

'The queen never explains,' Budge says. 'And *never* apologises.'

I nod. In truth, I do not really care.

He glances up the staircase. Leans in. 'Howard refused to agree terms unless you hanged. Twelve hundred pounds a year, control of his son, and no pardon for Thomas Hawkins. I do think she was *passing* sorry, sir.'

'And Betty? Was *she* sorry?'

Budge frowns. 'What choice was she given, do you think?'

The carriage rolls along the Strand. Kitty is so angry not to have met the queen that she cannot disguise it. She looks so furious and beautiful that I begin to laugh, for the first time in weeks.

'We were going to Italy,' Kitty grumbles. 'I have seen Yorkshire on a map. I believe it is *some distance* from Italy.'

Sedan chairs weave around us, chairmen trudging through the rain, water pouring from their hats. A merchant skirts past a stream of brown filth spewing from a broken gutter. I have not left London in three years. I cannot decide if I will miss it. 'The queen wants us to marry.'

Kitty looks down at her boots.

'Kitty. Are you afraid I will gamble away all your money?'

'Yes.'

'Are you afraid I will grow bored and leave you?'

Her boots are still of enormous interest to her. 'Yes.'

'Do you truly think that, my love?'

She looks up at last and stares deep into my eyes. 'I don't know.'

I smile at her. 'Well. That is progress.'

The carriage rolls over a hole in the road and she is flung forward. I grab her and pull her to safety, holding her close. She laughs, a little, and her shoulders soften as she settles against my chest.

The carriage moves on through the rain, the driver urging the horses forward with light taps of his whip. He is keen to travel as far north as possible today before the rain turns the roads to a sticking mud. He doesn't see the small, dark figure slip down from a sodden rooftop. The boy in the clean, patched clothes sprints after the carriage and climbs on the back. He tucks himself into a gap between the luggage until he is quite invisible. He's good at that.

THE HISTORY BEHIND
The Last Confession of Thomas Hawkins

The 'imprisonment' of Henrietta Howard

In the winter of 1727–8 the king's mistress, Henrietta Howard, was kept a virtual prisoner in her rooms at the palace of St James. Her husband, Charles Howard, had sent her stark messages, demanding that she return to live with him. When Henrietta refused to comply, Howard applied to the Lord Chief Justice for a warrant that allowed him to seize his wife 'wherever he found her'.

This was all play-acting on Howard's part, though no doubt he would have followed through if need be. The couple had lived separate lives for years and clearly loathed each other. But following George II's coronation in October 1727, Howard saw an opportunity to humiliate his wife and gain a fortune: irresistible for a man of his nature. While in public he continued to press – violently – for his wife's return, in private he made it clear that he would relinquish all claims to her for the enormous sum of £1,200 per annum. Although he applied to Henrietta for this 'fee', it was clear that – as she couldn't possibly afford it – his demands were really made to the king.

The implicit threat was clear. The more Howard insisted upon Henrietta's return, the more attention he would bring upon her intimate relationship with the king. It was generally accepted at the time that kings took mistresses, but they were expected to be discreet. This was messy and embarrassing. If the situation wasn't resolved swiftly, it could make everyone involved look weak and a little ridiculous.

However, Howard's plan had one flaw. He'd waited years for George to become king in order to ensure the maximum embarrassment and thus the best pay-off. But by this time, George had grown tired of his mistress. When he became king it turned out – much to everyone's astonishment – that Henrietta had no influence upon him whatsoever. People who had paid court to her for years in the hope of gaining a decent position under the new regime were left bitterly disappointed.

George refused to pay Howard's bribe. Perhaps it's not all that surprising: he was notoriously tight with money. He was also proud, stubborn and prone to terrible bouts of temper. (When very angry, he would snatch off his wig and kick it around the room, ranting and raging like a toddler.)

This left Henrietta in an intolerable situation. The early years of her marriage had been shockingly bad, even in the context of the time. Howard had married her for her large fortune and then gambled it away, leaving them with nothing. Far worse, he had abused and tormented her throughout their life together. Neighbours later testified that she had been beaten often and savagely, and that Howard would then abandon her and their young son Henry for months at a time, leaving them destitute and desperate. Henrietta even contemplated selling her hair, but could not agree a decent price. Howard taunted her about this when he learned the truth.

Henrietta's last hope, as a member of the nobility, had been to find a position at court. And so – ironically – it was Queen Caroline, then Princess of Wales, who had saved her, by making her a Woman of the Bedchamber. Howard meanwhile found a position with George I. Later, when the two courts split, Henrietta was at last given the perfect chance to escape her husband's control. But it meant leaving her son Henry in the hands of his father.

Now, ten years later, Charles had returned, swearing that he would seize his wife by force if he caught her. He even threatened to drag her from the queen's carriage if need be. And so Henrietta – terrified and powerless – was forced to remain within the sanctuary of the palace walls.

One of the fascinating things about studying the past is discovering how much has changed – and how much has stayed the same. Sometimes, this can be reassuring. Other times, it's heartbreaking. Henrietta's abuse at the hands of her husband is horribly familiar. Howard was clearly taking a sadistic glee in terrorising her. Even Lord Hervey, who disliked Henrietta, felt some pity for her 'extraordinary, difficult, and disagreeable' predicament, writing in his memoirs: 'She was to persuade a man who had power to torment her not to exert it, though it was his greatest pleasure; and to prevail with another [i.e. the king] who loved money and cared but little for her to part with what he did like in order to keep what he did not.'

Meanwhile Howard – frustrated by the lack of progress – arranged a meeting with the queen, alone. Her description of the tête-à-tête (as she termed it) in the novel is very close to the one she gave to Lord Hervey. He has a liking for camp drama, but the words ring true in this account:

> When Mr Howard came to Her Majesty, and said he would take his wife out of Her Majesty's coach if he met her in it, she had bid him 'do it if he dare; though,' said she, 'I was horribly afraid of him ... What added to my fear upon this occasion,' said the Queen, 'was that, as I knew him to be so brutal, as well

as a little mad, and seldom quite sober, so I did not think it impossible that he might throw me out of that window (for it was in this very room our interview was, and that sash then open just as it is now); but as soon as I got near the door ... [I said] I would be glad to see who should dare to open my coach-door and take out one of my servants ... Then I told him that my resolution was positively neither to force his wife to go to him if she had no mind to it, nor keep her if she had.'

In the end the king was persuaded to pay the £1,200 per annum after many weeks of stalemate. (The queen had drawn the line at paying the money herself, despite being asked by Lord Trevor on Henrietta's behalf. She pleaded poverty, but in fact she was insulted. It was one thing, she said, to allow her husband's *'guine-pes*' under her roof, but another to pay for them.)

It was in Caroline's interest to keep Henrietta at court – better the mistress you know. The queen had been the clear winner in the battle for influence over the king in the early months of his reign, and it suited her to have a mistress she could manipulate. Who was now, in fact, even more in her debt.

But before this resolution, Henrietta endured those long, dreadful winter months at St James's palace, trapped, humiliated and terrified as her husband made his demands and her lover ignored them. Within that gap, I imagined a situation where Howard's initial demands had been much higher and that per-haps there had been some form of compromise. I imagined the king growing more and more impatient about the situation, and increasingly bored with Henrietta. And the queen having to put up with this every night, and realising she might lose her tame mistress. Caroline was a politician and a pragmatist. Perhaps she

---

* basically, sluts

might put out secret enquiries to find something she might use against Howard?

That leap gave me room to create Tom's investigation and the final deal the queen makes with Howard – but the background is all based on fact.* I did allow myself one small piece of guesswork. Henrietta was deaf in one ear. Courtiers joked that this helped her to endure the king's infamously dull conversation – she simply turned her deaf ear towards him. But there is no record as to why she had become deaf in this one ear. Given the testimony from her neighbours and her own accounts of Howard's regular, brutal beatings, I have suggested that it was caused by a particularly severe blow to the head. I have no evidence for this, but it seems a possible explanation.

This was a time when it was perfectly acceptable for a husband to beat his wife. In fact Daniel Defoe (one of the few who spoke out against it) argued that beatings had become more common in his lifetime. Even so, Howard was recognised as an extreme case: 'wrong-headed, ill-tempered, obstinate, drunken, extravagant, brutal', according to Lord Hervey. Shortly after the events described in the novel, Henrietta finally won a legal separation from Howard – almost unheard of at the time.

There is more to this story – not all of it bad – and perhaps I will write a little more about it one day. But I would also urge anyone interested in this subject to read Tracy Borman's brilliant biography, *Henrietta Howard: King's Mistress, Queen's Servant*. I would also like to acknowledge my debt to her work here.

One thing I'm very sure about: it must have been Caroline who persuaded the king to pay Howard £1,200 per annum. For

---

* a small point by way of example: Henrietta's nickname really was 'The Swiss', because of her neutrality on court matters.

her own Machiavellian reasons, of course. But I like to think out of some fellow feeling with Henrietta, as well. The two women had been friends and confidantes before they were rivals. And I don't believe the queen would have delivered Henrietta into the hands of her monstrous husband. She was clever and strategic, but she certainly wasn't cruel.

Queen Caroline

Queen Caroline was a fascinating woman. Fiercely intelligent, she made up for years of poor education as a child by reading voraciously and seeking out the great thinkers of the day. She corresponded with Liebniz and Voltaire and, while Princess of Wales, took tea with Isaac Newton. Her husband, who couldn't really see the point of reading, used to grumble about the amount of time she 'wasted' on her books.

Caroline was a patron of the arts and also keenly interested in matters of science. She was a great early supporter of inoculation against small pox, encouraging research and later inoculating her own children. She also made sure that her children were educated in the arts, taking them to see private collections around London. (Her husband complained about this, too.)

Caroline really was the power behind the throne. First minister Robert Walpole relied on her heavily to persuade George to take up his policies. She was quite literally the voice of reason in the household. At the same time, she was careful never to let George suspect she had any power over him. She played a clever and no doubt exhausting dance of flattery, patience and at times humiliating deference to her husband. (Who she did, in spite of everything, truly love.) George would often brag:

'Charles I was governed by his wife, Charles II by his mistresses, James II by his priests, William III by his men, Queen Anne by her women-favourites . . . And who do they say governs now?'

And no doubt Caroline, hearing this, would compose her face and reply, 'you, my dear, of course'.

She must surely rate as the most intellectually engaged of British queens and she was also wickedly funny and mischievous. Is it likely she might also have hired spies to help out with certain private matters? Well, this was a woman who once chattered blithely to Lord Hervey about her concerns that her eldest son Frederick might be impotent, and pondered (playfully) about how they might sneak Hervey into the Prince of Wales' bedchamber to provide an heir. She had a mind for stealth and strategy and took secret meetings with Walpole. (She nicknamed him *le gros homme* behind his back, which given her own weight issues seems a bit rich.)

Caroline liked to be kept informed and she absolutely *adored* gossip. I'm pretty certain she would have had a number of informants about the town. She might not have taken quite such a direct interest in them, but then Tom is a gentleman. (Just.) And also – the legs.

I used a number of sources for my portrait of the queen, but by far her best biographer is Joanna Marschner. For more details see the select bibliography.

The Execution at Tyburn

The procession to Tyburn described in the book is based on a number of accounts. The shrouds for penitents, the black crêpe carts dragged through the town, the prisoners travelling backwards, leaning against their own coffins – these were all part of the theatre.

There was also something ritualistic – almost religious – about the procession. Perhaps, consciously or subconsciously, it was meant to mimic Christ's journey to the cross. The stop at St Sepulchre's steps for prayers and floral offerings; the offer of a cup of wine at St Giles; the final confession and chance for pardon beneath the gallows . . .

People were, occasionally, granted mercy at the last moment. And *very* occasionally, people were resuscitated after being hanged. There are various stories about this and they all helped to give me the idea of Tom's experience at Tyburn. One prisoner – for ever after known as 'Half-Hanged Smith' – was given a last-minute stay of execution when he'd already been hanged for several minutes. He was cut down and revived. Apparently, the process of being brought back to life was so excruciating (rather like waking up with a cramp, but all over your body, I imagine), that he wished those who'd cut him down would hang for it. Which seems a little ungrateful.

The point is that in this period, there was no 'drop' at a hanging. You didn't die instantly from a broken neck, but were slowly suffocated. It could take up to fifteen minutes. Hence slang ('cant') expressions for hanging such as being 'stretched', or 'kicking your heels', which is where the modern expression comes from. It was so painful, and took such a long time, that friends and family would often pull on the victim's legs to speed things along and end his or her suffering.

This act of kindness had an unfortunate result for Jack Sheppard, a legendary criminal who was a folk hero throughout the eighteenth and nineteenth century because of his daring escapes from prison. He was hanged in November 1724, and it's been estimated that 200,000 turned out for the procession and execution – about a third of the population of London at the time.

Sheppard had put in place careful plans for one final escape. He'd rented a room close to Tyburn and hired the services of a surgeon. The plan was to whisk him through the crowds as soon as he was hanged and smuggle him to the surgeon, who would revive him.

Unfortunately, because Jack was so popular with the crowds, they took pity on him and made sure to pull down hard on his legs to help him die more quickly. Even then he might have been resuscitated, but when people saw him being carried away, they thought his body was being taken off to be anatomised. Not realising these were Jack's friends hurrying him to the surgeon, they started a huge fight over the body. By the time the fighting was over, it was too late to save him.

The plan for Tom was a little different. Because the rope was knotted at the back of his neck, instead of pressing on the carotid artery, and because Hooper was paid to take him down early, Tom was not as far gone, so therefore didn't need a surgeon to revive him. None of this would be possible once the drop was introduced, of course.

Again, see the bibliography for further reading, in particular Christopher Hibbert's fascinating *The Road to Tyburn*.

The Society for the Reformation of Manners

This was a genuine society and particularly active in the 1720s and 30s. The term 'manners' was synonymous with 'morals'. The society's informers were responsible for sending scores of women to Bridewell for harsh, physical punishment. They also targeted 'molly houses' (gay brothels), and at least two men were hanged for sodomy because of the society's investigations.

John Gonson (later Sir John) was a prominent member of the society and the magistrate for Westminster. As a judge, he became infamous for giving harsh sentences to prostitutes. On the flip side of this moral crusading, he was a founding member of the Foundling Hospital for abandoned children.

He is depicted in plate three of Hogarth's *A Harlot's Progress* bursting in to arrest 'Moll Hackabout'. Moll is in a state of undress. Gonson has a rather startled, complicated expression on his face.

'Aunt Doxie's Brothel'

When I was doing publicity for my previous book, *The Devil in the Marshalsea*, the (wonderful) author Robyn Young asked if I'd uncovered anything particularly unusual or surprising during my research. 'I did find evidence of a fetish brothel,' I replied. We agreed this was surprising.

Then again: sex. Nothing surprising under the sun. It was more where I found it, and how casually it was dropped into the narrative. I'd spotted a reference in the British Library records of a short memoir by Thomas Neaves, hanged for theft in 1728, and called it up to read. It arrived in the rare books room, the fragile original pamphlet, looking as though it hadn't been read in years.

Convicted criminals would often write 'confessions' to sell at their hanging. The money would go to their family or to pay for a decent burial, away from the anatomists. As mentioned in the novel, they would sometimes hire a ghostwriter such as Defoe to write their story. (Which is no doubt how Defoe got his idea to write *Moll Flanders,* one of the first novels ever written. So you could argue that the British novel owes its very existence to criminal biographies, if you were feeling mischievous and ready for a scrap.)

Just like the more lurid true crime books and TV shows today, there was a certain voyeuristic element to these biographies. But Thomas Neaves clearly wanted to increase sales by adding in a rather surprising digression. He describes a brothel dedicated to what we would now call fetish – and in animated detail. There is a room where a dominatrix sits eating her supper, feeding little scraps to her customer, who barks at her feet like a dog. The next room . . . well, it's called coprophilia these days. I'll leave it there.

It was very strange to discover this hidden world described so openly in a prisoner's confession. It confirmed certain suspicions I had about the early Georgians – that they were fascinated by such things (hence the digression in the pamphlet) and that these brothels went relatively unchecked (hence the Society for the Reformation of Manners).

Cockpits and female gladiators

The description of Neala Maguire's fight is based closely on a description by a Swiss traveller to London called César de Saussure. The clothes, the coloured ribbons and the weapons all come from his memoir of London life in the mid 1720s. For the cockfight, I used Hogarth's 'The Cockpit' as a starting point. But then Hogarth is a good starting point for just about everything, and not just novels.

SELECT BIBLIOGRAPHY

This is a list of titles that were either particularly helpful to me, or might interest a reader keen to learn more about specific elements of the story. Or both.

Contemporary sources

Defoe, Daniel, *Street Robberies Consider'd: the Reason for their Being so Frequent*

Gay, John, *The Beggar's Opera*

Hayward, Arthur L., *Lives of the Most Remarkable Criminals* (original publication 1735)

Mudge, Bradford K. (ed.), *When Flesh Becomes Word: An Anthology of Early Eighteenth-Century Libertine Literature*

Ilchester, Earl of (ed.), *Lord Hervey and his friends 1726-38* (letters)

Neaves, Thomas, *The Life of Thomas Neaves, the Noted Street Robber*

de Saussure, César, *A Foreign View of England in the Reigns of George I and George II*

Sedgwick, Romney (ed.), *Lord Hervey's Memoirs*

Secondary sources

(These also included valuable references to primary material, of course)

Borman, Tracy, *Henrietta Howard: King's Mistress, Queen's Servant*

Cockayne, Emily, *Hubbub: Filth, Noise and Stench in England*

Cruickshank, Dan, *The Secret History of Georgian London*

Faller, B. Lincoln, *Turned to Account: the Forms and Functions of Criminal Biography*

George, M. Dorothy, *London Life in the Eighteenth Century*

Hay, Linebaugh, Rule, Thompson & Winslow, *Albion's Fatal Tree: Crime and Society in Eighteenth-Century England*

Hibbert, Christopher, *The Road to Tyburn*

Linebaugh, Peter, *The London Hanged: Crime and Civil Society in the Eighteenth Century*

Marschner, Joanna, *Queen Caroline: Cultural Politics at the Early Eighteenth-Century Court*

——, 'Queen Caroline of Ansbach: Attitudes to Clothes and Cleanliness 1727-37' in *Journal of the Costume Society No.31*

——, *Queen Caroline of Ansbach: The Queen, Collecting and Connoisseurship at the early Georgian court (thesis)*

Moore, Lucy, *Con Men and Cutpurses: Scenes from the Hogarthian Underworld*

Willett Cunnington, C. & Cunnington, Phillis, *Handbook of English Costume in the 18th Century*

Worsley, Lucy, *Courtiers: The Secret History of Kensington Palace*

ACKNOWLEDGEMENTS

I spent two years researching and writing this novel. During that time my first book, *The Devil in the Marshalsea*, was published. It's an exciting and terrifying thing, releasing your first book into the world. I had the most fantastic support from friends, work-mates and fellow authors – far too many people to list in full here. But to everyone who offered encouragement – especially readers – thank you.

At Hodder: huge thanks to Nick Sayers for being such a great champion of my work and for his extremely helpful editorial notes. Also for being the nicest man in publishing. (I have worked in publishing for many years and this is verifiably true.) Very special thanks, embossed and covered in glitter, to the brilliant Laura Macdougall. And to Kerry Hood – who hates a fuss – thank you.

At Conville & Walsh: love and thanks to my agent Clare Conville for her dedication, generosity and sage advice. I couldn't ask for more. Thanks, indeed, to the whole team, especially Alexander Cochran, Matt Marland, Alexandra McNicoll and Jake Smith-Bosanquet.

Thanks to my lovely L,B colleagues and friends, especially: Richard Beswick, Hannah Boursnell, Cath Burke, Sean Garrehy, Ursula Mackenzie, Clare Smith and Adam Strange. And most of all Rhiannon Smith.

Thanks to Eve Gutierrez and Paula Cuddy at Eleventh Hour productions for their enthusiastic support and for a fascinating trip to a modern prison. A warm hug of gratitude to Jo Unwin for giving me the confidence to keep writing in the first place. And to Mark Billingham for being such a kind and encouraging chap.

Big thanks to all my patient friends who have nodded politely while I regaled them with obscure eighteenth-century facts: Jo Krupa, Justine Willett and Victoria Burns; Ant, Vic and the Kirstys; Lance Fitzgerald and PJ Mark; Harrie Evans; Caroline Hogg; Val Hudson, and Andrew Wille. Love and thanks to my parents and to my sisters, Kay, Michelle and Debbie. Special thanks to Rowena Webb and Ian Lindsay-Hickman and also to Gordon Wise and Michael McCoy for much-needed and much-treasured weekends away. And to Ursula Doyle – again – for being such a loyal and supportive pal.

Thanks finally to any readers who read all the way to the end of this list of people they've never heard of. You may now leave the cinema. End credits.